A Regency Collection

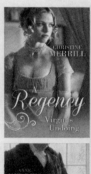

CHRISTINE MERRILL

A Regency Virgin's Undoing

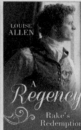

LOUISE ALLEN

A Regency Rake's Redemption

ANN LETHBRIDGE

A Regency Courtesan's Pride

DIANE GASTON

A Regency Gentleman's Passion

ANNE HERRIES

A Regency Lord's Command

CAROLE MORTIMER

A Regency Lady's Scandal

MARGARET McPHEE

A Regency Captain's Prize

SARAH MALLORY

A Regency Baron's Bride

AMANDA McCABE

A Regency Duchess's Awakening

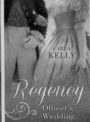

CARLA KELLY

A Regency Officer's Wedding

ISABELLE GODDARD

A Regency Earl's Pleasure

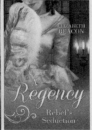

ELIZABETH BEACON

A Regency Rebel's Seduction

A
Regency
Baron's
Bride

SARAH MALLORY

MILLS
BOON

Published in Great Britain 2016
by Mills & Boon, an imprint of Harlequin (UK) Limited,
Eton House, 18-24 Paradise Road, Richmond, Surrey, TW9 1SR

A REGENCY BARON'S BRIDE © 2016 Harlequin Books S.A.

To Catch a Husband... © 2011 Sarah Mallory
The Wicked Baron © 2009 Sarah Mallory

ISBN: 978-0-263-91767-3

052-0316

Harlequin (UK) policy is to use papers that are natural, renewable and recyclable products and made from wood grown in sustainable forests. The logging and manufacturing processes conform to the legal environmental regulations of the country of origin.

Printed and bound
by CPI Group (UK) Ltd, Croydon, CR0 4YY

To Catch
a Husband...

SARAH MALLORY

Sarah Mallory was born in the West Country and now lives on the beautiful Yorkshire moors. She has been writing for more than three decades—mainly historical romances set in the Georgian and Regency period. She has won several awards for her writing, most recently the Romantic Novelists' Association's RoNA Rose Award in 2012 (*The Dangerous Lord Darrington*) and 2013 (*Beneath the Major's Scars*).

Chapter One

'I am off to London, to seek my fortune!'

Kitty Wythenshawe glanced up hopefully at the young farmhand driving the gig. He did not look overly impressed with her announcement, but perhaps that was because he had known her for years and had always thought of her as the seamstress's daughter—which, of course, she was— but now she was off to stay with her godmother. And her godmother was *A Lady!* Lady Leaconham, to be exact.

'Well, Joshua?' she demanded. 'Are you not pleased for me?'

The lad moved the straw he was chewing from one side of his mouth to the other.

'Nowt to do wi' me.'

Kitty sighed but did not allow her companion's indifference to damp her spirits. The overnight rain had given way to a beautiful spring morning, the sun had driven off the early mist from the moors and she could see the lapwings circling lazily over a distant field. It was as if Nature itself was smiling upon her adventure. Kitty glanced down at her olive-green walking dress with the yellow leaf motif embroidered down the front and around the hem. Mama and Aunt Jane had worked so hard for this occasion. She had never before had so many new clothes at one time.

'Dunno what tha wants wi' goin' t' Lunnon,' remarked Joshua, suddenly becoming loquacious.

'I have to find a husband,' said Kitty, clasping her hands together in a sudden moment of anxiety. If only she could marry well then she could provide for Aunt Jane and Mama. They were both widows, eking out their meagre savings with a little dressmaking. Their home was a little cramped, to be sure, but Kitty had grown used to that. However, she was painfully aware that Mama and Aunt Jane were growing older and the cold, damp cottage was not so comfortable in winter, when the water would seep up through the earth floor and Mama's joints would become stiff and painful, and Aunt Jane's cough always became much worse. They were the daughters of a gentleman and this was not what they had been born to. Kitty knew it was her duty to improve their fortunes and if she had to sacrifice herself at the Matrimonial Altar then she would do it—not that it seemed to Kitty much of a sacrifice to marry a rich man: it was all very well to read novels where the heroine gave up everything to follow her heart, but Mama had married for love and Kitty did not think that she was particularly happy, living in such straitened circumstances. Indeed, had she and Aunt Jane not scrimped and saved every spare penny to give Kitty this one chance to go to London expressly for the purpose of achieving a good marriage?

Letitia Leaconham had been a close childhood friend of Mama's and had gone on to make a brilliant marriage, while Mama had defied her family and married Walter Wythenshawe for love. He had been in possession of a moderate income, but he had not prospered, and as Mama was wont to point out at times of stress, strict principles and enlightened views were all very well but they do not pay the bills. Upon Papa's death there had been any number of accounts to be settled and so it had come to pass that Kitty and her mama had moved into the tiny cottage in Fallridge with Aunt Jane, the widow of an impecunious curate. Since then Mama had spent every penny she could spare upon Kitty's education in the belief that if only she could be launched into Society she would make a good marriage. After all, her birth was impeccable, even if she had no dowry. As Aunt Jane said, Kitty was their *Last Hope;* if she could only find a rich husband then they could all be comfortable.

'I'd marry thee.'

This utterance put an end to Kitty's ponderings.

'I beg your pardon?'

'I said I'd marry thee,' repeated Joshua. 'If tha needs a man.'

'Oh, Joshua, that is very kind of you!' Kitty put a hand on his rough sleeve. 'Indeed it is very generous, but you see, if I am to support Mama and Aunt Jane, that they may live out their years comfortably and without more suffering, I need to marry someone...someone...'

'A lord,' said Joshua, spitting out his straw. 'Some 'un richer nor me. Aye, well, me mam's set her heart on my marrying Lizzie Greenwood, since she will inherit the farm from her faither, so I suppose it wouldn't do fer me to be marryin' a lass with nowt to 'er name.'

For a few moments Kitty's sunny mood clouded: it was very lowering to think even Joshua considered her a poor prospect for marriage. Her spirits soon recovered, however. She was a gentlewoman by birth, and as Papa had always told her, it was a person's actions that were important. So Kitty pulled herself up and said graciously, 'No, but thank you for the offer. And it is very good of you to drive me to Halifax, and so kind of your father to let us use the gig. I am to meet with Mr and Mrs Midgley at the Crown. You may not know them; Mr Midgley is a cloth merchant, which is how Mama became acquainted with the family, for she often buys cloth from him. They are taking their samples to London, you see, and have agreed to take me with them, which was very fortunate, because otherwise Mama would have been obliged to send me on the stage and hire a maid to go with me. So you see everything has worked out very well.'

She ended on a cheerful note with a sunny smile for Joshua but he was not attending. He was staring ahead of him and frowning.

'Well?' said Kitty. 'What is it?'

Joshua scratched his head.

'I ain't right sure which road we wants.'

Kitty followed his stare. They were dropping down from the hills and she could see the junction in the distance, a large, open space where several highways converged.

'The road to Halifax will be the main route,' suggested Kitty, but even as she said it she realised that this did not help. All the roads leading away from them were in good order and wide enough for two carts to pass.

'Da said to keep goin' downhill 'til we get to Halifax.'

'That is all very well,' retorted Kitty, beginning to lose patience, 'but there are at least three of those roads leading downhill. Think, Joshua. Can you not remember which one you take?'

'Ah, well, I've never bin this road afore,' he confessed. 'Uncle Jed allus makes this run.'

Kitty closed her lips to prevent herself making a hasty exclamation. It would help no one and might upset her companion, who, after all, was going to considerable trouble for her. As they descended to the crossroads she spotted a large black horse standing at the side of the lane. At first she thought the animal unattended, but as they approached a man stepped into view. His serviceable buckskins and brown riding jacket were liberally spattered with mud and he was hatless, his black hair unconfined and hanging wild and disordered to his shoulders. He did not look around as they approached, but was concentrating upon securing the straps of his saddle.

'That fellow might know which is the correct road,' said Kitty. 'You should ask him.'

Joshua looked at the bedraggled stranger and pulled a face. 'Nay. No need for that.'

'To be sure he looks very rough, but he might know the way.'

'Tha can't be certain o' that.'

'Well, it would do no harm to ask,' said Kitty, trying to hide her impatience.

Joshua ignored her. When she realised that he had no intention of asking for directions she decided she would have to act. As they drew abreast of the man she leaned over the side of the gig and called out to him.

'I say, my man—yes, you: which one of these roads leads to Halifax?'

She was not used to accosting strangers, and a mixture of nerves and irritation at her companion's stubbornness made her tone much sharper than usual. The man turned slowly and looked up at her from beneath heavy dark brows. Kitty found herself facing the blackest, fiercest stare she had ever encountered.

It was as much as Kitty could do not to recoil from the stranger's angry glare. With some alarm she realised that Joshua no longer intended to drive past. He brought the gig to a halt and the man walked over to stand before them, looking very much as if he would drag her from the gig at any moment. Swallowing hard, she sat up straight, determined not to show fear. She said haughtily, 'Did you understand me, fellow?'

Those piercing black eyes held hers for a moment, then they swept over her, from the crown of her bergère bonnet down to the nankeen half-boots peeping out from under the hem of her walking dress. Kitty had the unsettling feeling that he could see right through her clothing to the flesh beneath. She felt thoroughly exposed and her cheeks flamed. She snapped her head up and stared straight ahead.

'Drive on, Joshua.'

The stranger's long arm shot out and one big hand caught the pony's bridle.

'Nay,' he said in a slow, deep drawl. 'First tha needs to know t'road.'

Kitty shot a furious look at him.

'Then perhaps you would be good enough to tell us!'

'I'll tell thee nowt afore I hears a civil word from yer ladyship.'

Joshua shifted uncomfortably beside her. Kitty wondered that he did not stand up to the stranger, but a moment's consideration told her that her companion, a stocky youth of sixteen, was no match for the tall, broad-shouldered stranger some ten years his senior. The man stood at their pony's head, one hand gripping the leather cheek-piece while the other stroked the animal's neck with slow, reas-suring movements. The pony, traitor that he was, turned his head and rubbed against the stranger's arm.

Kitty realised that, however angry the man might be with her, he was in control of himself and the situation. They could not move on until he allowed it.

She ran her tongue over her dry lips.

'I beg your pardon,' she said politely. 'Pray be good enough to direct us to the Halifax road.'

Silence.

It dragged on for a full minute. Kitty gave the stranger a challenging look but he did not move, merely stared back at her with his unfathomable black gaze. He looked as hard and immobile as the rocky granite outcrops that littered the moors.

Joshua rubbed his nose. A bullock cart lumbered up to the junction and turned along one of the lanes but still the stranger held Kitty's eyes. Then, just when she was wondering if Joshua would dare to use the shotgun that she knew lay beneath the seat, the man stepped back.

'That's thy road.' He pointed to the lane where the bullock cart was disappearing around a bend. 'Just follow yon wagon t'bottom of t'hill.'

With a slight nod of acknowledgement Joshua flicked the reins and they began to move.

'Thank you.'

Kitty felt obliged to utter the words as they drove away, but she kept her eyes fixed on the road ahead. From the tail of her eye she saw the man tug his forelock but there was nothing subservient about the gesture and she could not shake the horrible conviction that he was enjoying her discomfiture.

Daniel Blackwood watched the gig pull away, a deep crease in his brows. He was in the worst possible humour but he should not have taken it out on that young couple. He had been travelling since yesterday afternoon, his horse was lame and he had been obliged to spend the night on the moors. He was in a devil's own temper and it had not been improved by being addressed by an arrogant chit as if he was a lackey!

He had seen the gig approaching, but knowing the young couple could do nothing to help him he had ignored it, only to be summoned like a servant to give directions. True, the girl was young and pretty, but he was in no mood to appreciate the heart-shaped face, the large green eyes fringed with dark lashes or the dusky curls that escaped from beneath her wide-brimmed straw bonnet. He watched the gig rolling away down the hill, the little figure in her green robe and yellow bonnet sitting rigidly upright beside the boy who was driving. Probably some farmer's daughter trying to impress her swain by acting the great lady. Well, she had chosen the wrong man to try out her airs and graces!

With an angry snort he bent to pick up his greatcoat and hat from the grass verge and gathered up the reins of his horse.

'Come up, Marnie. I'll walk you to the inn and Fletcher can keep you there until you're fit to come home.'

Kitty arrived at the Crown and was informed by the landlord that she was expected: Mr and Mrs Midgley were waiting for her in the coffee room. Kitty nodded and he directed one of his servants to carry her trunk across to the travelling carriage standing in the middle of the yard. Before stepping into the inn she turned to say goodbye to Joshua, thanking him for his trouble and pressing into his hand a sixpence which he was somewhat embarrassed to take, but she insisted. She watched him drive away in the gig, a tiny pang of homesickness mingling with the excited anticipation she felt for the journey ahead of her.

Mr and Mrs Midgley greeted her with unfeigned delight, declaring that she had not kept them waiting at all, and begging her to sit down and join them for breakfast before they set off.

'For if I am not mistaken,' said Mr Midgley, twinkling at her, 'you were up before dawn, miss, and too excited to take a bite to eat.'

'Very true,' laughed Kitty, removing her bonnet and shaking out her dark curls. 'If you are sure we have time?'

'All the time in the world, my dear,' replied Mr Midgley. 'We travel to London in easy stages. I don't mean to press the horses, for we shan't be changing them again for some while, unlike the mailcoach.'

'Nor will we be careering along at such a breakneck speed,' added Mrs Midgley, chuckling. 'So come along, my dear, sit by me and you can tell me how your dear mother does.'

Kitty readily complied. She was not well acquainted with her hosts but their warmth and kindness soon broke down any reserve and she found herself chattering away quite naturally while they breakfasted upon freshly baked bread rolls and scalding coffee.

'So you arrived in style, Miss Wythenshawe,' remarked Mrs Midgley, when they had finished their meal and Mr Midgley went off to check if their carriage was ready. 'You say the farmer's boy drove you in his gig? I have no doubt your mama was very pleased you were not obliged to travel here with the poultry for market!'

'If I had done so then my driver might have known the way,' replied Kitty with a sigh.

She decided not to recount the incident at the cross-roads. The man had been odiously rude and not a little frightening, but Kitty was aware that her own conduct was not what it ought to have been. If she had not spoken in such a proud, disdainful way perhaps the whole unpleasant incident might not have occurred. She deeply regretted her own conduct but it was too late to apologise. She would learn from it and do her best to make sure she did not act in such an ill-mannered fashion again.

She gave Mrs Midgley a bright smile. 'But I am here now, and very much looking forward to our journey.'

'Bless you, my dear, then we shall be off directly,' declared Mr Midgley, coming in at that moment. 'If you would care to don your bonnets and cloaks, ladies, the berline is ready and we can be on our way! Oh, and we have a passenger for the first part of the journey: I'll just go and hurry him along.'

With that he was gone, leaving his wife to tut and direct a rueful glance at Kitty as they gathered up their belongings and headed out to the yard.

While they had been breaking their fast the clouds had gathered and now it was raining steadily, a fine, soaking drizzle. The ladies hurried across to the waiting carriage and made themselves comfortable on the forward-facing seat while they waited for Mr Midgley. He soon appeared at the door, standing back and addressing someone beyond her view.

'Get in, my boy, get in. You will find Mrs Midgley inside, and our young guest Miss Wythenshawe. This is Mr Blackwood, my love,' he called in through the open door. 'His mare is lame, so I said we would take him up as far as Hestonroyd.'

A large figure in a greatcoat and wide-brimmed hat filled the doorway, his shadow momentarily darkening the interior of the carriage, but as he sat down opposite her, Kitty bit back a gasp of dismay. It was the boorish stranger from the crossroads! He had washed his face and hands and tied back his hair, but there was no mistaking that strong jaw shadowed with its dark stubble or the coal-black eyes that now rested upon her with a look of cool disdain. Embarrassed, Kitty looked down and nervously twitched her skirts out of the way. He had such long legs that she was obliged to keep her feet tucked in to avoid dirtying her hem on his muddy boots. She knew her walking dress would not remain clean for very long, but it was new and she was determined to take care of it. She fully appreciated all the hard work Mama and Aunt Jane had put in, making all the gowns and clothes for her stay in London. She had helped, of course, but Mama had worked long into each evening, sewing by lamplight until her eyes were red and sore with strain.

'There, now, we are off at last!' declared Mr Midgley as he climbed into the carriage and they began to move. 'What a merry party we shall be.' He turned to his wife. 'Blackwood here lives at the Holme and—'

Daniel was quick to interrupt him, saying in a very broad accent, 'Nay, sir, I don't think the ladies is fetched to know about me.' He glanced at the young woman sitting opposite and added, 'They'd be more interested in frills and furbelows.'

Mrs Midgley chuckled.

'You are far too modest, Mr Blackwood. I take it you are Samuel Blackwood's son?'

'Aye, ma'am.' Daniel kept his response brief: if they knew his father they might well wonder why his son spoke in such an uneducated manner!

'We are well acquainted with your parents,' Mrs Midgley went on. 'If we had time I would suggest we call upon them when we drop you off, but Mr Midgley is determined to reach Market Harborough tonight, so we must not tarry. Do, pray, remember me to your mama.'

Dan nodded silently in response and earned a disapproving frown from Miss Wythenshawe. He returned her look with a cool one of his own and had the satisfaction of seeing her blush. As well she might, given her own behaviour towards him that morning.

He wondered if he should have hired a horse after all, but by the time he had walked Marnie to the inn the rain had set in and Mr Midgley had been most insistent. Daniel had seen the cheerful-looking gentleman with his full wig and bushy side-whiskers sheltering under the arch leading to the stableyard and he had nodded as he passed him. The man touched his hat.

'By Gad, sir, you look as if you have been through the wars!'

Daniel stopped. He looked down at his muddy clothes and gave a wry grin.

'My horse took a tumble yesterday evening and I landed in the dirt. I was unhurt but my mount was lamed, so I was obliged to spend the night on the moors.'

'And in the rain, too.' The gentleman shook his head.

Daniel shrugged.

'A little damp won't hurt me. I am even now going to find our host and hire a horse to take me back to Hestonroyd.'

The man looked up, his little bright eyes gleaming.

'Oh? Not the Holme, by any chance? Samuel Blackwood's place?'

'Why, yes, sir. I am his son.'

The gentleman gave a hearty laugh.

'Well met then, Mr Blackwood! My name is Midgley. I have known your father for many a year—a good man, and an honest businessman, too!'

'Indeed.' Daniel nodded. 'I will give him your regards, sir. Now, if you will excuse me, I must see if Fletcher can find me a horse...'

'No need, sir, no need,' cried Mr Midgley. 'I am going your way—that is my berline over there. We shall be setting off shortly—we have many miles to cover today!—but I should be delighted to take you up.'

'Indeed, sir, I would not wish to put you out...'

'Not at all, my boy, not at all. You do not want to be riding in this weather. And besides, we shall be driving through Hestonroyd and can drop you at the very gates of the Holme. Now, there is plenty of room in my carriage for another body, so let me hear no more arguments!'

Daniel hesitated, but only for a moment. His greatcoat was still wet and the idea of getting another soaking was not a tempting prospect, so he accepted Mr Midgley's offer. Now, looking across at Miss Wythenshawe's haughty profile, he thought that if he had known she was one of the party, he would have preferred to walk back to Hestonroyd in the rain rather than sit in a closed carriage with such a disagreeable wench.

Kitty stared resolutely out of the window. Heavens, she had thought Joshua taciturn, but this man had no conversation at all, except to be uncivil. Her conscience suggested that this might be her own fault. The thought made her uncomfortable, but she could not bring herself to utter an apology before Mr and Mrs Midgley: if she did that she would also be obliged to give them an explanation. She decided to put the matter from her mind and concentrate on the passing countryside.

The view could not fail to excite her. She had never been so far abroad before and as they travelled on, the harsh grandeur of the moors was left behind for a softer, greener landscape. Orderly fields stretched away on either side towards rolling, wooded hillsides. She was only a few hours from home and already everything looked strange: how much more diverting would it be in London? Mr Midgley said it would take two full days' travelling to reach the capital. A little tremor ran through her: how would she go on? She had never even been to school!

There had never been any money to send her to one of the select academies that taught young ladies how to behave. Not that her education had been lacking. Mama and Aunt Jane had seen to that. When Papa had died they had been obliged to release her governess but Mama and Aunt Jane had continued her lessons, which she had augmented by extensive reading of the books kept from her father's well-stocked library. Most had been sold to pay his debts but those suitable for a young lady's education had been retained—as well as less improving works. Mama might not wholly approve of novels, but she and Aunt Jane enjoyed listening to Kitty reading from the works of Mr Fielding or Mr Richardson while they sewed. They had managed to keep the little pianoforte for her to practise upon but there had been no money for a dancing master, so Kitty had joined the Squire's daughters for dancing lessons, repaying this kindness by helping their harassed governess with their schooling. Mama had been at great pains to teach her to be a lady. There had been extensive descriptions of life in a big house, lessons on how to address the various ranks of nobility and how to prepare tea, but Kitty suspected it would be very different practising all she had learned in London rather than in the tiny cottage in Fallridge.

She clasped her hands together. Mama had never taught her how to deal with rough, wild-looking gentlemen like the one now sitting opposite her. The only men she had met before had either been the young boys of the village or fatherly types like the Squire or Mr Midgley. In all her nineteen years she had never met anyone who had made her feel so ill at ease. She stole a glance across the carriage at Daniel Blackwood. He had removed his hat and was leaning back against the leather squabs, his eyes closed, his head moving gently with the swaying motion of the carriage. If, as Mr Midgley said, he had been travelling all night that would explain his wild, unkempt appearance. But it was clear that he did not favour a powdered wig, for he wore his own dark hair tied back at the nape of his neck and that, together with his heavy dark brows and straight nose, gave him a rather hawkish appearance. With his greatcoat hanging open she could see the broad width of his chest straining beneath his brown riding jacket and the outline of his muscled thighs encased within the buckskin breeches. He exuded strength and power. She thought back to their first meeting on the edge of the moors above Halifax: that, she realised, was the perfect setting for such a wild, vigorous creature. He was not a man to be crossed, but it occurred to her that he would be a good man to have as a friend.

At that moment Mr Blackwood opened his eyes and Kitty found herself once more staring into their coal-black depths. She had the oddest feeling that he was looking into her very soul and reading her thoughts. Blushing, she forced herself to turn away. She fixed her gaze on the window again. Really, the man was insufferable. She hoped they would be reaching Hestonroyd very soon, so that they would be free of his unsettling presence.

The carriage lurched and bumped as their route wound down through a steep wooded valley. The rain had stopped, but the leaves and the ground glistened in the watery sunlight, while tumbling streams ran down the hillside, creating frothy waterfalls between the trees. The carriage slowed and came to a stand. Mr Midgley let down the window and put out his head to direct an enquiry to his coachman. Kitty could not hear the man's reply, but it caused his master to climb out of the carriage, closely followed by Mr Blackwood. Kitty leaned across to look out of the open doorway.

They had reached the valley bottom where a new cobbled road had been laid to take vehicles through the ford. Now, however, the stream was swollen by the recent rains and it rushed and tumbled across their path. Mr Midgley came back to speak to them.

'Roberts doesn't want to drive across the ford with you ladies inside,' he told them. 'He is afraid of what might happen to you if the carriage should be overturned by the fast-flowing waters. You can see that it would not be unprecedented.' He nodded towards the far bank of the stream, where the remains of a farm cart protruded from the water. 'Roberts thinks it would be safer for us to use the bridge yonder.'

He pointed upstream, where an ancient stone bridge arched across the waters. It was wide enough for a single horse, but it was clear that it would not accommodate a carriage.

'Is it quite safe?' enquired Mrs Midgley, eyeing the bridge with some misgiving.

'Oh, aye, ma'am, the bridge is sound enough,' said the coachman cheerfully. 'It's not much used now we have the new road, but the pack-horses still cross by it.'

Kitty gave a little shrug. 'And so must we, it seems. Let us go to it.'

She followed Mrs Midgley out of the carriage and the party stood and watched as the coachman slowly drove across the ford. The water surged between the horses' legs and frothed around the wheels of the carriage, splashing up over the coach body and making it sway alarmingly, but at last the berline was drawn up safely out of the water on the far side.

'Excellent,' declared Mr Midgley, 'Well done, Roberts.' He held his hand out to his wife. 'Come along then, ladies. It is our turn!'

He set off towards the little bridge. The track was wet and overgrown and the ladies were obliged to hold up their skirts to keep them out of the mud. Kitty did her best to ignore Daniel Blackwood, who fell into step beside her but did not offer her his arm. The bridge was soon reached and they paused for a moment on the apex to gaze over the low parapet at the turgid water.

'I should not like to fall in there today,' remarked Mrs Midgley. 'The rains have swollen the stream so much it is in danger of overflowing its banks.'

'It has certainly flooded on this side,' said her husband, who had walked to the edge of the bridge and was prodding the grass with his cane. 'The ground is sodden here.'

Mrs Midgley followed her husband to where the cobbles of the bridge ended and the grassy track began.

'Well, we have to get across,' she said prosaically.

She laid her hand on her husband's arm and put one foot on the track. Immediately she sank ankle-deep into the mud.

'Oh, good heavens!' cried Mrs Midgley, picking up her skirts and stepping quickly back on to the cobbles. 'The ground is a quagmire. We cannot walk on that!'

'I am afraid we have no choice, my dear,' cried her spouse.

They watched as he strode purposefully forwards to the carriage, his feet sinking into the ground until the mud came halfway up his top-boots. When he finally reached the road he turned and looked back rather helplessly.

'Well, what else are we to do, my love? The carriage is on this side now, so we must cross somehow.'

Daniel Blackwood stepped forward.

'Allow me, mistress.' In one easy movement he scooped Mrs Midgley into his arms and carried her across the muddy stretch, setting her gently on her feet beside her husband, where she stood, a little red-cheeked and flustered by such cavalier treatment.

'Oh, well done, my boy!' cried Mr Midgley, clapping his hands. 'Now if you will do the same by Miss Wythenshawe we will be on our way.'

Kitty's throat tightened in alarm. That big brute of a man was bearing down upon her, a look of unholy enjoyment in his eyes. She looked at the mud and wondered if she dared run through it, but the thought of ruining her new half-boots and very likely muddying both her walking dress and her petticoats was too horrific to bear. Her dark tormentor stood before her, grinning.

'Well, Miss Wythenshawe, if tha's ready?'

She bit her lip and nodded. The sensation of being swept off her feet left Kitty feeling giddy and very helpless. She was held tightly against the man's chest, her face only inches from his jaw, so close that she could see the black stubble on his cheek and smell the damp wool of his greatcoat. As he turned his feet slipped a little on the cobbles and her hands flew up around his neck. His arms tightened even more. He held her firmly but he was not crushing her, yet for some reason she found it difficult to breathe. Her heart was pounding erratically, thudding against her ribs as if trying to escape her body. She had a sudden and inexplicable desire to lean her head against the man's shoulder. She had to admit it looked very inviting, and reassuringly wide. She realised that this was a situation she had dreamed of, a chivalrous knight coming to the rescue of a beautiful maiden. Only in her dreams her hero was a fair, handsome young knight, one deserving of his reward, not a big, brutish oaf with no manners. She peeped up at the strong, rather hawkish face of her rescuer, noting the long black lashes around his eyes, his straight nose and the smooth curve of his lips. Suddenly, surprisingly, Kitty found herself wondering what it would be like to kiss him.

He glanced down at that moment and she found herself staring into those dark eyes, unable to look away. For one alarming moment she thought he had read her mind and that he would actually kiss her. She was in his arms and completely at his mercy. Her heart raced. A moment's heady excitement was followed quickly by panic. To cover her confusion she said crossly, 'Pray do not hold me so tightly. You are crushing my dress.'

He chuckled.

His amusement only served to increase her discomfiture. She said angrily, 'I vow I cannot breathe! Loosen your hold, you oaf!'

The black brows snapped together and a dangerous gleam flared in his eyes. He released his grip on her legs and she gave a little cry as her feet touched the sodden ground.

'Ee, lass, seems I lost my grip on thee.' Her tormentor still had an arm around her shoulders, hugging her to him. She managed to free one hand and brought it up to his grinning face with a slap.

'How dare you do that to a lady?'

He looked down at her, his eyes narrowing. Then, very deliberately, he let her go. She gave a shriek, her arms tightening around his neck as she tried to lift her feet from the mud. Calmly he reached up and pulled her hands away and she was obliged to stand, the cold muddy water oozing around her ankles and into her boots.

'If that wants trettin' like a lady,' he growled, 'then that mun act like one.'

And with that he turned and walked to the carriage.

Kitty lifted her sodden skirts and pulled one foot clear of the sticky, cloying mud. With slow, unsteady steps she made her way to the road, biting her lip in rage and mortification. She had been very rude, to be sure, but how dare he drop her in the water? She looked down at her feet. Her new boots were ruined and instead of a jaunty yellow decoration around the hem of her walking dress, the bottom six inches of her skirts glistened with slick brown mud.

When Kitty reached the road she was too upset to speak and after scraping the worst of the mud from her boots and stockings she climbed silently into the carriage, biting her lip while Mrs Midgley clucked and fidgeted around her like a mother hen.

Daniel looked down at his legs. His topboots were almost completely covered in mud and it had splashed up over his buckskins. He walked to the edge of the ford to wash the worst of the dirt away before climbing back into the carriage. Mr Midgley gave the word and they set off again. The atmosphere inside the carriage was distinctly uncomfortable. Daniel looked at the young woman huddled in the corner: she was staring out of the window, her jaw set hard. He saw her blink rapidly and guessed that she was trying not to cry.

'I beg your pardon,' he said quietly. 'Miss Wythenshawe, I—'

'Now, now, my boy, you did your best,' put in Mr Midgley. 'I did not see quite what happened, as I was helping my wife into the coach, but I am sure it could not be helped. We must be thankful that one of our ladies at least was carried safely across the mud. I have no doubt Miss Wythenshawe is most grateful for your efforts, isn't that so, my dear?'

Daniel saw the little chin tremble. Miss Wythenshawe averted her face but he could not mistake the bitterness in her voice when she replied.

'Mr Blackwood's *efforts* will not be forgotten.'

'There, now, all's well, you see.' Mr Midgley beamed

around the carriage. 'Once the mud has dried, we can clean it off and your boots and your gown will be as good as new!'

Daniel sat back, closing his lips against further comment. Mrs Midgley did not look convinced by her husband's cheerful assurances and as for Miss Wythenshawe, she kept her gaze fixed firmly upon the passing landscape. He leaned forwards, his hand going out to her.

'Perhaps you will allow me to—'

'Pray do not touch me!' she said icily. 'I think you have done quite enough damage today!'

Daniel drew back immediately. He had been about to offer to pay for a new gown, but it was quite clear the young woman wanted nothing further to do with him. Stifling a sigh of exasperation, Daniel turned to stare out of the window beside him, praying that his nightmare journey would soon be over.

Chapter Two

The carriage slowed to negotiate a winding village street and Daniel sat up, relieved to recognise the familiar buildings.

'Hestonroyd.' He turned to Mr Midgley. 'This will do for me, sir, if you would direct your driver to stop.'

Mr Midgley pulled the check-string and Daniel jumped down. He bowed and offered his thanks to Mr and Mrs Midgley but when he touched his hat to Miss Wythenshawe she merely hunched her shoulder and looked away. With a shrug he waited until the carriage had moved off then walked briskly along the street until he arrived at the gates to the Holme, an imposing new house set back from the road. As he strode up the drive, the front door flew open and a young lady ran out.

'Daniel, at last!'

He caught her up in his arms, swinging her around and laughing.

'Have you been looking out for me, Bella?'

He set her back on her feet.

'Since daybreak. But what *have* you been doing, brother dearest? You are covered in mud.'

He grinned.

'That is a very long story. Let us go indoors. I need to clean myself up.'

'You must be quick, then, for Mama is waiting in the drawing room for you. Papa is at the mill, but he said we were to send word as soon as you arrived.' She twinkled up at him. 'He would not say so, of course, but he has missed you, and was mightily disappointed when you did not come home last night.'

Daniel put his arm around her shoulders.

'Well, you can send him a message now to tell him I am safe, and inform Mama that I will be with her as soon as I am presentable!'

The clock in the hall had chimed two more quarters before Daniel finally made his way downstairs to the drawing room. It was a large well-proportioned chamber, comfortably furnished, everything of the finest quality, and it had a quiet elegance that Daniel found very restful. His mother was seated at her new writing desk, her dark hair neatly confined beneath a lace cap.

'Well, Mama, I am home at last.'

She looked up, a smile lighting her face.

'Daniel, my love.' She rose to greet him, hugging him tightly. She would never admit it but he suspected she had spent a restless night worrying over his safety. He held her away from him.

'You are looking very well, Mama, and that is a very fetching coat. Is it new?'

'It is a *pet-en-l'air,*' she told him, smoothing her hands over the grey velvet of the loose jacket she wore over her morning gown. 'They are not so fashionable now, I'm afraid, but just the thing for these chill spring days.' She gestured to him to sit down with her. 'Bella tells me you have had an eventful journey.'

'Yes, Marnie is lame; we took a fall coming back from Barrowford. No, no, I suffered no injury,' he added quickly when he saw the alarm in her face. 'I was obliged to leave Marnie in Halifax but was fortunate to meet Mr Midgley and his lady on their way to London and they took me up. They send their regards, Mama, but would not stop.'

'That was very kind of them, but are you sure you are not hurt? No doubt you were cutting across the moors again. I wish you had kept to the roads, my son.'

'I wish I had done so, this time,' Daniel responded with a rueful grin. 'You will say I was well served, Mama, for I had to spend the night sleeping on the heather.'

'He was covered in mud,' added Bella, following him into the room. 'Up to his knees!'

'Not from my sojourn on the moor,' Daniel was quick to reassure his mother. 'The stream was in full spate across the ford and Midgley deemed it safer for us to walk across the bridge.'

'Heavens, if it was that muddy what did poor Mrs Midgley do?' asked Bella, eyeing the scalloped hem of her own gown.

'I carried her, since her husband could not.'

'Oh, famous!' Mrs Blackwood clapped her hands, laughing. 'A veritable hero! I have no doubt the lady was very pleased to have you with them.'

'*She* was, perhaps,' remarked Daniel, his brow darkening, 'but not her companion. Too high in the step for me. A right top-lofty piece...'

'Daniel!'

'I beg your pardon, Mama, but you know how I dislike it when people put on airs that don't become them! And this young miss, hah! Far too high and mighty *she* was! She took one look at me and wrote me off as a mere nothing.'

'I have no doubt she mistook you for a common labourer if she saw you in all your dirt,' remarked Bella sagely. 'I am sure she soon realised her mistake when she knew who you were.'

'Nay,' drawled Daniel, 'I weren't about to put 'er right.'

Mrs Blackwood frowned at his sudden lapse.

'My dear, I trust you were not uncouth.'

Daniel hesitated, thinking back over the events of the morning. He had behaved very badly by Miss Wythenshawe, he knew that, but it was too late to do anything about it now. He gave his mother an apologetic smile.

'Alas, Mama, I fear I was very uncouth.'

A deep, amused voice was heard from the doorway.

'What is this? Is my son up to his tricks?'

'Papa!' With a shriek Bella flew across the room and flung herself into the arms of the gentleman who had just entered.

'Father.' Daniel rose. 'I beg your pardon, I sent a message to assure you I was safe. I did not mean you to leave the mill early—'

His father smiled across the room at him.

'It was no hardship. 'Tis a poor manager I would be if my manufactories could not function without my presence! But what has been occurring, my son, to bring that black scowl to your face?'

'A minor irritation, sir, too trivial to bore you with.'

'Good manners are never trivial, my son,' put in Mrs Blackwood, a troubled look in her eyes. 'I had hoped your education had taught you how to mix with your fellow man, from humble labourer to the highest in the land. But

I know that temper of yours: you will act rashly if your will is crossed.'

'Oh?' Mr Samuel Blackwood raised his dark brows at his son. 'And who has had the temerity to cross you, my boy?'

'A young lady,' put in Bella before Daniel could reply. 'She saw Dan in all his dirt and mistook him for a rough, coarse fellow.'

'And is my son so lax in his manners that he is judged solely upon appearance?' asked Mr Blackwood gently.

A dull flush mantled Dan's cheek.

'Not generally, sir, I assure you.'

'I am very glad to hear it,' returned his father, smiling a little. 'Because your manners are going to be sorely tested, I fear.'

Daniel looked up.

'Sir?'

'Yes, my son, I have some matters of business for you to attend to.' Mr Blackwood reached into his pocket and took out his snuff box. 'I am sending you to London!'

Dearest Mama. You will know from my previous correspondence that I think Lady Leaconham the kindest, most generous godmother in the world! She delights in showering gifts upon me and will not hear of my spending the money you gave me upon anything other than little luxuries for myself—pin money, she calls it—and every time I remonstrate with her she merely laughs and says what else is she to spend her money upon, if it is not her goddaughter?

Kitty put down her pen. She had been in Portman Square for four weeks now, and already Lady Leaconham had spent more money upon her than Mama and Aunt Jane

earned in a year. Letitia Leaconham had been a widow for
a long time. Her husband had left her with a comfortable
income that allowed her to hire a house in London for several months each year and entertain her acquaintances in
lavish style. She had one son, Garston, but since attaining
his majority four years ago he had set up his own bachelor
establishment, leaving his mama to yawn over her morning
chocolate and bemoan the fact that she had no daughter
to comfort her in her twilight years. She was therefore
delighted to welcome her goddaughter into her house and
even more delighted when she discovered Kitty to be an
attractive young lady with very pretty manners. She began
immediately to make plans to introduce her goddaughter to
her friends, and wrote to Mrs Wythenshawe to assure her
that, despite Kitty's complete lack of fortune, she had no
doubt she would be able to secure for her a very advantageous marriage.

Since this was her sole reason for coming to London,
Kitty could only be grateful that her godmother entered
so fully into her concerns and therefore she stifled her
misgivings and threw herself into her new life. Kitty had to
be honest; it was not difficult to enjoy all the amusements
that London had to offer. Lady Leaconham took her to the
theatre, they attended concerts, and spent hours browsing
in shops that carried such a wide variety of merchandise
Kitty's eyes grew round in amazement. It was also very
pleasant wearing modish gowns and having my lady's *coif-
feuse* coax her soft dark hair into fashionable ringlets. It had
not taken Kitty long to realise that Lady Leaconham was a
wealthy woman with very little to do, and she looked upon
her goddaughter very much as a novelty, an amusement—a
doll to be dressed and petted and exhibited to her friends.
For the first week or so Kitty had found the experience
deliciously exhilarating, but a life dedicated to nothing but

pleasure was not something she could wholly approve. Her father had been a very religious man with a strong moral code. He had died before Kitty was twelve years old but by then she had been inculcated with his principles and a strong sense of social justice. She believed that the advantages of wealth and rank carried with them responsibility for those less fortunate, a belief that did not seem to be shared by many of the fashionable ladies she had met since arriving in Town. She took up her pen again.

> *Pray be assured that I carry out such errands as Godmama will allow and take her little dog for his daily exercise, but this is small recompense for her generosity.*

Kitty paused. She did not think Mama would quite approve of the number of times Lady Leaconham had taken her shopping, positively showering her with purchases until Kitty's room was overflowing with hats, bonnets, cloaks, pelisses, dancing slippers and half-boots as well as more day dresses, morning and evening gowns and walking dresses than Kitty could ever imagine having time to wear. She broke off from her reverie as the door opened and Lady Leaconham came in.

'Ah, so there you are, Kitty my love,' she greeted her with a smile as she drew off her gloves. 'Now, what are you about, here all alone in the morning room?'

'I am writing to Mama. I beg your pardon, Godmama: is there something you would like me to do for you?'

'No, no, child, you work far too hard as it is—no one should be writing letters so early in the day!'

Kitty laughed.

'This is not *work,* Godmama!'

'Perhaps not for you,' returned my lady, casting a dubious eye at the sheet of paper with its closely written lines. 'I have noticed that you like to read a great deal, too.' She looked at Kitty, a slight frown creasing her brow. 'My dear, I do hope you are not *bookish,* and pray tell me you do not wish me to get you an invitation to my neighbour Mrs Montagu's blue-stocking parties! Nothing would be more fatal to your chances of making a good match, you know.'

Kitty hastily disclaimed and Lady Leaconham gave a very visible sigh of relief.

'Very well, my love, put away your letter now, if you please: you may finish it later. I have just come from Bond Street where I saw the prettiest pair of sandals! I just had to buy them for you. I thought they would go very well with your yellow muslin. I had Meakin put them in your room so perhaps you would run upstairs and try them on. I am expecting my sister Lady Harworth to call shortly and thought you might like to change your gown for her visit.' Kitty looked down at her closed robe: it was one of the gowns Mama had made for her. As if reading her thoughts, Lady Leaconham said quickly, 'I know how hard your dear mama and your aunt worked, making all those lovely gowns for you, and while they are perfectly suitable for quiet days at home, I do believe you should wear something a little more...stylish when we are entertaining guests such as Lady Harworth. And I do so want you to make a good impression upon her.'

'Oh, why should that be, Godmama?'

'Well, she is very well connected, and she has a daughter only a year or so older than you; I should like her to think you a fitting companion. Also...' My lady slipped off her pelisse and gave her attention to laying it carefully over the arm of the sofa. 'Also, she has a son, and Lord Harworth is unmarried.'

Kitty was not deceived by her airy tone.

'Surely you do not think a *lord* would look at me, Godmama.'

'I do not see why not,' returned Lady Leaconham. 'Now that Meakin has cut your hair and dressed it a little more stylishly, you look exceedingly pretty, and your manners are very good, so I have no doubt that if you exert yourself a little you could make yourself very agreeable—you must not talk about your family, of course.'

'Oh, must I not?'

'No, my dear. It is not the thing in Town to chatter on about people known only to oneself.' My lady clasped her hands together, her pale eyes taking on a dreamy look. 'Only think how pleased your mama would be with both of us if we were to catch you a lord!'

Kitty did not think it worth trying to reply, so she obediently slipped away to her room to change into her new gown of lemon-coloured muslin with the blue sash and to put on the soft yellow kid sandals that her godmother had purchased for her. When she returned to the morning room some twenty minutes later she found her godmother sitting with her visitors.

'Ah, my dear, come in.' Lady Leaconham drew her forwards. 'Clara, may I present my goddaughter Katherine to you?'

'Why, she is quite charming,' cooed Lady Harworth as Kitty dropped into a deep curtsy. 'And how old are you, child?'

'Not yet twenty, ma'am.'

'Oh, how wonderful. You must talk to Ann, my daughter. She is only a little older than you. She will attain her majority in June. I have no doubt you will have much in common.'

The fair-haired young lady sitting beside Lady Harworth rose to her feet, smiling.

'Mama says that of every young lady we meet. But in your case I think she may be correct.' Ann Harworth took Kitty's arm and led her away to the other side of the room. 'There is a liveliness about your countenance that I like very much.'

Kitty blushed and laughed.

'Thank you, Miss Harworth, I hope I do not disappoint you.'

'I am sure you will not. You come from Yorkshire, you said? We have estates there, or rather my brother does, which is the same thing. Come, sit here in the window with me and tell me how you like London!'

Kitty happily obliged and after a half-hour's lively discussion was pleased when Miss Harworth declared that she had found a friend.

'I am so glad to have discovered someone with a wit to match my own. And someone who knows their own mind, and is not afraid to say so, Miss Wythenshawe.'

'Am I so unusual, then?' asked Kitty, her eyes twinkling. 'I must learn to guard my tongue if I am not to be labelled an oddity.'

'No, no, you must say exactly what you mean. I always do. We are holding a ball on Friday and—Mama, have you invited my aunt?'

'Manners, my love.' Lady Harworth frowned at her daughter's impetuous interruption. 'As a matter of fact we were just discussing it, as well as the little party we will be holding next month to mark your birthday, Ann.'

'So your son will be there on Friday?' enquired Lady Leaconham, flicking a small, triumphant glance towards Kitty.

'I would not consider such an event without his being

there,' replied Lady Harworth. 'It is his house now, after all, and while he says I must continue to treat everything as my own until such time as he takes a wife, it is so very difficult, for I no longer feel like the true mistress now I am a widow. But you must understand that, dear sister, since you are in very much the same position.'

'Well, Garston is somewhat younger than his cousin, Clara, and he is content to leave everything as it was when his dear father was alive,' replied Lady Leaconham.

Kitty heard the faint note of dissatisfaction in her voice and closed her lips tightly to prevent herself from expressing her own opinion. She had not yet met Lord Leaconham but she could not help thinking that at five-and-twenty, her godmother's only son was more than old enough to be taking responsibility for his inheritance.

'But you will come?' Ann implored her. 'Do say you will, *dear* Aunt!'

'Lady Leaconham has agreed to attend, and to bring Miss Wythenshawe with her,' replied Lady Harworth, a touch of impatience creeping into her well-modulated tones. 'Now, pray you go away with your new friend and talk quietly so that your aunt and I may enjoy a little conversation.'

Ann turned to address Lady Leaconham.

'Perhaps Miss Wythenshawe and I could take your dear little dog for a walk, Aunt.'

'But Kitty took him out this morning.'

'I am sure he would enjoy another airing,' Ann persisted. 'It is such a lovely day. I am sure the fresh air would do us good.'

'Oh, do let them go out, sister,' begged Lady Harworth. 'My maid is sitting in the hall with nothing to do, so she may accompany them.'

In the face of such enthusiasm Lady Leaconham capitulated. Ten minutes later the girls were stepping out into Portman Square with the little Scottish terrier trotting merrily along beside them on his silken leash.

Ann gave a noisy sigh and slipped her arm through Kitty's.

'It is so good to be on our own, where we may say what we please. Oh, you need not worry about Norris,' she added, as Kitty glanced back towards the maid following silently behind them. 'She has been with us for ever and is *very* discreet. And I am so pleased that you will be coming on Friday.'

'It will be my very first ball,' Kitty admitted.

Ann gave a little squeak of excitement.

'How wonderful! I shall be able to introduce you to everyone! How long will you be staying in Town?'

'I do not know…as long as Lady Leaconham is pleased to have me with her.'

'I hope it is for ever!' cried Ann. They had reached the gate in the low railing that surrounded the gardens and she stopped. 'This is very pretty, but shall we go instead to Hyde Park? There will be so many more interesting people there.'

Kitty hesitated. 'I do not think…'

'Oh, do say yes,' Ann squeezed her arm. 'We have only to slip across Oxford Street to get there.'

'I do not know London as well as you, Miss Harworth, but I do not think one can *slip across* such a busy thoroughfare.'

'No, but there are crossing sweepers, and we have Norris, so there can be no objection. Oh, do say yes, Miss Wythenshawe!'

Kitty was not proof against her new friend's entreaties. They left the square, safely negotiated the traffic of Oxford Street and soon found themselves in the relative peace of

the great park. Although it was not the fashionable hour
there was a considerable crowd and several carriages to be
seen, but once they had crossed the broad carriageway and
walked some distance from the gates they found themselves
alone. Kitty released the little dog and watched him running happily amongst the bushes.

'Oh, this is infinitely better than a dusty street,' declared
Ann.

Kitty turned her face up to the sun, so much warmer
here than in her native Yorkshire.

'I have to agree, Miss Harworth.'

'Let us be done with this formality. You must call me
Ann and I shall call you Katherine.'

'Kitty, if you please—apart from when Godmama intro-
duces me to new acquaintances the only time I am called
Katherine is when I am in disgrace.'

'Very well, then, Kitty! And since we are now such good
friends, you can tell me if you have a beau.'

'Goodness me, no,' replied Kitty, laughing and blushing
at the same time.

'What, is there no gentleman waiting back in Yorkshire
for you?'

Kitty shook her head. 'There were no gentlemen in Fallridge. None that Mama approved,' she added, thinking back
to the occasions when she had seen the carriages driving
up to the King's Arms for the monthly assembly.

'Farmers and tradesmen,' her mother had said, dismis-
sively. 'Very good people, I am sure, but not suitable companions for *you,* my love.'

'Were you very lonely?' asked Ann.

Kitty looked up quickly, and Ann smiled at her.

'You looked so wistful that I thought, perhaps...'

'Yes, I *was* lonely,' Kitty confessed. 'I should have liked
to go to school—'

'Oh, I went to school,' broke in Ann, pulling a face. 'It was the most horrid experience and of very little use, for apart from learning to dance what do I need with history, or the use of globes, or even to speak French, when we are forever at war with that frightful country?'

'But surely you made friends there?'

'Well, of course, although most of them are married now. Or betrothed.' She flicked a glance at Kitty. 'I am considered quite old to be still unwed, you know. Poor Mama is beginning to despair.'

'And do you not wish to marry?

'Oh, yes,' replied Ann casually, 'eventually I suppose I must accept someone. Poor Mama is even more desperate for Bertram to wed, because he is nearly forty and Mama says we must have an heir. As for me, I am enjoying myself far too much flirting with all the gentlemen of my acquaintance! Do you like flirting, Kitty?'

'I do not think I have ever tried it.'

Her frank reply brought Ann's astonished gaze upon her.

'Never?'

'No, never. I know so few gentlemen, you see. The Squire and Reverend Denny are the only gentlemen who called upon Mama, and they are both very old.'

'But surely you must have come into contact with younger gentlemen?' said Ann, appalled.

Kitty considered for a moment.

'Well, there is Joshua, of course: he is the local farmer's son who drove me to Halifax.'

'No, a farmer's boy does not count,' declared Ann firmly. 'But you must know others. *Think,* Kitty.'

Kitty tried to think, but the only other man who came into her mind was the fierce-eyed Mr Blackwood, and he had not even liked her. At last she shook her head, saying ruefully, 'I fear I am not the sort of girl that gentlemen like to flirt with.'

'Gentlemen will flirt with any female,' Ann retorted. 'It is quite clear to me that you have lived far too sheltered a life, Miss Kitty Wythenshawe, so we must do what we can to make it more exciting!'

Kitty laughed at her. 'I shall be delighted if you can do so! For now, though, we had best return to Portman Square before Godmother thinks we have been kidnapped!'

Kitty called the little dog to her and fastened him on the leash, then the two young ladies set off to retrace their steps in perfect harmony. When they reached the edge of the park Kitty noticed something white fluttering against the trunk of one of the trees. As they drew closer it became clear it was a printed sheet, secured to the trunk with a nail.

'It will be a handbill,' said Ann, when Kitty directed her attention to the paper. 'Perhaps there is a new play at Drury Lane!' She stepped closer, peering up at the words. 'No, it is one of Mr Clarkson's meetings.'

'Thomas Clarkson the abolitionist?'

'You have heard of him?'

'Why, yes,' said Kitty, coming forwards to stare at the paper. 'He travels the country with his talks on how badly the slaves are treated. I have never attended a meeting, however. I have only read reports.'

'Then perhaps we should go to this one,' said Ann slowly. 'It is at the Red Lion in Lombard Street—in the City, where the banks are.' She turned to Kitty, her eyes shining. 'Shall we go? We have a week to concoct a story that will please Mama and Aunt Leaconham. We will take a hackney carriage to the City. It will be so exciting.'

'Now, that's enough, miss,' said Norris, stepping up. 'You know her ladyship will never allow it.'

'She will not know,' replied Ann. 'Not a word of this to anyone, Norris, or I shall have you turned off for insolence.'

The maid snorted loudly. 'I should like to see you try that, miss. What, when her ladyship knows just what a handful you are?'

'You are right, of course, and I should never let you leave me, *dear* Norris!' Ann put her arms about the older woman and hugged her ruthlessly. 'But I am quite determined to go to this meeting, so you must come with us, Norris, to make sure we are safe!'

Kitty could not but admire her tactics. The maid argued for a few moments, but soon gave in to Ann's cajoling, saying bitterly that if she refused then her mistress was quite capable of sneaking off alone and unprotected.

'And what her ladyship would have to say about that, I don't know,' she ended, shaking her head.

'No more do I, Norris,' chuckled Ann, turning to take Kitty's arm again. 'Come along then, we had best make haste back to Portman Square or Mama will be demanding to know just what you were about to let us tarry so long in the gardens!'

They set off, Ann taking no notice of the maid's out-raged mutterings. Instead she began to describe for Kitty the gown she would wear to the forthcoming ball. As they prepared to cross Oxford Street Kitty found her attention caught by someone standing on the far side. There was something familiar about the tall, commanding figure encased in a close-fitting coat of dark superfine wool and nankeen knee-breeches. As they approached the gentle-man turned and with dismay Kitty recognised the dark, aquiline countenance of Mr Daniel Blackwood. He was deep in conversation with another gentleman and Kitty lowered her gaze, hoping they would be able to walk by unnoticed, but her companion broke off from her talk of shell-pink satins with old rose ribbons and scalloped hems to give a delighted cry.

'Bertram! Oh, by all that is famous, what luck is this! Kitty—it is my brother!'

With a sinking heart Kitty watched the gentleman standing with Daniel Blackwood turn towards them. She was struck immediately by the similarity between brother and sister, both fair-haired and grey-eyed, although Lord Harworth was much older and his countenance was the more serious of the two.

Introductions could not be avoided. She allowed Ann to present her to Lord Harworth but all the time she was aware of Daniel's dark, piercing gaze fixed upon her. When at last Lord Harworth drew his companion forward she raised her eyes, opening her mouth, ready to admit they had already met, but Daniel was there before her.

'Miss Wythenshawe and I are already acquainted.' He spoke calmly, with no hint of the broad Yorkshire accent she had expected. Stunned, she could only watch as he reached out for her hand and lifted her fingers to his lips with all the practised ease of a gentleman. 'So we meet again, ma'am.'

Kitty tried to think of something to say, but was distracted by the shrill barking of her canine companion. She looked down to see that the little dog was greeting Daniel like a long-lost friend, jumping up and emitting a series of ecstatic yelps.

Kitty jerked on the lead, saying sharply, 'Down, Titan!'

Daniel raised an enquiring eyebrow. *'Titan?'*

Kitty bridled. 'Be careful,' she said in a voice of rigid self-control. 'He bites.'

Daniel looked down and uttered one quiet command. 'Sit.'

To her surprise Titan sat down immediately, obviously recognising a voice of authority.

'Oh, how sweet,' declared Ann. 'He likes you, Mr Blackwood.'

'Yes, he does,' Daniel responded. He bent to scratch Titan's ears. 'Very intelligent animals, dogs. They have an instinct for a fellow's true character, while humans are so often misled by appearances.' He straightened. 'Would you not agree, Miss Wythenshawe?'

The wicked glint in his black eyes made her seethe inwardly. She put up her chin and gave him back look for look.

'I have always maintained that *actions* are the real mark of a gentleman, Mr Blackwood.'

He bowed. 'Ah, but even a gentleman may fall from grace if the provocation is great enough,' he murmured.

Kitty glared at him, guilt and anger bringing a flush to her cheeks.

'But what are you doing here, Bertram?' Ann demanded of her brother. 'Are you on your way home from your club?'

'No, no, I have been meeting with Blackwood. He is advising me on a—ah—business venture that I am considering. When I found he was staying in Greenwich, I told him it was foolish of him to remain at the Spread Eagle when there is so much I want to discuss with him, so he has agreed to be my guest for the remainder of his stay.'

'You never told me about this, Bertram,' said Ann, smiling up at Daniel in a way that Kitty considered to be far too friendly.

'We have only this minute decided upon it,' replied her brother. 'We are on our way back to Harworth House now, to send a messenger to Greenwich with instructions for Blackwood's man to pack everything up and bring it here. But what are you doing out, Ann?' asked Lord Harworth. 'Does Mama know?'

'Oh, yes,' came the airy reply. 'She is visiting Aunt Leaconham. Aunt is Miss Wythenshawe's godmama, you know. We offered to take her dog for a walk and are on our way back to Portman Square now. Why do you not come with us? You can say hello to Aunt Leaconham and I am sure Mama would be glad of your escort back to Cavendish Square.'

'An excellent idea,' declared Lord Harworth, holding out his arm to Kitty. 'What do you say, Blackwood, will you help me escort these two young ladies to Portman Square? It is not far out of our way and there will still be plenty of time to get a message to your man and have him back here with your bags before dinner.'

Kitty's hopes rose a little when Daniel hesitated.

'Will that not be an imposition? After all, I do not know Lady Leaconham...'

'Then we shall introduce you,' cried Ann. 'I am sure she will be pleased to meet an acquaintance of her goddaughter. Besides,' she added naughtily, as she took Daniel's arm, 'I am intrigued to know more of you, sir. Miss Wythenshawe assured me she had no personable gentlemen amongst her acquaintance.'

'Did she indeed?' Again those coal-black eyes quizzed Kitty. 'I suppose our meeting slipped her mind. It was quite a trivial event, after all.'

Trivial! Kitty's eyes blazed with fury. She had been picked up and dropped, quite callously, into cold, muddy water that had quite ruined her gown and boots and stockings. If Godmama had not been so generous she would even now be obliged to walk out in skirts stained quite six inches deep at the hem!

'You are right.' She threw the words over her shoulder as she and Lord Harworth led the way back to Portman Square. 'I had quite forgotten you, Mr Blackwood.'

Kitty turned her attention to her escort, forcing herself to converse with Lord Harworth as they made their way back to Lady Leaconham's house, but all the time part of her mind was racing with conjecture about Daniel Blackwood. Just to know he was behind her made her spine tingle, as if he might pounce upon her at any moment. What was he doing in London, and what had happened to the rough country voice he had used in Yorkshire? She thought she knew the answer to her last question and her conscience pricked her when she remembered how uncivil she had been towards him. She had assumed he was a rough labourer and he had responded in kind. She deserved that trick, she acknowledged, but she had *not* deserved his subsequent treatment of her! Her indignation grew with every step and by the time they arrived at Lady Leaconham's door Kitty was full of righteous fury. When they entered the hall she left all the explanations to Miss Harworth and stalked past the wooden-faced butler to hand Titan over to a hovering footman. By the time she turned back the rest of the party were divesting themselves of hats and surcoats. Daniel took advantage of the confusion to step up to her.

'I have long wanted to offer you an apology, Miss Wythenshawe,' he said quietly. 'My actions when we last met were inexcusable.'

'I do not want your apology!' she said in a fierce whisper, and immediately regretted her incivility.

'But I would like to make some recompense to you—I fear I ruined your gown—'

A mixture of anger and remorse combined in Kitty and

she answered recklessly, 'My gown is of no consequence. I have *trunks* full of clothes, so you need concern yourself no further with me!'

With that she put her nose in the air and sailed into the morning room.

'After you, Blackwood.'

Lord Harworth was standing back, waiting for Daniel to follow the ladies.

'Thank you, I really do not—' Daniel bit off the words. He wanted to tell Harworth to go to the devil and storm out of the house, but that would be the height of incivility, and, however little Miss Wythenshawe might think of him, he had been brought up a gentleman and would act like one. Curbing his temper, he nodded and strode into the room, forcing himself to smile and say everything that was required of him, but all the time he was aware of Kitty standing in the corner, biting her lip and darting fiery looks at him from those stormy green eyes. He had offered her his apology and it had been rebuffed. He clenched his jaw, smiling with even more spurious interest at something Ann Harworth was saying. If the chit could not bring herself to act in a civilised manner than he would have to show her how it was done!

Kitty could barely suppress a sigh of relief when at last the visitors took their leave and it was the greatest trial for her to sit quietly while her godmama declared herself delighted with the success of the visit.

'And what a sly little puss you are, my love,' Lady Leaconham chuckled, tapping Kitty's knuckles playfully with her fan. 'I send you out for a little walk and you return with two eligible gentlemen in tow!'

'Mr Blackwood is not in the least eligible,' protested Kitty.

'He is my nephew's guest, is he not? To be sure a mill-owner's son is not what your mama would like for you, but he is very gentlemanlike, *and* he is related to some of the wealthiest shipping families in Liverpool.'

'It smacks of trade, Godmama.'

'It smacks of a fortune, my dear,' responded Lady Leaconham drily. 'However, I will grant you that a man like Mr Blackwood should only be considered as a last resort. Lord Harworth would be a more prestigious match for you.'

'He is indeed more what Mama had in mind,' agreed Kitty. 'But is he not a little…old, Godmama?'

'At eight-and-thirty? Not at all, my love. It makes it all the more likely that he is looking in earnest for a wife. But we must be practical. Every cap in Town will be set at such an eligible *parti*. However, not every young lady will have an invitation to the Harworth ball, so I have great hopes for Friday, my love. Great hopes indeed!'

Chapter Three

Any hopes Kitty might have had for her very first ball were eclipsed by apprehension. Mama had insisted that learning to dance was a prime requirement for every young lady but Kitty was very sure that dancing with the Squire's daughters in the privacy of Fallridge Manor was a very different matter from standing up with a gentleman in a crowded ballroom. And she would have to stand up at least once because Lord Harworth, prompted by his sister, had requested that she save a dance for him.

When Friday arrived Kitty resolved to wear the evening gown that Mama had made for her rather than any of the dresses purchased by Lady Leaconham. Politely but firmly she rejected her godmother's suggestions of the pink sarcenet or the blue spider gauze and insisted on wearing the simple white crape gown ornamented with silver embroidery to the sleeves and hem. Aunt Jane had embroidered a silk shawl to match and she had a pair of white satin dancing slippers to complete the ensemble. Kitty was quite satisfied with the result, but she was more than a little nervous when she joined her godmother in the drawing room

'Well, Godmama, what do you think?'

She spread her skirts and gave a little twirl before fixing her anxious gaze upon Lady Leaconham.

'To be sure it is a much simpler design than the evening gowns I had made for you,' said my lady, studying her closely. Kitty held her breath. At length her godmother smiled. 'But is looks quite perfect upon you, my love. And no one will recognise the seamstress, you may be sure of that.' She blinked rapidly and began to hunt for her handkerchief. 'You look like an angel, my dear.'

'She does indeed!'

Kitty spun round to see a rather portly young gentleman in the doorway, regarding her through his quizzing glass.

'Garston!' Lady Leaconham flew up from her chair in a flutter of lace. 'My dear boy, when did you return to Town?'

'At noon, Mama,' replied Lord Leaconham, suffering her embrace. 'Thought I should come and tell you I was back. Didn't know you had company...'

'My love, this is my goddaughter Katherine, come to keep me company for a few weeks,' said Lady Leaconham. 'Kitty, my dear, allow me to present my son Garston to you.'

Kitty dropped into a curtsy, blushing a little as Lord Leaconham bowed over her hand.

'Delighted, Miss Wythenshawe. Proule informs me that you are about to go out, so I know that all this splendour is not in my honour.'

'We are off to Harworth House,' replied Lady Leaconham, a note of triumph creeping into her voice. 'Your cousin Ann has taken a great liking to dear Kitty. Why do you not come with us, my son? I am sure your aunt would have invited you, had she known you were back in Town.'

Lord Leaconham was still casting an admiring eye over Kitty, who found the prolonged scrutiny a little unnerving.

'I am dining with friends at my club tonight but I may well look in later.'

'Well, if you are coming, pray be in time to dance with Kitty and do not spend all your time in the supper room,' replied his mother, picking up her wrap. 'Now, we must be off. Come along, my dear, we will go downstairs to wait for the carriage.'

Lady Harworth might complain that her house was not situated on the magnificent west side of Cavendish Square but it seemed to Kitty that the whole of fashionable London was intent upon attending the ball. The square was crowded with vehicles. Coachmen and postillions traded insults while liveried footmen directed the carriages to the entrance before tenderly handing down the occupants and escorting them into the house.

Kitty followed Lady Leaconham up the wide sweeping staircase, her nervousness somewhat alleviated when she saw Ann waiting for her at the top of the stairs, a beaming smile upon her face as she held out her hand to Kitty.

'Is this not wonderful? I have never seen so many carriages in the square before. It is going to be *such* a squeeze, and Mama has hired a whole host of musicians to play for us. I cannot *wait* for the dancing to begin!'

'Well, you must contain yourself a little longer,' put in her mother, directing a smile towards Kitty. 'There are any number of people still to arrive. Now pray, Ann, allow Miss Wythenshawe to move on, that the other guests may approach.'

Kitty glanced behind her: a column of gorgeously gowned ladies and elegant gentlemen stretched all the way down the stairs. It was quite unnerving to see so many strange faces. She knew so few people, despite having been in Town for a whole month. Kitty was so daunted by this thought that when she saw Daniel Blackwood enter the house and join the line she could not suppress a smile of relief.

It was unfortunate that the gentleman should glance up at that moment, raising his brows when he saw her smiling down at him. Kitty quickly turned away, blushing furiously. What had possessed her to smile at the man? Resolutely putting this aberration aside, she followed her godmother into the ballroom, only to stop on the threshold and gaze about her in astonishment. The lofty room was ablaze with light from several glittering chandeliers. Everywhere was colourful and noisy confusion, the sounds of the musicians tuning up adding to the laughter and chatter of the guests.

'Good evening, Aunt, Miss Wythenshawe.' Lord Harworth stepped up to them and bowed. He gazed at Kitty, appreciation in his slightly protuberant grey eyes. 'I hope, Miss Wythenshawe, that you have not forgotten you have promised to dance with me later this evening?'

Kitty gave him a shy little smile. 'No, indeed, my lord.'

'Good,' responded his lordship. 'Capital. I shall look forward to it.'

'Well, that is an exciting start,' declared Lady Leaconham, as Lord Harworth moved off to greet more guests.

'It is, ma'am,' said Kitty, feeling rather overawed. 'At least I shall have one dance partner tonight, and if Lord Leaconham should turn up and dance with me as well I shall think myself very content.'

'Oh, I do not think we need to rely upon Garston tonight,' declared her godmother, her voice rich with satisfaction. 'I have already noticed several gentlemen looking at you with interest, my love. I shall introduce you to everyone I know, and with you looking so very pretty this evening I have no doubt that we shall soon find you any number of partners. And with luck a good many of them will be unmarried!' She took Kitty's arm and began to look around her. 'Now, where shall we begin?'

Between them, Lady Leaconham and Miss Harworth introduced Kitty to so many people—turbaned matrons, bewhiskered lords and eager young gentlemen—that there was no possibility of her remembering all their names, but she should not complain, for when the musicians finally began to play she had the satisfaction of walking out on to the dance floor to join the very first set. Her initial anxiety soon disappeared as she realised she was familiar with all the steps and she uttered up a silent prayer to the squire for employing such an excellent dancing master. After that first dance, she found there were a number of gentlemen eager to partner her and she began to enjoy herself. Rather to his mother's surprise, Lord Leaconham arrived in time to stand up with Kitty for a minuet and even came back later to escort the two ladies to the supper room, where he remained to entertain them until it was time to return to the dancing.

It was towards the end of the evening when Lord Harworth came to claim his dance with Kitty. He appeared to be in the very best of spirits, although she suspected that the high colour in his cheeks was partly the result of the rather potent punch being served at supper. After a particularly lively country dance he pulled her hand on to his arm.

'Well done, Miss Wythenshawe. My sister informs me this is your very first ball, but to see you dance one would never know it.'

'Thank you, my lord,' Kitty replied. 'I did not expect to enjoy myself half so much. Everyone has been most kind, especially you, sir, and your sister.'

'Phshaw!' Lord Harworth puffed out his chest. 'Think nothing of it, Miss Wythenshawe. Now, where shall I take you, who is your next dance partner?'

'Why, sir, I do not think I have one, so perhaps you could escort me back to Lady Leaconham…'

'What, no partner?' cried my lord. 'But these will be the last dances of the night. We cannot have you sitting out! I promised m'sister we would keep you amused tonight, so we must see what we can do…'

Lord Harworth raised his head and began to look about him.

Kitty disclaimed and declared herself perfectly ready to join her godmother, but her escort merely patted her hand as he raised his voice to address someone.

'Blackwood—just the man! You are not dancing?'

The press of people had prevented Kitty from spotting Daniel Blackwood, but she saw him now as he stepped towards them, unsmiling, towering over her, a dark and brooding figure in the colourful crowd.

He said briefly, 'No, my lord. I do not dance.'

'Nonsense, man, you trod a very pretty measure with Ann earlier this evening, I saw you! I have here a delightful partner for you.'

Kitty went cold.

'Believe me, my lord,' she began, 'there is no need—'

'Nonsense, you will be doing Mr Blackwood a great

service,' cried Lord Harworth jovially. 'I am appalled to think he has been standing around all evening.'

'I assure you, my lord,' Daniel began, his tone clipped, 'I have partnered more than one young lady tonight—'

'Then you must dance again, sir!' Lord Harworth took Kitty's hand and held it out. 'Come along, Blackwood, take Miss Wythenshawe to the floor!'

Kitty thought she might die of embarrassment. Daniel, his face cold and shuttered, held out his arm to her and when she slipped her fingers on to his sleeve he silently led her away.

'I am sorry,' she managed, biting her lip. 'I know you want this as little as I do.'

'Society has its rules, madam, and we must both adhere to them.'

His indifferent tone had its effect in rousing Kitty's spirit. She put up her chin.

'For either of us to walk away would have given rise to conjecture.'

'Quite,' he replied. 'So let us get through this dance as best we may.'

'Certainly,' she said icily. 'After all, we need only stand up for one dance, and there is no necessity for us to speak to one another.'

However, once the music started and she put her hand into his, something very strange happened. It was as if she had danced with Daniel Blackwood many times before: their steps matched perfectly as they followed the traditional movement of the country dance and when they were required to separate their fingers seemed reluctant to part. Bemused, Kitty raised her eyes and regarded her partner, only to find him watching her with a fierce glow in his eyes that brought the colour rushing to her cheeks. She had danced with many gentlemen that evening, she had even performed a very stately minuet with one fair-haired young man reputed to be the epitome of a fashionable Adonis, yet none had had the same effect upon her. Not one of them had infused her with the soaring elation she experienced now, the feeling that she and her partner were alone in the room, the only people in the world.

The dance drew to its conclusion. He bowed, she made her curtsy, but neither made any move to leave the floor. The cry went up for the last dance and suddenly they were surrounded by even more couples, all jostling to find space. With so many dancers on the floor Kitty found herself very close to Daniel, so close that she could not move without her arm brushing his sleeve. Kitty looked up and saw the rueful smile upon his face as if he, too, realised there could be no possibility of maintaining a cool reserve once the lively music began. With a jolt of surprise Kitty realised she did not mind. Suddenly all the hurt and anger she had felt for the man melted away. He took her hands.

'Are we ready, Miss Wythenshawe?'

She found herself smiling up at him.

'Perfectly, Mr Blackwood.'

Kitty would never forget that final country dance at Harworth House. It was hot and noisy and it seemed as if all the world was crushed into the ballroom, everyone bouncing and skipping, laughing and shouting and deter-mined to expend every last ounce of energy before they went home. Garston and Lord Harworth were on the floor, each squiring a handsome young lady, and at one point she came close to Ann dancing with the fair-haired Adonis, but Kitty hardly noticed them. All her attention was on Daniel. She no longer thought him dark and menacing. She could see beyond the rather austere cast of his countenance to the warmth in his dark eyes, the faint curve of his lips that was not quite a smile yet told her he was happy to be at her side. He was not the tallest man in the room yet to Kitty he stood head and shoulders above every other gentleman. He held her hand and led her confidently about the room, skilfully manoeuvring to put himself in the way and prevent her from being buffeted by the jostling dancers. He bore no resemblance to the boorish brute who had treated her so abominably, but instead was more like a guardian angel, strong, gentle and protective. She stole another look at him as he danced her down the line. No, *not* an angel: the strong jaw and athletic frame were more those of a warrior. A hero. By the time the music ended Kitty was the victim of such conflicting emotions that she dare not even look at her partner. She wanted to appear calm and assured, but she suddenly felt extremely shy.

Daniel was enjoying himself. It surprised him, for the stately minuets of the first part of the evening had been a lifetime away from the lively dances he had enjoyed at home and, although he had partnered one or two of the blushing young ladies Lady Harworth had brought up to him, he had found the evening a little dull. He had even considered how soon he would be able to make his excuses and retire. If Harworth had not persuaded him to stay in Cavendish Square he could have excused himself on the grounds of the long journey back to Greenwich. To leave the party and travel no further than the next floor would be the height of incivility.

He had been aware of Miss Wythenshawe from the first moment he had looked up and seen her at the top of the stairs, such a delightful smile on her face that his heart had flipped over, until he came to his senses and realised that there was no possibility that she could have directed such a smile at him, and he looked around him, trying to discover just who was the lucky recipient of her favour. He had done his best to prevent his eyes dwelling on her as she glided about the room in her sparkling white gown, her dark curls glowing in the candlelight. She had made it very plain that she despised him and thus she was not worth his notice. When Harworth had insisted he lead her on to the floor Daniel had fully intended to leave her after that first dance together, to make some excuse to quit the ballroom, but she had been so light on his arm, had danced so beautifully that he had forgotten she was the proud disdainful woman who had scorned him. He saw only an entrancing, ethereal creature that bewitched his senses. So he persuaded himself that it was only polite to remain for the last set. Harworth would expect it of him.

The final, energetic measure of the evening was much more like the assemblies he attended at Hestonroyd: too many dancers, too little space. He remembered standing up with his sister Bella, leading her through the movement of the dance and all the time trying to protect her from the other couples who were charging up and down the room. But this silver and white creature beside him was most definitely not his bouncing, boisterous sister! He was almost sorry when the music ended. He stood beside his partner as they joined in the spontaneous applause for themselves and the musicians, then he held out his arm, ready to escort her back to Lady Leaconham. Some of his good mood evaporated when he looked down at the still little figure beside him. Her lips were firmly closed and she laid only the tips of her fingers on his sleeve, as if she could not bring herself to touch him. He was disappointed at the change from his lively, sparkling dance partner. Silently he delivered her back to Lady Leaconham but in response to his parting bow her thanks to him were uttered in a cold, stilted manner and she turned away immediately. Daniel's jaw tightened. So much for enchantment!

'An excellent evening, eh, Blackwood?' Lord Harworth came up to him, his mother leaning on his arm. 'I hope you enjoyed yourself, sir. 'Twas your first ball here in Town, was it not?'

'It was, my lord.'

'I doubt you have such glittering occasions in the north, Mr Blackwood,' remarked Lady Harworth.

'Certainly we cannot boast such elevated society as one finds in Town, ma'am,' returned Daniel, 'but we have our balls and assemblies.'

'Indeed, Mama, they ain't savages,' chuckled Lord Harworth. 'And we shall soon be adding to the society, ma'am, will we not?' He turned to Daniel, smiling. 'Mama has suggested that we should open Kirkleigh Hall and take a party to Yorkshire in July. You suggested we should travel north to look at the mills and Kirkleigh is perfectly placed between Hestonroyd and Arkwright's mills at Cromford, less than a day's ride from either place. No harm in mixing a little business with pleasure, eh, Blackwood?'

'No indeed, my lord,' said Daniel. 'Although I had planned to show you more than just Cromford: if you are serious in building a mill of your own we shall not have a great deal of time for society—'

'Nonsense, sir, there is always time for society!' declared Lord Harworth. 'We shall take a little longer over the business, that is all, and I have no doubt Mama will like to entertain while we are there—even a ball, eh, Mama, now you have seen Blackwood dance? I am sure we can find you a few pretty girls to stand up with, although none to surpass your last partner.' He gave Daniel a playful dig in the ribs. 'Exceptionally pretty little thing, ain't she?'

'Miss Wythenshawe?' said Daniel coolly. 'She is far above my touch.'

'Indeed?' said Lady Harworth, suddenly showing an

interest. She turned to watch Kitty as she walked out of the room. 'Letitia was not very forthcoming about her family. I believe she comes from the north, too—do you know her family, Mr Blackwood? Are they very wealthy?'

Lord Harworth laughed.

'Must be as rich as Croesus if they won't look at Blackwood, Mama. His family owns half of the West Riding!'

Daniel disclaimed, but Lady Harworth was not listening. She excused herself, saying, 'I believe my dear sister is about to leave, and I must go and say goodbye to her.'

'Well, that was a success and no mistake!' Lady Leaconham settled herself back into the corner of her carriage and gave a satisfied sigh. 'You danced every dance, and I cannot tell you how many compliments I received for you, my love! You were enchanting.'

Kitty gave a little nod but said nothing. She knew that at least one person was less than delighted with her. She had been quite dismayed by her behaviour towards Daniel Blackwood at the end of the evening, when she had suddenly been overcome with nerves. She had intended to be charmingly grateful for his standing up with her, yet when she spoke she had been cool to the point of rudeness. Even now she was embarrassed to think of it.

So she would not, she decided quickly. She would concentrate instead upon what her godmother was saying.

'Yes, Kitty dear, I could see from the first that Lady Harworth was disposed to like you. I was afraid she might think you a little *too* pretty, but with your dark hair you are such a contrast to Ann's fair beauty that you complement one another perfectly! And nothing could have exceeded Clara's affability, when she came up to us just as we were leaving. She hinted at many more invitations this summer.'

'How delightful for you, Godmama.'

'For *me?* Kitty, you little goose, the invitations will be for you, too.'

'But I have already been with you for a whole month, ma'am. I thought I should be thinking of returning home very soon...'

'Nonsense,' retorted her godmother briskly. 'A month is nothing, and if my niece has taken to you then nothing could be better than for the two of you to be seen together—so much more attractive than to be always accompanied by a matron!' Lady Leaconham paused while she smoothed the wrinkles from her long gloves. 'My sister can seem a little...cold to those she thinks beneath her notice, but I know she takes her responsibilities very seriously. I have no doubt she would like to see Bertram settled and raising a hopeful family, but Ann must be causing her some anxiety, to be nearing one-and-twenty and still unmarried! So I can quite see why Clara is happy to promote your friendship with her daughter. Two such pretty young ladies out on the Town together will be sure to attract any number of gentle-men.' Lady Leaconham reached out and placed a hand on Kitty's knee, saying urgently, 'Think of it, my dear: if we can secure a gentleman of good birth with even a modest fortune, the settlements will allow your mama and her sister to give up their sewing and live in the manner more suitable to their stations!'

'Yes, I suppose so,' said Kitty, brightening. 'And you think it is possible, Godmama?'

'I think it very likely,' returned Lady Leaconham, lean-ing back in her corner. 'You charmed a number of gentle-men this evening, even my nephew. What a great thing it would be if he were to offer for you.'

'Lord Harworth? Oh, no, ma'am, surely not. He

was merely being kind to me, because I am your god-daughter.'

'He showed you a great deal of attention, my love. But perhaps you are right: we must not be too ambitious for you. But neither must we settle for anything less than your equal in birth—whoever we choose for you *must* be a gentleman!'

From the number of callers at Portman Square over the next few days it did indeed appear that Kitty had made a good impression at her very first ball, as her godmother was quick to explain to Ann when she came to see Kitty.

'I am delighted to hear it,' declared Ann, smiling. 'I have never known Mama to be so taken with any of my friends before.' She added, when Lady Leaconham had left the two young ladies alone, 'Was it not the most wonderful ball? I was engaged for every dance, and whenever I looked across you were always dancing, too!'

'Yes, I was very fortunate. I had not looked for such attention.'

'And you even persuaded dour Mr Blackwood to stand up with you.'

'Why do you call him dour?' asked Kitty, intrigued in spite of herself.

Ann wrinkled her nose. 'Well, he is perfectly *polite*,' she said slowly, 'but he is so very quiet, and only seems to want to talk business with Bertram.' Her eyes twinkled and she added ruefully, 'He makes no attempt to flirt with me. In fact, he makes no attempt to engage my attention at all! I am most impressed that he danced with you.'

'That was your brother's doing.' Kitty felt the colour rising to her cheeks. 'I think, since he is staying in your house, he could hardly refuse to dance with me when Lord Harworth suggested it.'

'Yes, that will be it.' Ann nodded. 'They have become wondrous great friends. My brother wrote to old Mr Blackwood when he first conceived the idea of building a mill and they were corresponding for several months before Mr Daniel Blackwood came to London. Bertram says that with the exception of Mr Arkwright, no one knows more about mills and manufacturing than the Blackwoods. But this is very boring talk! Let us discuss instead the Abolition meeting tomorrow evening. Have you given any thought to how we shall get there?'

'I confess I have not,' admitted Kitty. 'Perhaps we should not go, if your mama disapproves...'

'Mama disapproves of everything except achieving a great match for Bertram and the same for me,' declared Ann. 'I am determined to go. It is quite the fashion now, you know, to support the abolition of the slave trade.'

'My family have been fighting against slavery since before I was born,' replied Kitty. 'My father was vehemently opposed to it, and my mother still does what she can—we do not buy sugar from the West Indian plantations, you know.' She wanted to add that Mama could not afford to buy very much sugar at all, but remembered her godmother's warning that she should not chatter on about her family. Ann was regarding her with admiration.

'How good you are! I have no idea whether Bertram has any slaves, but I am even more determined that we shall go to the meeting tomorrow. Now all you need do is to tell Aunt Leaconham that I am taking you to join us for dinner tomorrow and that we will not be returning until late. What time shall I call for you?'

'It cannot be too early,' replied Kitty. 'I have an engagement tomorrow. With Lord Leaconham. He is going to take me driving in the park.'

She ended a little hesitantly. Garston had issued the

invitation and Kitty had accepted quite happily without reference to her godmother, but when Lady Leaconham heard of her plans she had looked a little shocked.

'I am sorry, Godmama,' Kitty had said, anxious and bemused. 'I thought there could be no harm in going out with Lord Leaconham in an open carriage.'

'No, of course not. It is just that...' Lady Leaconham bit her lip and gazed at Kitty, a shadow of unease in her eyes. 'It is just...I do not want you to develop a *tendre* for Garston, my dear. I had planned on finding him, um...'

'You want him to take a rich wife,' Kitty finished for her. She had been in Town long enough to know that every man and woman of marriageable age was intent upon making a brilliant match. 'Yes, I quite see that, Godmama, and you need have no fear: I am sure Lord Leaconham only offered to take me out in order to please you.'

'I expect you are right,' said Lady Leaconham, much relieved, 'and it will give you the opportunity to be seen in the park at the fashionable hour.'

So Lady Leaconham gave the outing her blessing.

Kitty set off with Lord Leaconham, knowing that her godmother would be far more disapproving of her engagement with Ann Harworth, if ever she learned the truth of it.

It was a beautiful summer's day and much as Kitty wanted to turn her face up to the skies and feel the sun's warmth on her skin, she knew that this would be frowned upon. Instead she unfurled her parasol, looking around her with interest as Lord Leaconham drove his phaeton through the busy London streets. Her initial apprehension at riding so high above the ground soon disappeared and she relaxed, looking forward to her excursion.

'Heavens, how crowded it is,' she remarked, as they

turned in through the park gates. 'I thought it busy enough when Miss Harworth and I brought Titan here for a walk one morning.'

'Oh, I have seen it ten times worse than this,' cried Garston, gaily flourishing his whip. 'I have been here when we have been forced to crawl along at a snail's pace because there is so much traffic. But it is not yet five o'clock. We are early. I have no doubt it will fill up later.'

Kitty heard this with dismay. She had been expecting the great park to offer some peace and solitude after the hustle and bustle of the busy streets but all she could see was a host of fashionably dressed people riding, driving or walking, everyone intent on seeing and being seen.

Their own progress was slow for the park was full of Garston's friends, some of whom she knew, but many she did not, so that each stop necessitated explanations and a few moments' conversation.

'Well, Miss Wythenshawe, are you enjoying yourself?' Lord Leaconham enquired as they moved off from yet another introduction.

'Why, yes, my lord. Very much. Although I am afraid that with so many of your acquaintances here today we shall not complete even one circuit of the park.'

He laughed. 'What a jokesmith you are, Miss Wythenshawe! One does not come to Hyde Park for the drive! No, no: when I go to White's this evening I shall be complimented on the fine new rig I was driving this afternoon, and of course upon my charming companion. To be seen here will bring you to the attention of a great number of useful people, I assure you.'

She did not know what to reply; she was not at all sure she wanted to be brought to anyone's attention.

Kitty was beginning to wonder if she would be back

in Portman Square before Ann called for her when she suddenly heard her escort give a low whistle.

'By heaven, that is a most beautiful piece of horse-flesh.'

Kitty looked up to see two riders approaching and had no difficulty in recognising the creature that had drawn Garston's admiration—a sleek black horse with a deep chest, refined head and a bold eye. The animal seemed well aware that it was a handsome beast for it carried itself proudly, almost as proudly as the straight-backed gentleman in the saddle: Daniel Blackwood. He was accompanied by Lord Harworth but to Kitty's mind neither the older man's bearing nor his glossy bay hack could compare with the dark grandeur of Daniel and his mare. But Kitty remembered seeing the very same horse and rider when they had looked much less grand, covered in mud in a lane above Halifax. Once again the mortification of that encounter overwhelmed her and she hoped fervently that the two riders might not see them in the crowd, but Lord Leaconham pulled up the team, waving his whip to attract their attention. She smothered her dismay as the gentlemen drew rein and turned their mounts towards the phaeton.

Lord Harworth greeted Kitty in his usual friendly way but his companion gave only a slight nod of recognition.

'Blackwood, ain't it? We met at the ball the other night. By Jove, that's a fine horse you have there, sir,' declared Garston. 'Broad chest, good sloping shoulders, intelligent eye—magnificent!'

Daniel acknowledged the compliment with a nod.

'Thank you. She's Yorkshire bred, of course.'

'Of course.' Garston laughed. 'We've a few good hunters at Leaconham but nothing as fine as that.' He cocked an eyebrow at Daniel. 'How much d'you want for her? She looks up to my weight. Yes, I'd like to buy that mare.'

Daniel's dark brows rose.

'What, when you haven't seen her put through her paces?'

'No need, Blackwood. I can tell just by looking that she is a good all-round mount, certainly at home here in Town, but I have no doubt she comes into her own in the hunting field. Well, Blackwood, what d'you say? Name your price, sir!'

'Thank you, my lord, but no. Marnie has been with me for so long I believe she will see her days out in my company.'

'As you wish,' replied Garston, shrugging. 'But I'm not beat yet. Mayhap you will give me a chance to win her from you one night, when we've had a few glasses of wine together. Now what d'ye say to that, sir, eh?'

Kitty saw the faint hint of contempt creep into Daniel's dark eyes.

'I never gamble—'

'Never gamble?' cried Garston, 'why, man, you will be telling me you don't like cock-fighting next!'

'As a matter of fact, I don't,' Daniel replied curtly. 'But I was going to say that I never gamble with what is important to me.'

'Ha, very wise,' agreed Lord Harworth. 'That's a lesson we could all learn, eh, Leaconham? But we are holding you up, sir, and we should not keep the horses standing. Nor should we keep a lady here in this heat. You will want to get on, Miss Wythenshawe.' He smiled at Kitty. 'Has that madcap sister of mine acquainted you with her latest scheme?' Kitty's eyes widened. Had Ann told her brother of their visit to Lombard Street that evening? She was about to speak when Lord Harworth continued, saying jovially, 'A picnic! My mother has a small property a little way out of town, on the Cambridge road. She rarely uses it but the grounds are very pretty and Ann has decided we should dine there, *al fresco.*'

'Miss Harworth has said nothing to me, my lord,' replied Kitty, thanking Providence she had not mentioned the Abolition meeting.

'Well, depend upon it she will. I have no doubt that she is even now plaguing my mother to write the invitations.' He touched his hat. 'Good day to you, Miss Wythenshawe. Leaconham.'

As the gentlemen moved off, Garston turned in his seat to watch them.

'Do you know, I was not that enamoured of Blackwood when I first met him. Far too serious for me, and he drinks hardly anything—Bertram tells me he never goes beyond the third bottle. Not the sort to go out on a spree! But having seen his horse, damn me, I think he can't be such a bad fellow after all! I can even forgive him for not liking to gamble! Seems to be great friends with Harworth.'

'I believe Mr Blackwood is a manufacturer,' said Kitty carefully.

'Ah, that might explain his gloomy looks,' nodded Garston, setting his team in motion. 'Not brought up to enjoy himself, or to appreciate the finer things in life.'

'He is a very good dancer,' she responded, determined to be fair.

'Ah, well, that might give him an advantage with the ladies, but a man without a taste for gambling, or cock-fighting, well—'

He broke off as he negotiated the busy road leading out of the park and Kitty was pleased to let the subject drop. She had come perilously close to defending Daniel Blackwood, and that would never do!

There was little time for conversation when she returned to Portman Square. By the time she had changed her gown and tidied her hair, Lord Harworth's carriage was at the door. She had told her godmother that Ann had invited her to dine since her mother and brother were to be out that evening. This was perfectly true, but what she did not explain was that they would be having a very hurried dinner before setting out for Lombard Street.

During her short time in London Kitty had never been further east than St Paul's, but now they were venturing deep into the City and she felt a little apprehensive as their hired cab trundled over the cobbles in the narrow streets.

'Is this not exciting?' exclaimed Ann, her eyes shining. 'I have never been to a public meeting before!'

'I am not sure that your mama or your brother would approve,' murmured Kitty, regarding the garishly painted inn where the carriage had drawn up.

'No, that is why I suggested we should be veiled,' Ann replied, unabashed. 'And why I did not want to use one of our own carriages with the crest upon the door.' She laughed. 'Do not look so anxious, dear Kitty. We shall be perfectly safe for we have Norris with us, do we not?'

Kitty nodded, trying to look more cheerful, but a quick glance at Ann's maid sitting silent and tight-lipped in the corner was far from reassuring. However, when they had pulled their veils down over their faces and descended from the cab Kitty was heartened to see that the people making their way up the stairs to the meeting room looked most respectable. It was, after all, early evening, she told herself. They would be safely back in Cavendish Square before the long summer's day had drawn to a close.

Kitty would have preferred to slip on to one of the benches at the back of the room but Ann had spotted empty chairs much nearer to the dais where the speaker would be standing and was already making her way towards them,

so Kitty had no alternative but to follow. At the front of
the room a tall gentleman with a shock of red hair was
opening up a large trunk in the centre of the dais and she
heard someone address him as Mr Clarkson. Kitty regarded
him with interest, for she had read a great deal about the
fiery speaker who travelled all over the country promot-
ing the abolition movement with evangelical zeal. He was
very pale and there were dark circles beneath his eyes: she
suspected he was worn down by the arduous task he had
set himself.

'Oh, goodness,' hissed Ann suddenly. 'Look who
has walked in! You see how wise we were to disguise
ourselves.'

Kitty turned to see Daniel Blackwood striding towards
the front of the room. As he approached, Mr Clarkson
looked up and greeted him with every appearance of
delight.

'Well, of all people I did not expect to see Mr Blackwood
here,' Ann whispered. 'Bertram told me he is connected
to one of the foremost shipping families in Liverpool, and
they derive a great part of their fortune from slaves, you
know. However, he does seem to be on the best of terms
with our speaker.'

There was no opportunity for Kitty to reply because at
that moment a large bewhiskered gentleman banged on the
table to bring the meeting to order. From behind the safety
of her veil Kitty allowed her eyes to follow Daniel as he
retreated to a chair at one side of the room. The audience
hushed as Mr Clarkson began to address the crowd.

Kitty had not known what to expect from the meeting:
she had read in the newspapers about the Abolition meetings held in Manchester and Leeds, but when Mr Clarkson
began to explain about the horrific conditions endured by
the slaves during their long sea voyage from Africa to the

West Indies she found her indignation growing, and when he reached into the trunk and took out the thumbscrews, shackles and branding irons that he had collected during his investigations into the cruelty of the trade, she felt physically sick. Kitty was not alone in her sentiments: murmurs of outrage ran around the room during the meeting and she heard cries of anguish from some of the other ladies present. She was so incensed that when the meeting ended she ignored Ann's whispered protests and joined the queue of people waiting to sign their name to a petition that would be presented to Parliament.

'What is the point in our coming here so secretly if you are going to declare yourself?' demanded Ann, standing beside her.

'I do not think my name will stand out amongst the hundreds already written on the paper,' she replied as she took up the pen. 'Besides, I want to show that I am opposed to such cruel practices. My father certainly would have approved of my actions. There...it is done.'

Ann grasped her arm. 'Very well, now let us get out of here before we are discovered.'

They were forced to walk in line between the rows of empty chairs that stood between them and the door. Ann led the way and Kitty followed, head bowed, lost in her own thoughts. Suddenly she realised that her friend had stopped and she looked up to find Daniel Blackwood blocking their way. He towered over them, unsmiling, as he inclined his head.

'Miss Harworth, Miss Wythenshawe.'

'M-Mr Blackwood, what a pleasant surprise!' replied Ann, quick to recover her composure. 'If we had known you were coming here—'

He interrupted her, saying drily, 'You would not ask

me to believe that Lord Harworth knows you are here unattended.'

'Well, no,' confessed Ann, while Kitty stood silently behind her. 'However, we were determined to come, and it is *such* a worthy cause!'

'It is, of course,' he responded gravely. 'But you will notice that all the other ladies here are accompanied by a gentleman. If you will give me a moment, I shall escort you home.'

His tone brooked no argument and he went off to take his leave of Thomas Clarkson. Ann turned to Kitty.

'Well, it was unfortunate that he recognised us, but I think we may yet persuade him not to give us away.' She added philosophically, 'And if Mama does learn of our coming here, at least she will be comforted to know that we had Mr Blackwood's escort.'

By the time they left the meeting room the crowd had disappeared and it was a matter of moments to find a cab to take them back to Cavendish Square. They were still settling themselves into the worn leather seats when Ann threw back her veil and demanded to be told how Mr Blackwood had recognised them.

'I made sure with our cloaks and veils no one would know us,' she added.

'As a guest in your house you should expect me to recognise your maid, Miss Harworth,' he replied with the glimmer of a smile. 'And since I was in the room when you asked your brother to send the carriage for Miss Wythenshawe, I deduced that she was your companion.'

Kitty put up her veil: there seemed little point now in disguise.

'And did Lord Harworth know that you were attending the meeting this evening, Mr Blackwood?' she asked him.

Daniel's dark brows went up.

'I had made no firm plans before Lord Harworth went out this evening so no, he did not. But even if I had told him it would make no odds; Lord Harworth is not my guardian, after all.'

'No, but there will be no need to tell him you saw us, will there, sir?' said Ann, giving him a coaxing smile. 'After all, no harm has been done.'

'No harm this time, but such meetings can turn ugly. We were fortunate that the slave-traders did not send in a mob to break up the meeting, as I have heard they are wont to do. But in any case I would never advise you to travel into the City unescorted, Miss Harworth. These streets can be very dangerous: there is more to be lost than your reputations, you know.'

Kitty knew he was speaking the truth. They had been foolish to take such a risk. With her impeccable lineage and large fortune, Ann might be regarded as high-spirited or eccentric if their escapade was made public. For Kitty, however, the consequences could be disastrous. As her godmother constantly reminded her, if she wished to make a good marriage she would need to protect her reputation.

At that moment Daniel's gaze shifted to her face. The harsh features relaxed slightly and again Kitty saw the smile lurking in his eyes.

'I will not lie, Miss Harworth, but I shall not say anything about this evening, unless I am taxed directly.'

'Oh, thank you, sir! Kitty, are we not greatly indebted to Mr Blackwood? And you must be sure to accompany us on our picnic, sir. I shall insist that Bertram brings you along. We shall be as merry as grigs!'

Perhaps it was because her own mind was still struggling over the plight of the slaves that Kitty thought she saw a shadow cross Daniel's face when Ann spoke with such frivolity. Ann was chattering on about her plans for the forthcoming picnic, but when she drew a breath Kitty said quickly, 'May I ask how you know Mr Clarkson, sir?'

'Cambridge,' said Daniel. 'We were there together when he won the Latin Essay contest.'

'And were you both concerned for the plight of the slaves then?' asked Ann.

Daniel shook his head.

'I doubt if either of us gave it a thought at that time. Clarkson started looking into the subject of slavery to write his essay.' He shrugged. 'We were not close friends: when we left Cambridge, I went back to Yorkshire to join my father running the family business. But it seems that Clarkson could not forget what he had learned about the slave trade. Instead of going around the world as he had intended he came to London and has been working with the Society for the Abolition of the Slave Trade ever since, travelling the country setting up sub-committees and organising petitions. I have followed his career from the reports I have read, but have not seen him for years. Then I heard of the meeting this evening, and as I was not engaged elsewhere I thought I would look in.'

'But does not the Abolition run contrary to your own family interests, sir?' asked Kitty. 'I understand you have connections with shipping…'

'Not at all,' he replied coolly. 'My concern is manufacturing. It is true the cost of cotton may rise if slavery is abolished, but we will weather that storm, I am sure. Those members of the family more closely connected with the slave trade must look to their own consciences.'

'Let us pray that they do, sir.'

Kitty's earnest response brought his hard eyes upon her.

'And what is your interest in this matter, Miss Wythenshawe?'

She met his gaze without flinching.

'Hardship and suffering such as we have heard about tonight should be the interest of every Christian, Mr Blackwood!'

'It *should* be, Miss Wythenshawe,' he agreed, 'but so many prefer to turn a blind eye and enjoy a life of ease and enjoyment.'

She bristled at that.

'My father was a great supporter of the Abolition. He died when I was a child but I hope I have not lost sight of his principles.'

'Well, I will insist we no longer purchase sugar from the West Indies,' declared Ann. 'I shall tell Aunt Leaconham to do the same. Only...what of my sorbets and sweetmeats?' She looked up at Daniel. 'Oh, dear, shall I be obliged to give them up completely?'

Her look of dismay was so comical that both Daniel and Kitty laughed.

'There are other sources of sugar, Miss Harworth,' Daniel told her, 'but they may not be quite so plentiful, or so cheap. You may still have your sorbets and sweetmeats, but fewer of them.'

It was agreed they should take Kitty to Portman Square before Daniel escorted Ann and her maid back to Harworth House.

'There is no point in your coming back with me just to go home again,' reasoned Ann.

The carriage rolled up to the door of Lady Leaconham's house and Daniel jumped down, ready to hand Kitty out of the carriage.

'Now remember, Kitty, tell no one where we have been tonight!' Ann warned her, but Kitty hardly heard the words. She was very conscious of her hand lying snug in Daniel's strong grip as he helped her to alight and she was not a little alarmed at the effect his proximity was having upon her breathing.

'Well, Miss Wythenshawe, will your conscience allow you to lie?'

She saw the gleam of amusement in his eyes. There was no animosity there, no attempt to belittle her. She ventured a small smile.

'I shall do my best to avoid the subject.' She added, as he had done, 'Unless I am taxed directly!'

He executed a little bow and squeezed her fingers. Kitty dropped a curtsy. Peeping up at him, she found he was smiling down at her and she was unable to tear her eyes away. She wanted to speak, but words would not come to her. The breath caught in her throat: some silent message was passing between them. She could not comprehend it, but it left her excited, exhilarated and frightened, all at the same time. Her pulse was galloping, thudding through her body. Did he feel it, too?

'Kitty, make sure you tell Aunt Leaconham to look out for Mama's letter, inviting you both to our picnic.' Ann's voice from the carriage recalled Kitty's wandering senses. With a final, tremulous smile she pulled her fingers free and hurried indoors, hoping the servants would not notice her burning cheeks.

Daniel climbed back into the carriage. He was only dimly aware of Ann chattering away to her maid in the corner. In his mind he was going over again the recent exchange with Kitty. So there was another side to the proud and disdainful Miss Wythenshawe. She appeared to be deeply affected by what she had heard at the meeting. Not that there was anything so unusual there, for Clarkson was a great orator and could soften the hardest heart, but what she had told him of her father hinted at deep-seated liberal opinions, something he had not even guessed at.

There had also been a moment of shared humour. Daniel flexed his fingers, feeling again the shock of excitement he had experienced when he had taken her hand. His reaction unsettled him, the more so because it was very rare for him not to be fully in control of any situation. Silently he stared out of the window: he was intrigued to learn more of Miss Kitty Wythenshawe.

Chapter Four

Two days later Lady Harworth's letter was delivered to Portman Square, inviting Lady Leaconham and her goddaughter to join her picnic party at Wormley.

'Well, this is excellent,' she told Kitty as she perused the note with a smile of satisfaction. 'My dear Clara has never invited me to one of her *al fresco* parties before, even though we are sisters!'

Lady Leaconham's pleasure at the forthcoming trip was somewhat dimmed when she discovered that her son had no intention of accompanying them. Lord Leaconham was dining at Portman Square when his mother mentioned the forthcoming picnic.

'Devil a bit, Mama,' protested Garston, looking pained. 'I'm engaged to join a party of friends for a beefsteak dinner at Chipping Barnet.'

'But surely, escorting Kitty and myself to Wormley Hall should take precedence? Lady Harworth's hospitality will not be stinting, I am sure.'

Lord Leaconham pulled a face.

'Perhaps not, but she will not be serving beefsteak and oysters, now will she? And I can't say I want to wander about the gardens all day before dining *al fresco* on cold meats, Mama. Not my style at all.'

Regarding Lord Leaconham's substantial figure, Kitty considered that wandering around a garden might be more beneficial to the young man than sitting indoors drinking porter and eating beefsteak, but she held her peace.

However, Lady Leaconham was not to be put off. She continued to refer to the picnic throughout the evening.

'But my love, surely you do not want your mama driving out of town without a gentleman's escort? Why, it is not done.' Lady Leaconham resorted to her finest weapon, her handkerchief. She flicked it out and dabbed at her eyes. 'I should never be allowed to travel unescorted if your father was alive.'

'Very well, I will tell you what I shall do,' said Garston, exasperated. 'I will come with you as far as Barnet—it is on the way, after all.'

'On the way?' retorted my lady, in a far from lachry-mose tone. 'What nonsense is this? We will be taking the Cambridge road!'

'Well, if you take the Great North Road instead you could drop me at the Rising Sun. After that it would not take you long to cross Enfield Chase to pick up the Kentish Lane. There, what do you say to that?'

It was not ideal; Lady Leaconham would much have preferred to have her son's company for the whole day, but he was not to be moved so she had to be satisfied.

'After all,' she said to Kitty once Garston had left them, 'my son is a dear, dear boy but he is so very much like his father: not *stubborn* exactly, but a man of fixed views, and once he has made up his mind, there is no changing it.'

Kitty did not see Ann again before the picnic, and since she heard nothing more about their outing to Lombard

Street she hoped their attendance at the Abolition meeting had gone unnoticed. Although she was relieved at this, Kitty was nevertheless anxious to support the cause, but apart from persuading her godmother to refrain from buying sugar imported from the slave plantations there was little she could do as a single young lady. Judicious enquiries of her godmother elicited the information that the Leaconham fortune came from estates in England and Ireland and although an earlier Lord Leaconham had dabbled in investments in the West Indies these had not been a success and the link had been broken. A suggestion to Lord Leaconham that he should raise the matter in the House brought the daunting response that he had not yet taken his seat, being far too busy. However, the subject raised a dilemma for Kitty and when she next sat down to write to her mother she voiced her concern that since so many of the families in Town had connections with the slave trade she could not, as Papa's Daughter, consider an alliance with any of them. Not that she had as yet received any offers, she hurried to point out. Her mother's response was typically pragmatic: much as she applauded her daughter's liberal views, Kitty must do and say *nothing* to discourage any advantageous offer, but to remember that as the wife of a rich man she would be much better placed to influence both her husband and the debate.

Lady Leaconham said much the same thing and, while she agreed that they would no longer use cane sugar from the West Indies, she begged Kitty not to voice her opinions in public.

'It is a very worthy cause, I am sure, and I have read that Mr Wilberforce is very eloquent on the subject, but it is not something to be discussed in my drawing room.'

'I beg your pardon, Godmama,' replied Kitty, anger bringing a warm flush to her cheek, 'but it should be discussed in *every* drawing room!'

'Well, perhaps when you are with your close friends,' conceded Lady Leaconham, 'but it makes people uncomfortable to think about it, and that will make them shy away from you. My dear, the reason for you being here is to find you a husband, and we shall not do that if you do not *conform*. And while we are talking of such things, perhaps I should just drop you a word of warning.' Lady Leaconham began to fidget and pluck at the skirts of her gown. 'I have been very careful not to be too explicit about your circumstances.'

'My...circumstances, Godmama?'

'The fact that you have no fortune, my dear. It is nothing to be ashamed of, and you have such pretty manners that people cannot fail to like you, but we do not want to prejudice anyone against you.'

'Are you saying that people will not wish to be acquainted with me if they know I am *poor?*' said Kitty baldly.

'My dear, there is no need to be quite so blunt,' protested Lady Leaconham. 'All I ask is that you refrain from discouraging eligible gentlemen by being too truthful—about your country upbringing, for example—or expressing your more...liberal views.'

Kitty bit her lip. She very much wanted to say that she did not want a husband if he did not share her opinions, but then she had a vision of poor Mama and Aunt Jane, sitting in their cold little cottage, struggling to set their stitches in the failing light and unable to afford to buy good candles and coal from their meagre income. They had scrimped and saved, forgoing all luxuries to send her to London. The more she thought about it the more she realised that, having spent their savings on this trip, Mama and Aunt Jane were now in a very perilous position, for if they could no longer make a living from their sewing then they would have nothing at all to live on. Fearful visions of them being thrown onto the streets began to haunt her. She must not let them down. Kitty fought down a sigh: her resolution to marry well had not seemed quite so problematic when she had been in Yorkshire.

Kitty saw that Lady Leaconham was regarding her anxiously and she gave her a reassuring smile. 'Very well, Godmama, I promise you I shall try to avoid saying anything that would make you uncomfortable. I will do my best to do my duty.'

Lady Leaconham gave a very audible sigh. She smiled and patted Kitty's cheek.

'There. I knew you were a good girl! Oh, and I almost forgot to tell you that your new walking dress has arrived.'

'Another dress? Oh, ma'am, you are spoiling me!'

'Nonsense. We were agreed that you should have a new one, were we not? After all, you walk out every morning when you take Titan for his exercise.'

Kitty laughed.

'No one sees me at that time in the morning, Godmama!'

'Nevertheless you cannot have too many walking dresses. And when I was with Madame Sophie last week I saw the most beautiful sprigged muslin that I knew would look lovely on you. It is for our picnic tomorrow. I want you to look your best for Lord Harworth.'

'But I am sure Lord Harworth has no interest in me, except as his sister's friend.'

'Perhaps not, but there is no harm in your looking your best for the picnic,' responded Lady Leaconham. 'And since you will be together for most of the day tomorrow, it would do no harm to make yourself agreeable to him, now would it? After all, he is by far the most eligible bachelor we know, and even if he is only a baron think how happy your mama would be if you were to become Lady Harworth!'

With her godmother's words ringing in her ears, Kitty rose the next day and made her preparations for the picnic. She dressed carefully in the new gown of pale primrose, its bodice embroidered with tiny flowers in a deeper lemon, and she allowed Meakin to style her hair so that her glossy dark curls would peep out beneath the shady brim of her villager straw hat. When a servant scratched upon the door to tell her Lord Leaconham had arrived and that Lady Leaconham was waiting for her in the morning room, she took a final look in the mirror, picked up her parasol and hurried downstairs.

'My dear, you look charmingly,' smiled Lady Leaconham as she entered the morning room. 'Well, Garston, what do you think of my protégé now?'

'By Jove, Mama, she's a veritable diamond!' declared Lord Leaconham. 'Been thinkin' so for a while now.' He raised his quizzing glass to stare at Kitty, who wished she had draped a neckerchief around the low neckline of her gown.

'Yes, well I am hoping we can fix Lord Harworth's interest,' put in Lady Leaconham, adding pointedly, 'It is not so important for *him* to find a rich wife.'

'Dash it, Mama, he is not that much wealthier than me!' muttered Garston but his mother was not listening.

She swept up, put her arm through Kitty's and carried her towards the door. 'The carriage is here—shall we go?'

In recognition of the sunny weather, Lady Leaconham had elected to travel in the open landau, and once the busy streets were left behind Kitty had to admit that it was very pleasant to be bowling along with the sun shining down upon them. There was just enough breeze to make it necessary for her to pull her Norwich shawl about her shoulders, which had the added advantage of screening her décolletage from Lord Leaconham's admiring gaze. She was not sorry when at last they reached the steep hill leading to Chipping Barnet, where they were to part company with the young lord and she had the impression that her godmother, too, was relieved he was not now accompanying them further. Lady Leaconham had taken the precaution of hiring outriders, two liveried servants on horseback who would accompany them to Wormley and as they drove away from Barnet she now declared herself perfectly satisfied with their escort.

'And who knows,' she ended with a hopeful little smile, 'you are looking so pretty today, my dear Kitty, that Lord Harworth might decide to accompany us on our homeward journey!'

Kitty said nothing. She could not recall Lord Harworth paying her any particular attention, and she hoped for nothing more from the day than a pleasant time spent in congenial company. The image of Daniel Blackwood flashed into her mind and in an unguarded moment she hoped he would be there. She quickly stifled the thought: she had come to London to find and marry a gentleman, not a blunt Yorkshire manufacturer!

Wormley Hall was a beautiful old manor house set in large grounds that had been landscaped some fifty years ago. The trees had matured, the gravel paths and artificial lakes were somewhat overgrown and the whole now possessed the beautiful, slightly neglected air that was fashionably romantic. Several carriages were drawn up on the drive when they arrived and it was not long before

Kitty was being introduced to Lady Harworth's guests, those considered worthy of sharing the treat of an *al fresco* dinner. Several young people were present and Ann soon carried Kitty away to join them.

'I am so glad you could come,' she declared, linking arms with Kitty. 'I do so love to eat out of doors. We are going to dine down there.' She waved her arm in the direction of the lake, where a dozen or so servants were following a lumbering wagon to the far bank. 'But before we walk there Mama wants to show everyone the formal gardens.' Ann giggled, then lowered her voice. 'Mr Grant has written an ode that he is going to read to us.'

Kitty followed her glance towards a very thin young man with a mop of brown hair. He was even now poring over a notebook.

'Do not expect too much, Miss Wythenshawe,' laughed another member of the party, a stocky young man with a florid complexion. 'Julian's poems are never very good.'

'Y-you w-will eat your w-w-w-words one day, Ashley,' retorted Mr Grant, pushing his hair out of his eyes. 'Just w-w-wait until my work is published!'

Laughing and chattering, the group of young people followed their elders round the house to the south front, where the formal gardens stretched before them. They gathered round while young Mr Grant read them his 'Ode to a Fallen Rose' and applauded politely, then Lady Harworth conducted them around the gardens, pointing out the new plants and marble statues that had recently been introduced.

'I wonder that you will take so much time over these gardens, Mama, when you never stay here,' said Ann, smothering a yawn.

'One never knows what might happen,' replied Lady

Harworth, leading them back towards the house. 'I am minded to live here, should Bertram take a wife.'

Lady Leaconham was looking about her anxiously. She waited for Ann to come up to her and said casually, 'Ann, dear, is your brother not joining us today?'

'Oh, Bertram is around somewhere...yes, here he is now.'

Kitty found herself smiling at her godmother's look of relief when Lord Harworth emerged from the house, Mr Blackwood walking beside him.

'My apologies that I was not here to greet you, ma'am,' said Lord Harworth, bowing over his aunt's hand. 'Blackwood and I were looking at the new range we have installed in the kitchen—the latest thing, you know, enclosed firebox, bigger hot-water tank...'

'Oh, Bertram, our guests are not interested in that,' protested Ann.

'Not yet, perhaps,' put in Daniel. 'It may not be so necessary on a warm day like today, but imagine yourself coming in after a day's hunting, muddy and dirty and wanting a bath before going down to dinner. By keeping a small fire in the range there will always be hot water for you.'

He was smiling directly at Kitty, who found herself wanting to smile back until Lady Harworth's voice cut across the moment.

'Very interesting to *you*, I am sure, Mr Blackwood, since you understand these things and are always talking to my son about spinning jennies and water frames, but I do not think our guests wish to concern themselves with the domestic arrangements of the house, what do you say, Miss Wythenshawe?'

Everyone's attention turned to Kitty. Her godmother was watching her and she read the appeal in her eyes—she must not appear provincial. She thought of her mother and her aunt in their cottage in Fallridge, cooking on the little hob-grate with only a maidservant to help them.

'You must excuse me,' she said quietly, 'I know nothing of cooks and kitchens.'

'That is not to say she is not an excellent housekeeper,' Lady Leaconham rushed in, giving a nervous laugh. 'But I doubt my goddaughter has ever had the need to venture into a kitchen. Am I correct, Kitty?'

'No, I have not.'

'Then Miss Wythenshawe is very fortunate,' murmured Daniel.

His smile had disappeared and Kitty wanted to protest, to explain that it was not because she had an army of servants at her beck and call that she had never entered the kitchen of a grand house, but Lord Harworth was turning towards her, offering her his arm.

'I think we should be making our way to the lake. May I escort you, Miss Wythenshawe?'

Kitty did not need the little nudge in the back from Lady Leaconham to remind her of her duty, but she did try to smile a little more warmly at Lord Harworth as she tucked her fingers into the crook of his arm and walked off. She would not think of Daniel and his black looks, nor the fact that when she had put her hand on Daniel's arm at the recent ball she had felt a little buzz of excitement run through her body. She could remember even now the feel of the hard sinews beneath his sleeve, the coiled energy of the man in the solid muscle. Lord Harworth's arm merely felt...solid.

The party making its way around the lake to the picnic site was a very jolly one, with plenty of chatter and laughter and Kitty did her best to join in, responding in kind to her escort's jovial remarks. She tried not to think of Daniel, who was following some way behind. When they reached the designated dining area Lord Harworth excused himself and rushed off to instruct the servants on the placing of the remaining tables and Kitty was left to wait for the others to come up. Daniel and Ann were the first to arrive and as they approached she was somewhat surprised to hear Ann alluding to the Abolition meeting.

'Kitty has successfully persuaded my aunt to give up plantation sugar, but I have not been able to help at all,' Ann was saying to Daniel. 'Bertram has investments in the West Indies, you see, so it is impossible for us to purchase our sugar elsewhere. And as Bertram says, if we all stop buying sugar then the poor plantation workers will starve, and what good will that do?'

'It might force change,' Daniel replied, but Ann was not listening.

'Besides, if you consider what we use in one household,' she continued reflectively, 'it is not so very much, after all, so what good would our little protest do?' She smiled at Kitty. 'We would be inconveniencing ourselves to very little effect, do you not agree?'

Kitty hesitated; her godmother's warning was still fresh in her mind.

'I think, if there were enough *little protests,* they might have a profound effect,' she replied carefully. She excused herself and moved away, determined not to be drawn into the argument, but not before she heard Daniel's comment.

'Miss Wythenshawe does not appear quite so eager to support the movement now. Perhaps her enthusiasm has waned since the meeting.'

'We were all moved by Mr Clarkson's talk that evening,' replied Ann. 'But when the heat of the moment is passed then rational thought returns. I tried to dissuade her from signing the petition, but she was adamant she would do it...'

Kitty heard no more. She moved away quickly to join her godmother, who was being invited by Lord Harworth to sit at his table. It would do no good to assure Ann that she was as passionate as ever about the evils of slavery, and such a public declaration could only upset her godmother, so she tried to put the conversation out of her mind and concentrate upon the picnic.

The sun continued to shine and the party was in excellent spirits as the footmen served them with a delicious assortment of dishes, most impressive of which were the sorbets and chilled lemonade brought down from the house in a wagon full of ice.

'Oh, this is delightful,' cried Ann. 'I do hope the fine weather holds a little longer. Perhaps we could dine out of doors for my birthday, Mama.'

'And where would you suggest we do that, miss?' retorted her mother. 'The terrace is not wide enough and Harworth will not allow you to trample all over his flowerbeds.'

'No, indeed,' chuckled Lord Harworth. He turned to Kitty. 'You must know, Miss Wythenshawe—indeed, I am sure Ann has told you, such good friends as you have become!—that my sister has persuaded me to hold a little dance for her birthday before we go north for the summer. I hope you will be able to come?'

'Oh, I—um—'

'Of course we shall, Bertram dear.' Lady Leaconham smiled. 'And I am sure Leaconham will come, too.'

'But why is my nephew not here today?' demanded Lady Harworth. 'I made sure my invitation included him.'

'He is engaged to join a party of friends today, at Barnet,' explained Lady Leaconham, helping herself to another dish of sorbet.

'Barnet,' cried Lord Harworth. 'Ah, that will be at the Rising Sun, no doubt. They are famous for their dinners.'

'That is correct,' affirmed Lady Leaconham. 'We shall drive back that way and collect him on our return to Town.'

'I hope he has a good head then,' laughed Mr Ashley, sitting at a nearby table. 'I believe the wine and brandy flow pretty freely at those affairs!'

'Not sure I'd want *my* m-mother to see me after such a meal!' remarked Julian Grant.

'Heaven forbid,' muttered Mr Ashley. 'It might give you inspiration for another of your dreadful odes!'

Lady Leaconham was busy conversing with her sister and Kitty was thankful she did not hear this interchange.

'Tell me, Miss Wythenshawe…' Lord Harworth turned to address her '…how does this compare with your life in the north?'

'It is very…different, my lord,' she replied.

'A little warmer, I don't doubt,' he chuckled. 'My mother always bemoans the fact that when we are at Kirkleigh the weather is rarely conducive to dining out of doors. So how do you amuse yourself at home? Balls, assemblies…'

Kitty was at a loss to know how to reply and was thankful when her godmother came to her aid.

'My dear Kitty has lived very retired, my lord. Her mother is a widow now, of course, but Mr Wythenshawe was a man of *very* strict principles. Not,' she added hastily, 'that he had any objection to parties, but only in *select* company.'

'And are you well acquainted with Mr Blackwood's family?' enquired Ann.

'Not at all,' Kitty replied hastily.

'Oh?' Ann looked up, surprised. 'But when we met him in Oxford Street you said—'

'Yes, but we do not move in the same circles.'

Kitty hoped in vain that her words had not carried across the table to Daniel. She saw his dark frown descend.

'I told you, my lord,' he said, 'Miss Wythenshawe is far above my touch.'

The icy words coincided with a small cloud crossing in front of the sun and a sudden, uneasy hush fell over the company. It lasted only a couple of seconds, but Kitty was mortified.

'No, no, I never meant—'

Her anguished protest was no more than a whisper and it was lost as Lady Harworth rose from the table, signalling the end of the meal. There was a sudden flurry of activity as everyone followed suit and Kitty looked towards Daniel, hoping she might be able to apologise and explain herself, but he was already moving away, giving his arm to a dashing young matron.

'Miss Wythenshawe?' Lord Harworth was holding his arm out to her. 'Shall we walk?'

Silently she put her fingers on his arm, responding mechanically to his remarks while inwardly berating herself. It was so difficult! In trying to please her godmother and conceal her impoverished circumstances she appeared proud and conceited. Suddenly she could restrain herself no longer; she burst out, 'My lord, when I spoke just now, about my family in the north, I fear I offended Mr Blackwood—'

'Blackwood, offended?' exclaimed Lord Harworth. 'No, no, I am sure he is not. After all there is no denying that he is a manufacturer and while you might bump into him at Harrogate, perhaps, it is not surprising that you have not met him at any of the grander houses. Not but that the situation might change in the future,' he added and when Kitty looked an enquiry he tapped his nose. 'Meetings in Whitehall, m'dear! Can't say more, but let us just say that I am not averse to furthering my acquaintance with the Blackwood family.

'Now, Miss Wythenshawe, if we take this path you will find we have a very good view of the house across the lake…well, what do you think of that? Magnificent, eh?'

Kitty duly admired the view, but even while she was conversing with her escort she was thinking of Daniel. She must talk to him. Despite their past differences and the fact that he had treated her abominably, her conscience would not allow her to rest until she had explained herself. However, Lord Harworth and his guests were in no hurry to conclude their rambles through the woods and it was a good hour before the party gathered again at the house and carriages were summoned. Kitty spotted Daniel standing by himself and resolutely made her way across to him, steeling herself for her apology. She needed all her nerve to keep going, for the look he bestowed upon her when he saw her approaching was not at all encouraging. Kitty squared her shoulders, bracing herself to meet his harsh stare.

'Mr Blackwood, if I may have a word with you.' He regarded her with eyes as hard as stone. She took a breath. 'I w-wanted to beg your pardon. I think my words earlier might have been misconstrued.'

'Oh, I understood you perfectly, Miss Wythenshawe.'

'No! I never meant to imply that my family was above yours,' she told him earnestly. 'I know nothing of your circumstances.'

'That much is very true!'

'And you know nothing about me!' she retorted. 'I am

sorry for it if I appear to you to be bent upon nothing but pleasure.'

His lip curled.

'Why should you be any different from all the other fashionable young females in Town? And do not think that your attendance at Clarkson's meeting gives you any reason to feel especially self-righteous: I am well aware that it is currently a fashionable cause.'

Kitty's cheeks flamed. She said angrily, 'Not for me!'

She saw the disbelief in his eyes and was surprised at how much his contempt stung her. She hated arguments and wanted desperately to turn and walk away: after all, what did it matter what he thought of her? But she found it *did* matter. She forced herself to speak.

'My father died ten years ago, Mr Blackwood, when I was but a child, yet I remember his liberal views, and his correspondence with like-minded acquaintances on the subject of slavery. A number of pamphlets on the subject remain amongst my father's papers. I have always considered the plight of those less fortunate than ourselves to be of the utmost concern.'

Kitty held her ground, steadily meeting his dark, unfathomable gaze. At last he said coldly, 'Then perhaps you should be committing your energies to the cause of abolition, madam, rather than looking out for a rich husband!'

Daniel turned on his heel and strode away. Hell and damnation, could he never meet the woman without quarrelling? She had come to him to apologise for her ill-chosen remarks. He should have received her apology with a dignified silence. After all, he was used to being snubbed by those who considered themselves to be his superiors, regardless of the fact that they had little to their name except a title. Their ancient houses were for the most part crumbling and impoverished. He had thought himself above such considerations, proud of his heritage, knowing that his father had earned his money with honest toil and now held the welfare of hundreds, if not thousands, in his hands: spinners, weavers, carders, combers and silverers— the list of those involved in the manufacture of cloth was endless. As he himself became more involved then the responsibility fell upon his shoulders, too.

He strode through the ornamental gardens and on around the side of the house, and as he worked off his anger in exertion, he found himself considering the situation more rationally. He stopped, his head coming up as the realisation hit him. It was not Miss Wythenshawe's comments that had angered him, but seeing her hanging on Harworth's arm. By God, he was jealous!

Daniel began to walk again, more slowly this time, while he tried to understand this new emotion. Damnation, Miss Katherine Wythenshawe had got under his skin. She was nothing like the ripe beauties who had caught his eye when he had first come to Town, women with whom it was possible to pass an enjoyable hour or so, but who were then so easy to forget. No. Katherine—Kitty—was proud, self-opinionated and extremely annoying, but one could not forget her!

He had reached the stable block by this time. Through the arch he could see the yard was full of activity as the teams of horses were brought out from the stables and harnessed to the respective carriages, each one under the watchful eye of the coachman. It had been agreed that Daniel would accompany Lord Harworth and his party back to Town later, when the rest of the guests had departed, so he saw no reason to add to the workload of the grooms by demanding his horse should be saddled up immediately. He perched himself on a mounting block just outside the entrance to the yard, intending to regain his composure in this shady spot before rejoining the main party. The noise from the stables spilled out of the yard and the clatter of hooves echoing under the arch told him that the first of the carriages was about to leave. He turned to watch Lady Leaconham's coachman overseeing the stable boys as they pulled up and secured the hoods of the landau, while the two outriders stood to one side, drawing on their gloves. None of them noticed Daniel, sitting still and silent in the shadow of the wall.

'So we're to pick up his lordship at the Rising Sun,' said one of the outriders.

The other gave a short laugh.

'That's what 'er ladyship thinks.' He turned to spit on the ground. 'I'd wager he's caught a fox by now!'

'The mistress won't like that,' growled the coachman. 'She told him to be ready to come home at six o'clock.'

'Aye, she might've *told* 'im but he'll have been drinking since she set 'im down. And let's be honest, his lordship ain't one to hold his drink well.'

The coachman chuckled.

'There'll be fireworks at Barnet, then,' he said, climbing up onto the box. 'Come on, lads, mount up, else 'er ladyship will be after your hides, too!'

Daniel sat back against the wall and watched the carriage drive past him, the two outriders trotting smartly along behind. He remembered the chit's look of horror when he had climbed into Mr Midgley's carriage in all his dirt. A grin tugged at his mouth: how much more uncomfortable would she feel making the journey back to Town in the company of the drunken Lord Leaconham!

Chapter Five

The drive back to Chipping Barnet was accomplished in good time, with Lady Leaconham expressing herself highly satisfied with the day.

'To dine *al fresco* with the Harworths is an honour not afforded to everyone,' she told Kitty. 'And that my nephew should choose to spend so much time with you is very encouraging. I was pleased to see you making yourself so agreeable to him.'

'I hope I did not seem too forward, Godmama,' replied Kitty, alarmed. 'I had no thought other than to be polite. I would not like Lord Harworth to think I was encouraging his advances...'

'That is exactly what you were doing, you silly puss,' chuckled Lady Leaconham. 'I admit when you first came to me I had no thought of aiming so high for you. I had hoped to find you a gentleman of comfortable means, but a *baron,* and my own nephew at that—well!'

She subsided into her corner, engrossed in her own happy thoughts and leaving Kitty prey to much more disturbing reflections. There was no doubt she was enjoying her time in London, although she missed Mama and Aunt Jane. She found the society diverting, but although she knew her mother had sent her to Town in the hope that she would find a husband, the idea of spending more than a day in the company of any of the gentlemen she had met, even Lord Harworth, filled her with dismay. Sadly she had discovered that most of the eligible gentlemen were empty-headed and so full of their own conceit that she found them positively disagreeable after a half-hour's conversation. Others, like Lord Harworth, were perfectly agreeable but, she was ashamed to admit it, rather *dull*.

The thought flashed into her mind that Daniel Blackwood was neither dull nor empty-headed. He was infuriating, of course, and arrogant, and outspoken, but one could never accuse him of being boring.

The carriage began to slow and Kitty saw that they had arrived at the Rising Sun. The shadows were already lengthening in the cobbled yard as they drove in. The landlord came bustling out to greet them, grinning broadly and wiping his hands on his apron as he addressed them through the open carriage window.

'Good day to you, ma'am—and you, miss! 'Tis very busy here today, but I am sure we can find you a room…'

The man's genial smile disappeared when Lady Leaconham demanded to see her son.

'L-Lord Leaconham, m'lady? He's one of those who came for the beefsteak dinner in the upstairs dining room, I believe. I am afraid they are not yet concluded.'

He cast a glance upwards, where sounds of raucous merriment could be heard coming from an open window on the first floor.

'Then you will inform him I am here!' commanded my lady.

'Aye, ma'am.' He flicked his head and a young boy scampered away into the inn. 'Will you not come in and take some refreshment, madam...?'

'No, I want to collect my son and go home.'

'Well, ma'am, you see...' The landlord shifted uncomfortably.

Lady Leaconham waved to him to open the door and she alighted from the carriage, Kitty following close behind her.

'What is the matter with you—he is here, is he not?' demanded Lady Leaconham.

'Aye, he's here. That is—'

'Well, let us to him!'

Lady Leaconham swept towards the inn, the landlord hurrying after her, but before they had gone more than a few steps Garston appeared in the doorway, looking flushed and bleary-eyed.

'Oh, so it *is* you, m'm.' He placed one hand on the doorframe to steady himself. 'Wasn't expectin' you yet.'

'I think you have lost track of the time, my son,' replied Lady Leaconham. 'Come along now, fetch your things and let us be off. I want to reach Portman Square well before dark.'

'Ah, well, that's the thing,' replied Garston, enunciating his words with enormous care. 'Not sure I'm up to travellin' at the moment.' He gave his mother a smile of great sweetness. 'Excuse me, Mama. Rather fancy I'm about to cast up my accounts.'

With that he swung round and vomited at the side of the doorway.

Kitty gasped, while Lady Leaconham remained rooted to the spot, staring at her son. Behind them, one of the outriders gave a short laugh.

'Told you 'e wasn't one to 'old 'is drink.'

Lady Leaconham whirled about.

'How dare you be so impertinent! You are dismissed, both of you!'

'But, Godmama, we need their escort—'

'I will not tolerate insolence!' retorted Lady Leaconham, white with fury. 'How dare they suggest my son is... is inebriated! Go, I say! You will be gone from my service by the morning—and leave your livery behind you, or I shall have you arrested for robbery!'

In dismay Kitty watched the two outriders clatter out of the yard. Lady Leaconham took a few steps towards Garston, who was still leaning against the wall, groaning. Tentatively she put her hand out to him.

'Come along, my son, get into the carriage and let us be gone from this place. What were your friends about, could they not see you are unwell? Come, my love, let me help you.'

'Don't think...anyone...can...' muttered Garston.

He turned, leaning his back against the wall as his legs crumpled under him and he slid to the floor, unconscious. Lady Leaconham gave a little scream.

'Oh, good heavens—oh, my poor boy! Quickly, someone, run and fetch a doctor!'

The landlord stepped forwards, shaking his head.

'Nay, my lady, I'm sure if we was to get him upstairs and into a bed—'

'No, no, fetch a doctor! Oh, I shall go distracted,' cried Lady Leaconham, reaching out to grip Kitty's arm. 'Quickly, child, where is my vinaigrette? I fear I am going to faint.'

'Now that won't help anyone, madam,' said a deep, calm voice behind them.

Kitty looked round to see Daniel Blackwood jumping down from his horse.

'And the landlord's right,' he continued bluntly. 'Leaconham is drunk: best to take him upstairs and let him sleep it off.' He signalled to the coachman and footman, who ran forward to pick up Garston and carry him inside.

Kitty felt Lady Leaconham sag against her, but even as she struggled to support her, Daniel stepped up to take the matron's free arm.

'Come, ma'am,' he said. 'Allow us to escort you inside.'

The landlord led them to a small parlour where Kitty and Daniel half-carried Lady Leaconham across the room to a cushioned armchair beside the empty fireplace.

'Have a bottle of wine brought in,' ordered Daniel. He glanced at Kitty. 'Will you look after Lady Leaconham while I go upstairs and see what I can do for her son?'

Kitty nodded and as he strode away she searched in her godmother's reticule for her smelling salts.

By the time Daniel returned Lady Leaconham had recovered a little and was sipping at a glass of wine.

'How is Leaconham?' she asked him anxiously.

'Sleeping,' he said shortly. 'He is unlikely to stir before the morning.'

'Then perhaps we should go home, Godmama,' suggested Kitty. 'There is still time to reach Town before dark.'

'And leave my son here, alone?' declared my lady, setting her glass down with a snap. 'Never. The poor boy has obviously eaten something that disagreed with him. Did he not say he would be dining on oysters? I have no doubt that was it. I make it a rule never to touch shellfish.'

As Daniel opened his mouth to reply Kitty met his eyes and gave a tiny shake of her head. He shrugged.

'Whatever the cause,' he said, 'Lord Leaconham is in

no condition to travel today. The inn is very busy.' Loud voices and a burst of raucous laughter from the room above added weight to his words. He continued, 'You are best to go home, ma'am. The landlord here can be trusted to look after Leaconham.'

But Lady Leaconham merely shook her head and dabbed at her eyes with the wisp of lace that was her handkerchief.

'I do not think I could travel another yard tonight,' she said querulously. 'Seeing Garston in such distress has completely destroyed my nerves. Kitty, my dear, go and find the landlord. Tell him we need rooms for the night.'

'But, ma'am, it is not far to Town,' protested Kitty, 'I am sure you would be more comfortable in your own bed.'

'You forget, Katherine my dear,' said my lady in reproachful tones, 'that we have no outriders to escort us, and the sun is already setting.'

'I would be very happy to escort you to Town, madam,' put in Daniel, stepping forwards.

'That is very kind of you, Mr Blackwood,' came the gracious reply, 'but I cannot contemplate leaving my poor boy here alone. What if he should wake in the night, calling for his mama?'

Kitty saw Daniel's lips twitch and she said, trying to keep the laughter out of her own voice, 'My dear ma'am, Garston is five-and-twenty. He has had his own establishment for years now.'

'That is not the point,' returned my lady in dignified accents. 'I am still his mama, and I am the person he needs when he is ill.'

'He is not ill, ma'am, he is dead drunk!' retorted Daniel with brutal frankness.

Lady Leaconham gave a little shudder and collapsed

back in the chair. Kitty stepped up and took her hands, chafing them gently between her own.

'Now look what you have done!' She cast an angry glance towards Daniel. 'How can you be so unfeeling?'

'Well, you know I am an insensitive, uncouth, northern fellow!'

'And you can stop that nonsense this minute,' she told him crossly. 'I know very well it is all play-acting designed to annoy me.'

He laughed suddenly.

'So it is, Miss Wythenshawe. Very well, tell me what I can do to help.'

'Bespeak rooms for us, if you please, and ask the coachman to stable the horses. If Lady Leaconham is determined to stay, then we must do so, I think.'

He disappeared, coming back a few moments later to inform her that a room was being prepared.

'I hope you will not object, but they are very busy tonight so I have arranged for you to share a room. I thought you would prefer that to having separate rooms at opposite ends of the building, which is all they have free.'

'Yes, thank you, sir. That is very satisfactory is it not, Godmama?' Kitty looked to Lady Leaconham, who was leaning back in her chair, her vinaigrette clutched in one hand.

'And is my room near my son?' asked the widow in a faint voice.

'I am afraid not, but I have directed the landlord to have someone sitting up with him tonight.' said Daniel. 'There is a very small chamber available next to Lord Leaconham, so I have taken that for myself. If he wakes in the night and—er—calls for you, ma'am, I will be able to send word.'

Kitty frowned.

'That is very good of you sir, but I am sure there is no need for you to stay—'

'Oh, but there is,' Lady Leaconham interrupted her. 'Surely you would not expect Mr Blackwood to abandon us in this horrid place when my son is too weak to act as our protector? As for Garston...' She hesitated, a look of distaste crossing her face. 'I shall wait until the morning and then if I think it necessary I shall summon a doctor. I am in your debt, Mr Blackwood, and gladly accept your protection for myself and my goddaughter. I am very grateful.'

'Think nothing of it, my lady. They have tea here, so I have ordered them to send in the Black Bohea, to restore your nerves.'

'Now that *is* kind of you, Mr Blackwood,' murmured Kitty, allowing herself to smile at him for the first time.

'It is my mother's remedy for most ills,' he told her, with the flash of a smile.

The sudden transformation in his dark features momentarily robbed Kitty of her breath, and she was relieved that the maid came in with the tea tray at that moment and she could give her attention to the ritual of making tea for them all.

The hour was quite advanced when Lady Leaconham put down her cup and declared she would retire. She struggled to her feet.

'Kitty my dear, give me your arm. We will ask the landlord to direct us to our bedchamber.'

Daniel opened the door for them.

'Would you like me to have a little supper sent up to you, my lady?'

Kitty felt her godmother shudder as though even the thought of food made her feel unwell. Daniel observed it, too, and inclined his head.

'Very well, ma'am, but do not forget that this parlour is at your disposal until the morrow, should you wish to make use of it.'

Murmuring her thanks, Kitty accompanied her god-mother to the chamber allocated to them. It was a large room overlooking the street, where Lady Leaconham declared that there was so much noise she would not get a wink of sleep.

'I have no nightgown,' she complained tearfully. 'And no maid. Who is to undress me and look after my clothes? I would not trust them to a common inn servant!'

'Oh, dear, if we had thought of that earlier we might have sent to Portman Square for Meakin to come here and to bring you a change of clothes,' said Kitty, dismayed. 'We are not so very far from home, after all.' She summoned up a smile. 'No matter, Godmama, I will look after you. I shall help you out of your gown and you may sleep in your shift.' She added cheerfully, 'This is a very respectable inn, ma'am. Look, the sheets are clean and they have even used the warming pan in the bed.'

An hour later Lady Leaconham was sleeping peace-fully. Kitty had helped her to undress, carefully folding her gown and placing it with her stays, petticoats, shoes and stockings in readiness for the morning. She pinched out the candles and moved the solitary lamp so that the light did not fall directly upon her godmother's face. However, Kitty herself was reluctant to go to bed. It was not late, the summer twilight was still evident outside the window and she was aware of a gnawing hunger. She would not risk disturbing her godmother by ordering a meal to be sent up to the room, so she decided to go in search of food.

The inn was quieter now, the noisy diners had left or retired to their beds to sleep off their potations and there was no one on the stairs as she made her way down to the ground floor.

She found the little parlour illuminated by candles on the mantelpiece and a branched candlestick on the table, where Daniel was sitting before a mouth-watering array of dishes. He rose as she entered the room.

'Miss Wythenshawe!'

'I came in search of supper…'

He pulled up a chair.

'There is more than sufficient here for the both of us, if you would care to join me. Sit down and I will send for another plate and glass.'

In two strides he was at the door, calling for the waiter. She heard the rumble of voices in the passage before Daniel returned.

'Our host has promised to lay a cover for you immediately. It should not take more than a few minutes.'

'I am interrupting your meal…'

'Not at all,' he said politely. 'I have only just begun and will now wait until you can join me. Will you not sit down?'

Kitty moved over to the chair he was holding for her and sat down with a quiet word of thanks. Daniel resumed his own seat and silence filled the room.

At last Kitty said, 'You have not told us, sir, why you were travelling this way. This is not on your route back to Town.'

He looked down at the table, intent upon straightening his knife and fork.

'I overheard your coachman talking. It seemed pretty clear that he did not think Leaconham would be fit to travel: I thought you might need assistance.'

The entry of a serving maid caused a diversion and they watched silently while she laid another place at the table.

When they were alone again Daniel poured Kitty a glass of wine.

'Will you take a little of the lamb?' he asked her. 'It is very good. You will note I have not ordered the oysters.'

Kitty chuckled.

'We both know they were not the cause of Lord Leaconham's malaise.' She sighed. 'Poor Garston. Poor Godmama! I doubt she has seen her son in that condition before.' He made no reply. Kitty put down her glass. 'I know you think him weak and foolish. After all he knew we were coming back this way to collect him, but have you no compassion at all? No, obviously not.' She bit her lip, then said with difficulty, 'I beg your pardon, that is unjust. You have shown great kindness in following us to this place.'

He looked across the table and held her gaze.

'My opinion of Leaconham is not high. The man may go out and drink himself into oblivion every night for all I care, but to do so knowing that he was needed to escort two ladies back to Town, I find that foolish and irresponsible.'

'You are right, of course. Which makes it all the more generous of you to look after us.'

'I am not doing this for Leaconham, nor for your godmother.'

Kitty caught her breath, wondering if she had misunderstood him.

'I do not deserve that you should be so kind to me,' she said in a low voice. 'Every time we meet I am impolite to you.'

The corners of his mouth lifted a fraction.

'You certainly like to remind me of my place.'

There was a heartbeat's pause before she spoke again.

'I made an assumption about you on that first morning we met. I was wrong. I beg your pardon.'

'And I beg *your* pardon for reacting as I did,' he said. 'Will you cry friends with me now?'

Kitty looked up to respond and found him smiling at her. Once again she was aware of her heart behaving erratically. Like a wild bird in panic, fluttering against its cage. The first time it had happened she had thought it the result of fear and alarm, because she had been trapped in his arms as he carried her through the mud. Here in this candlelit room there was no such danger.

Was there?

'F-friends?' she managed to say. 'Yes, of course.'

She lowered her eyes and fixed her attention upon her plate. Nerves had diminished her appetite, but her companion's quiet good manners did much to calm her. He wasted no time on small talk, but proved himself a considerate host, serving her himself and encouraging her to partake a little of each dish. She declined the roasted pigeon but managed to eat a little of the lamb and a few French beans, and by the time she had finished her glass of wine she was feeling much more relaxed and able to enjoy a small portion of gooseberry syllabub. She even accepted a small glass of Madeira wine.

'I hope you do not suspect me of trying to make you drunk?' said Daniel as he refilled her glass.

'No. I know you now for a gentleman.'

His brows went up, but at that moment the servant returned to clear the table, and he said merely, 'Shall we move over to the window? The armchair there will be more comfortable for you.'

Kitty hesitated. She was suddenly aware that she and Daniel were alone, and the chair he indicated was well away from the candles' golden glow.

'I should perhaps retire.'

'Are you weary?'

'No.' The blood was singing through her veins. She felt more like dancing than sleeping. 'No, not at all.'

'Then sit with me for a while. After all, your godmother has accepted my protection for you both. And you yourself said I was a gentleman.'

The glint of amusement in his eyes as he said this made Kitty laugh and did much to ease the tension. She sank down into the cushioned armchair and sipped at her wine. He carried a chair across from the table and placed it opposite her.

'I am not at all high in the instep, you know,' she said as he sat down.

'You surprise me, Miss Wythenshawe.'

'No, really. Before, I would have mistaken your tone for condemnation but now I know you are teasing me, are you not?' she looked up a trifle anxiously. 'I think I have given you a false impression, and…and would like to explain, if I may.' She wrapped her hands around her glass and braced herself for a confession, thankful for the dim light. 'You see, I am…not rich.'

She looked up, waiting for his reaction. He said mildly, 'I am not sure Harworth knows that.'

'Perhaps he is not aware of my *exact* circumstances.' She blushed. 'Godmama suggested we should not give out such information too freely. I doubt if she would approve of my telling you so much.'

'You do not need to disclose anything further, Miss Wythenshawe—'

'But I want to!' she said quickly. 'I thought it might help you to understand why, why I acted as I did. Why I was so rude to you when we first met.'

'Very well. If you wish to talk, I will listen.'

She paused, gathering her thoughts.

'I was very excited by the thought of coming to London.

The gown I was wearing the day we met was a new one. It was my only walking dress. At that time I did not know Lady Leaconham, that she would buy me another gown and positively shower me with gifts and clothes. She is so very, very generous. I was nervous, you see: so eager to make a good impression when I arrived in London that I am afraid I quite forgot my manners on the journey.' She looked up suddenly and said with spirit, 'You will admit, sir, that you were extremely dirty!'

'I cannot deny it. I had spent a night on the moors, in the rain.' He spoke gravely, no hint of a smile, but she perceived the softening of his look.

'I thought you very ill mannered, and I was afraid that... contact with you would make my gown dusty.'

His lips twitched.

'I did much more than that, and I am very sorry for it.'

She waved aside his apology.

'If I had not been so uncivil to you—! I was puffed up with conceit, as if I had been a very fine lady, which I am not.' She settled into her chair, determined on a full confession. 'If you will allow me to explain: Mama is the widow of a gentleman, a very good man, but unfortunately a series of ill-judged investments meant that when he died suddenly, poor Mama was left with almost nothing and we were obliged to live with my aunt in Fallridge.' She held up her head and added, a hint of defiance in her voice, 'Mama and Aunt Jane earn a living with their sewing.'

'Very commendable,' remarked Daniel.

'Yes, it is,' agreed Kitty. 'Mama used all her savings to ensure that I had an excellent education and that I learned all the accomplishments a young lady might require— dancing, singing, playing the pianoforte. I speak French excellently and know a smattering of Italian—'

He put up his hand to stem this recital.

'I have not been in Town very long, Miss Wythenshawe, but I know that many young ladies get by with far fewer accomplishments.'

'Yes, but *they* have dowries,' replied Kitty drily. 'It is much easier to find a husband if one has a fortune.'

Daniel settled himself back in his chair.

'Is that why you came to London, Miss Wythenshawe, to find a husband?'

'Yes. Mama taught me how to make my curtsy to a duke or to an earl, to hold my fan just so and how to address everyone, from a duchess to a dairymaid.' She took another sip of her wine. The sweet nutty flavour of the Madeira was very pleasant and she was beginning to feel a warm glow spreading through her. 'Everything, you see, to make me fit to marry a lord. It has been my dream since I was a very little girl.'

'I fear you are aiming at the moon, Miss Wythenshawe.'

She put up her chin.

'Perhaps, but I have been given this opportunity and I must make the most of it.'

'Of course.'

A little of her certainty drained away. She said pensively, 'I am Mama's only hope, you see. I *have* to marry well, because I need my future husband to make such settlements that Mama and Aunt Jane will be able to live out the rest of their lives in comfort. Mama said it is very important that I act like a lady, because she is very particular about the sort of husband I should have.' She saw his brows twitch together and added, 'I know, it sounds quite ridiculous, but you see, Lord Harworth has been so kind to me that Lady Leaconham is encouraged to think an alliance might be possible and she has written to Mama to say so! And he is her nephew, so she cannot think me too unsuitable, can she?'

'Is that why you went off into the woods with Harworth this afternoon?'

Kitty nodded.

'Godmama suggested I should be friendly, and it is not at all difficult, for Lord Harworth is most agreeable. He was most kind, explaining all about the park and the woods at Wormley, and the new planting he wants to do there—' She broke off as Daniel gave a shout of laughter.

'Are you telling me that he took you along that secluded path and did nothing but talk of landscaping the gardens? What a cod's head.'

'Why, yes, he—' She broke off, her eyes widening. 'Do you mean he should have *flirted* with me?'

'It's what any man would do with a pretty girl.'

'Oh...' She blushed, momentarily diverted. 'Do—do you really think I'm pretty?'

His eyes rested on her for a moment, a look in them that she could not interpret.

'As a matter of fact, I do.'

'Oh,' she said again. 'Well, perhaps he did flirt with me, and I didn't know it.' She got up and walked to the window, staring out into the yard, which despite the late hour was still bustling with activity beneath the light of a dozen flaming torches.

'What did he say to you?' he asked.

She frowned, trying to remember.

'I really cannot recall, we merely strolled along the path.'

'And did he walk very close to you?' asked Daniel.

Kitty did not need to turn her head to know that Daniel was standing behind her; his body was only inches from her own. She could feel his presence, it made her spine tingle. She kept her eyes fixed firmly on the view from the window and forced herself to stand still.

'I held his arm,' she said carefully.

'But did he at any time stop and direct your attention to the view? Like this, perhaps.'

He rested his hands lightly on her shoulders. His touch was warm on her skin and it took all her will-power not to drop her head to one side and rub her cheek against his fingers. She was so tense she felt as brittle as glass. At any moment she might shatter. She had to struggle to answer him.

'No, he did not.'

'Then the man is most decidedly a fool,' murmured Daniel.

The vibration of his warm, deep voice was carried through his hands and into her bones. Her insides became an aching void, the ache spreading quickly into her thighs. Even her breasts felt taut. She knew she should make some flippant comment, slip out from under his hands and put distance between them, but she was no longer in control. She heard herself saying, 'Oh, and why is that?'

'Because from here it is the work of a moment to turn you, like this, and then…'

Gently he pulled her round to face him. Kitty turned, like one in a dream, and obedient to the pressure of his fingers beneath her chin she raised her head and found herself gazing up into his face. She watched the amused glint disappear from his dark eyes. They seemed to blaze, burning into her. The aching void was instantly filled with white-hot fire. Daniel swooped down, enveloping her. He crushed her against him, imprisoning her lips beneath his own, his arms binding her close. She was overwhelmed, confused, as if she was flying, drowning and burning all at the same time. Her knees felt weak, she clung to his coat, and all the while her senses were reeling under the onslaught of his kiss. It was as savage and wild as the Yorkshire moors and it drew from her a shuddering response. When Daniel loosened his hold and raised his head she gave a little cry and threw her arms about his neck, pulling him back to kiss her again.

Daniel found himself locked in a fierce, passionate embrace. Being alone in the candlelight with a beguiling young woman was certainly a temptation, and he had given in to it, but he had intended nothing more than a light kiss. However, when he had pulled her into his arms all conscious thought disappeared and a violent, uncontrollable desire ripped through him. That had surprised him, but what had completely thrown him off balance was that when he had tried to apologise for frightening her, Kitty had pulled him back and shown herself eager for his kisses. He found her inexpert but ardent response more arousing than the practised arts of any courtesan. She was so damned alluring. Dangerously so. He summoned every ounce of his will-power to break away. Gripping her arms, he pushed her gently but firmly back into the chair.

'Did, did I do something wrong?' She looked up at him, her eyes troubled.

'No, sweetheart.' He dropped to his knees in front of her and gave her what he hoped was a reassuring smile. 'I am at fault for taking advantage of you.' His hands slid down and he caught her fingers. 'I should never have allowed you to sup alone with me.' Shouts and the clatter of hooves in the yard made him look up at the unshuttered window. 'I only hope the stable lads were too busy with their work to notice what was going on in here. Thankfully it is brighter in the yard than in this parlour.' He glanced back at Kitty, his heart turning over when he saw the anxious look on her face. He said bluntly, 'I am afraid I may have damaged your reputation, Miss Wythenshawe.'

'Because you kissed me?'

He squeezed her fingers.

'Just being alone here with me is enough to compromise you.'

She considered this for a moment. He was pleased to see the bemused look had gone and she was more in control of herself.

'I am sure Lord Leaconham and my godmother will not wish to talk about this evening.'

'But there is the landlord, and the servants.'

She shrugged.

'I am not known here, sir, neither are you. Who are they likely to tell?'

'A few judicious coins in the right hands might secure their silence. Are you willing to trust that no one will find out about our being here together?'

She gave him a little smile.

'What is the alternative, Mr Blackwood?'

He shrugged.

'That we marry, I suppose.'

Daniel cursed silently even as the words left his lips. Devil take it, what was he saying? He had surely imbibed more than he had intended tonight! He saw her eyes widen, felt the little hands tremble and a moment later she gently withdrew them from his grasp.

'Out of the question, sir,' she said crisply, leaving her chair and walking away from him. 'Why, we hardly know each other. And I am sure your family has no idea of your marrying a penniless bride.'

Daniel rose to his feet, not knowing if he was more relieved or disappointed at her response. Did she think so little of him that he was not even to be considered as a husband?

'No, of course not, but neither would they have me compromise a young lady.'

She was standing with her back to him but at this she turned. The lighted candles behind her framed her dark head with a golden halo, but the shadows concealed her expression.

'Then we must hope word does not get abroad,' she said quietly. 'Perhaps you would be good enough to—what is the term?—*grease a few palms* to ensure it does not. I shall retire now, and in the morning we may behave as if this evening never occurred.'

'If that is what you want.'

'It is.' She added lightly, 'Have I not told you that I intend to marry a lord?'

She gave him a little curtsy and went out, leaving Daniel staring at the empty space.

Chapter Six

Kitty entered the bedchamber quietly to find Lady Leaconham still sleeping soundly. She undressed quietly and slipped between the sheets, careful not to disturb her godmother.

The noise from the street had died away almost completely but despite this and the lateness of the hour, it was some time before Kitty fell asleep. Her body was still tingling with the excitement of being crushed in Daniel's arms, her lips still bruised from his kiss. It had been shocking, yes, but she had not been frightened. She had found it fiercely exhilarating. Even now she felt more alive than ever before. She did not want to sleep, she wanted to stay awake and relive that startling, earth-shaking embrace over and over again. The mere thought of it sent an aching excitement shooting through her. She turned on her side and curled up, hugging the feeling to her. She wanted to remember for ever those few short hours spent with Daniel, because they could never be repeated. It was not allowed for respectable young ladies to kiss gentlemen they were not going to marry, and Daniel had no intention of marrying her. He had suggested it, but only because he thought he had compromised her—had he not agreed that his family would not want him to take a penniless bride? And her own family, her mother, Aunt Jane, Godmama—they all expected her to make a very good match. She had been sent to London with the express intention of finding a husband, and she knew that in her mother's eyes at least, a mill-owner's son was not an eligible suitor. Kitty sighed and closed her eyes. Images of Daniel Blackwood filled her mind and another delicious tingle ran through her.

Stop this, she told herself fiercely. His actions were *not* those of a gentleman. No man of honour would have pounced on her in such a savage way. A man of honour, she decided, would have treated her with respect and even if he had been violently in love with her—which Daniel most definitely was not—he would have suppressed his feelings and done nothing more than plant a fervent kiss upon her fingers.

Kitty put her hand to her lips. There had been nothing suppressed about Daniel's embrace. He was clearly not an honourable gentleman. She had the daunting feeling that no honourable gentleman would ever be so exciting.

Despite the clatter of traffic from the street below their window, Lady Leaconham enjoyed a good night's sleep, waking refreshed and eager for news of her son. In contrast, Kitty's spirits were heavy and lethargic but she tried to conceal this as she helped her godmother to dress and then followed her down to the private parlour, where they had been informed that Lord Leaconham was waiting for them.

They found Garston and Daniel seated at the table, which had been laid for breakfast. Although Garston replied breezily to his mother's anxious enquiries, Kitty thought he looked decidedly pale and drawn. By comparison, Daniel appeared full of vigour and vitality and it was with some trepidation that Kitty took her seat beside him. In the bright light of a summer's morning the parlour seemed a different world from the cosy, candlelit room she and Daniel has shared, but she was painfully aware of him beside her, his long fingers wrapped around a coffee cup where last night they had been warm on her shoulders. His very presence was like a magnet, tugging at her body. She wanted to lean towards him, to be touching him…

'Kitty, my love, you are shivering,' observed Lady Leaconham. 'Perhaps you should run upstairs and fetch your shawl.'

'I am quite warm enough, ma'am,' said Kitty hastily, aware of Daniel's keen eyes turned towards her. 'I am a little tired, that is all.'

'That is no wonder,' remarked Lady Leaconham, helping herself to a slice of bread and butter. 'I woke some time before midnight and you were not in your bed.'

Beneath the table Daniel's knee touched hers and Kitty jumped. Her whole body was a tingling, jangling mass of nerves. She stole a glance at Daniel. He had not looked up but his studied indifference made her wonder if the contact had been accidental. She struggled to concentrate upon her reply to Lady Leaconham.

'I came downstairs for a little supper, ma'am.'

'Oh? And what did you eat? After Garston's experience yesterday I am reluctant to break my fast here, but I cannot think there is any danger in taking a little bread and butter.' She cast a doubtful glance at her son's plate, piled with thick slices of ham and cold beef. 'You certainly seem to have regained your appetite, my love.'

Garston's mouth was too full to reply but Daniel

said coolly, 'I believe a good breakfast will aid Lord Leaconham's recovery.'

Garston gave him a rather sheepish look and swallowed hard.

'Aye, it will indeed,' he agreed. 'Just what I need. I shall be well enough to travel back to Town with you today, Mama, never fear.'

'And I shall ride with you,' said Daniel. He turned to Kitty. 'May I pour you a little more coffee, Miss Wythenshawe? And perhaps you would like another bread roll?'

'Coffee, thank you, but no more to eat.'

'I hope your…supper did not prevent you from sleeping,' he remarked as he filled her cup.

Kitty felt the blood rushing to her cheeks.

'N-no.' His countenance was impassive but she observed the glint in his dark eyes and added firmly, 'I slept very well. I know of no reason why I should not do so.'

'Do you not?'

The blush on Kitty's cheeks deepened and she could only pray that the others were too intent upon their breakfast to notice her discomfiture. She shot Daniel an angry look.

'No,' she said in a tight voice. 'Nothing worthy of comment at all.'

With a smile, Daniel returned his attention to his breakfast. Was it cruel of him to tease her? Perhaps, but she looked so delightful when she was flustered. The touch of her leg against his had not been deliberate, she was far too respectable for that, but it had taken all his will-power not to react. That brief contact had sent a warm thrill rushing through him, reminding him again of the excitement he had felt when he kissed her. But he must be careful. He picked up his cup. There would be the devil to pay if last night's little encounter should be discovered. Doubtless he would be expected to marry the chit.

It was a sudden shock to realise that the idea rather appealed to him.

'Mr Blackwood, you have spilled your coffee!'

Lady Leaconham's voice recalled his wandering thoughts.

'I beg your pardon.' He looked down. The coffee had slopped on to his empty plate. 'That was very careless of me.' He shot a quick, apologetic glance at Kitty. 'Thankfully there is no harm done. This time.'

She met his eyes fleetingly.

'You must be careful to make sure it doesn't happen again.'

Her tone was cool but he was certain she was not talking about the spilling of his drink but of that blazing, explosive kiss they had shared last night. They had agreed the matter was best forgotten but after a night's reflection Daniel found he did not want to forget it. Kitty's reaction when he had kissed her convinced him that she was not indifferent to him, but could he be wrong? Was it possible that she had put the matter from her mind? He did not think so. He wanted to talk to her but she gave him no opportunity to do so, staying close to her godmother for the remainder of the morning and ignoring him when he tried to hand her into the carriage, turning instead to Leaconham to perform that duty. After that he could only ride beside the carriage, knowing Kitty was only feet away from him.

'I trust Lord Harworth will not be too put out with you for your absence last night, sir,' said Lady Leaconham when they arrived at Portman Square and she took her leave of him. Kitty, he noticed, said nothing, merely standing on the doorstep with her eyes downcast.

'I sent a messenger to him yesterday evening, to explain the situation.'

'Ah, of course. And I hope you will escort my son to his rooms—'

'Dash it all, Mama, I ain't in need of a nursemaid!' cried Garston, poking his head out of the carriage window. 'I am perfectly capable of getting myself home. Drive on, Dawkins!'

He dragged his hat from his fair head and waved it towards the coachman. Daniel nodded to Lady Leaconham.

'You need not worry, ma'am. I'll see him home safely.'

Then with a nod of his head he turned his horse and rode off. There would be no tête-à-tête with Miss Kitty Wythenshawe today. Perhaps that was for the best, he thought as he rode out of Portman Square, for the very unsettling idea was taking hold of him that where Miss Wythenshawe was concerned, he was standing on the edge of a precipice.

'Well, there is no doubt about it,' declared Lady Leaconham, leading the way into the house, 'Mr Blackwood is much more gentlemanly than I had at first thought. To be sure, he does not smile a great deal or go out of his way to make himself agreeable, but his stopping at the inn to look after Garston, and escorting us home was uncommon kind!' Her brows drew together. 'Do you think he has formed a *tendre* for you, my love?'

'F-for me?' said Kitty, forcing a laugh. 'What an absurd idea! He never speaks to me but to pick a quarrel!'

'Well, I am relieved to hear it,' said her godmother. 'Pleasant Mr Blackwood may be, but he is nothing compared to Lord Harworth. He is in trade and thus not to be considered at this stage. I think we had best concentrate on securing Bertram's interest in you. Ah, Meakin, there you are.' She turned to address her maid who was hurrying down the stairs and she continued in a much weaker voice, 'I need you to help me to my room. What with the anxiety over my son, and being obliged to remain overnight in a common coaching inn, my poor nerves are in shreds...'

She tottered to the stairs and into the arms of her waiting dresser. Realising that her assistance was not required, Kitty made her way to the servants' hall. She was far too tense to lie down in her room so she decided that she would take Titan for a walk and enjoy a little solitude in which to examine her own reaction to the previous evening.

The memory of Daniel's kiss kept jumping into her mind, bringing back that weakness in the knees and the feeling of her bones turning to water. She had no experience of being kissed before, and the thought that these sensations occurred every time a young lady allowed herself to be embraced by a gentleman alarmed her. No wonder anxious parents warned their daughters never to be alone with a man. It was also very daunting to think that not only had she allowed Daniel to kiss her, but she had responded in a most unladylike way. Indeed, she could not deny that she had enjoyed the sensation of being in his arms.

For the rest of the day guilt and shame raged within Kitty. She dare not tell anyone of her transgression, but she was determined that nothing like it should ever happen again. She would make sure in future that she was always suitably chaperoned. She would avoid the company of all men and especially, *especially* Daniel Blackwood!

Lady Leaconham was laid low with her nerves for a few days following the picnic and Kitty was glad of the excuse to remain indoors, even declining an invitation to drive out with Ann Harworth. However, the following week brought no hint that the events at the Rising Sun were known by more than those closely involved and Kitty was encouraged to hope that no one other than she and Daniel knew of their taking supper together.

She had not seen Daniel since that night and was nervous of meeting him again, so when Lady Leaconham informed her that her sister had invited them to the opera she was reluctant to accept.

'But, my dear, we must go!' cried Lady Leaconham. 'It is so near the end of the Season this may well be our last opportunity to visit the theatre. And Lord Harworth has hired a box for us all.'

'But I thought you were not a lover of opera, Godmama,' said Kitty, clutching at one last straw.

'Well, in general I am not, but this is a new working of *Dido,* and the review in the *Herald* says that there is to be a procession with an ostrich and an elephant! There, that will be something to see, will it not, my love?'

'Yes, it will indeed. Do you know who is to be in Lady Harworth's party, ma'am?' Kitty asked, trying to keep her voice casual.

'Well, Ann will be there, naturally.' Lady Leaconham gave a little chuckle. 'I have no doubt the two of you will have your heads together as soon as you meet.'

'And...and will any gentlemen be present?'

Kitty flushed as Lady Leaconham reacted to her question with a knowing smile.

'My sister does not say but I have no doubt that Lord Harworth will be escorting us. So we must make sure you are looking your best!'

Kitty did not reply. To ask more questions might make her godmother suspicious. She could only hope that Daniel Blackwood was not musical, and would stay away.

Alas for her hopes, when they arrived at the King's Theatre, Kitty immediately spotted Daniel amongst the crowd. Catching her eye, he smiled at her but she immediately looked away, pretending she had not seen him. Lord Harworth was in good spirits and genially escorted them to the box, where he insisted upon directing his guests to their seats. His sister, however, immediately objected.

'I will not allow you to monopolise Kitty,' she cried. 'We shall sit together, at the front of the box where we may see everything.'

'And where you may be seen by all your beaux,' replied her brother, in high good humour. 'Very well, if that is what you want! Mama, you and my aunt should sit here, where you will have an excellent view of the stage. Blackwood and I will sit behind you. We can stand if we wish to see more.'

With everything arranged, the ladies made themselves comfortable. Kitty knew Daniel was watching her but she avoided his gaze as she disposed her skirts carefully around her. Unfortunately her nervousness made her drop her fan and it was Daniel who immediately stooped to retrieve it. As he leaned over to return it he said quietly, 'I think you are avoiding me, Miss Wythenshawe.'

She tried to look at him to make her denial, but her eyes stopped at his mouth. She could not help admiring the beautiful, curving lines of his lips, remembering the feel of them pressed against her own. She found herself growing hot at the memory. A sudden fanfare heralded the start of the performance and gave her the excuse to turn her attention to the stage, but she was all too aware of Daniel's warm breath on her cheek as he murmured, 'I hope you will oblige me by taking a stroll with me in the interval.'

The idea set Kitty's pulse racing, and she sat through the first part of the opera hardly taking in anything she was witnessing on the stage. She was conscious of Daniel sitting behind her and she resisted the temptation to turn and look at him. She longed to know if he was enjoying the performance or if he, too, was distracted. The thought that he might be studying her made Kitty feel a little light-headed. Despite her resolution to avoid him, she decided if he repeated his invitation to stroll out in the interval she would accept. After all, what danger could there be in walking together in a crowded foyer?

As soon as the front curtain was lowered a general buzz of conversation and movement ran through the audience. Kitty collected her fan and her reticule, anticipating Daniel's invitation.

'Miss Wythenshawe, will you walk outside with me?'

'Oh, that is very kind of you, sir,' said Lady Leaconham quickly, 'but I think Lord Harworth is before you...'

Kitty was dismayed at her godmother's interruption, but at that moment a number of visitors arrived in their box and it was clear that Lord Harworth would have to remain to talk to them. There was an added distraction as Lord Leaconham appeared, saying, 'I saw you from the pit, you know, and thought I should look in.'

'Garston, how delightful!' Ann waved an imperious hand towards him. 'Come and sit by me and tell me what you thought of the singing. Was it not dreadful?'

The small box was suddenly full of people, all talking at once.

'Shall we go, Miss Wythenshawe?' Daniel murmured in Kitty's ear.

She looked around. No one raised any objection when Daniel held out his arm to her and they slipped out to join the noisy crowd parading through the vestibule. It was so busy that Kitty was obliged to cling tightly to Daniel's arm, thankful for the strong, protective presence of her escort.

'I thought I might not get you away,' remarked Daniel. 'I haven't seen you since Barnet.'

She raised her hand in a small, defensive gesture.

'Please. We agreed not to mention it again.'

'Can you forget it so easily then?'

'Yes,' she lied. 'I have quite put it from my mind. It is an incident that could ruin my reputation.'

'Because you intend to marry a lord.'

'It would make *any* gentleman think twice about marrying me,' she responded frankly.

'Not if he really cared about you.'

'But I must not deter a suitor before he has a chance to care for me,' she reasoned.

'And must you have a title?'

'Yes, if I can.'

There. It was out, she was acknowledging her ambition. She wondered why she should feel so ashamed of it: after all, it was commonly expected that every young lady would make the best marriage she could.

Papa would not have liked such worldly ambition. The thought popped into her head unbidden, but almost immediately she imagined her mother's response: "Yes, and look where your father's lack of worldliness has landed us—in poverty!"

After a slight pause she said, 'Please, Mr Blackwood, do not think too badly of me: a good marriage is my mother's dearest wish and I must not disappoint her.'

She held her breath. There was no explosion, no angry retort.

After a moment he said coolly, 'If that is what you want then I wish you every success. There is the interval bell— shall we return to the box?'

Kitty awoke the next day to find the early morning sunshine flooding into her room, but she was conscious only of a dull depression. She sipped thoughtfully at her hot chocolate, trying to work out why there should be such a cloud over her spirits.

The visit to the opera had been a success: nothing had occurred to mar the good humour of the party. Lord Harworth had been an attentive host; the performance had been entertaining—the ostrich and the elephant most diverting—and her companions agreeable. There had been no cross words or spiteful comments to spoil her enjoyment. She allowed her mind to dwell upon Daniel. He had said nothing out of the way, had been polite and gentlemanlike during their brief walk together and after that first mention of Barnet had assured her that the matter would not be mentioned again. His manner for the remainder of the evening had been no less gentlemanlike and he had taken his leave of her with his usual calm friendliness, but Kitty had the uncomfortable feeling that he had withdrawn from her. It did not matter, of course: despite what he had said at the Rising Sun they were not really friends—no more than mere acquaintances—but she was disturbed to find that she did not like the thought that somehow she had disappointed him.

The depression did not lift all day, but Kitty was able to push it to the back of her mind while she accompanied her godmother on a shopping expedition and later drove in the park with Ann, who was full of excitement over the forthcoming birthday celebrations her mother had arranged.

'Bertram is taking us north to Kirkleigh Hall the following week so this will be our last party of the Season,' Ann told her. 'I do hope the dry weather holds, for Mama is going to throw open the doors to the garden and hang coloured lamps from the trees. I think it will look magical, do not you? I cannot wait for you to see it. Bertram tells me that Mr Blackwood is engaged to dine out that evening so there will only be family sitting down to dinner beforehand.

I am sure Mama can be persuaded to invite you and Aunt Leaconham…'

'That will not be necessary,' Kitty replied. 'Garston is taking me to Somerset House that afternoon and I doubt we would be back in time.'

'Garston?'

Kitty giggled.

'I am afraid I rather bludgeoned him into it. It is a lecture, or more properly a debate, on slavery and I knew that Godmama would not allow me to go unattended, so I persuaded Garston to accompany me.'

'But you will not miss our party?' cried Ann, alarmed.

'No, no,' said Kitty soothingly. 'Godmama and I will be there, I promise.'

She did not disclose to her friend that Lady Leaconham had almost collapsed in tears of despair and frustration when Kitty had told her of her determination to attend the debate.

They had been alone in the morning room when Kitty had mentioned the matter.

'I may as well wash my hands of you now, you unnatural girl,' Lady Leaconham had replied, falling back in her chair with her vinaigrette clutched in her hand. 'What is Garston thinking of to agree to such a thing?'

'He wishes to make up to me for his behaviour at the Rising Sun,' Kitty explained patiently.

'He would do better to make up to *me* by refusing to take you,' retorted her godmother, taking another sniff of her smelling salts. 'Oh, dear, what am I to do? Do you not realise the damage to your reputation if word of this gets out?'

'My dear ma'am, surely there can be no harm in my

attending a lecture,' responded Kitty, amused. 'It is at Somerset House, and perfectly respectable.'

'On slavery!' declared Lady Leaconham. 'You have no business to be involving yourself in such matters.'

'My father would not have agreed with you, ma'am,' returned Kitty, a slight edge to her voice. 'He considered it every man's duty to reduce the suffering of others.' She dropped to her knees beside her godmother's chair. 'Dear Godmama, you have such a good, kind nature and you were happy that we should avoid buying sugar from the plantations, were you not? You would not have done that if you did not support the abolition.'

Lady Leaconham eyed her doubtfully.

'Far be it from me to see any poor creature suffer,' she said, 'but with the situation in France, the poor rising up against their masters—it makes people nervous, Kitty. Support for the abolition is fading. It is not so fashionable now.'

'I do not support it because it is *fashionable*,' retorted Kitty through gritted teeth.

'No, of course not, my love,' said Lady Leaconham hastily. She closed her eyes, took another sniff from the enamelled phial in her hand then sat up, sighing. 'Well I suppose you will go, whatever I say.'

'Yes, ma'am, unless you expressly forbid me to do so.'

Lady Leaconham softened immediately.

'Bless you, child, I will not do that. But Garston must bring you straight back, and we will dine here quietly before going to the party. And for heaven's sake, my love, when we are at Harworth House, do *not* voice your opinions, or you will be quite cut out!'

Kitty had been too relieved to have her godmother's approval to argue further and she had set out with Lord

Leaconham for Somerset House, promising to be back in good time for dinner. The lecture was a lively one, and she returned to Portman Square, her head ringing with arguments and ideas which she was eager to share with her godmother. Garston was less enthusiastic.

'Can't say I took a lot in,' he said frankly as they sat down to their dinner. 'Difficult to get worked up about something that is happening so many miles away. Besides,' he added, smiling at the ladies, 'it ain't as if I employ any slaves. No need, since I have no plantations, and I pay my servants to do everything that is required.'

'But you take snuff,' objected Kitty. 'Slaves are used to grow the tobacco. And think of all the cakes and sweet-meats you like so much. They are full of sugar, much of it grown by slaves.'

Lady Leaconham put up her hand.

'Now, Katherine, my love, you promised me if I allowed you to go to Somerset House that would be an end to it. Let us have no more discussion, if you please. And pray, if you have any feeling for me at all, you will not refer to it again this evening. My sister would not appreciate you bringing such contentious issues to her party.' Kitty bit her lip and nodded, knowing she had stretched her godmother's good nature to the limit. 'Garston, your aunt assures me you are very welcome, if you wish to attend this evening.'

He gave his mother a pained look.

'Devil a bit, Mama, I am engaged to meet up with friends this evening—I am sure I told you of it.'

'You did, of course, but I wondered, since you have spent the afternoon with Kitty, that you might wish to escort her to Harworth House…'

Kitty hid a smile when she saw the look of horror on Lord Leaconham's chubby countenance. She was not at all offended: she had made shameless use of Garston to accompany her to the lecture that afternoon, but she was happy to admit that they had very little in common. Ann had confided to her cousin about their attendance at Mr Clarkson's meeting and Kitty knew Garston had been disapproving, regarding her ideas as dangerously liberal. Their exchange of views as they returned from Somerset House that afternoon had become quite heated.

'Don't know why you are botherin' your head with all this abolition business,' he had told her as he followed her into the coach. 'We have laws and preachers who deal with the rights and wrongs of the case.'

'Then they are woefully neglecting their duty!' she had retorted, frustrated by his refusal to discuss the matter. 'As a peer of the realm you could influence the government.'

'They know what they are about,' replied Garston, bored with the subject. 'I let Pitt and his cronies go about their business and I go about mine.'

'And just what *is* your business, Garston?' she asked him. 'Just what is it that you do every day?'

He regarded for a moment, uncomprehending.

'Do? I don't understand you.'

'You are a rich man, Garston—'

'Not that rich!' he put in quickly.

'Then let us say you have a comfortable fortune,' she amended. 'But what do you *do* for that fortune? How long each year do you spend on your estates, making sure everything is in order, looking after your land and your tenants?'

'But I have no need to do that, m'dear. I have an excellent steward who looks after everything. He would not thank me for interfering, I assure you.'

'So your days are spent in pleasure and idleness—'

'Pleasure, yes,' he retorted, sitting upright, 'but not

idleness! I'll have you know there are some days when I barely have time to think! You can have no idea how long it takes me to get ready each morning—deciding what coat to wear, which invitations to accept.'

'Whether to attend a cockfight or a mill!' she threw at him.

'Well, yes, there is that,' he said defensively. 'When one has so many friends, it's impossible to spend time with 'em all.'

'I suppose today is the first time you have been called upon to give serious thought to anything for a long while.'

'Yes, it is,' he replied, eyeing her indignantly. 'And jolly poor sport I thought it, too. Why should I bother my head with matters I know naught of?'

'That was the point of attending, to learn more.'

'Well, that seems a pretty foolish notion. I have given up my whole day to you for this—'

'If it did not take you 'til noon to dress it would not have been your *whole* day!' she flashed.

Garston ignored that.

'I can't see that this outing has been of any use at all. Why should we make ourselves uncomfortable over it? It ain't our business. Let those who enjoy politics argue about these things!'

Kitty had realised that it was futile trying to persuade Garston. Her godmother had been a little more sympathetic but she was aware that her views filled Lady Leaconham with unease, especially when events in France were so disturbing. If the mob could rise in Paris and bring down the old order, who was to say the same thing might not happen in England?

Kitty understood Lady Leaconham's concerns and when, after dinner, she went off to change into her gown of white organdie with apricot sprigs and to drape her shawl of fine, apricot muslin about her arms, she determined that for the rest of the evening she would be the perfect goddaughter.

Chapter Seven

Ann was waiting for Kitty when they arrived at Harworth House and she was profuse in her thanks to Kitty for her birthday gift.

'Handkerchiefs!' she cried, tearing off the wrapping paper. 'Oh, how pretty, and you embroidered them yourself, did you not? How clever you are, Kitty! I do not have the patience for sewing, I rush my stitches too much, but these are exquisite, and just what I need. Thank you, my dear. Now, you must come and see the ballroom. Mama has lined it with ells and ells of blue silk draped across the ceiling to look like the summer sky. There.' Ann stopped in the doorway. 'What do you think of that?'

Kitty looked around her, amazed at the transformation of the elegant, rather austere ballroom with its pale walls and gilded plasterwork into a heavenly chamber. Candlelight from the chandeliers was reflected in the huge gilded mirrors that hung around the room and it glittered on the silver ribbons holding up the celestial blue silk. She glanced back at Ann, laughing.

'It will be like dancing in the sky. And your dress is an exact match for the silk! How clever of you. The colouring is perfect with your fair hair.'

'Thank you. Your own gown is very pretty, too.'

'It is one of the gowns I brought with me from York-shire,' explained Kitty. 'I thought it the height of fashion until I arrived in Town and saw how high the waistlines had crept up, and how low the necklines had dropped!'

'It is still very fashionable,' Ann assured her. She put one hand to her bodice. 'You do not think my gown *too* low cut? I know Mama would much prefer me to be wear-ing a high neckline such as yours—although at one and twenty perhaps I should be wearing a cap and sitting with the dowagers.'

They giggled at the thought.

'No, your gown looks perfect on you,' said Kitty. 'I wish you enough partners to keep you dancing all night.'

'Thank you, but we will not only be dancing,' said Ann, leading her into the room. 'There will be music and sing-ing, too—I have asked Martin Hamilton to join me in a duet and I shall be playing a new piece I have learned for the harp. Do you play or sing?'

'A little, but not well enough to perform here without practice. Pray do not suggest to anyone that I should do so!'

'No, of course not, if that is your wish.' Ann grabbed her hand again and dragged her across the room towards the tall windows. 'Let me show you the garden while the servants bring in chairs for the recital. Mama has had lamps strung between the trees and along the paths, and as dark-ness falls they will all be lighted so that the guests may step out of the room on to the terrace and even walk down into the cool garden. Aren't you glad the evening is so warm? It means that the windows can remain open: I do

not know what we would have done if it had rained today.'
Ann led the way on to the terrace and down the steps to
the garden. 'I used to play here in the garden when I was a
child. Look, my swing is still there, hanging from that tall
beech tree. And come and look at the pretty little summer
house. It is built in the style of a Roman temple.' She led
Kitty through the trees. 'I wanted Mama to hang lamps in
here, too,' said Ann, dancing between the pillars before
sitting down on the wooden bench that ran along the back
wall. 'Mama refused, saying she did not wish her guests
to wander so far from the main path.'

'They should not need to,' observed Kitty, sitting down
beside her friend. 'The flower gardens are delightful,
and there are more than enough paths to accommodate
everyone.'

Ann jumped up. 'I suppose we must go back. I have
no doubt most of the guests will have arrived by now and
Bertram will want to secure a dance with you.'

'Oh, I expect he is far too busy to think of that.'

Ann stopped.

'No, Kitty, he is very taken with you!' She caught Kitty's
hand. 'Come along, let's find him.'

They hurried back to the house and were running up the
steps to the terrace when a figure stepped out from one of
the long windows and blocked their way.

'Miss Harworth.' Daniel bowed. 'I believe your brother
is looking for you.' His dark, unsmiling gaze moved to
Kitty. 'Miss Wythenshawe.'

Kitty inclined her head. She put one hand on the stone
balustrade to steady herself. She could not deny the sudden
bolt of pleasure at the sight of his tall, elegant figure but
she was determined not to reveal how much his presence
unsettled her. His athletic form was well suited to the tight-
fitting black evening coat and satin knee-breeches and his

hair, brushed until it glowed, glinted blue-black in the evening sunlight. She tried desperately to think of something witty to say, but her brain refused to work.

'Mr Blackwood!' Ann exclaimed. 'I was not expecting you to be here tonight. Bertram said you had other plans for this evening.'

'I changed them.' He looked at Kitty. 'I set off for Yorkshire tomorrow and Lady Harworth persuaded me to join you for one last evening.'

'I am very glad she did so,' replied Ann, voicing Kitty's thoughts, although with perhaps a little less intensity than Kitty was feeling. 'We are going to have such a jolly time, I know you will enjoy it.'

Kitty followed Ann back into the house, her spirits unaccountably lifted by the knowledge that Daniel was present. She found herself looking forward to the evening.

When Ann left to prepare for her harp recital, Kitty went off to find her godmother. As she stood wondering in which direction to go first, a passing waiter mistook her hesitation and held out his tray towards her. It was her custom at such parties to drink lemonade or orgeat but there was only wine in the glasses in front of her. Rather than refuse and wave him away, she picked up a glass and moved on. She was searching the crowd for the tall purple ostrich feathers adorning Lady Leaconham's turban but they were nowhere to be seen and she wandered through the reception rooms, which were growing more crowded by the minute. As Kitty eased herself past a particularly tall, rotund gentleman she found herself face to face with Daniel. He bowed and she was emboldened to stop.

'So you are going home, Mr Blackwood. Is your work here concluded?'

'It is.'

His response was curt but she pressed on, knowing it might be her last chance to talk to him.

'And are Lord Harworth's plans for a new spinning mill complete?'

'The mill? No, but I can do no more until I have seen the site.'

'You did not come to London solely to advise Lord Harworth, I think.' His brows drew together and she added quickly, 'You were staying at Greenwich when you first came to Town.'

'You remember that, do you?' His distant, shuttered expression softened into one of surprised amusement. 'My family has connections with several shipping families, and not only in Liverpool. With the unrest in France it is important we keep our shipping routes open.'

'But you use local wool in your mills, do you not, Mr Blackwood?'

'We spin worsted,' he corrected her. 'It is from the longer fibres of the wool: a fine, strong yarn suitable for greatcoats and pelisses but not the soft, fine cloth you would want to wear next to your skin.'

Something happened to Kitty's breathing. She had been listening to Daniel with interest but now, watching him, she had a sudden conviction that he was imagining her naked, draped only in a soft woollen shift. Perhaps it was the way his voice slowed and deepened as he finished his sentence, or the dangerously dark look in his eyes as they moved over her body. She was afraid to look down lest she discover that her fine, opaque muslin gown had disappeared. The air crackled around them, heavy and charged with an excitement. Daniel had brought his eyes back to her face and was staring at her with such intensity she thought she must burn up. It seemed a lifetime before Daniel looked away.

He seemed to gather himself, giving a very slight shake of the head before he cleared his throat, saying brusquely,

'We...um...we export much of our cloth. And we have the cotton mills, too, that depend upon imports.'

'I beg your pardon,' said Kitty, trying to speak normally yet aware that her cheeks were aflame. 'I fear I am very ignorant of what you do.'

He shrugged.

'Manufacturing is not something often discussed in society's drawing rooms.'

'Very true, unlike politics!' declared Lord Harworth, coming up and overhearing this last remark. 'Although some like to keep silent on their true opinions.'

'I admit my views are more...reformist than yours, my lord,' said Daniel. He was smiling slightly and Kitty wondered if he, too, was glad that the conversation had moved on. 'But I would not be so ill-mannered as to quarrel with my host.'

'No, damn your impudence, but you didn't offer up the information when we first met, did you?'

'The subject did not arise,' was Daniel's mild reply.

Lord Harworth laughed heartily and clapped him on the shoulder.

'Very true, my boy! I suppose I was too keen to discuss building my mill to think of anything else!' He turned to Kitty. 'Miss Wythenshawe, did Blackwood tell you he was in favour of Grey's motion for electoral reform? Dashed poppycock. Wasn't best pleased when I found he had come to London to offer his support to Grey, but in the end it all came to nothing, so I didn't have to throw him out of the house.'

Lord Harworth threw back his head and laughed at his own joke. Daniel merely shrugged.

'I made no secret of it, nor of the fact that I would

like to see the laws against Nonconformists and Catholics relaxed.'

'Whatever his faults, Pitt won't make a stand on that in the present climate,' returned Lord Harworth, shaking his head. 'He's too busy making sure we avoid a revolution like the one in France.'

'Do you think there is any risk of such a thing?' asked Kitty.

'Not if we contain the mob and keep the poor in their place,' replied Lord Harworth.

'Surely the poor should be encouraged to better themselves,' put in Kitty. 'We should educate them; teach the parents to read, perhaps, and open schools for the children...'

'Now, now, Miss Wythenshawe,' cried Lord Harworth genially, 'you are beginning to sound very like Blackwood here!'

'So I have found you at last, my love!' Lady Leaconham's exclamation forestalled Kitty's response. She addressed their host with a soft laugh. 'You must forgive my goddaughter, Bertram, she does not understand the complications of politics. You know what young ladies are, their kind hearts rule their heads and they are all too fond of expressing opinions on matters they know little about.' Kitty opened her mouth to protest but met with a warning glance from Lady Leaconham, who pinched her arm and began to pull her away. 'Come, Kitty, my love, we must find a seat in readiness for the recital. I believe Lady Celestine is to play for us upon the pianoforte, including something by Signor Clementi and I know you have been practising one of his pieces yourself...'

As she was almost dragged away, Kitty cast one last look back at Daniel. He met her eyes for an instant and nodded. Perhaps that earlier, incendiary moment between them had been in her imagination: certainly he gave no sign of it now, only reassurance that he understood what she had been trying to say and did not regard her as a foolish young girl, talking out of turn. The thought warmed her as she sat beside Lady Leaconham, listening to a series of musical performances including Ann's lively if not always accurate rendition on the harp of a piece by Mr Handel.

When at last everyone who wished to perform had done so, Lady Harworth announced that the room would be cleared for dancing. Ann was nowhere to be seen, so Kitty followed her godmother away to the supper room in search of refreshments. She saw Daniel standing alone and could not resist taking the opportunity to speak to him again. She refused to be intimidated by the rather severe cast of his countenance as he sipped at his wine: she was growing used to his sober mien and the fact that he was not scowling blackly she took as a good sign.

Daniel's heart sank as he saw Kitty coming towards him. Damnation. Surely his expression should tell her he did not want to speak to her—did the woman not know the effect she had upon him? His irritation passed. Of course not: she was such an innocent she did not realise how adorable she looked, gliding about the room in a cloud of pale gauze, curls tumbling artlessly about her head and her green eyes sparkling like emeralds. She attracted every man's eye, made every male pulse race. She had no idea that while he was trying to talk to her about serious subjects such as spinning and exports all he really wanted to do was to take her off somewhere and ravish her! She had told him herself that she was set on achieving a good marriage, possibly even ensnaring a lord, so he should not waste his time even thinking about such a woman. The problem was that he could not help himself. He squared his shoulders: he was no moth to perish at her flame—this would be the last time he spoke to her. After that he would make damned sure he kept away from Miss Kitty Wythenshawe.

Daniel schooled his features into what he hoped was a look of polite indifference as she came up to him, refusing to allow himself to respond to her shy smile.

'What time do you leave tomorrow, sir?'

'Directly after breakfast. I am travelling on horseback and expect to make good time.' He paused. 'And you, Miss Wythenshawe? Do you remain in Town?'

'I do not think my godmother has plans to leave just yet.'

'Perhaps she is remaining here in the hope that Harworth will offer for you.' He clipped off the words, angry that he had spoken of it. He had meant to remain aloof, to cut short this conversation and move away from her. Kitty did not appear to notice the bitterness of his tone and merely shook her head.

'I do not think that is likely.'

'But you would accept him, if he did propose to you?' She hesitated.

'Yes. I do not think I have a choice.'

Daniel put his glass down with a snap; the tight rein on his temper had slipped a little further.

'We all have a choice, Miss Wythenshawe,' he said harshly.

Blinking, Kitty watched him walk away. She was confused by his anger: could it be that he did not wish her to marry Lord Harworth? Why should that be—did he not consider her good enough for his friend? Or—her mouth was suddenly very dry—could it be that he was jealous? Absently she took another glass of wine from a passing waiter. She must be mistaken: Daniel had never shown any sign of preferring her. In fact he went out of his way to quarrel with her every time they met—with the exception of that evening at the Rising Sun.

They had agreed the events of that evening meant nothing, but a tiny spark of excitement flickered within her as she accompanied Lady Leaconham back into the ballroom. *If* he liked her, *if* he wanted to talk to her, then surely he would ask her to dance with him.

Lady Harworth brought a young gentleman forwards to partner her for the first two country dances, then Lord Harworth claimed her hand for the next. From the corner of her eye she saw Daniel watching the dancing, and her spirits lifted when he led Ann on to the floor to join the next set. Kitty finished her last dance with Lord Harworth, who then asked his sister to be his partner. They went off, laughing, and Kitty waited expectantly. Daniel hovered for a moment then, his face set, he made his bow and walked away.

Disappointment and humiliation seared through Kitty. Tears threatened but she fought them down. She had been foolish to hope that he liked her. Daniel Blackwood had never given her reason to think it, save for one, fierce kiss that had shaken her to the core but obviously meant nothing to him. She put back her shoulders and pinned a smile in place as she walked across to join her godmother at the side of the room. If he did not wish to pursue the acquaintance, then neither did she.

'There you are, Kitty. I have someone here who is anxious to dance with you.' Ann came up, dragging a stocky young gentleman behind her. 'This is Mr Leonard Ashley, Kitty. You may remember he came to our picnic.'

'By Jove, yes!' declared the young man, making her a

flourishing bow. 'I'd be honoured if you would stand up with me for the next set, Miss Wythenshawe.'

Kitty looked at the young man. She remembered him from Wormley Hall as the gentleman who had made such disparaging remarks about Mr Grant's poetry. Her impression then had been of a very square gentleman, for he was not above average height with a broad chest and a thick neck. That impression was reinforced now when she saw him in evening dress. He wore a bushy curled wig that made his head as wide as it was long. He was regarding her with blatant admiration in his rather small eyes. It was nearing midnight but Kitty was still smarting from Daniel's defection and she ignored the small voice within that urged caution. Mr Ashley's attentions were balm to her wounded spirits.

'Why, thank you, sir.' She gave him a wide smile. 'It would be my pleasure.'

Mr Ashley bowed again.

'Is it not the most wonderful party, Kitty?' cried Ann, clapping her hands. 'I vow I am quite out of breath with dancing so much, but I would not have it otherwise—oh, Bertram!' She looked up, smiling. 'What are you come for? If it is to ask Kitty to dance then you are too late, for you see that Mr Ashley has beaten you to it! Now, I have danced with Martin Hamilton, and George Camber—who else is there? Ah, yes, I must go and find Julian Grant: he is promised to me for the next dance.'

'If he can tear himself away from his poetry!' replied Mr Ashley with a loud snort of laughter.

Ann dashed away, leaving Kitty feeling quite breathless. She had time for a small, apologetic smile for Lord Harworth before Mr Ashley escorted her to the dance floor just as the musicians were striking up. Two energetic country dances followed and at the end of them Kitty was feeling flushed and very warm. She moved towards one of the open windows, fanning herself vigorously while her partner went off to fetch her a glass of lemonade. She could not see Daniel anywhere and wondered if he had gone out into the garden, where the coloured lamps shone brightly in the darkness. Not that she really cared where he might be. The sooner he took himself back to the north the happier she would be. A movement beside her made her turn and she found Mr Ashley had returned and was holding out a wine glass.

'Oh, but I wanted lemonade.'

'I know and I am very sorry for it but I could only find this.' Mr Ashley pushed the glass towards her. 'It is champagne—have you tried it?'

'But of course.' Kitty raised her brows and tried to look as if she drank champagne every day. She took the glass from him and sipped it cautiously. The light, refreshing taste was very pleasant. She took another sip: the way the bubbles burst on her tongue was really quite delightful. She drank some more and gave a sigh of satisfaction.

'It really is frightfully hot in here,' remarked Mr Ashley. 'Would you care to take a stroll outside?'

He was smiling at her and holding out his arm. Kitty looked out of the window. Below the terrace she could see a number of couples wandering along the illuminated paths.

'I *should* like to see the lamps,' she admitted. She put down her glass, pulled her thin wrap over her shoulders and gave him a smile. 'So, yes, Mr Ashley, I would like to walk through the gardens.'

It was the work of an instant to step out on to the terrace, and another to descend into the gardens, where the night air was cool after the heat of the ballroom. For a moment Kitty felt quite dizzy.

'Steady, Miss Wythenshawe!' Mr Ashley laughed as she clung to his arm.

'I beg your pardon,' she muttered, breathing deeply as she tried to control her balance.

The gardens of Harworth House were extensive and the paths criss-crossed between the flowerbeds that filled the centre space. The area was bounded by the house on one side and the high walls on the other three sides were obscured by a belt of tall trees. It was from the branches of the innermost trees that the coloured lamps twinkled and shone. As they strolled along the outer path, Kitty could hear laughter and voices coming from the darkness. Peering through the gloom, she could just make out a ghostly figure moving gently back and forwards, a noisy group of gentlemen gathered around her.

'Ann is on the swing,' she remarked, pausing. 'Shall we join her?'

'Oh, I think not,' said her companion, gently drawing her on. 'I do not think she is in need of our company. Let us explore.' He led her away from the house until they reached a point where the main path turned to follow the edge of the flowerbeds, while a smaller track stretched off into the trees. 'I wonder where this leads?'

'To the summerhouse,' Kitty responded. 'I saw it earlier.'

'Splendid, just what we need.'

Kitty did not understand the remark but she accompanied him along the path and up the shallow steps. The light from the coloured lamps had not penetrated the trees and Kitty stopped between the tall pillars, loath to enter the shadows beyond.

'I do not think our hostess intended the guests to come here,' she said, trying to withdraw her hand from his arm. Mr Ashley gripped her fingers.

'Not all of them,' he replied. 'But now we are here, perhaps we should make the most of the solitude.'

He pulled her into his arms and with a jolt of surprise Kitty realised he was going to kiss her. She had experienced none of the awareness she had felt when alone with Daniel at the Rising Sun: there was no pleasant if guilty anticipation. Quite the opposite—she felt a definite aversion to the idea. She turned her head and tried to hold him off, but he was too strong and merely laughed at her struggles.

'Do not play the innocent now, Miss Wythenshawe. We both know this is why we came out into the dark!' He pushed her back against one of the pillars, trapping her with his body while his hand caught her face, turning it up so that he could kiss her.

Kitty shuddered and tried to pull away but she was powerless to move. She felt his knee pushing between her legs while his free hand began to pull up her skirts.

Thoroughly frightened, her hands pummelled ineffectually at his back. But her struggles only seemed to inflame him; his mouth moved savagely against hers and through the thin muslin of her gown she could feel his body hardening. Her knowledge of the coupling between a man and a woman was incomplete, gleaned from the books she had read and a few overheard conversations between Mama and Aunt Jane, but instinct told Kitty that Mr Ashley was beyond reason and meant to force himself upon her. In a panic she brought up her hand and raked her nails down his cheek. He gave a howl of fury and, gathering up all her strength, Kitty pushed him off enough to wriggle free. There was a ripping sound as his fingers caught the delicate lace of her bodice. She had barely reached the bottom of the steps when his hand grabbed her arm. 'Oh, no, you don't. I haven't finished with you yet.'

He tried to pull her back but Kitty's knees buckled and

she sank to the earth, too exhausted to fight him again. She shrank from his loathsome touch.

'Take your hands off her!'

The words cracked like a whip through the darkness. The grasp on her arm loosened.

'Who the hell are—?'

The smack of a fist on his chin sent Mr Ashley crashing to the ground. Silence followed, then Kitty was aware of a pair of white-stockinged legs standing before her. Strong hands were helping her to her feet.

'Are you hurt?' Daniel's voice was full of concern. Kitty shook her head, unable to trust her voice. Behind her she heard her assailant grunting and she shrank against Daniel. He put his arms around her and spoke over her head, saying coldly, 'You will leave now, sir, if you know what's good for you.'

His tone was so menacing that Kitty trembled. From the corner of her eye she saw Mr Ashley dust himself off, glaring at them.

'She was willing enough,' he said sullenly. 'Why else would she come off the path with me—?'

With a growl Daniel released Kitty and lunged towards his opponent, but Kitty clung on to his coat, begging him not to fight. He stopped, saying savagely, 'I suggest you take yourself off immediately, before I forget there is a lady present and give you the thrashing you deserve.'

Mr Ashley hesitated, glaring pugnaciously at Daniel. 'Take her then, and welcome to her,' he snarled. 'Strumpet!'

Daniel moved so quickly that Kitty did not have time to protest. Again there was a sickening thud and again Ashley was stretched out on the ground. This time Daniel stood over him, his fists clenched.

'You will leave the house now, sir, and if I ever find that

you have spoken a word about this, I swear I will call you out and cut you down like a dog.'

Daniel spoke quietly, but there was so much menace in his voice that his opponent made no attempt to rise. Instead he scrabbled away on all fours until he was out of reach of those punishing fists before clambering to his feet and hurrying away.

In the silence that followed Kitty did not move. Daniel turned back to her.

'He is gone now. You are safe.' He held out his hand. 'Shall I take you back?'

Kitty shook her head.

'N-no, not yet. I do not think I could face...' Her voice trailed away. With shaking fingers she lifted the shred of muslin that was hanging down from her gown and pulled it across the exposed linen of her under-bodice.

'Here, let me.' Daniel scooped her muslin shawl from the ground and wrapped it about her shoulders. 'If we cross it like this and tie the ends at the back, no one will know there is anything amiss.'

'Yes. Yes, of course, how...how sensible. Why did I not think of that?' She put a hand up to adjust the folds of the shawl but her fingers shook too much to be of use.

'You are trembling.' He took her arm. 'There is a bench in the summerhouse. You must sit down until you are feel-ing better.'

He led her into the little shelter and guided her to the seat. She clutched at his arm.

'Do not leave me!' Her voice shook pitifully and she was relieved when he sat down beside her.

'I am not about to leave you.'

'I d-did not know what he was going to do.' Kitty leaned against his shoulder, the soft, fine wool of his evening coat beneath her cheek. 'He s-seemed such a gentleman.'

She felt him take a long breath, as if controlling his anger.

'Have you not learned yet that it is dangerous to be alone with any man?'

'There were so many people in the gardens, I didn't think we *were* alone. I thought it would be quite safe...' She shuddered. 'It was horrible—'

'Hush now.' He put his arm around her. 'He is gone.'

She gave a sob and turned her face into his coat, one hand clutching at his jacket.

'I am so ashamed! To put myself into such a situation—I feel so foolish!'

'The fellow will say nothing, you may be sure of that. And no one else need know anything about it.'

'But *you* will know,' she said in a low voice. 'I did not w-want you to think ill of me.'

With a soft laugh he held her away from him and drew a handkerchief out of his pocket.

'I do not think ill of you,' he said, taking her chin between his fingers and turning her face up so he could wipe her cheeks. 'I think ill of that blackguard for his behaviour.'

He had turned her face to catch what little light there was and Kitty kept very still, gazing up into his shadowed countenance. Mr Ashley was forgotten. She was only aware of being very close to Daniel, of his thigh pressed against hers, his fingers holding her chin, the soft scented handkerchief sliding gently over her cheeks. She was tingling through the length of her body and her heart had begun to thud painfully against her ribs. Nervously she ran her tongue across her lips.

'Don't do that!' ordered Daniel.

Her eyes widened. Her tongue flickered again over her lips before she could speak.

'Do what? I do not understand you.'

He dropped the handkerchief and cupped her face in his hands, running his thumb gently along her bottom lip.

'Kitty, you little witch, stop it! You have no idea how adorable you are.' His voice had softened and the words wrapped themselves around her, deep and warm as he said, 'You do not know how much I want to kiss you.'

She might not have known the perils of stepping off the path with Mr Ashley, but Kitty was well aware of the danger Daniel posed to her. It was not safe to be alone with him. She should run back to the safety of the crowded salon, but the temptation to move even closer to Daniel was far, far too strong.

Torn between what she wanted to do and what she *should* do, Kitty did nothing. She remained very still, gazing up into Daniel's dark eyes, enjoying the feel of his hands on her face, aching for the touch of his lips against hers.

It never came. He gave a slight shake of his head; she heard a long exhalation as he gathered her in his arms and pulled her close.

'For me to take advantage of this moment would make me an even bigger scoundrel than the fool I found molesting you. We would both regret it, for I am going north tomorrow and you...' she felt his chest rise and fall on another sigh '...you are going to find a lord to marry.'

'You must think me very mercenary,' she whispered.

He laid his cheek briefly against her hair.

'No, you are doing the same as every other young lady in the Town; the difference is that you are honest about your goals. So I wish you well with your quest, Miss Katherine Wythenshawe.'

'You do?' Safe within his arms, Kitty turned her face up to look at him.

'Of course.' Daniel did not glance down but continued

to gaze out through the trees towards the starry sky. 'Harworth is already showing an interest in you. With his fortune he has no need to marry money. He is a gentleman and I believe he will treat you well. What more could you want?'

A cloud had settled over Kitty's spirits. Perhaps everything she had hoped for was within her grasp but here, now, sitting in the little stone temple with Daniel, all she knew was that he was leaving in the morning and she would never see him again.

'You have been very kind to me, Mr Blackwood.'

'It is nothing.'

His dismissive tone was unsettling. She wanted to thank him, to make him know how much she would miss him. He was still gazing out at the night sky and suddenly Kitty was overwhelmed by the desire to kiss him. She lifted her head and strained to touch her mouth to the only bare flesh she could reach, the soft hinge where the column of his throat rose up from the folds of his snowy neckcloth and met the strong line of his jaw. A steady pulse was beating there and she felt it jump when her lips grazed his skin. He drew back and stared down at her, deep shadows concealing his expression.

'I beg your pardon,' she whispered. 'I know I should not—'

Her words were cut short as he bent his head and covered her mouth with his own. Like a spark in a tinderbox the white-hot flame of desire ignited within her. She clung to him as a drowning man might cling to a wooden spar. Indeed, she felt as if she was drowning in the pleasure of his kiss, which seemed to tug at her very soul. He teased her lips apart and began to explore her mouth with his tongue. The wild pleasure at her core intensified, pooling somewhere between her thighs. Her hips tilted restlessly towards him. His hold tightened and he pulled her on to his lap. He began to cover her face with kisses, then his mouth moved over the line of her jaw and trailed down the column of her neck, the feather-light touch of his lips making her moan with pleasure.

Gently he pushed aside the muslin shawl that he himself had tied over her shoulders. Little shivers of excitement coursed through Kitty as his fingers brushed her skin. The moonlight glinted on his hair as he bent his head to kiss the soft swell of her breast at the point where it emerged from the confining stays. She arched towards him, gasping. Every inch of her was alive and aching to be touched. If he had started to undress her there and then on the bench she would not have resisted him.

'Oh, Daniel!'

The words were little more than a breath. She ran her fingers through his silky hair, trailing them across his cheek as he raised his head.

'This has gone far enough,' he said, his voice cracking with strain. 'I came here to your rescue, not to ruin you.'

'Perhaps I do not wish to be rescued,' she whispered, her hand cupping his cheek, trying to draw him back down to her.

With a sigh Daniel slid her off his lap. The jolt of hitting the hard wooden bench was sobering. The thrilling tingle was replaced by the sudden, stark realisation of her situation. She put her hands to her mouth.

'Oh, heavens, what have I done?'

Daniel was adjusting his coat but he paused at her anguished cry.

'Why, you have done nothing, my dear. *Yet.* That is why I must get you back to the house before it is too late.'

Tears burned Kitty's eyes. She felt chilled, unwanted. Undesirable.

'Come.' He held out his hand to her. 'We will slip back on to the path and no one will be any the wiser. Your reputation will be secure.'

Kitty tried to stand. She was surprised to find her legs still obeyed her will. She put up a hand to straighten the folds of her shawl but Daniel reached out and grasped her fingers.

'It looks very well,' he assured her. 'Come now, we must get back to the house.'

He led her through the trees and they stepped out on to the deserted path. He pulled her arm through his just as another couple came into view. Raising his voice, he said loudly, 'The grounds were designed by Switzer some sixty years ago for the third Baron Harworth, you know. A little formal for our modern tastes, but delightful nevertheless.'

Kitty replied in kind, conscious of the chattering couples around them. The air was suddenly very heavy and oppressive, weighing down on her spirits. She was relieved to hear a low rumble of thunder in the distance.

'A storm.' She looked up. 'I am glad it is not my imagination. I thought perhaps this oppression was some terrible presentiment of my disgrace.'

He glanced down at her.

'It is no such thing. I am returning you to the house with your reputation—and your dreams—intact.'

Not my dreams!

The words echoed through Kitty's head. She realised with a bitter clarity that her duty and her dreams were two vastly different things.

As they approached the terrace the laughter and chatter from the ballroom spilled out towards them. Everyone sounded so happy, so different from the tumult of regret, misery and despair that warred within Kitty. She stopped at the bottom step and Daniel turned to look at her, his brows raised in enquiry.

'Pray, Dan—Mr Blackwood, let us take our leave of each other here.'

'If you wish.'

She put out her hand.

'Then, goodbye, sir. I wish you a safe journey tomorrow, and...and thank you.' She added, determined to be truthful, 'I am only sorry our first meetings were so...stormy.'

He carried her hand to his lips and pressed a kiss upon her fingers.

'We made a wretched beginning, did we not? For my part in that I humbly apologise, Miss Wythenshawe.'

'I should like to have known you better,' she confessed.

He gave her a wry smile.

'Nay, ma'am, how should that be? When tha'art a fine lady and meself but a manufacturer!'

'Will you never forgive me for that slight?'

'It is no slight,' he told her. 'I am proud of what I am.'

And I am ashamed I ever thought ill of you!

She wanted to utter the words but a sudden flurry of laughter told her that another couple was upon them, pushing past to ascend the steps. The moment for confession was gone.

Daniel took her arm and led her up to the terrace. Lady Leaconham and her sister were standing by one of the open windows, fanning themselves vigorously.

'So there you are, Kitty!' cried Lady Harworth, reaching out for her. 'The dancing finished some time ago and your godmother has been looking for you.'

'I beg your pardon, I—'

'The blame is mine,' Daniel interrupted her smoothly.

'I persuaded Miss Wythenshawe to give me the pleasure of her company in the gardens.' He gave Lady Harworth the benefit of his rare, charming smile. 'We have been admiring the decorative lamps, ma'am.'

'They are very pretty, are they not?' replied his hostess, beaming. 'I have been very pleased with the effect and will use them again, I think. Not this Season, of course, for the house will soon be shut up for the summer.'

'They were a splendid idea, my lady, and one I will take back to the Holme,' said Daniel. 'I think my mother will like the idea of being able to use the garden on warm summer nights. And I have no doubt my sister will consider it a splendid notion!'

'Sisters, hah!' chuckled Lord Harworth, coming up at that moment. 'They are always troublesome at parties, ain't that so, ma'am?'

Lady Harworth looked a little put out but she managed a smile.

'Alas, young people can get a little out of hand,' she admitted. Lady Leaconham's politely enquiring look obliged her to continue. 'I had to send Bertram out to fetch Ann away from the swing, Letitia. That little group was becoming far too raucous.'

Lady Leaconham smiled and tucked her hand through Kitty's arm.

'I am pleased to think my dear Kitty was not of their number.'

'No, she preferred to stroll in the gardens with a handsome young man, ain't that so, Miss Wythenshawe?' said Lord Harworth, clearly in the best of spirits. 'And I have no doubt that Blackwood, the young dog, was trying to cut me out!'

'No such thing, my lord, I assure you,' returned Daniel.

With another fat chuckle his host gave him a playful punch in the ribs.

'Oh, don't stiffen up so, my boy, I am roasting you—I know I have nothing to fear from *you!* I am delighted that you showed Miss Wythenshawe the gardens. As host I am afraid I did not have as much time to spare for my own pleasures as I would have liked.' He beamed at Kitty for a few moments. 'So you see, Blackwood, I am grateful to you, truly I am!'

'Thank you, my lord.'

Kitty watched as Daniel gave a stiff little bow to include them all and walked away. She felt very low. A cold chill had settled around her heart, like the mist that sometimes clung to the moors, blotting out the sun for days on end. He was leaving. They would not meet again and she must smile and say all that was proper as she followed her godmother through the crowded rooms to take their leave. They had reached the hall and were waiting for their wraps to be fetched before Lady Leaconham turned to give Kitty a long look.

'My child, I did not like to say anything before my sister, for I would not draw it to her attention, but what are you doing with your shawl crossed over your bosom in that fashion? It makes you look like a matron rather than a young lady in her first Season.'

Kitty had been expecting the question and had had time to work on her explanation, but she could not prevent the colour stealing into her cheeks.

'I spilled red wine on my bodice, Godmama. It looked very unsightly.'

'Oh, I see. Well, we must see if Meakin can wash it out when we get home—' She broke off as the footmen arrived with their cloaks and Kitty hoped she would say no more about it, but when they were shut up in the carriage and making the short journey back to Portman Square Lady Leaconham said suddenly, 'Just when did you spill the wine, my love? I hope you were not...carousing with Mr Blackwood.'

'No, ma'am. It was Mr Ashley.' Kitty was not sorry she could put some of the blame for the spoiled gown in its rightful place. 'He offered to fetch me some refreshment and I had asked for lemonade...'

Lady Leaconham gave a little huff of displeasure.

'My sister has only herself to blame if Ann and her friends grow a little wild at these parties,' she said severely. 'It is always a mistake to allow young people too much freedom. And the idea of *encouraging* guests to walk in the gardens! I cannot pretend that I am very happy about you going off with Mr Blackwood, but there were so many people strolling out of doors I am sure there was no harm in it.'

'No, Godmama. And you need not worry about Mr Blackwood. He is leaving for the north in the morning.'

'Yes, so I understand, and a very good thing, too. I know I am very much obliged to him for his services to us at Barnet, but I would not have him set himself up as a rival to Lord Harworth for your affections. I admit I was encouraged by the number of compliments I received upon your behalf this evening, my love, and several gentleman commented most favourably about you, but I have hinted them away, for the present. I will not say anything too final, of course, until we are sure of Harworth, but I am satisfied he is very interested in you.'

'Thank you, Godmama.'

'So you must be careful to keep gentlemen like Mr Blackwood at a distance in future, my love.'

'Since Mr Blackwood will be hundreds of miles away I think that is distance enough, Godmama, do not you?'

replied Kitty, trying to make light of a fact that weighed on her spirits.

'Well, of course it is, for the next two weeks, until Lord Harworth goes north, but he is sure to come to Kirkleigh to discuss Bertram's schemes for his new mill.'

Kitty shrugged.

'That can have nothing to do with us, Godmama.'

'Heavens, child, if he would be confined to the steward's office I should not worry, but you have seen how Harworth treats him, almost as an equal! He lives too close to be invited to stay, so that's a mercy, but Bertram will ask him to dine with us, I am sure.' She paused, frowning at Kitty's look of bewilderment. Then her brow cleared. 'But of course, you do not know, for you were not with me when the invitation was issued. My sister has invited us to spend the summer with her at Kirkleigh! You look amazed and well you might! I have no doubt that it was Bertram that put her up to it and all because of you, you clever little puss! We are to go to Yorkshire.'

'No!'

'*Yes!* It is all arranged, we are to follow a fortnight after my sister. Garston, too, is coming with us and there is every reason to believe that Harworth means to propose to you!'

Chapter Eight

*My dearest Kitty, how your aunt and I look forward
to receiving your letters, with news of all the parties,
routs and balls that you have attended! And now
your godmother tells me you have been invited to
Kirkleigh, as the guest of Lady Harworth no less! My
dear child I am so* proud *of you. Letitia has hinted of*
An Alliance. *How wonderful that would be! And if
the settlements could be drawn up before the winter,
perhaps it might be possible to move out of our cottage here at Fallridge, for there is no doubt that
the damp does not agree with your Aunt Jane. Her
cough has returned and she is not in spirits. I fear
another winter here may well prove too much for her,
although she does not complain. Of course, we shall
not try to influence you, my darling child, except to
say that to see you* well established, *possibly as* a
lady, *is the* dearest wish *of our hearts.*

*But of course, my love, our greatest concern is
for your happiness…*

'How is your dear Mama, Kitty?'

Kitty looked up from her letter, forcing herself to smile.

'She is well, Godmama, although she says Aunt Jane is coughing again.' She looked down at the bread and butter on her breakfast plate, her appetite quite gone. There was such a weight of responsibility on her shoulders. Her godmother was so sure that Lord Harworth would offer for her and if he did, then it might be possible to find a new home for Mama and Aunt Jane before the winter. Perhaps they might even be allowed to live with her, but certainly she must do what she could to remove them from the cottage, which was cold in summer, draughty in winter and always damp. She glanced again at her letter. Mama insisted that she wanted Kitty to be happy, and by marrying Lord Harworth she *would* be happy, would she not, because she would be fulfilling the hopes of those she loved most...

'Now, we must finish packing today, my dear, because it is an early start tomorrow.' Lady Leaconham helped herself to another hot muffin. 'Garston has promised me he will be here at nine tomorrow and I must say I am not a great traveller, but I am looking forward to visiting Kirkleigh. I have not been there since my dear Leaconham died. My sister Harworth has her own circle of friends, you see, and I have mine. Since I have been widowed the time has never been right for her to invite me...' She paused for a moment to consider this, then looked up again, saying cheerfully, 'So I am convinced that this invitation is due to you, my love.'

Kitty glanced at her mother's letter again, her eyes drawn to one particular section.

It delights me to think that by the end of the month you will be less than fifty miles from us, my love. Not

*that we shall expect you to visit while you are with
your noble friends at Kirkleigh. In fact, I expressly
forbid it...*

'Lord Harworth knows nothing of my family, does he,
Godmama? More to the point, Lady Harworth thinks I
come from a family of consequence.'

'Well, I have not gone into detail...'

Kitty waved an impatient hand.

'Have you told her I am rich, ma'am?'

'No, of course not!' Lady Leaconham concentrated on
pouring herself another cup of coffee. 'I may not have told
her *precisely* of your condition, but if my sister thinks you
wealthy then she cannot claim that I told her so!'

'Perhaps I could visit Fallridge while we are there—'

'No!'

'My dear ma'am, I have nothing to hide. My birth is
perfectly respectable, and if my mother has not the means
now to live in the manner in which she was raised, that is
not her fault...'

'No, of course not, my love, and you know I am excessively fond of your mama, but this visit is not the time to
introduce her to Lord Harworth.'

'But, Godmama—'

'Once my nephew has made you an offer, then of course
your circumstances must be explained,' said Lady Leaconham firmly. 'As a man of honour he will not consider your
lack of fortune an impediment.'

'You mean once he has offered for me it will be too late
for him to cry off.'

'My dear, how you do twist my words! That is not at all
what I meant!'

'Then perhaps it would be best if I explained everything to him and to Lady Harworth before we travel north,' persisted Kitty.

Lady Leaconham put down her cup and bent a serious look upon her goddaughter.

'Now, Katherine, listen to me. My sister Harworth is naturally anxious for her only son to marry well. If she knew you to be penniless she would do everything in her power to prevent the match. I merely want her to—to give Bertram the opportunity to become acquainted with you. There is nothing so very wrong in that, is there? Especially when such a match would mean so much to your mama. She has only ever wanted one thing for you, my dear, and you have the chance now to make her dreams come true.' The look softened into one of entreaty. 'I know you abhor pretence, Kitty, and I would not have you *lie* to Lord Harworth, but, my dear child, pray *consider.* If you announce to the world that you are a pauper, you give up all hope of a good marriage.'

'Is that what I am, Godmama, a pauper?' asked Kitty in a small voice.

'Of course not, it was thoughtless of me to use the term. You are a gently born young woman who lacks a dowry. It is not a crime, and all I ask is that you hold back from explaining the true state of your finances until Bertram proposes to you. So—' Lady Leaconham beamed across the table '—that will not be so very bad, will it?'

Reluctantly Kitty gave her assurance to her godmother that she would say nothing and went off to finish her packing. She tried to console herself with the fact that Lord Harworth might not propose, but she was honest enough to admit that recently he had given her sufficient hints— drawing her aside for a few moments' private conversation whenever they met, squeezing her hand when taking his leave of her, and now this invitation to Kirkleigh, when

Lady Leaconham freely admitted she was not in the habit of being invited to her sister's summer home. It seemed depressingly clear that Lord Harworth was singling her out. As she watched the coachmen carrying the heavy corded trunk out of her room she determined that if Lord Harworth made her an offer she would explain her situation. She would do so immediately, before any official announcements could be made, before he had time to tell his family. That way she could give him the opportunity to withdraw, if he so wished. She would not trap him into an unequal marriage.

These thoughts came back to her when, after three days of weary travel, Lady Leaconham's lumbering carriage arrived at the gates of Kirkleigh House. The entrance to Lord Harworth's main seat had been designed to impress. A long straight drive led off the road towards a high, battle-mented stone wall where tall pillars topped with eagles flanked a pair of ornate iron gates. There was no lodge but a small gatehouse was built into one side of the wall and her godmother informed her that when the family was in residence a gatekeeper was on duty at all times. Even as she said this, a liveried servant dashed out to throw wide the gates and they entered the grounds. They drove through a good half-mile of landscaped parkland before passing through another set of gates and approaching the house itself. Kitty gasped, her eyes widening as she took her first look at Kirkleigh House.

It was a vast building in the Palladian style, the entrance front decorated by a series of columns built into the walls between the windows. A high-pitched roof extended behind a central pediment which proudly displayed the Harworth coat of arms.

'Well, Kitty, what do you think?'

Kitty did not know how to answer Lady Leaconham's question. The house was so large, so magnificent, that her heart sank within her. Could the owner of this vast pile really want her, little Kitty Wythenshawe, to be its mistress?

'It is very...grand,' she managed at last and drew a soft laugh from her companion.

'It is indeed, but you must not let that deter you. The house is run by an army of servants and there are house-keepers and stewards a-plenty to attend to everything.'

'If that is the case, ma'am, then what would there be for me to do?'

Lord Leaconham, sitting opposite, found the question highly amusing.

'Why, there will be nothing for you to do but to please your husband and enjoy yourself!'

The carriage drove past the first of two flights of steps leading up to the first-floor entrance and stopped at a wide doorway at ground level, where a series of liveried servants waited to hand them out of the coach. Kitty would have found their presence very daunting if at that moment Ann had not flown out of the house and enveloped her in a warm embrace.

'Oh, Kitty, I am so glad you are here! You are the first of our guests to arrive. It has been so very dull here with only Bertram and Mama to talk to! And Aunt Leaconham, too: welcome to you, dear Aunt! And Garston! I am delighted you could join us, Cousin. Now we shall be a merry crowd! Come in, come in, all of you! Bertram is out riding and Mama is resting in her room. She gave instructions that you were to be shown to your rooms first so that you might rest and change before we all met up at dinner, but I could not wait for that so I came out to meet you!'

Bemused by this enthusiastic but unconventional

welcome Kitty was not sure how to react, but a glance at the butler's face showed her that that august personage was smiling benignly upon his young mistress, so she allowed herself to be marched off, leaving Lady Leaconham and Garston to follow at a much more dignified pace.

'Oh, I have missed you so,' declared Ann, leaning happily on Kitty's arm. 'I know it is only two weeks since we were in London but it feels so much longer than that! Tell me all that I have missed. Has everyone left Town now?'

'It is much quieter,' responded Kitty, adding with a twinkle, 'I think your departure signalled the beginning of the mass retreat!'

'No! Have all the gentlemen gone, then? I expected Mr Duffey to propose to that plain Jane he was courting, and Mr Ashley seemed determined to pay court to you at my party...'

Kitty did not wish to be reminded of Mr Ashley, but it was clear that she would need to give some sort of answer.

'He was interested only in a flirtation, which did not please me at all—'

'Oh, my poor little Kitty, did he try to make love to you?' Ann laughed. 'He is a rattle, but quite amusing.'

'Well, I did not find him amusing at all,' retorted Kitty, remembering her torn dress, and the lies she had told. 'I wish you had not introduced him to me.'

'Oh, dear, you are really upset. Pray do not be angry with me, I thought he might amuse you. Did you send him away? I cannot recall seeing him at the house after the dancing.'

'I think he left early,' said Kitty, eager to change the subject. 'As for Mr Duffey, I believe he has gone into Devonshire, following his plain Jane.'

'Well, I wish him luck. He has been head over heels for

her all Season, which made him very poor company, I can
tell you. He was convinced everyone would think he was
marrying her only for her fortune, because he has not a
penny to fly with, but I told him no one cares for that any
more! But enough of that—here is your room!'

It seemed to Kitty that they had walked miles up stairs,
through elegant chambers and along echoing corridors to
reach a large sunny bedroom.

'It is next to mine,' continued Ann, leading the way in.
'We are quite a distance from my Aunt Leaconham, but
I hope you won't mind that, and I thought my maid could
look after you, if you would not object. Then Meakin won't
have to trail all the way up here from my aunt's chamber
every time you change your dress.'

'You have thought of everything,' Kitty, responded, a
laugh trembling in her voice. 'And, no, I have no objection
at all to being here, if that is what you wish. As for a maid,
I am very used to dressing myself, you know. I never had
a maid until—' Even as the words spilled out, Kitty had
a vision of her godmother's horrified countenance. With
barely a pause she continued, 'I mean, I never had a maid
of my own until very recently.'

'Norris will be more than sufficient for us both. And
you know she is *very* discreet,' added Ann with a naughty
twinkle.

She continued to chatter for a while longer until she saw
Kitty trying to hide a yawn.

'Oh, dear, here I am talking non-stop and you will be
wanting to rest before dinner!' She stepped up to give Kitty
another hug. 'I shall leave you now, and I will send Norris
to unpack your trunk while you sleep!'

If Kitty did not actually go to sleep before dinner she did
at least rest, and when Ann came to collect her to take her

down to the dining room she was feeling much refreshed and ready to see more of Kirkleigh.

Many of the windows had been opened and a cool breeze flowed through the house. Kitty might never have moved in such exalted circles, but she had grown up with the reminiscences and instructions from Mama and Aunt Jane, so the high rooms with their gilded ceilings and thick carpets, the bustling activity of the servants, even the call of the peacock coming in from the open window, seemed familiar. Ann had told her that several other guests had been invited to join them at Kirkleigh later that week, and she was relieved to think she would have a few days to become accustomed to the house and its ways before meeting new people.

Dinner was served in the small dining room, and although the mass of silver in the centre of the table resembled a small mountain range to Kitty, she knew this was an informal dinner. Everyone appeared to be in the best of spirits, even her godmother making light of the long journey north with its lame carriage horses and unaired sheets.

'It is even worse if one is travelling without a gentleman,' observed Lady Harworth. 'Bertram wanted me to bring Ann here on my own while he stopped off in Derbyshire, but I would not agree to it. I said if he could not come here directly with us then we would go with him.'

Lady Leaconham turned a smiling enquiry upon her nephew.

'And what was there in Derbyshire that required your presence, Bertram?'

'Mr Blackwood wanted him to visit Cromford and see Mr Arkwright's cotton-spinning mill,' put in Ann. 'Mama and I did not go into the mill, of course, but Bertram said it was a vast, noisy place, and everything is powered by water.'

'And you'll soon see we have plenty of that here,' declared Lord Harworth. 'Water and the hills make Kirkleigh ideal for a mill.'

'But you will not be building your mill anywhere near the house, my dear,' put in Lady Harworth. She turned to address her sister. 'I have never seen such a place as Cromford, Sister. The mill stands like a huge stone fortress, grey and forbidding.'

'It could well be the Castle of Otranto,' giggled Ann.

'And is Cromford itself a pretty village?'

Lady Harworth shook her head.

'Everywhere is dust and noise, because they are forever building. We were obliged to put up at the Greyhound. I have to admit it was very comfortable, nothing like the usual coaching inn. It is far more commodious: Mr Arkwright himself built it for his many visitors. I understand his mill attracts a great deal of interest, although I cannot see why that should be.'

'It is the future, Mama,' said Lord Harworth. 'With the new mills and machinery to spin cotton we can make cloth better and quicker than anywhere else in the world, and make a fortune to boot. Several fortunes!'

'I am not sure it is quite as easy as it sounds,' remarked Kitty.

Lord Harworth smiled at her.

'You are quite right, Miss Wythenshawe, which is why I have engaged Blackwood to help me! In fact, he will be riding over next week to look at the new plans my man is drawing up, so you will be able to renew your acquaintance with him—I shall ask him to stay for dinner!'

The news roused mixed feelings for Kitty. Much as she

wanted to see Daniel again, was it wise, when he awoke such passion in her yet she knew nothing could come of it?

She had struggled with the problem throughout dinner, but when she carried a dish of tea across to Lady Leaconham later in the evening she discovered that her godmother was also unhappy.

'I cannot understand Bertram inviting that young man to eat with the family,' she said, drawing Kitty down beside her on the sofa. 'He says himself he has engaged him, so he is in some ways an *employee*. And to have the man mixing with his own sister, who is at a very impressionable age!' She shook her head. 'I do not understand it,' she said again. 'And my sister, to allow it with never a word of reproach. She is usually such a stickler for propriety.'

Kitty listened to her in growing dismay. It seemed that as her godmother's hopes of a match between Kitty and her nephew had grown, so had her prejudice against Daniel Blackwood and despite her attempts to remain neutral, Kitty found herself more and more wanting to defend him.

'But the Blackwoods own several mills,' she said now. 'I believe they are a family of considerable standing in the north. And you said yourself he is quite eligible.'

'That was when I first met him, and I did not understand that he is still so involved in trade. Nor did I know Bertram was employing him. And as for his family—you knew nothing of him before you met in Town? Your mama never mentioned the Blackwood family?'

'Well, no, but we lived far to the west, and Mama...' Kitty paused for a moment '...Mama showed no interest in anyone except the very highest society. We had very few acquaintances.'

Lady Leaconham did not appear to notice the wistful note in Kitty's voice, too intent upon her own train of thought.

'But if the family is so well to do, then *why* is he working for Bertram?' she said. 'No, it does not make sense. But then, nothing makes sense any more in a world where the poor king and queen of France can be locked up by their own people. And now we must have tradesmen at our table!'

'But, ma'am, you were happy enough to recognise Mr Blackwood in Town.'

'But I never invited him to dinner, my dear. Oh, dear me, no. He may be an acquaintance of my nephew, and I do not deny that he behaved like a gentleman when he came to our assistance at Barnet, but that does not mean we should sit down to dinner together!'

The remainder of Lady Harworth's guests arrived the following day and soon Kitty found herself caught up in the busy routine of a Kirkleigh house party. With half-a-dozen young people in the house Ann was very happy, organising drives and picnics on fine days, theatricals and charades when the weather was inclement. The ladies would spend afternoons at their sketching and painting while the gentlemen took themselves off riding, mostly to inspect the woods and discuss the new coverts with Lord Harworth's gamekeeper, but the ladies knew that they sometimes went off to watch a cock-fight or a mill in a nearby village.

There were protracted breakfasts and noisy dinners and by the end of the week Kitty was relieved to slip away to spend a quiet hour alone with her books. She wrote long letters to her mother, describing life at Kirkleigh, but even as she wrote of the delights of having nothing to do all day but please oneself, Kitty knew she was not being quite truthful. She longed for an occupation; even helping the governess with the squire's children had made her feel more useful than idling away each day as she was doing now. However, she could tell her mama that she was learning one new accomplishment.

Many of the ladies went riding each morning, and when Ann discovered that Kitty had never learned the art, she was shocked.

'But everyone rides in the country! This must be remedied immediately: we shall teach you!'

'And how long with that take?' asked Kitty, torn between amusement at her friend's enthusiasm and alarm at the thought of joining Ann on one of her rides: she had heard Lord Harworth describe his sister as a bruising horse-woman, afraid of nothing.

'Not long. I shall have my old pony saddled up for you tomorrow morning. You need not look so anxious, Kitty: you will not be expected to jump fences or anything dangerous—at least, not for the first few weeks.' She twinkled mischievously. 'I shall have my groom lead you around the stable yard each morning until you are at home in the saddle.'

'That is very kind of you,' said Kitty. 'I confess I should like to ride with you in the mornings.'

'I am sure you will pick it up very quickly,' Ann reassured her. 'Dapple is very steady, you will find her as comfortable as sitting on a sofa.'

'Only considerably higher,' laughed Kitty.

Thus, on the very next fine morning, Kitty donned the riding habit that Ann insisted she should borrow and went off for her first lesson. She was quick to learn, and two days later they progressed to the park. The groom led Kitty around the perimeter, complimenting her on her improvement and suggesting that they could now dispense with the leading rein.

'Oh, not quite yet, if you please,' begged Kitty.

'Well, mebbe not, then, miss, seeing as someone is coming through the park. We don't want Dapple takin' off with 'ee.'

Kitty became aware of the sound of hoofbeats behind her and turned her head to see a rider cantering in the direction of the house. As he drew nearer she recognised Daniel Blackwood and her heart gave the now familiar little skip. He slowed and turned his horse towards them, raising his hat as he approached. She was a little disappointed that no flash of pleasure illuminated his countenance, nor did he look surprised to see her, but she thought it very likely that Lord Harworth had informed him that she was at Kirkleigh.

'Good morning to you, Miss Wythenshawe.'

She nodded, smiling as his eyes ranged over the pony. She felt compelled to explain. 'Miss Harworth tells me that everyone rides here so, as you see, I am learning!'

'A very useful accomplishment,' he said gravely.

Kitty continued to smile, inordinately pleased to see him again. She wanted to keep him with her, to begin a conversation, but he was smiling back at her now and her poor brain refused to work properly. Dapple shifted from one leg to another, unbalancing Kitty who clutched anxiously at the reins.

Daniel touched his hat.

'I will leave you to your lesson,' he said. 'Lord Harworth is expecting me: no doubt I will see you at the house later?'

'Yes, yes, I hope, I mean, I am sure—'

She broke off, covering her confusion by giving her

attention to the mare who was objecting to having the reins twitched so nervously. With a nod, Daniel rode away.

'Oh, how embarrassing that he should see me thus!' she exclaimed, watching his retreating form.

'Nay, it ain't so bad,' said the groom, grinning. 'We all have to start like this. And if you'll forgive me, miss, I'd say that you will make a good horsewoman, given time. You have a good seat, and good hands, when you ain't distracted.'

'Thank you, Selby.' Kitty flushed, pleased with the compliment. 'I really would like to be able to ride well.'

'No reason why you shouldn't, miss. Now, shall we try going round the park without the leading rein?'

The groom's praise spurred Kitty to try even harder and she stayed so long in the park that breakfast was finished by the time she returned to the house and she was obliged to ask for a little bread and butter to be sent up to her room.

She found it difficult to settle to anything, knowing that Daniel was in the house.

'You may not see him,' she told herself. 'It is such a large, rambling building, and he is closeted with Lord Harworth in his office on the lower floor. There is not the least reason why you should meet.'

Despite this she found herself taking extra time over changing her gown, deciding upon her sprigged muslin decorated with ivy leaves embroidered around the neck and sleeves. Norris suggested dressing her hair in a new style, catching it back with a bandeau and leaving just a few dusky curls to escape and frame her face. Kitty allowed herself to be persuaded, and as soon as the maid had worked her magic Kitty hurried down to join the other guests.

The new look immediately found favour with Ann,

whom she found in the garden where the younger members of the party were playing at bowls.

'I do wish my hair was fashionably dark and curled as yours does,' sighed Ann, tucking her hand in Kitty's arm and drawing her towards a table laden with lemonade, pastries and delicate little cakes. 'And you have a delicious colour in your cheeks—your morning riding lessons are agreeing with you! Selby tells me you are making good progress.'

'He thinks I will be good enough to ride out with you in the park soon.'

'That is excellent news, because Mr Hamilton has a plan to ride over to Titchwell and take luncheon at the Star next week.'

'That's right,' declared a lanky young man with a shock of yellow hair. 'I thought we should make up a party and ride out for the day, if the weather holds.'

'I can always follow in the barouche with Godmother and Lady Harworth,' offered Kitty.

'Oh, we are not intending to have Mama or Aunt Leaconham with us,' said Ann quickly. 'We shall have much more fun if we are on our own.'

'We?'

Ann began to count on her fingers.

'Well, me, you, and Garston of course. And Martin—that is, Mr Hamilton—plus Lizzie Camber and her brother George—those of us here now.'

'Will your mama allow us to go alone?' asked Miss Camber.

'Of course,' came the airy reply. 'Titchwell is part of our estate: Mama knows we shall come to no harm.'

Kitty glanced doubtfully at the little group. She knew Elizabeth Camber was barely sixteen and her brother little more than a year older, and although Mr Martin Hamilton was several years older than herself, Kitty thought him rather immature. She watched him now as he teased Lizzie Camber and laughed immoderately at something Garston was saying to him.

'You will of course be taking Selby?'

Ann wrinkled her nose.

'Oh, no, he is far worse than Bertram, always criticising! We should not have a minute's peace if we take him with us. No, this will be a party of *pleasure*. We shall be free to do as we wish for the day!'

'Well, I am not sure I shall be able to ride well enough...' began Kitty, but Ann stopped her.

'Of course you will. You must not worry about that. We will all look after you, won't we, Garston?'

'You may be sure of it,' declared Lord Leaconham, coming up. 'A gentle ride and a good lunch, it will be a splendid day.'

'Well, not too gentle a ride,' put in Mr Hamilton, grinning. 'George and I will want to try our horses over a few fences. But the ladies need not follow,' he added hastily, when Ann hissed at him and glanced in Kitty's direction. 'We shall all please ourselves!'

Kitty could not be easy. She had thought that Lady Harworth would not allow them to ride out unaccompanied, but when they all met in the drawing room before dinner she was surprised to find that Lady Harworth had already given her permission.

'Leaconham will be with them and I am sure the rest of us have no wish to drive out to Titchwell.' She smiled around at the assembled group. 'Young people have so much more energy, and they must be allowed to use it up. And after all, there are enough of them to look after each other.'

'I cannot like it,' opined Lady Leaconham. 'I am not at all sure that Kitty should go, not without a maid to give her countenance.'

'Oh, Aunt, none of the maids can ride,' cried Ann. 'And you know how tedious you would find it if you were obliged to come with us! We are only riding out to the Star. We will send ahead and have a luncheon prepared for us and when we have done we shall ride back.'

'And we will not be obliged to leave Harworth land at any time,' added Martin Hamilton. 'It will be *quite* unexceptional.'

'So you see, Letitia, there is nothing for us to worry ourselves over,' said Lady Harworth, smiling serenely at her sister.

Kitty had to admit that none of the older occupants of the room looked keen to join the young people on their outing. Most of the other guests were considerably older than their hostess and liked to spend their afternoons reading or dozing in the morning room until the dinner hour. She wondered if Lizzie and George's parents might object to their children riding off unattended, but when Kitty glanced in their direction she saw that they were both smiling and nodding benignly at Lady Harworth. Since they were both so corpulent that they took up a whole sofa each, Kitty had to stifle a giggle at the thought of either of them on horseback. She wondered if Lord Harworth might refuse his permission, but when their host did at last join them and Ann told him of the proposed expedition, he did no more than pat her arm and bid her enjoy herself.

'I would come with you myself, but I am meeting Reverend Miller and the churchwardens that day: we are to discuss a new church roof.'

'Poor Lord Harworth, he works so hard,' gushed Mrs

Camber, beaming at her host. 'My dear sir, we have not seen you all day.'

'Business, ma'am,' returned Lord Harworth. 'Out riding on the estate for most of the day. But it's done now so I am free to enjoy myself. And we have an extra guest for dinner! I said I would ask him and Blackwood has agreed to join us. No need to trouble yourself, Mama, I saw Strutt on my way in and told him to lay another place at the table.'

Even as he finished speaking the door opened and Daniel entered. Lady Leaconham's countenance tightened with disapproval, but Kitty observed that Lady Harworth was showing no concern and her son was cheerfully introducing Daniel to his other guests. She had to admit that there could be no fault found in Daniel's appearance. His tight-fitting dark coat was beautifully made, not a wrinkle or a puckered seam in sight. His buff-coloured waistcoat and knee-breeches enhanced his athletic figure and the snowy froth of linen at his neck was immaculate. When he turned to greet her she could not resist asking him if he had been expecting the invitation to stay to dinner.

'Lord Harworth usually asks me so I always come prepared with a change of clothes.' He hesitated, as if he might move away, then he said, 'You are looking very well, Miss Wythenshawe. The country air agrees with you.'

'I think you are right, Blackwood,' said Lord Harworth, overhearing his comment and coming up. 'Plenty of fresh air and exercise, eh, miss? And m'sister tells me you are learning to ride, too!'

'Yes, sir. Ann has kindly loaned me one of her riding ponies.'

'Selby says she is an excellent student,' said Ann. 'We are making up a party to ride to Titchwell next Tuesday.'

'After only a week's tuition?' said Daniel. 'I am impressed.'

A smile tugged at Kitty's mouth, responding to the gleam in his eyes.

'Ann has promised me it will be a very easy ride. I shall not be expected to jump any fences.'

'I am sure you will manage very well,' he told her.

'And if you are at the Star around noon on Tuesday, Mr Blackwood,' put in Ann, 'you will be able to see for yourself, for we are taking luncheon there. You might even join us...'

Lady Leaconham stepped up.

'I have no doubt Mr Blackwood is far too busy to ride out on a whim.' She took Kitty's arm and led her away. 'Mrs Camber was complimenting me upon your gown, my love,' she murmured. 'She was most impressed with the embroidery. If she asks you about it pray do not tell her that your mama made it herself!'

This reminder of her humble state effectively robbed Kitty of all power of conversation and she was thankful when they went through to the dining room, where the elegant settings and superb food commanded everyone's admiration and attention.

Kitty found herself sitting between Mr Hamilton and Mr Camber. Since the former flirted with Ann for the duration of the meal and the latter devoted himself to his food, Kitty was left to enjoy her meal and her thoughts in peace. Daniel was too far away to converse with her, almost hidden from sight by a large silver epergne, but he seemed to be at ease. Whenever she looked at him he was engrossed in conversation with one or other of his neighbours. She was relieved. They, at least, did not seem to share her godmother's reservations about his suitability as a dinner guest.

Kitty heard her name and looked up to find Lady Harworth was asking a number of questions of her sister about

Kitty's family and birth, all of which Lady Leaconham deftly turned aside. Kitty had to admire her tactics. She gave the impression that Kitty's parents were very rich but eccentric, refusing to give their daughter the lavish presentation she deserved and hinting that such a come-out was unnecessary for someone of Kitty's birth and fortune. It was subtly done and it satisfied her hostess, but it made Kitty uncomfortable, especially when she realised that Daniel was listening to the conversation, a sceptical look in his hard eyes.

What in hell's name am I doing here? Daniel was beginning to wish he had not accepted his host's invitation to stay for dinner. The knowledge that Kitty was at Kirkleigh had been gnawing away at him ever since Harworth had mentioned it. He had returned from London determined to forget Miss Kitty Wythenshawe. She had set her heart on marrying well, so let her get on with it. There were many girls far prettier: Miss Harworth, for example, with her generous figure and golden hair was generally acknowledged to be a beauty, but Daniel found his eyes drawn towards Kitty, with her dusky curls and expressive mouth and those deep green eyes that could darken and flash with anger.

When they had parted in London he had vowed he would never see her again: at the time it had seemed an easy promise to keep, since he was leaving Town. He had hoped that once he was home he would be able to forget her by throwing himself into his work, but he had not succeeded. She was always in his thoughts. It did not matter if he was surrounded by the deafening clatter of machinery in the mill, silently poring over the ledgers in the office or even riding over the moors, he found himself thinking of her, wondering what she was doing, if she was happy. Harworth had mentioned that she and Lady Leaconham were amongst his summer guests so he had not been surprised to see her in the park that morning, but he had been taken aback by his own soaring elation when he had ridden up and she had smiled at him with such obvious pleasure. She had looked very good sitting on the horse, too, the tight-fitting riding jacket accentuating her tiny waist and straight back. He smiled slightly, remembering her nervousness. That would go in time, of course. He had no doubt that she would be a good horsewoman. In his imagination he saw them riding out together over the moors in high summer, galloping along the paths lined with purple heather, the sky a vivid, unbroken expanse of blue...

Daniel caught himself up. What was he thinking of? That would only happen if she remained in the north— as Lady Harworth. He looked at his host, sitting at the head of the table. Harworth was sitting back in his chair, his eyes fixed on Kitty and a faint, satisfied smile on his face. A shiver rattled Daniel's spine. Had he offered for her already? No, he thought not: Lady Leaconham was still fending off her sister's questions about Miss Wythenshawe. If an offer had been made and accepted Daniel was certain Lady Leaconham would be looking much more complacent. But it was only a matter of time. He ground his teeth in frustration.

After dinner they gathered in the drawing room, where it was expected that the young ladies would each take their turn upon the pianoforte. He watched Ann drag Kitty forward, insisting that she should play. Daniel chose to stand at the edge of the room where he could watch her without being observed himself. As her fingers flew over the keys he was impressed. She played well, due no doubt to a good teacher and a willingness to apply herself—he was well aware of the tussles between his mother and Bella when it came to music lessons! All too soon the performance was over and Ann bounced up, declaring that they had been practising a duet. It was not yet dark enough for candles but the summer evening was drawing to a close, the setting sun casting a golden glow over the drawing room and adding an extra radiance to the two young ladies seated together at the pianoforte.

'Do they not make a beautiful picture?' murmured Lord Harworth, coming to stand beside him. 'Two fine girls, one so dark, the other fair: I would like to have their likeness captured, just as they are now. What do you say, Blackwood, they would look well hanging on the wall here, eh?'

'Very well, my lord.'

'Aye, I think so.' Lord Harworth turned towards him, saying confidentially, 'I am minded to offer for Miss Wythenshawe, you know.' Daniel clenched his jaw, not trusting himself to speak. 'I have been thinking for some time that I should settle down. There's the title to think of, I need an heir, you see. And Miss Wythenshawe is a pretty little thing. Besides, my mother likes her.'

'Does she?'

'Oh, yes. Well, she's her sister's godchild, so we know she comes from a good family. It's an anxious time,' continued Lord Harworth, shaking his head. 'Her godmother is very obliging, of course, but you said yourself the gel was above your touch: I only hope she doesn't turn her nose up at a mere baron! Oh, bravo, ladies, bravo!'

A smattering of applause told them that the duet was ended and Harworth walked away, clapping loudly. A bank of heavy cloud had blotted out the sun, and there was a break in the entertainments as servants hurried in to light the candles. Daniel remained in the shadows. He wished the evening was over so he could take his leave, but to set out before the moon had risen would cause comment. He must endure this torture a little longer.

The room was settling again. Over by the piano he could see Kitty shaking her head, politely declining to play more and she moved away as Miss Harworth prepared to display her expertise at the harp. Daniel drew a sharp breath: she was coming towards him.

'Do you play for us tonight, Mr Blackwood. Or sing, perhaps?'

'No, not tonight.' Thank heavens she had not asked him what she thought of her performance, he could not recall a note, only that he had been spellbound.

'I understand you have been out riding all day with Lord Harworth.'

He relaxed slightly. This was safer ground.

'Yes. We were looking at sites for his new mill. There are several that would be suitable.'

'It would require many men and women to work in such a place, would it not? Where would they come from?'

'From the surrounding farms and villages. Harworth is already improving the farming methods used on his estates so there is less work on the land. The people will make a better living in the mills.'

She nodded. Her eyes were fixed upon Ann, playing the harp, but he could tell that she was thinking of other things, and he watched her, entranced by the tiny crease in her brow, the slight quirk of her lips as some new thought came to her.

'Mr Blackwood, may I ask you a question?' She turned her disconcertingly clear gaze upon him and his heart skidded erratically within his chest. His brows snapped together: better that he should frown at her than she should know the effect she had upon him! She ran her tongue over her bottom lip in that nervous little habit of hers, rousing the demon desire in him. He had to steel himself not to reach out for her. She started to turn away. 'I beg your pardon. I can see you think it an impertinence...'

'No!' He put his hand on her arm. 'No,' he said again. 'Please. Ask me.'

His fingers seemed welded to her flesh. It took an immense effort to remove them when he saw the startled look in her eyes.

'Please,' he said again, giving her what he hoped was a reassuring smile. 'What is it you wish to ask me?'

'I wonder, sir, why you are working for Lord Harworth? From what I know of you...' She blushed a little. 'And I confess it is not very much! From what you have told me, you do not need this employment. And will not another mill be competition for you?'

'It will be competition, yes, but the industry is young, there is room for more manufactories. But if Harworth is determined to set up a mill, I am concerned that he should set about it in the right way. Soon he will need to bring in extra workers—whole families. I want to make sure they have proper housing, a school for the children, a doctor to look after them.'

He read approval in her face, but even as it made his heart soar he knew he must defend himself. He said curtly, 'Do not think of me as a saint, Miss Wythenshawe. This is not charity, it is good business sense. If men are sick, or ill fed, or worrying about their family, they do not work so well.'

There were more questions in her head, he knew it, and part of him wanted to draw her aside and continue their discussion, but that was madness: the longer he spent in her company the harder it was to tear himself away. A movement caught his eye and he looked up to see Miss Harworth approaching with her brother and Martin Hamilton at her side.

'Well, now, Blackwood, what did you think of that?' demanded Lord Harworth. 'Hamilton here says she plays like an angel, what?' He threw back his head and gave a loud laugh. 'Harps, angels—what a good joke.'

Ann tapped his arm with her fan and tried to frown.

'Martin meant it as a compliment, Bertram, and I shall take it as such.'

Kitty looked around, startled. Daniel wondered if she had even noticed that her friend's performance had ended.

'Having heard you perform on the pianoforte, Miss Wythenshawe, I know you are musical, too,' remarked Hamilton, in what Daniel considered to be far too familiar a fashion. 'What did *you* think of Miss Harworth's performance?'

Kitty stepped away a little before replying.

'It was delightful,' she said. 'I did not notice one wrong note.'

'And *you* are truly delightful to say so, Miss Wythenshawe,' chuckled Lord Harworth. 'Ann has only been learning the harp for a few months and I tell her she needs to practise more if she is to become really proficient.'

'But there are so many other things to do, Bertram, especially when we have company.'

'You cannot expect your sister to neglect her guests, my lord,' said Hamilton with a little laugh.

'Of course not, and I, too will now devote myself to our guests.' Lord Harworth bowed towards Kitty. There was no mistaking the warm, intimate smile he gave her. 'A task that will give me no small enjoyment, I assure you!'

Daniel thought it a clumsy compliment but it made Kitty

blush rosily. She murmured, 'We must not take up all your time, my lord.'

'Nonsense! What are we here for if not to enjoy ourselves! In fact, I am thinking I should put off the meeting on Tuesday and ride with you to Titchwell.'

'Oh, no, my lord,' said Kitty faintly. 'If you are otherwise engaged…'

'I thought that meeting was arranged for some weeks,' put in Daniel, irritation sharpening his voice. 'Surely you will not rearrange it to accommodate an outing of pleasure?'

Lord Harworth blinked at him.

'I do not see… Well, perhaps not, I shall have to consider carefully, of course.' He bent another beaming smile at Kitty. 'I admit the temptation is very great!'

'We should of course be delighted to have you join us,' said Ann, not quite truthfully. She gazed up more hopefully at Daniel. 'Perhaps you, too, would like to ride over and join us, Mr Blackwood? It promises to be a very jolly party.'

Ann's smile awoke no response in Daniel. He scarcely heard her, his mind working out an excuse to get away before he said something he would regret.

'Alas, no,' he said shortly. 'I have engagements that day that cannot be put off. In fact, I have work tomorrow that requires an early start so I must take my leave of you now. If you will excuse me.'

Kitty's feelings were mixed as he gave a stiff bow and walked off. His presence unsettled her, but with his departure the room seemed a little less bright. Ann gave an uncertain laugh.

'Well, do you think I frightened him off, that he dashed away so suddenly? He looks so serious.'

'No, no, sister, Blackwood *always* looks serious!'

'He is a manufacturer,' said Mr Hamilton, raising his quizzing glass to watch Daniel's retreating figure. 'Such men would have us believe there is no time for anything but work.'

'I believe supervising the proper running of a mill does take a great deal of effort,' observed Kitty.

Ann pouted.

'Then I do not think you should build one, Bertram, if it leaves you no time for pleasure.'

'Pho, that is why we have managers and overseers,' declared her brother. 'Have no fear, Ann my love. Once the mill is up and running I do not expect it to take up much of my time at all. In fact, I mean to ask Blackwood to find me a good man to run the mill for me.'

'So you are serious about this mill business,' remarked Mr Hamilton.

'Yes, most certainly. The improvements I have made on my estates here mean that we no longer need so many people. Best to employ 'em to my benefit than to have them a burden to the parish. Blackwood's invited me to see his own mill over at Hestonroyd tomorrow. Perhaps you should come with me, Hamilton, to see for yourself how these new manufactories are run.'

'Not I, my lord!,' laughed Hamilton, throwing up his hands. 'I never had any head for business.'

Ann shook her head and laid a hand on her brother's arm.

'Oh, Bertram, surely you saw enough of mills and machinery at Cromford! How can you think anyone would be interested in such things?'

'I am,' said Kitty, greatly daring. Her spirit quailed as every eye turned in her direction. She swallowed. 'I would very much like to see a spinning mill, my lord.'

'Would you now, Miss Wythenshawe?' After his initial shock, Lord Harworth beamed at her.

'Yes, I would,' she declared bravely. 'Very much.'

'But, Kitty, we are going to take our sketchpads and easels into the park tomorrow and paint views of the house,' Ann reminded her.

'You can easily do that another day,' put in Lady Leaconham, coming up. 'I am sure Bertram would be delighted to have company tomorrow.'

'I would indeed,' declared her nephew. 'Perhaps we should make up a party...'

Kitty noted with wry amusement that this suggestion found little favour with the other guests, who all found reasons why they should remain in the luxurious surroundings of Kirkleigh Hall the following day.

'Well, if Kitty is determined to go then I shall go too,' declared Ann. 'You will not object to that, will you, Brother? And that way Kitty and I can chaperon each other. There will be no need for Mama or my aunt to come with us.'

Thus by the time the tea tray was carried in, the visit was arranged to everyone's satisfaction and the carriage was ordered for early the following morning.

'Well, what a clever little puss you are,' murmured Lady Leaconham, tucking her arm through Kitty's and taking her off to sit with her on a sofa by the window. 'I should never have thought of suggesting you go to the mill with Bertram, but it was very well done of you. He could not fail to be flattered by your interest.'

'I had no idea of flattering Lord Harworth,' Kitty protested. 'I truly want to see the mill.'

'Of course you do,' replied her godmother with a maddening smile. 'And nothing could make it plainer to my nephew that you are just the wife for him!' She patted

Kitty's hands. 'Do not look so dismayed, my love. It was a little bold of you, to be sure, but it may be just the nudge Bertram needs to offer for you!'

Chapter Nine

After an early breakfast the next morning Kitty set off for Hestonroyd with Ann and Lord Harworth in an open carriage. As the miles sped by it occurred to her that they would not have to travel much further to reach Fallridge and her home, but she kept these thoughts to herself, remembering her promise to her godmother not to talk of her family. She longed to see Mama and Aunt Jane, imagining their pleasure at all she would be able to tell them, but it was not only Lady Leaconham's wish that she should not visit Fallridge while she was a guest at Kirkleigh. Mama too had expressly forbidden her to call.

Lord Harworth was addressing her and she looked up to respond. She was a little embarrassed in his company, conscious that by expressing her interest in visiting Hestonroyd everyone assumed she was determined to become Lady Harworth. Kitty thought of her mother's letters, the constant reminders that she should strive to find a suitable husband, but even the thought that Mama would approve of her actions brought her little comfort. Kitty sighed.

Papa had always insisted that high rank and titles counted for very little, but it seemed that everyone else she knew, including Mama, thought they counted for a great deal. Her family would be very disappointed in her if she threw away her chance to marry a lord.

'Ah. We are nearly there now.'

Lord Harworth's words recalled her wandering thoughts. The carriage had slowed and now turned off the main highway to follow a well-made, winding road that led down into a thickly wooded valley. There was no opportunity to see very far ahead as the road twisted back and forth in its descent, but eventually they rounded the final bend and there before her was Hestonroyd Mill. She gasped, staring wide-eyed at the huge building that filled the narrow valley bottom. The stone walls were punctuated with dozens of windows on each of its four floors and the slate roof was surmounted by an elegant bell tower, not to call the faithful to worship, she knew, but to summon the workers to their posts.

The road descended to run alongside the mill, separated from it by a fast-flowing stream. They crossed the bridge and drove under the arch that led into a large courtyard, bustling with people and wagons. The clatter of hooves echoed against the stone walls, for the mill continued on three sides, while on the fourth was a series of smaller buildings. The carriage drew up outside the biggest of these, a square house that looked very much like a gentleman's residence but which Lord Harworth declared would be the offices. A sound like distant thunder reverberated through the yard and Ann looked around nervously.

'What is that noise?'

'The machinery,' said her brother. 'Water frames that turn dozens, even hundreds of spindles at a time, producing more yarn in a week than a woman could spin in a lifetime.'

As Kitty followed Ann down from the carriage, Daniel appeared. Lord Harworth hailed him, saying easily, 'Hope you don't object, Blackwood, but the ladies wanted to come with me. Miss Wythenshawe especially is eager to see inside your mill!'

Kitty's cheeks grew warm as Daniel's dark, unfathomable glance rested upon her.

'No,' he said at last. 'I have no objection at all, but I would warn you that the noise and bustle of a mill can be overwhelming.'

'You employ women here, do you not, Mr Blackwood?' asked Kitty, brows raised. 'I am sure if they can live with it day after day then we can put up with the...*noise and bustle,* as you put it, for an hour or so.'

Daniel looked surprised, but she read approval in his hard eyes and felt a faint glow of satisfaction.

He nodded.

'Very well then. If you would like to come this way?'

They crossed the yard, keeping close to Daniel. Looking about her, Kitty saw that everyone was working busily, loading wagons or pushing handcarts across the cobbles, while all around them the mill rumbled and growled like some huge, sleeping monster. The noise of the machines grew louder as they stepped into the mill.

'We have spinning shops on all four floors,' said Daniel, leading them towards a heavy wooden door. 'No need to see them all, but I'll take you through a couple of them. Please be sure to stand clear of the mules—'

'Mules?' Ann repeated.

'The spinning mules—machines,' explained Daniel. 'They travel out over the floor and have moving parts that can snatch at your gown if you stand too close.'

He opened the door. As Kitty stepped into the spinning shop the deafening noise was like a physical assault. She glanced at Ann, who was clinging to her brother's arm, looking about her wide-eyed. The floor shook beneath their feet and the whole room seemed to be one seething, boiling mass of movement. It was very bright from the many windows on all sides. Banks of machines—the mules—ran the width of the building, each one carrying large spools of creamy-grey yarn.

Daniel was explaining the process to Lord Harworth and Kitty had to draw closer to hear anything at all. She heard him mention creels and bobbins, tops and roving and headstock, but it was difficult to concentrate with the incessant clatter of the machinery. She watched, fascinated, as the lower part of the mule moved out slowly. The thick yarns were paid out and twisted, then as the mule stopped and returned, the twisted thread was gathered up on the spindles.

She jumped when strong hands gripped her arms.

'You are too close.' Daniel's mouth was close to her ear. He was pulling her back away from the machines. 'Please, stand over here with the others, out of the way.'

Mortified, Kitty stood in one corner with Ann and Lord Harworth, watching the slow process of the spinning being repeated over and over again. She had not intended to draw attention to herself, but now she feared Daniel would think her troublesome. Another black mark against her. She allowed her eyes to shift to Daniel. He was walking between the machines, surveying the room, his keen eyes taking in everything. He stopped occasionally, exchanging a word here, issuing an instruction there. He stood tall, his black-coated figure conspicuous against the lighter, dust-covered clothes of the spinners. He was master here and it showed in the proud line of his bearing. She glanced at

Lord Harworth, who was trying to hide a yawn behind his hand. She doubted he could ever be as at home in this noisy, busy place.

They moved on, taking the stairs to another spinning shop then on to the packing rooms. Daniel pointed out the joiners' and mechanics' workshops, and then took them off to see the huge water wheel that provided the power for the machines. His pride in the mill was evident. He was familiar with every process, every machine within his mill. He knew every man's name and it was apparent to Kitty that they esteemed him. There was no servile bowing and scraping when he was near, they were all too busy for that, but they responded with alacrity when he spoke to them, regarding him with respect.

'Well, I think we must have seen everything now,' declared Lord Harworth, taking out his watch. 'Do not forget we were going to discuss the returns I can expect on my investment, Blackwood. The wages you pay, working hours and the like.'

'We will go back to the office for that,' said Daniel. 'James Stoodley is my mill manager and I think it would be useful for him to be present.'

'Very well, then. Lead on, sir!'

'I have instructed that refreshments should be brought to the office,' said Daniel as he took them back across the yard, stopping to allow a string of pack-ponies to pass. He pointed to the large bundles wrapped in oil-cloth strapped to each pony. 'That's the tops, the rough wool that we spin into yarn. It has been sorted and combed by families in the outlying villages, then my agents collect it up and bring it here for spinning.'

'It is my head that is spinning,' replied Ann, throwing a humorous glance up at Daniel. 'I vow I shall be glad to sit down for a little while.'

Kitty, too, was thankful when they reached the manager's office. It was a large panelled room overlooking the yard and it was mercifully cool and quiet. The large desk had been cleared and it now held a tray laden with decanters and glasses and a small plate of macaroons.

'I am afraid I only have wine, ratafia or water to offer you,' said Daniel. 'If I had known you were bringing ladies with you, my lord, I would have arranged for some lemonade to be prepared. I am sorry, too, that my father is not here to meet you. He has taken my mother and sister to Harrogate and will not be back until next week.'

Lord Harworth dismissed his apology with a wave of his hand.

'You know this was not intended as a social visit, Blackwood, but the ladies would insist upon coming!'

'I hope they have found it of interest.'

Daniel's eyes were upon Kitty. She felt obliged to respond.

'Yes, very much, sir, thank you. It was very informative.'

She accepted a glass of water and retired to a seat by the window, glad to have a few moments to think over all she had seen.

'But why worsted, Blackwood?' enquired Lord Harworth. 'Surely cotton is the thing now.'

'Our cotton mills are in Lancashire,' replied Daniel, handing him a glass of wine. 'We have been producing worsted here for generations—it makes sense when we are surrounded by sheep and we have the wool on our doorstep. Besides, I do not like to have all my eggs in one basket.'

'And your people here work only ten hours a day? They could do more, surely.'

Daniel shrugged.

'They could, but tired people do not work so well.

And tiredness brings carelessness. That is when accidents happen.' He looked up as a stocky man in a brown coat entered. 'Ah, Stoodley, come in. This is James Stoodley, my mill manager.'

Once the introductions were complete Daniel moved away, leaving Lord Harworth deep in conversation with his manager.

'What were the buildings we passed on the way here?' asked Kitty. 'I thought I glimpsed a house and a garden, too—is that your own house, perhaps?'

'No, Miss Wythenshawe, I live a mile away on the edge of Hestonroyd village. The building you saw today houses the nursery and school. Perhaps, when you have rested a little you might like to see it?'

Kitty hesitated.

'I—I am sure you have other business to attend to, Mr Blackwood.'

'No, I was going to show Lord Harworth the ledgers and explain something of the costs involved in running a mill this size, but Stoodley can do that much better than I, if you ladies would like to walk to the nursery building?'

'I do not think I could walk another yard!' cried Ann, selecting a second macaroon from the plate on the desk. 'You go, Kitty, then you can tell me all about it later. I will wait here with Bertram.'

'Yes, off you go, my dear,' nodded Lord Harworth, sitting down at the desk and pushing the tray aside to make room for a large ledger. 'Stoodley can tell me anything I want to know here.'

Kitty was still undecided. Daniel held out his arm to her.

'Then shall we go, Miss Wythenshawe?'

After the briefest hesitation she placed her fingers on his sleeve and he led her out into the yard again.

'Do you wish me to summon the carriage to take us up the road?'

'No, no, it is not that far to walk, I think?'

She glanced up at him, looking quite enchanting with her dark curls peeping from under the straw bonnet that framed her face. He was struck again by her eyes; their colour reminded him of the vivid green of the moors after a summer rainstorm. It took a moment for him to realise she expected an answer.

'No—um—it will only take us ten minutes.'

He escorted her out of the yard and along the road. He had walked this way many times but rarely had the sun shone so brilliantly, nor had he noticed so many birds singing in the woods, or the merry babble of the stream. Kitty made some remark about the mill and he responded mechanically, but her interest was genuine, the questions she posed were thoughtful and soon he found himself telling her of his plans to expand, to develop and improve the spinning machines and add a loom shop—he even mentioned the idea of installing a steam engine, something he had not even discussed with his father.

'It all sounds very exciting,' she remarked. 'But some believe innovation is dangerous. Are there not risks involved in all these changes?'

'Of course. But there is even more danger in standing still. I hope that by the time the children in the nursery here are grown, not only will we be spinning but we will also have weaving sheds here at Hestonroyd.'

They had reached the path leading down to the square, whitewashed building that housed the nursery and school. Daniel opened the gate for her to enter the neat gardens that surrounded it.

'This is much bigger than I thought,' she told him. 'I had imagined perhaps a small schoolroom...'

'I do not allow very young children in my mills,' Daniel explained. 'The parents leave their children here when they come to work. They are taught to read and write, and help in the garden, where they grow vegetables for their meals.'

'And when they are older?'

'Most of them come to work in the mill.' She did not reply but he knew she was thinking of the noisy, dusty spinning shops. He said, 'It is a harsh world, Miss Wythenshawe. They are free to find work elsewhere if they can. Those who master their letters might find work in the towns, but somehow they must earn their keep. If their parents did not work in my mill then these children would most likely be toiling in the fields now or helping in the home, rather than being schooled. I like to think that this way I am giving them a chance to better themselves.' He glanced down at her. 'You and I were fortunate, Miss Wythenshawe, we have never known poverty.'

'I am aware of that,' she responded quietly. 'And I am profoundly grateful.'

They had reached the house and the door to the school-room stood open. Inside the children were sitting at their benches, practising their letters. Daniel allowed the school-teacher to show Kitty around. They disappeared briefly into the nursery where a nursemaid looked after the very young children before coming back to spend some time in the schoolroom. Kitty removed her bonnet and sat down with the children, talking to them and using her own dainty finger to draw letters in the sandtray on the bench before her. The afternoon sun was streaming through the window and as Kitty moved about the room the sunlight caught her hair. Strange that he had never noticed the hint of red in it before, an occasional glint of fire. He folded his arms and leaned back against the wall. She was so at ease here, coaxing even the shyest child to talk to her. He imagined her running just such a school as this, or even with a child of her own in her arms. She would want several, he thought idly, and he would wander into the nursery of an evening to find her there...

Hell and damnation, this was madness!

Daniel snapped himself upright. She was as good as promised to Harworth. Her coming here with him today was undoubtedly a declaration of intent. Daniel had been surprised when he had seen the ladies arrive with Harworth, but pleasantly so and he had enjoyed showing them around the mill. Ann Harworth had evinced little interest but Kitty had been eager to learn. He had noticed how she had moved closer when he was talking to Harworth and the questions she had posed today had been intelligent and apposite. If Harworth did marry her she would take an interest in his mill and its workers, he was sure. Daniel stifled the tiny voice in his heart whispering that Harworth didn't deserve her. He acknowledged his jealousy, but he would overcome it. He cleared his throat.

'I think we should be getting back, Miss Wythen-shawe.'

Kitty looked up as Daniel's deep voice cut through the light chatter of the schoolroom. She had quite lost track of the time in talking with the teacher and the children. For the first time since coming to Kirkleigh she could see a purpose to her future life. Her concerns that as mistress of Kirkleigh she would have nothing to do were at an end. If Lord Harworth should offer for her then she would interest herself in his people. There were already his tenants and those who worked on his land to care for, but once his mill was working there would be even more families arriving, and many would have young children.

Kitty's head was buzzing with ideas as she walked back

to the mill beside Daniel and they had gone more than halfway before she realised that her companion had not said one word to her since leaving the nursery building.

'Thank you for bringing me here,' she said earnestly. 'Is it very unusual to set up such a school as this one, Mr Blackwood?'

She was idly swinging her bonnet by its ribbons, too preoccupied to think of putting it on, or to consider the effect of the sun on her complexion.

'It is becoming more common,' he replied. 'Mill owners recognise the benefits of looking after their workers. This was my mother's idea. She visits frequently to assure herself the children are well cared for.'

'Yes, I can see that such a role might fall to the mistress,' murmured Kitty, frowning a little.

'Do you think men are so lacking in kindness?' he challenged her.

'I think they are more motivated by profit, and can forget the more civilised aspects of life,' she replied, thinking of Lord Harworth, poring over the ledgers in the office.

'It is not impossible for profit and philanthropy to go together, Miss Wythenshawe!'

Kitty stopped.

'I beg your pardon,' she said, her colour heightened. 'I did not mean to imply any slur upon you, Mr Blackwood.'

'I am well aware of what you think of me,' he muttered. 'I am hardly a gentleman in your eyes!'

He went to walk on but she caught his sleeve.

'Now what nonsense is this? I thought we had done with that misunderstanding. You know how much I regret ever thinking ill of you.'

He shook off her hand.

'That is not the point. Nothing can change the fact that I am a manufacturer.'

She was confused by his anger, and a little hurt, too.

'You told me you were proud of what you are,' she retorted. 'Do you think we came here out of idle curiosity, to look at your mill as one might look at a freak show? Lord Harworth wants to build a mill and has consulted you because your family knows more about the subject than anyone. *That* is why he came to Hestonroyd today.'

'And you insisted upon accompanying him,' he threw at her. 'Still toadying up to him, I don't doubt, showing him you are the perfect helpmate, entering into all his concerns!'

'No!' cried Kitty. What could she say? He was only repeating what everyone else thought of her. She moved a step closer, forcing herself to meet his eyes. 'That is not how it is. I wanted to come, I wished to see the mill. I wanted…I wanted to discover why it means so much to you, why you are so proud to be a manufacturer.'

The anger still smouldered in his eyes, his mouth fixed in a thin line.

'And are you satisfied?'

Kitty's anger melted. He looked so much like a sullen schoolboy that she wanted to reach out and brush the stray lock of hair from his forehead, to pull his face down to hers and kiss away his sulks. She dare not allow herself to do any of these things so she merely nodded.

'I think you should be very proud of what you have achieved here, Mr Blackwood.'

He continued to stare at her but she would not look away. She needed him to know she was sincere.

'You must think me a boorish fellow,' he said at last.

She smiled. 'I think you have a temper that is not always under control.'

His lips curved a little and the dangerous light faded

from his eyes. The wind had whipped an errant curl across her face and he lifted one hand to catch it.

'You are right,' he said, tucking the curl carefully behind her ear. 'My mother despairs of me.' The touch of his fingers set Kitty's heart knocking painfully against her ribs, but when he dropped his hand the lack of contact was even more agonising. She forced herself to stand still while every nerve screamed to reach out for him. The world no longer existed, she was no longer aware of the rumble of the mill, the sound of the stream or the singing of the birds, there was only Daniel, standing so close, holding her eyes.

His face softened, he lifted his hand again. 'Miss Wythenshawe—Kitty—I...'

'There you are!'

Lord Harworth's jovial cry echoed over them. Daniel dropped his hand and Kitty was filled with an intense disappointment. As one they turned, schooling their features to smile as Lord Harworth approached with his sister hanging on his arm.

'You were gone such a time that we decided to walk out and meet you,' said Ann. 'What kept you so long? '

'I'm afraid I could not tear myself away from the children.' Kitty responded calmly, hoping the turmoil within her did not show in her face. To her relief Ann merely released her brother's arm and reached out her hand.

'Bertram thinks it is time we were going back to Kirkleigh, so I think we should walk ahead and let the gentlemen talk business. I know Bertram has one or two final questions he wishes to put to Mr Blackwood.'

Kitty dare not look at Daniel to see if he was happy with this suggestion. She allowed Ann to take her arm and walk with her back towards the mill entrance but all the time she was aware of Daniel and Bertram behind her and although they spoke of nothing but business her ears strained to catch every syllable that Daniel uttered, revelling in the sound of his deep mellow voice and knowing that she would forever wonder what he would have said to her, if they had not been interrupted.

Chapter Ten

Kitty did not know whether to be glad or sorry that the visit to Hestonroyd Mill attracted so little interest from Lord Harworth's guests. On the one hand she would have been glad to discuss all she had seen there, but she was aware that any such discussions must involve mention of Daniel Blackwood and she would much rather not talk about him. She did not even want to think about him, but the wretched man kept coming into her head and cutting up her peace quite dreadfully.

He had not spoken a word to her once Lord Harworth and Ann had joined them on the road outside the mill and when he escorted them back to their carriage she heard him tell Lord Harworth that he would be too busy to call at Kirkleigh again for several weeks.

Kitty was determined to put him out of her mind. She knew the best thing to do was to stay busy so she made great efforts to keep herself occupied. The dry sunny weather continued and the guests at Kirkleigh whiled away their time with pleasant diversions. The younger members of the party played bowls and amused themselves in the gardens while the gentlemen rode, fished and shot and the older ladies spent most of their time reclining in easy chairs, fanning themselves and complaining of the heat.

Ann was determined that nothing should spoil their ride to Titchwell and resisted Lady Leaconham's suggestions that they should postpone the visit until the weather was cooler.

'Pho, Aunt, we are not such fragile creatures that we shall melt under a little sunshine. What say you, Kitty, are you not bored with sitting around the house? Do you not long to ride out in this glorious weather?

'No, I am not bored,' said Kitty, who was spending the long, lazy days at Kirkleigh practising upon the pianoforte, writing long letters to her mother or filling her sketch-book with scenes to show Mama and Aunt Jane when she returned home. 'I am a little nervous of riding out with you,' she confessed. 'Selby is very encouraging about my ability, but I am still very much a beginner...'

'You will be perfectly safe with us,' Ann assured her. 'We will enjoy the odd gallop but in the main we will keep to the lanes, so there will be no fences or ditches to cross.' She dropped her voice so that only Kitty could hear her. 'And think how wonderful not to have my aunt, or Mama or even Bertram telling us how to go on!'

Tuesday dawned fine and clear, and spirits were high when the young people gathered at the breakfast table. Lady Leaconham was still uneasy and pointed to the strong sunshine as a reason for deferring the ride.

'To be out of doors in the height of summer, exposed to the elements for hours on end,' she said. 'Just think of the damage to your complexions.'

Ann was quick to disclaim.

'We will have our bonnets, Aunt, and we can always stop under the trees if we need to rest.'

'But you cannot dismount,' objected Lady Leaconham. 'Who will look after your horses if you do not take your groom?'

'You may be easy, Mama,' put in Garston. 'Hamilton, Camber and I will be there to take care of the ladies.'

'Let them be, Letitia,' said Lady Harworth before her sister could speak again. 'Young people must be allowed a little freedom. And what harm can they come to as long as they are on our land?'

'But what if one of them should fall...?'

Kitty could see that her godmother was not reassured and she gave her a quick hug.

'Do not worry, ma'am, we will be riding directly to Titchwell and back again. I am not proficient enough for anything more than the gentlest of rides, is that not so, Ann?'

'We will proceed with great decorum, I promise,' said Ann, twinkling. 'You may expect to see us back here in very good time for dinner!'

In high good humour the riders gathered in the stable yard an hour later. There were several minutes of noisy confusion as the horses were brought out and everyone mounted up. Kitty looked askance at Selby as he walked up to her, leading a very pretty grey mare.

'Dapple has cast a shoe,' explained the groom. 'The mistress ordered Bianca to be saddled for you.'

Kitty eyed the mare doubtfully. She had grown used to the little pony and although the grey mare looked beautiful, she doubted she would be quite as docile as Dapple. She was obliged to take an extra step up on the mounting block to reach the saddle and she tried not to feel too nervous as she gathered up the reins.

'Just remember all I've taught you, miss,' said Selby as he adjusted the stirrup and checked the girth. 'She's a sturdy little mare, and will carry you all day without flagging, never fear.'

'I seem so much further from the ground,' said Kitty, trying a little laugh.

'You will be safe enough on Bianca,' said Ann soothingly. 'She has no vicious habits. And if we get separated,' she added, as she turned to lead the way out of the yard, 'just give Bianca her head: she knows her way home!'

It did not take Kitty long to settle on to her new mount and she soon felt very comfortable in the saddle. Ann suggested they should gallop through the park and Kitty found the mare's speed exhilarating. It was gratifying to be able to keep up with her friends and their compliments upon her ability helped her to relax and enjoy the long ride into Titchwell. The landlord of the Star was looking out for them and his stable lads were waiting to take charge of the horses as soon as they arrived.

Kitty allowed one of the diminutive stable boys to catch at the reins, holding the mare steady while Mr Hamilton ran over to help her dismount. Ann had already jumped nimbly to the ground and was gazing intently at a paper nailed to the doorpost as Kitty and her escort walked across the yard.

'Now what is that, Miss Ann?' demanded Mr Hamilton, laughing. 'What has caught your attention?'

Ann quickly tore down the paper handed it to Garston, who uttered a laugh.

'A little added entertainment,' he said, tucking the paper into his pocket as they all followed the landlord into the hostelry. Miss Camber and her brother immediately demanded to know what he meant, but Garston merely shook his head, and when they applied to Ann she would only smile mysteriously.

'Come now, tell us what is on that paper,' cried Mr Hamilton as they settled themselves around the table in their private dining room.

'Something very dear to Miss Wythenshawe's heart,' announced Ann.

Kitty looked up.

'I am sure I do not know what that might be.'

Garston pulled out the paper.

'An Abolition meeting,' he read. 'At Harper's Field, Chapeltown, this afternoon. Members of the Anti-Slavery Movement will address the meeting.' He looked up. 'These meetings are happening everywhere: I think it is time I attended one. Doesn't do to be behindhand, you know.'

'Chapeltown is not far from here,' said Ann. 'We could go there this afternoon.'

'But we promised Papa we would go directly back to Kirkleigh,' objected Miss Camber.

'It is only a little deviation from our route,' said Garston, studying the paper. 'The meeting is for two o'clock: no doubt it will be over by three and if we do not tarry, we will still be back in plenty of time for dinner.'

'Is Chapeltown part of Lord Harworth's estate?' enquired George Camber.

Ann waved one white hand.

'It is only a couple of miles outside the boundary.' She pouted. 'I should have thought that you of all people would want to go, Kitty. You were very keen to support the cause in London.'

'I am still a supporter, but this is not what we planned...'

'We planned to spend the day riding.' Mr Hamilton

grinned. 'If we were to take a look at the meeting on our way home it can do no harm.'

'Perhaps Mr Clarkson will be there with his box.' Ann turned to Miss Camber, her eyes wide. 'You should have seen him, Lizzie, he pulled out thumbscrews and leg-shackles, all designed to subdue the poor slaves. I vow I almost fainted at the sight of such gruesome articles.'

'By Jove, I wish I had been there!' declared George Camber. 'By all means let us ride over after lunch and take a look.'

'We need not stay long,' added Garston, ' We do not want to be late for dinner.'

'And I should like to see what this Clarkson has to say,' added Mr Hamilton.

'Let us take a vote upon it!' cried Ann. 'Who would like to ride over to Chapeltown when we have finished our meal?'

Kitty remained silent, but the others were all in favour. She tried to hide her unease. She guessed that a large crowd meeting in the open air might not be quite so well behaved as those gathered in Lombard Street. Something of her thoughts showed in her face, for Ann reached over and gripped her hand.

'Do cheer up, Kitty. You were doubtful about the meeting in London, were you not? And those fears were quite unfounded.'

'It did pass off very well,' Kitty admitted.

'And so will this one,' said Ann. 'Besides, this time we have three gentlemen to look after us.'

Mr Hamilton reached for the bottle of wine.

'Don't you worry, Miss Wythenshawe,' he said comfortably. 'We will take care of you all. And if we don't like the look of the meeting, we can always ride away.'

'Good notion, Hamilton.' Garston nodded. 'Is that the last of the bottle? Waiter, bring us more wine, and hurry!'

Because of their proposed detour the little party did not tarry over their lunch and they were soon on their way again, not riding back towards Kirkleigh but taking the road south to Chapeltown. It was a glorious day and the trilling song of a lark accompanied them as they rode between the thick green hedges that marked the lower valleys and provided a contrast with the dry stone walls of the hill farms. As they approached Chapeltown the road became noticeably busier.

'No need to fret about getting lost,' grinned Mr Hamilton, bringing his horse alongside Kitty's mare. 'I have just spoken to one of the men. He is a local, and says everyone is going to Harper's Field. All we need do is to follow the crowd.'

Ahead of them Kitty could see the people stepping off the road and into a field, where a number of carts and carriages were already drawn up close to a small copse, taking advantage of the shade. One farm cart had been stationed out in the open, and Kitty guessed it was to act as an improvised stage for the group of serious-looking gentlemen standing close by. She looked around. From her vantage point in the saddle she had a good view of the whole area. There were one or two better-dressed gentlemen sitting in the carriages under the trees, but the large crowd comprised mainly working men. Farm labourers, she guessed, with a few women amongst them and a noisy crowd of very young men in one corner that she thought could well be apprentices.

'You see,' said Ann, 'everyone is perfectly amiable.'

'They are also perfectly noisome,' giggled Lizzie

Camber, holding a handkerchief to her nose. 'Let us move away from the crowd, shall we?'

'Aye,' agreed her brother. 'We could tether the horses in the shade. That fellow over there has a flagon of ale. I wonder if he would sell it to me. It's dashed hot here today.'

'Good idea, George. Let's get the ladies into the shade and we'll come back and ask him.'

They began to walk their horses towards the trees. Kitty noticed that more people were arriving, one or two on horseback but most were walking, including a large group of rough-looking men who strode purposefully into the field. Very quickly the festival atmosphere disappeared. The late-comers were carrying thick sticks that they brandished threateningly. The air was now full of menace and Kitty watched, horrified, as they began to force their way through the crowd, lashing out at anyone who got in their way. Angry roars replaced the laughter and chatter as fighting broke out amongst the men. Kitty looked towards the apprentices. With a loud halloo they charged into the crowd, fists flying. Behind her she heard Garston utter an oath.

'We should get out of here,' he said sharply. 'Camber, look to your sister. Ann, Kitty, come along.'

They turned towards the gate, but Kitty could see that their exit was blocked by even more people pouring into the field. Behind her, shouts and yells filled the air: men were grappling with each other, women screamed and people were running in all directions, trying to avoid the rough-looking men brandishing the cudgels.

'This way!' shouted George Camber, turning his horse about, but everywhere they looked there were groups of men, fighting. Lizzie Camber began to cry.

The crowd was spilling out around them. A man

cannoned into Ann's mare, which reared and snorted nervously. Garston pushed his own horse closer and urged Ann to move away. Kitty fought down her nerves, trying not to snatch at the reins as Bianca sidled and fretted beneath her. A scream made her look round. A woman with a baby in her arms was being pursued by a black-jowled man in a leather waistcoat. The woman was turning, using her body to shield the child from the blows he was aiming at her with his short staff. The man was gaining on his victim; another few strides and his huge paw would close on her shoulder and she would be lost.

Without thinking Kitty kicked Bianca, forcing the horse between the woman and her attacker.

'No! Leave her alone, you fiend!'

The man pulled up quickly and narrowly avoided crashing into Bianca. He raised his head and glared at Kitty, his face contorted with rage. With a snarl he lifted his stick, whether to attack Kitty or Bianca she did not know, but even as she tried to move the mare out of the way, a huge black horse thundered up, its rider kicking out one booted foot to knock her assailant to the ground.

'Daniel!' Kitty gazed at her saviour, dizzy with relief.

He said nothing, merely grabbed at her reins and led her away from the immediate danger. Ann and the others trotted up. Kitty noticed that George Camber was riding very close to his sister, who was sobbing quietly.

'Blackwood, thank heaven—' began Mr Hamilton, but Daniel cut him short.

'We need to get out of here, immediately.'

Garston nodded, looking pale.

'I know,' he said, 'but the gateway is blocked with carriages and men fighting...'

'We will have to jump the hedge,' said Daniel shortly. 'The longer we delay the more chance that we will be attacked. Go on,' he ordered as George Camber began to protest. 'We must get the ladies out of here!' He held Bianca's rein to prevent her following as the others set off towards the far corner of the field. He turned to Kitty. 'You will have to jump, too. What practice have you had?'

She swallowed, her eyes fixed on Ann as she galloped up to the hedge and flew over it, skirts billowing around her.

'A few small jumps with Dapple, nothing at all with this horse...'

'This is Miss Harworth's mare, is it not? I cannot imagine her keeping a horse that could not clear a barn.' Daniel let go of the rein and rested his hand briefly over hers. 'You can do it, Kitty. Follow me, hold on tight and leave everything to the mare.' Kitty nodded and Daniel squeezed her fingers. His eyes crinkled as he gave her a quick smile. 'Good girl!'

Another shout told them the mêlée was closing in on them again. Daniel kicked his horse into a trot and Kitty followed. Soon they were cantering across the grass. They were obliged to swerve to avoid a running man, but Kitty kept her eyes fixed on Daniel riding ahead of her, trying not to think of the hedge looming like a solid green wall in the distance. It was not high; she could see the others gathered on the far side, waiting for them. She forced herself not to pull on the reins and instead tried to push down on to the saddle, tightening her leg firmly around the pommel and struggling to remember everything Selby had taught her.

Daniel's horse took the hedge with barely a break in its stride, then it was Kitty's turn. She felt Bianca check slightly and gave her a little flick with her whip, urging her forwards. Suddenly the mare pushed off from her haunches and they were flying through the air, clearing the hedge easily and landing gracefully on the far side. The jolt as they hit the ground almost unseated Kitty, but she clung on, aware of her friends' cheers as they applauded her. She realised she had been holding her breath and let out a huge sigh as she straightened in the saddle and pulled on the reins to bring Bianca to a walk.

Nothing happened.

Bianca continued to canter across the field with Kitty pulling ineffectually on the reins. She heard Lizzie Camber scream, her brother shouted in alarm, but Bianca's pace only quickened. They were galloping away from Harper's Field and Kitty could do nothing to stop the mare's head-long flight.

Kitty tried to relax her tense hands on the reins and commanded herself not to panic. She needed to concentrate upon keeping her balance and staying in the saddle. Bianca showed no inclination to swerve or buck but she had the bit between her teeth and was in no mood to slow down. Kitty managed a quick look behind and was relieved to see Daniel pursuing her. She settled into the saddle: his horse was so much bigger and faster, he could not fail to catch her very soon, she knew it.

By a cruel twist of fate the short turf was giving way to bracken and rough heathland with a narrow track through it, wide enough for a single horse. Kitty's heart sank a little: Daniel would only be able to follow her. She tried tugging on the reins again, but Bianca's neck was rigid, her ears flattened and she had no intention of stopping. There was nothing for it but to hang on.

'Very well,' muttered Kitty. 'Run if you must, you will tire eventually.'

On and on they went, the mare negotiating the twists and turns of the path with sure-footed ease. The others would follow her, she was sure, even though she dared not look around: she needed to keep her eyes on the path if she was not to be thrown off balance with any slight change of direction. The shouts and screams of the crowd had long ago disappeared and now the only sound was the thud of hooves and the creak of leather. The wind tugged at her bonnet, the ribbons came loose and she was unable to take a hand from the reins to prevent it being whipped away. As they rode further on to the moors she felt its chill seeping through her riding jacket. The path took a sudden upward turn and the mare's headlong pace began to slow. Kitty seized her chance. She pulled hard on the reins and felt the mare respond, slowing to a walk just as the track widened.

Almost immediately Daniel was beside her. He reached over and caught the mare's bridle, bringing both horses to a stand. Kitty realised she was shaking.

'I c-couldn't stop her.'

'You did very well not to fall off.'

She managed a small smile.

'Yes, I think so, too. Where are the others?'

'I sent them home. If none of you arrives in time for dinner there will be panic at Kirkleigh.'

She nodded, then frowned at him.

'But what were you doing in Harper's Field?'

'I know several members of the Anti-Slavery Society in this area. I had heard there was to be an open-air meeting at Chapeltown but it was only this morning that I realised how close you would be if you rode to Titchwell.'

'So you came to join us?'

'No! I came to get you away,' he retorted. 'These outdoor gatherings often end in rioting. I rode to the Star to tell you that you should avoid Chapeltown on your return journey, but I arrived too late. The landlord told me you had already set out for the meeting.'

'I did not realise.' Kitty shivered. 'Everything started so well...'

'Aye, that's the devil of it. The innocent and the curious find themselves caught up in violence. Those opposed to the movement often pay gangs of men to break up open meetings such as this one. There's more than one man in this area that would not be above such tricks.'

'Do—do you mean they c-came with the sole purpose of fighting?' Kitty shook her head, trying to clear her thoughts. 'I thought it was merely the heat, and too much ale...' She swayed in the saddle and Daniel quickly slipped from his horse.

'Come,' he said. 'You should rest a little.'

She kicked her foot free of the stirrup and slid down into his waiting arms.

'I d-do not think my legs will hold me.'

'They will not need to.' In one smooth movement he swept her up, just as everything went black.

When Kitty opened her eyes she could not at first remember what had happened. She was lying on a bed of soft bracken, the smell of peat and hum of insects filling her senses. She moved her head and saw Daniel standing beside the horses. He had removed his jacket and waistcoat and was wiping the sweat from Bianca with handfuls of dried grass, his arm sweeping over the mare's flanks in a smooth, graceful arc. As if aware of her eyes upon him he turned, and after giving the mare a final pat he threw away the makeshift brush and strode towards her.

'So you are awake.' He dropped down beside her. 'How do you feel now?'

She did not answer immediately and instead looked sleepily at the way the slight breeze rippled the fine linen of his shirt, outlining the muscled body beneath. She closed her eyes again as the pleasant image was marred by returning memory. She struggled to sit up and immediately his arm was around her shoulders, supporting her.

'Oh, dear,' she muttered, 'how...how *feeble* of me to faint off like that. I must get up...'

'Do not try to stand just yet. There is no hurry.'

'But there is! I must get back to Kirkleigh before dark.'

'Impossible.' Kitty stopped struggling. He said, 'It is at least two hours' ride and the sun is setting. We will ride as far as we can while it is still light, then we must take shelter until the moon rises. You are very pale,' he added quietly. 'I wish I had something for you to drink...'

She dragged up a smile.

'I will be very well again in a moment. You have done more than enough for me already, coming to my rescue.'

He shrugged. 'That was nothing; you had already regained control when I reached you.'

'No, not for following after me, although I am very grateful to you for doing so! I meant back at the meeting, when that man was about to attack...'

She shivered and as his arm tightened around her it seemed quite natural to shrink towards him and rest her head against his chest.

'I would not let anyone harm you.'

His words and the solid, steady thud of his heart beneath her cheek was very soothing. She closed her eyes, breathing in the familiar, reassuring scent of him, a mix of wool, soap and spices.

'You are a good friend to me, Daniel.'

He did not reply, merely squeezed her fingers and for several minutes they sat together in silence, staring out across the heath. It was so peaceful that Kitty was almost disappointed when Daniel suddenly jumped to his feet.

'We should move on, if you are able.'

He put on his waistcoat and shrugged himself into his jacket. His tone was brisk and Kitty felt a stab of guilt. No doubt he had made plans for this evening and they would now be ruined.

'Yes, of course,' she said quietly. 'I feel much better now.'

Silently she took the hand he held out to her and allowed him to pull her up. He walked her over to the grey mare and without ceremony he put his hands about her waist and threw her up lightly into the saddle. She looked down at him, a slight frown creasing her brow as he adjusted her stirrup. His face was stern, almost forbidding, but as if aware of her gaze he glanced up.

'Do not look so anxious,' he said gently. 'You will be back at Kirkleigh soon after midnight.'

'Yes, of course. It is very good of you to give up your time for me like this.'

His brows rose.

'Would you have preferred to find your way alone?'

'No, of course not, but the others...'

'They were all shaken by what they had witnessed. Miss Camber especially was very distressed. I thought it best they should return together. Besides, Marnie was by far the fastest horse, so it was logical for me to come after you.'

His answer was so matter of fact she felt quite daunted and did not venture to speak again. He scrambled into the saddle and led the way across the heath towards the road that could be seen snaking through the valley below them. As they rode Kitty watched a line of thick grey cloud bubbling up in the west. As soon as the path widened she brought Bianca alongside Daniel's black mare.

'When the sun drops behind that cloud it will very soon grow too dark to go on.'

He nodded. 'We have a little time yet: we will head for the road. It will be easier to find shelter down there. I doubt you had anticipated such an adventurous day's ride, Miss Wythenshawe.'

'Certainly not!' She tried to match his bantering tone. 'I expected the most exciting part of the day would be a short gallop.'

'Lord Harworth will take care not to let you go out alone in future.'

'Will he be very angry, do you think?'

'No, no. He will be anxious, of course, but you may have noticed that his sister can wind him around her finger.' A smile tugged at one corner of his mouth. 'My own sister is just such a minx!' He paused. 'Harworth is a good man at heart, and a responsible landlord. However, there is a lot he has to learn about running a mill.'

'And can you teach him that?' she asked, turning her head to look at him.

'I shall try. It is something I have grown up with.'

'Has your family always been involved in spinning?'

'With cloth, certainly. My grandfather was a merchant. He was obliged to travel widely throughout the north, collecting pieces—woven sections of cloth—from the weavers who lived in the little villages throughout the area. He traded in all sorts of cloth, calimancoes, serges, camlets and so on. Grandfather encouraged his younger sons to build a mill, just over the Pennines in Lancashire. Using Arkwright's new cotton machines they soon had a thriving business. My uncle still owns that mill, but my father wanted to return to Hestonroyd so he built his first mill there. I grew up with the business. I have worked beside my father in each new venture.'

'It must be very rewarding.'

'It is, but it is not to be undertaken lightly.'

Daniel began to explain to her about the responsibilities of a mill owner and she listened, fascinated as he told her how his father had built sturdy new cottages for the workers, schools for the children, about the doctor he employed to make regular visits to his mills. She put in questions occasionally, but they were hardly necessary: he was eager to talk.

'Why are you telling me all this, Mr Blackwood?' she asked him, when at last he fell silent. 'Do you explain your business to everyone in such detail?'

He did not answer her immediately, but kept his eyes fixed on the road ahead of them.

'Lord Harworth has excellent intentions,' he said at last. 'But I fear that he may not understand that a mill requires constant supervision. It is easy to be tempted into cutting costs and making short-term profits at the expense of the workers. I believe that you will be in a position to remind him of his duties, when other interests distract him.'

'I—I fear I do not understand,' she stammered.

'You will be able to look after the welfare of your people, when you are Lady Harworth.'

The sudden disappearance of the sun made Kitty aware of the chill breeze cutting through her riding jacket.

'I...I think you are mistaken,' she muttered. 'L-Lord Harworth has not made me an offer.'

'Perhaps not, but it is his intention to do so.' He glanced at her, his face shuttered. 'It is what you want, is it not?'

'I—' Kitty swallowed. 'Why...yes, I suppose...'

'As Lady Harworth you will be in a position of influence,' he said. 'You will be able to ensure your mill-workers are treated well. Yours will be a very important role.'

Kitty was silent. So Daniel, too, thought Lord Harworth would offer for her. She bit her lip. Surely she should be happier than this at the prospect, but all she felt was confusion. The darkness that was enveloping them seemed to enter her very being, weighing her down.

'We will have to stop soon.' He pointed to a rocky out-crop looming over them. It had been quarried away to form a large semi-circular space beside the road. 'We could shelter there for an hour or so, or we could go on; there should be an inn somewhere along this road...'

'Let us stop here,' Kitty begged, exhausted as much by the tumult raging within as by her ordeal.

They moved into the shelter of the rocks and Daniel lifted Kitty from her horse. This time he released her almost before her feet touched the ground, increasing her feeling of desolation.

While Daniel saw to the horses she walked over to sit on a low ledge that formed a natural bench, the stone rising smooth and sheer at her back. Night fell rapidly. Bianca became a vague grey shape and she could not make out the black horse at all. When Daniel turned and walked towards her she could see only the pale blur of his face and his white neckcloth.

'What if the cloud moves in to cover the sky?' she asked him, a slight edge of panic in her voice. 'What if there is no moonlight?'

'There will be. The cloud is breaking up already.' He sat down beside her and they both leaned back against the hard stone. Kitty was very conscious of the gap between them. It was only a few inches but it was as if Daniel had put up a barrier between them. He continued, 'The moon will rise in a couple of hours. As soon as it is high enough to light our way we will move on.'

'Until then we must sit here.'

'Yes.'

Kitty shivered.

'Are you cold?'

'A little.' She put out her hand, saying quickly, 'No, I would not take your jacket! If we could sit a little closer...'

He put his arms around her.

'Is that better?'

'Yes, thank you.'

She leaned into him, resting her head on his chest. Would any other man make her feel so comfortable? she wondered.

'You are always coming to my rescue, Daniel,' she said sleepily. 'In another life you would have been a knight, I think. A knight in armour. Rescuing damsels.'

There is only one damsel I would ever wish to rescue.

Daniel glanced down. He could see very little in the darkness but he felt her curls tickling his chin. Desire stirred within him and he cursed silently. Damnation, did she not realise the temptation she presented?

'I am not as chivalrous as you think me,' he muttered.

She raised her head.

'Why do you say that?'

Her face was very close, a pale blur in the darkness. He could feel her warm breath on his cheek.

'Because being here with you in my arms, I want to...'

He turned his head slightly and his mouth brushed her soft lips, as he had known it would. She trembled but did not recoil and he kissed her gently, savouring the taste of her, the scent of fresh flowers that clung to her skin. Her lips parted beneath his even as she melted against him, the movement slight but deliciously inviting. Slowly and with great care he lowered her down on to the ledge, half-hoping, half-dreading that she would protest and he would be obliged to draw back. Instead she gave a little moan and clutched at his coat, pulling him down with her. They were stretched out together and Daniel thought he would never want a more comfortable bed than this stone ledge with Kitty nestled against him. Passion threatened to consume him. By sheer force of will he contained it. With infinite tenderness he kissed her eyes, her cheek. He had no idea when she had removed her gloves but he felt her fingers driving through his hair, tormenting him with thoughts of how it would feel to have those same hands on his skin, stroking his chest, the fingers raking down his back. He sought her mouth again and while he kissed her he smoothed his hand over the tightly fitted riding jacket, following the curve of her waist up to the swell of her breast. Kitty shivered and arched towards his hand. His pulse leaping, Daniel unbuttoned the jacket. He gently pulled aside her neckcloth and opened the mannish shirt she wore beneath. It was too dark to see anything but shadows so he lowered his head and pressed his lips to the bare flesh of her neck. Kitty moaned as his fingers slipped beneath the shirt and found her breast. She shifted restlessly against his hand, her body arching when his mouth slid downwards, his tongue circling and teasing one erect nipple while his fingers caressed the other. Kitty gasped. Her hands clutched at his hair but she did not try to pull him away, rather she held him closer. She moaned and writhed beneath him, every movement an invitation for him to go further. If only she knew it.

Daniel's hand stilled. Her responses were instinctive; she had no idea how she inflamed him. Any man could be excused for taking this to its natural conclusion.

But he was not any man.

'Daniel?'

She whispered his name, her hand reaching out. He

caught it and pressed a kiss into its palm, trying to control his ragged breathing.

'We must stop now, my dear, before we do something we will regret.' It was too dark to read her face but he sensed her confusion. He leaned down to kiss her one last time. 'You are too, too alluring.' He spoke lightly, not wanting to embarrass her. 'I confess this is a delightful way to pass the time but it will not do. You are as good as promised to another man.'

He waited for her to contradict him. When she remained silent his disappointment was bitter as gall. She struggled to sit up.

'We—we are destined to bring out the worst in each other, are we not?' There was a catch in her voice, as if she was trying not to cry.

The worst? Is that what she thought of his love-making? He was aware of her every move as she sat beside him, re-tying her neckcloth and fastening her jacket. His senses were heightened so much that when she touched his arm he flinched.

'Do you mind if we sit like this?' Her tone was hesitant, anxious. 'I am not comfortable, alone in the dark, but if it disturbs you…'

He put his hand over her fingers.

'There is nothing to be afraid of here.'

'You are not angry with me?'

'Angry with you? No, never.'

'Then you will let me sit here, beside you?'

He signalled his acquiescence by squeezing her hand.

'It will not be long now.' He stared up at the sky, a vast velvet curtain studded with diamonds. 'Look, the cloud has dispersed. As soon as the moon rises we will move on.'

Daniel settled back on the ledge and beside him Kitty made herself comfortable. When her head dropped to his shoulder he did not move away. Nothing stirred. The starlight was sufficient to see a faint line where the land ended and the sky began but little else. A few feet away the horses stood quietly, Kitty's grey mare a paler blur in the darkness.

Daniel did not sleep. His senses remained alert to the sounds of the night, the distant call of a night bird, the rustle of some animal in the bushes. A sigh escaped him. He could wish for nothing more than to be allowed to sit here for ever with this girl-woman beside him, but all too soon they would have to return to their worlds—very different worlds, for she was destined to be Lady Harworth. It was her wish, her dream, was it not? Sometimes he thought she cared for him and when she returned his kisses he was aware of the passion within her, but that was for her husband to awaken, not him. She snuggled closer and he had to grit his teeth to keep his desire for her under control, to sit perfectly still when he really wanted to pull her into his arms and cover her face with kisses.

Why did he not do just that? Why not keep her here all night? She would have given herself to him earlier this evening, so why did he not kiss her again, re-awaken her desire and make love to her? If they did not return to Kirkleigh until morning her reputation would be ruined—there could be no question of Harworth marrying her then. He gazed up at the stars but although they winked and twinkled at him they gave him no encouragement.

Daniel closed his eyes. If he took advantage of her, what future could there be for them? He would make her his wife, but would she always resent him for forcing her into marriage? With sudden, blinding clarity he knew what he wanted: he wanted Kitty to choose him and only him. But it had to be her free choice; he did not want to force the decision on her.

So he would ask her to marry him. Not now of course, when she might think he was only doing it to save her reputation, but once they were back at Kirkleigh. He would make her an offer; present himself as a suitor to rival Bertram Harworth. A silent laugh shook him. He had never made any great show of his family's wealth but perhaps it was time to puff himself off a little. Even without the land and mills he would inherit from his father, his own fortune was comparable with Harworth's. He would tell Kitty as much: she should choose her own future.

And his.

The decision made, Daniel was impatient to be moving. Beside him, Kitty's regular breathing told him she was sleeping and he turned his head to press a light kiss on her tumbled curls before settling back to watch the horizon for the first signs of the rising moon.

Kitty heard Daniel's voice calling her. As she awoke she realised her head was resting on his shoulder, the soft wool of his jacket pressing against her cheek. She was reluctant to open her eyes: it was so comfortable to be snuggled up beside Daniel, just the two of them alone together. She really did not want to think about anything else. He spoke her name again and reluctantly she sat up, yawning.

'Oh!' A fat, butter-yellow moon was resting on the rim of the far hills. 'Is it time to go?'

'Very soon. You have been asleep for some time: perhaps you would like to stretch your legs a little before we begin our long ride back?'

He stood up and held out his hand to her. She allowed him to pull her to her feet.

'Daniel, what happened here, earlier—I was too forward, I must apologise…'

He put a finger to her lips.

'Hush. There is no need to say anything.'

'But I want to—'

'Once we are back at Kirkleigh this will all be forgotten.'

She gazed up at him, trying to pierce the shadows that masked his face. Did he mean that *he* wanted to forget? She wanted to talk about it, to know if he too felt that irresistible tug of attraction whenever they were together. That he desired her she had no doubt, but Mr Ashley had desired her, and she knew that did not mean he really *liked* her. She wanted to ask him to explain himself but Daniel was already leading her across to Bianca. Silently she allowed him to throw her up into the saddle. Then, with the moon climbing in the night sky and turning the world from black to silver-blue, they set off along the road to Kirkleigh.

Kitty had never been on a horse for more than an hour before today and now her body ached, but that was nothing compared to the pain inside. When she thought of Daniel kissing her she found herself melting all over again. She could not deny that she had wanted him to kiss her. Once again she had offered herself to him and once again he had been the one to break away. She thought that he must indeed care for her to be so protective, but that was small consolation and the heavy cloud settled more firmly around her heart. He did not desire her sufficiently to declare the world well lost when she was in his arms. She glanced across at him as he rode beside her. There was no sign of fatigue in his upright figure; his face in the moonlight was unsmiling, as still and inscrutable as stone. He might have been hewn from the quarry where they had taken shelter.

'Is anything amiss, Miss Wythenshawe?' He looked across at her.

Kitty hesitated. Should she ask him why he had not taken advantage of her? Perhaps she had disgusted him.

Her godmother had talked with contempt of the forward behaviour of some of the young ladies in Town, and had not Mama told her that on no account was she to allow a gentleman to go any further than kissing the tips of her fingers? She had allowed Daniel to do a lot more than that!

'I am very tired,' she managed at last. 'I have never ridden so far before.'

'And you have done very well. Look, there is Kirkleigh village ahead of us. Another half-hour and this nightmare will be over. You will be home.'

She nodded, too miserable to speak. So he thought of this whole episode with horror. For her, once the danger was past she had thought of it as a glorious adventure: the elation of successfully jumping the hedge, galloping head-long across the heath, kissing Daniel. Especially kissing Daniel.

I am undoubtedly a very wanton young woman, she told herself miserably. *And after tonight I should not be surprised if Godmama sends me back to Mama and wishes to have nothing further to do with me!*

Chapter Eleven

Her unhappy thoughts kept Kitty occupied until at last they clattered into the stableyard at Kirkleigh. She was surprised to see so many torches burning. Selby came running out to meet them.

'Right glad I am to see you, Mr Blackwood, and you, miss! When t'others returned and said what had happened I was that put out. His lordship was all for setting out immediately but Lord Leaconham said as how you had gone after her, sir, so we decided we should wait 'til morning before getting up a search party. I should never have saddled up Bianca for you, miss, whatever the young mistress said. If that mare runs away with you then there's no stopping her. I was that afraid you had been thrown.'

'No, I am quite safe,' she said as he helped her to alight. 'Bianca carried me very well.'

'Miss Wythenshawe even took a hedge in her stride,' added Daniel, coming to collect her. 'You are a good teacher, Selby.'

'I allus said miss had the makings of a clipping rider,'

responded the groom, grinning widely. 'Off you go indoors, now. You'll find her ladyship and all the others waiting up for you.'

'I wish I could just creep away to my room,' admitted Kitty as she accompanied Daniel into the house.

'Everyone will want to assure themselves that you are unharmed.' They stopped to allow the lackey to run ahead and open the door to the drawing room. 'Come, you have been very brave until now.' Daniel turned to her, encouragement glinting in his eyes. 'After you, Miss Wythenshawe.'

Their reception was rapturous. As soon as the door opened the room erupted in cries of relief. Ann flew out of her seat and enveloped Kitty in a tight hug before insisting that she come and sit down with her on the sofa. Everyone was talking at once, demanding to know what had happened. After the calm silence of their night ride Kitty found the cacophony of voices far too confusing. She was content to remain still and silent, sitting between Ann and Lady Leaconham while Daniel explained everything.

'Well, I am relieved that no harm has been done,' declared Lord Harworth, pouring brandy into a glass and handing it to Daniel.

'Except poor Lizzie,' put in Ann. 'She was so distraught that she took to her bed as soon as we got home.'

'I was obliged to give her a little laudanum,' added Mrs Camber, nodding. 'I am sure she will be fully recovered by the morning.'

'This would all have been avoided if they had stuck to their original plan and come straight home,' stated Mr Camber, frowning direfully at his son.

George Camber shrank down in his chair, looking sheepish.

'In Harworth's absence I should have taken responsibility,'

put in Garston. 'I should never have agreed to it. It was a mistake, and I admit it.'

'You were not solely to blame, Cousin,' added Ann, 'we were all of us eager to go to Chapeltown, except Kitty.'

'Then she showed more good sense than the rest of you put together,' retorted Lord Harworth. 'I can only thank Providence that Blackwood was on hand.'

'If I had not been there I am sure Hamilton or Lord Leaconham would have gone after Miss Wythenshawe,' remarked Daniel.

'Aye, of course we would.' Martin Hamilton nodded. 'Not that we didn't have the devil's own job finding our way back to the road, even in daylight.'

'But we were only a little late for dinner.' Ann cast a soulful look at her brother.

'Aye, well, that was some relief, to have most of you home,' he agreed. 'And when it grew dark and the ladies began to fret about Miss Wythenshawe I told 'em not to worry. "Mark my words," I said, "Blackwood will look after her. And when darkness falls you may be sure he will take shelter at some inn or tavern until there's moonlight enough to see the way." And I was right, you see. But you'll not be riding back to Hestonroyd tonight, my boy? The least we can do is give you a bed for the night.'

'Thank you, my lord, I would like to stay,' replied Daniel. 'Very much.'

Kitty knew his eyes were upon her but she dared not meet his gaze.

'Did you dine on the road?' enquired Garston.

'No, we did not stop to eat,' said Daniel.

'Oh, how remiss of me!' declared Lady Harworth, tugging at the bell-rope. 'You must be quite famished! I will order something to be brought in immediately.' Kitty disclaimed, wanting only to go to her bed, but Lady Harworth insisted and when the servant came in she gave orders for soup to be prepared and sent up to Kitty's room. 'And for Mr Blackwood, too, but ask Cook to send up a plate of ham and some pickles as well for him. I am sure you must be very hungry, sir,' she added as the servant withdrew. 'But now it is very late, and I am sure we should all be in our beds...'

'Not quite yet, Mama, if you please, I would like to say something.' Lord Harworth moved to the centre of the room. 'In all the anxiety of this evening we have not been able to divert ourselves with charades, or billiards as is customary, and it has given me time to consider. I have made a decision and do not wish to put things off a moment longer. My mother and Aunt Leaconham are well aware of my intentions, and approve, so I think it is time to speak.'

Kitty was looking at her host, trying to appear attentive when all she wanted was to go to sleep. From the corner of her eye she saw Garston lean down to whisper something to Ann, who giggled. She hoped Lord Harworth would hurry up and finish whatever it was he had to say so that she could retire to her bedchamber.

'Mama has been telling me for years that I should do this, and since I am assured by my aunt that there is no impediment I see no reason to wait. We'll have the lawyers discuss settlements and jointures and what-not later but I want to get this off my chest so I might as well do it now, while everyone is here, eh?' Bemused, Kitty watched as Lord Harworth crossed the room and lowered himself on to one knee before her. 'Miss Wythenshawe, will you do me the honour, very *great* honour, of accepting my hand in marriage?'

Kitty stared at him. Beside her, Ann was clapping and

laughing, her godmother gave a gusty sigh and everyone else crowded round, eagerly awaiting her answer.

All except Daniel. Briefly raising her eyes from the figure kneeling before her, she looked across the room. Daniel remained by the door, his face pale and drawn with fatigue. Apart from a muscle twitching in his cheek he might well have been made from marble, so cold and indifferent was he. Lady Leaconham gave her a little nudge.

'Well, Kitty, answer his lordship.'

'I—um—I am honoured, my lord, and, and flattered that you should think me worthy...' She cudgelled her brain for the right words but it appeared she had said enough.

'Oh, my dear, I am so *pleased!*' cried Ann, enveloping her in another of her fierce hugs. 'Now I shall be able to call you sister!'

As soon as she emerged from Ann's embrace, Lady Leaconham pulled her close and kissed her cheek.

'Kitty, my love, how happy I am about this! And I cannot *wait* to tell your mama—you know how delighted she will be.'

Lord Harworth, having risen to his feet, held out his hand to her.

'Miss Wythenshawe—Katherine—*Kitty*.' He pulled her up to stand beside him. 'You have made me the happiest man on earth!' He raised first one hand then the other to his lips before leaning forward to plant a kiss on her cheek.

'My lord, this is not—I mean—I must speak with you.'

He beamed at her.

'Of course, my love, of course, but everything else can wait until the morrow. We must let our guests go and get some rest now, eh?' He looked around. 'But where's Blackwood? Gone to bed already, has he? Young dog, not staying to congratulate me, but there, I suppose he is tired after all the adventures of the day!'

'I was concerned for a while today that he might cut you out,' remarked Lady Harworth, stepping forward to give Kitty a congratulatory peck on the cheek.

'Goodness, yes,' cried Ann, putting her hands to her mouth. 'Just think. If you had not returned until the morning then Mr Blackwood would have been obliged to offer for you!'

'Do not look so horrified at that, my dear,' said Lady Harworth drily. 'He would not be such a bad catch, rich as he is.'

Lady Leaconham bent an enquiring eye upon her sister.

'But, Clara, a manufacturer...'

'Not just a manufacturer, Letitia, although he has some very wealthy connections in the trade—one of his uncles is the richest wool merchant in Leeds and another owns several cotton mills in Lancashire, not to mention his father's interests in both wool and the cotton spinning. But not only that, he is to inherit a very sizeable property. Harworth tells me his father bought the Hartleydale estate last year.' She glanced speculatively at her daughter. 'Mr Daniel Blackwood stands to inherit a business worth in excess of forty thousand a year. To my mind that makes him a *very* eligible bachelor.' She added after a moment, 'He does not have a title, of course.'

'Well,' exclaimed Lady Leaconham, fanning herself briskly. 'I never would have thought it. He is extremely well presented, of course, but there is never anything ostentatious about the man.'

'But he is very much a gentleman, Aunt, do you not think so?' said Ann, looking thoughtful. 'A few more fobs and seals, a little more time in Town...'

'Enough, enough!' cried Lord Harworth jovially. 'What care I how rich Blackwood may be? There is one prize he does not possess.'

He lifted Kitty's hands to his lips again, then stood beaming down at her. Realising she was expected to respond, Kitty could only think of one thing to say.

'Sir, I am very tired...'

'Oh, my poor child, of course you are!' Lady Leaconham was on her feet in an instant. 'Say goodnight, my love, and I will take you upstairs immediately. A betrothal, and after such a day of excitement, it is no wonder you are worn out.'

'Yes, I am, Godmama. If you will all excuse me...'

Lady Leaconham put one arm about Kitty and led her away and as she picked up a bedroom candle from the bottom of the stairs she gave a little chuckle of delight.

'Oh, my dear, was anything so fortunate? I was afraid at first that it was all up with you when Garston returned with the others and told me what had happened, but once it became clear that no blame was attached to you then Bertram was all concern. And to make you an offer here, in front of everyone—'

'He does not know my circumstances,' muttered Kitty. 'It must be explained to him how very poor I am—'

'Yes, of course, my dear, but what can that matter now?'

'It matters to *me,*' said Kitty, close to tears. 'I am sure he will not wish to marry me once he knows the truth.'

They had reached the door of her bedchamber and Lady Leaconham led the way inside.

'There can be no objection to your birth.' She went around the room, lighting all the candles from her own before coming to stand before Kitty once more. 'He has proposed to you most publicly, Kitty. Bertram would be a complete scoundrel to cry off now!'

Despite her exhaustion, Kitty's sleep was disturbed by dreams and she rose late the following morning. She was still pinning up her hair when Ann bounced into the room.

'Good morning, *sister!* You cannot know how happy I am to call you that. And I heard Bertram go downstairs this morning *singing,* so you have made him happy as well!'

'I am very glad of it,' said Kitty, forcing herself to smile.

'Shall we go down to breakfast together? There is so much to discuss. Mama says Bertram wants to hold a ball to announce the betrothal and Aunt Leaconham will be planning your trousseau already. We must make sure we have our say—'

'You go on,' Kitty broke in, 'I—um—I am not at all happy with this gown and will change it before I go downstairs.' Ann was looking very keenly at her and she added beseechingly, 'Pray go ahead of me and I will join you as soon as I am able.'

'My dear, you are very pale, are you sure you are not ill?'

'No, no, it is merely a headache.'

'Poor Kitty. After the exertions of yesterday it is no wonder you are looking hagged. I shall send Norris up to you with a tisane and you must go back to bed. And I shall have breakfast sent up to you, as well!'

Ann flew out of the room and Kitty dropped her head in her hands. She had been quite truthful when she had said she had a headache, but she did not think any tisane would cure it. Tears pricked her eyelids. All her life she had dreamed of becoming a lady, and now it was actually going to happen, but instead of elation Kitty only felt anxiety. She told herself that it was because she had not been honest with Lord Harworth. Once she had explained to him about her family and her lack of fortune she would feel much better. Stepping out of her dress, she lay down on her bed again and stayed there until the maid arrived with her tisane. She drank it, but she sent her breakfast away, saying she wanted to sleep again until her headache had eased.

Kitty was surprised to find that after another hour's sleep she did indeed feel better. She decided that her first task must be to find Lord Harworth and confess everything. She wandered over to the window and threw up the sash, leaning her head against the frame as she breathed in the fresh morning air. Of course there was always the possibility that once she had informed him of her true circumstances he would no longer wish to marry her, but she would face that problem when it arose.

A movement below caught her eye and she glanced down to see Daniel's tall figure striding through the garden, his dark coat a startling contrast to the colourful flowerbeds. She heard a faint call and saw Ann hurrying along one of the paths towards him. Daniel stopped to wait for her. He offered Ann his arm and they continued to stroll together, Daniel bending his dark head to catch something Ann was saying. With a sigh Kitty turned away from the window. Bertram's not wishing to marry her because she was poor was suddenly not the problem. It might be the solution.

'My lord, may I come in?'

Kitty peeped around the door of Lord Harworth's study and waited anxiously for his reply. He jumped up, smiling broadly.

'My dear Katherine, come in, come in! I was just writing

out the notice for the newspapers. I cannot wait to tell everyone of my good fortune!'

'Before you do that, sir, I think there is something you should know.'

Twenty minutes later Kitty emerged from the study exhausted and depressed but still engaged. She had been at pains to explain to Lord Harworth how her father's misjudged investments had robbed the family of its income, how her mother and aunt now lived at Fallridge in their damp, cramped little cottage, and were obliged to take in sewing to make ends meet. Lord Harworth had indeed looked serious, but he was not inclined to call off the engagement.

'I cannot recall that you have ever told me anything of your family that was not true,' he said. 'You have not misled me, my dear. My mother will be disappointed, naturally, but if she was under the apprehension that your family were affluent then I am sure such a rumour did not come from you. What is not in doubt is that your birth is impeccable. Whatever hardships may have befallen your family you cannot be blamed for. It would not behove anyone who called himself a gentleman to think your lack of funds a reason to cry off from our engagement.'

So Kitty had retired, secure in the knowledge that Lord Harworth had no intention of casting her aside. She went in search of her godmother and found her in the morning room, engaged in writing letters. Kitty described her interview with Lord Harworth and watched the anxious look upon Lady Leaconham's countenance turn to delight when she told her of its conclusion.

'You see, my dear Kitty, I knew everything would turn out well in the end! I will pen a short letter to your mama today, and perhaps you would like to write a note to her yourself and enclose it inside mine; she will want to hear all the details. In fact, perhaps we could prevail upon Bertram to invite your mother and your aunt to Kirkleigh to join us. What do you say to that?'

Kitty mumbled some reply and Lady Leaconham shot her a frowning look.

'My dear Kitty, I do not know what is the matter with you! You have made a most excellent match and yet you look as if you had lost sixpence and found a groat!'

'I—I am sorry, Godmama, I am afraid I cannot quite believe it is happening to me.'

'I confess I have been pinching myself all morning, to make sure I am awake,' replied my lady, giving a very girlish giggle. 'Now go and write to your mother, Kitty: I cannot wait for her to hear the news—this is something she has dreamed of since you were a baby.'

Perhaps that was the truth of it. The thought shot through Kitty's head like a revelation. This had always been her mother's dream, much more than her own. She glanced up as Lady Harworth sailed into the room. Judging by the happy look upon her rather austere countenance Kitty did not think that Bertram had told her of his bride's impecunious state. Lady Harworth greeted her sister warmly, solicitously enquired if Kitty's headache had gone, then sank down on to a sofa.

'Well, this is turning out to be a most eventful morning!'

'What is it, Clara, what has happened?'

'My dear Letitia, you would never credit it! As if there was not enough to do organising next week's ball—Bertram is determined that we use the occasion to announce his betrothal and I am sure it is only right, and just what dear Katherine deserves, but I had barely left my room when—but here is Ann now. She must tell you herself!'

Ann came in, closely followed by Daniel. Kitty shrank back into one corner, wishing the ground would open and swallow her. She did not feel at all comfortable amongst so many happy people.

'Well, Mama, have you told them?' demanded Ann, giving a little skip.

'No, dear Niece, she has told us nothing,' cried Lady Leaconham impatiently. 'She is leaving that to you!'

Ann gave her beaming smile. 'Kitty is not the only one to find a husband, Aunt Leaconham, I am engaged!' She turned and held her hand out to Daniel. 'Mr Blackwood has proposed to me!' Her eyes fell upon Kitty standing in the shadows. 'Kitty, my love, I did not see you there! Is this not wonderful, will you not congratulate me?'

Kitty swallowed and forced her stiff lips into a smile. 'I am sure I w-wish you both very happy.' Her voice sounded strained, but Ann did not appear to notice. She was already turning to receive her aunt's good wishes.

'Of course there will be no announcement until after the ball,' stated Lady Harworth. 'Bertram is adamant that nothing should detract from his own betrothal. He wants me to invite even more people to dine with us beforehand, which means a great deal more work, of course, for everyone must be told. Letitia, my dear, perhaps you would help me to write out the invitations.'

'By all means, Sister. Let us go now and I will collect your lists.'

'And you must let me see them,' said Ann. 'There are several of my particular friends that I want to come!' She turned to Daniel. 'You will not object if I disappear for a few minutes, will you, dearest? I will be back even before you have time to miss me!'

She swept out of the room behind her mother and her aunt, all three of them forcefully voicing their thoughts on the forthcoming ball. As the door closed behind them there was silence. Kitty and Daniel were left facing one another.

'I had no idea...' began Kitty.

Daniel cleared his throat.

'Nor I. At least, not until this morning, in the garden. Miss Harworth came to find me, she left me in no doubt of her sentiments... I confess I had not been aware...'

He did not look at her, but instead began to toy with a small vase on the side table. Strangely the confusion in Kitty's head had lessened. It did not matter what Daniel thought of her. There were no longer any half-acknowledged hopes. She felt very calm, but as fragile as the porcelain he was twisting between his restless fingers.

'Kitty—'

'No, please.' She put up her hand, holding herself together with an effort. She felt so brittle that one wrong word and she might shatter. 'Let us say nothing more now. I am sure you wish for my happiness, just as I wish for yours. If we understand that then there is no need to say anything more.' She put up her head. 'What a h-happy outcome after yesterday's horrid events. I am s-sure we could not have expected anything half so good to come of it. Now, if you will excuse me, I should go.'

He stood silently, his dark head bowed as she left the room. She would not cry, she told herself over and over as she made her way to her bedchamber. There was nothing to cry about. She had made a splendid match—how could she deny Daniel the same good fortune? His family had made their money by honest toil: marriage to the sister of Lord Harworth would be a splendid alliance for him. She slipped into her bedchamber and closed the door, leaning against it, as if to keep out the world.

'You see?' she said to the empty room. 'Everyone is happy.'

So why, then, did she feel as if something inside her had died?

Chapter Twelve

The succeeding days passed like a dream for Kitty. It was as if someone else inhabited her body and she was a mere spectator. She smiled and said all that was proper to the many visitors that came to Kirkleigh House, agreed with all her godmother's suggestions for which gowns she should wear and spent hours with her smile in place, listening to Ann chatter on about her own engagement.

She had not seen Daniel since the announcement. He had left that day for Hestonroyd and had no plans to return until the ball. She could not be sorry, for without his presence she found it much easier to pretend that she was happy. And she must *be* happy, a letter from Mama told her it was so. The news of her engagement had been greeted in Fallridge with much rejoicing, although the invitation to Mama and Aunt Jane to travel to Kirkleigh and attend the betrothal ball was regretfully declined: Mama had not yet recovered from a bout of influenza. Kitty thought that the decision not to travel might also be due to her mother thinking that she had nothing fine enough to wear on such a grand occasion. That would all change: Lord Harworth had told Kitty he would give her an allowance to buy her clothes for the wedding, and she had already determined to send a portion of it to her mother.

'So you see what a good thing your marriage will be,' she told her reflection, as she prepared for the ball that evening. 'Everyone will benefit, so you must look happy.'

She tried out a smile. The young lady smiling back at her from the mirror certainly looked well enough: Kitty's dusky curls had been brushed until they glowed and were caught up in a bandeau of gold ribbon to match the embroidery on her white muslin gown. Emeralds glittered around her neck and from her ears, a betrothal present from Lord Harworth, purchased at the same time as the large diamond that now flashed and twinkled on her finger.

'Are you ready, Kitty?' Ann appeared at the door. 'Shall we go downstairs together? Norris says that Daniel has arrived.'

With her eyes still on her reflection, Kitty saw her smile slip a little. She quickly pinned it back in place as she picked up her fan.

'Yes, I am ready now.'

The noise and chatter from the drawing room drifted up to them as they descended the stairs. Lord Harworth had told her there were only thirty sitting down to dinner, but the idea frightened Kitty more than the thought of the hundred or so guests who would be arriving later for the ball. The first person she saw as she walked into the room was Daniel, his tall figure commanding attention. He was deep in conversation with a group of gentlemen but the flurry of movement by the door caught his eye and he looked across the room. For a moment he looked towards Kitty, his gaze fixed somewhere above her head, his face showing neither pleasure nor pain, then his eyes shifted to Ann and he smiled a little as he came forwards to greet her.

'Well, my dear Katherine, you are looking magnificent, magnificent!' Lord Harworth was beside her, leading her away from Ann. 'Damn me if Blackwood wasn't right about emeralds being the stones for you.'

'M-Mr Blackwood suggested you buy these?' asked Kitty, surprised.

'Aye. He was with me in Leeds, you see, the day I bought 'em. We had been visiting one of his business acquaintances and afterwards I told him I was going to get your ring and a little something to mark our engagement. "Emeralds," he said. "Buy her emeralds, to match her eyes." And for Gad he was right! Come along, m'dear, there's any number of people here you have to meet!'

Kitty accompanied him around the room, saying what was proper, smiling, always smiling, but Daniel dominated her thoughts. She wanted to look for him, she longed to hear his voice, but Bertram kept her by his side, presenting family and friends to her. Everyone wanted to congratulate the happy couple, the ladies wanted to gasp and sigh over the ring, the gentlemen winked at Lord Harworth and declared he was a lucky dog.

At dinner Kitty found herself sitting opposite Daniel. For once she was grateful for the mountains of silverware in the centre of the table. Much as she longed to look at Daniel she was afraid that thoughts she wanted to remain hidden might show in her eyes. So she kept her gaze averted, trying to concentrate upon what her neighbour was saying and to respond in kind. She had no idea what she ate, even less what was said during the protracted meal and she could only be thankful when at last they rose from the table.

Even then her ordeal was not over. Kitty stood beside Lady Harworth at the top of the stairs to receive the guests, then Bertram carried her off to dance with him. And all the time she was obliged to smile. She was grateful that Daniel did not ask her to dance: it was painful enough watching him across the room and when she saw him smile at Ann she felt sick at heart. Occasionally she was aware of Daniel's eyes upon her, but when she looked up he would quickly glance away. It was like some bizarre ritual: they circled the room, painfully aware but always avoiding each other. And smiling. Constantly smiling.

A steady stream of partners had kept Kitty on the dance floor until late into the night but at length she had had enough and as the music ended she slipped away before her godmother or Lady Harworth could present her with another partner. She had been at Kirkleigh long enough to know the layout of the house and made her way to a small sitting room on the ground floor. It was used by the ladies of the house as a sewing parlour and, knowing it would not be occupied, she picked up one of the double candlesticks from a hall table and carried it into the room. The glow from the candles was not sufficient to light the room but it was enough for Kitty. She placed the candlestick on the mantelshelf and sat down in one of the worn armchairs beside the empty fireplace. As she clasped her hands together the diamond on her finger flashed, reminding her that she must not tarry long here or she would be missed.

A sudden flickering of the light made her look up. Daniel was standing in the doorway.

'I saw you leave,' he said, coming into the room and carefully closing the door behind him. 'I wanted to be sure you are not ill.'

'No, I am well. I needed to be quiet for a little while.'

She rubbed her aching cheeks. 'I seem to have done nothing all evening but smile and exchange pleasantries.'

'I know.' He walked across the room to sit down opposite her.

She said, 'Ann is very happy tonight.'

'Yes.'

He sat forward, elbows resting on his knees and his hands clasped. He was so close she could have leaned over and touched him. Her knuckles gleamed white as she resisted the temptation.

'Your betrothal was very sudden.'

'Yes.' She thought he would not speak again and berated herself for her remark. It was no concern of hers what he did. Exhaling, he straightened, saying slowly, 'She came to me in the garden, the morning after you had announced your engagement to Harworth. She made it very plain that she would welcome an offer from me. I thought, why not? It would make Ann happy. You are going to marry Harworth. This way at least I shall know where you are, how you go on.'

Kitty's hands went to her mouth. The knife that had been twisting within her all evening now cut even deeper.

'You…you do not…love Ann.'

For the first time that evening he looked straight at her.

'No. I love you.'

His image blurred as tears filled her eyes. She tried to blink them away. If only she had known.

You did know! the voice screamed in her head. *You did know. Every act of kindness, every kiss…*

'Oh, Daniel.' She had to breathe very carefully to keep her unhappiness under control. 'Does it help to know that… that I love you, too? Only I did not realise it until it was too late.'

'No, that does not help at all.' His mouth twisted into a humourless smile. 'I thought you had achieved your dream.'

She shook her head.

'I realise now it was not really my dream, but my mother's: she had such hopes for me.'

'She is happy, then.'

She heard the bitter note in his voice and said quickly, 'Please do not blame her; Mama's life is very hard and she did not want that for me.'

The steady tick, tick of the clock reminded her that she must not stay away from the ballroom for too long.

'Soon we will be brother and sister,' she said carefully. 'How will we manage, meeting as if we mean nothing to each other?'

He rubbed a hand across his eyes.

'We must.'

A rogue tear escaped and she dashed it away.

'I am not sure I can,' she whispered.

With an oath Daniel was on his feet, dragging her up and into his arms.

'Then let us not even try!' he muttered, covering her face with kisses. 'We can both cry off. Surely it is better to tell the truth now than to make the four of us unhappy?'

He kissed her savagely and Kitty clung to him, responding with all the pent-up longing that had been slumbering within her.

'If you cannot face telling them then I'll carry you off now,' he muttered between kisses. 'We will go away; I'll write to Harworth and tell him what has happened…'

Steeling herself, Kitty put a hand to his mouth to silence him.

'You know we cannot do that.' She gave him a misty smile and reached up to brush back a lock of dark hair, her fingers trailing lovingly over his brow. 'You are too much of a gentleman, Daniel Blackwood. You cannot cry off.'

'Despite what she says I swear Ann Harworth doesn't love me—'

'That is not the point. You have promised to marry her. How could you live with your conscience if you broke off your engagement?'

'How can you live with *your* conscience,' he threw at her, 'knowing you married Harworth for his title and his money?'

She looked at him, saw the tortured anguish in his eyes. The confusion that had been banging around in her head for days suddenly resolved itself.

'I am not going to marry him,' she said quietly. 'Lord Harworth does not love me: when I told him I had no money of my own he decided the honourable course was to continue with the engagement, but I think he would be quite relieved if I were to withdraw.'

'But if you cry off, if you are free—'

'No!' She pushed away from him. 'I am nothing. If I cry off everyone will say Lord Harworth is well rid of me. His pride may suffer a little, and Lady Leaconham will be embarrassed, but that will pass, it will be forgotten. Society may want to punish me but that will not be possible, for I am not really a part of that world. I can retire to Fallridge and obscurity. I shall be no worse off than when I began. For you to jilt Ann Harworth would bring shame and embarrassment upon her and social ruin upon you and your family.'

'But I love you!'

'And I love you too much to bring disgrace to you.'

'But it needn't be like that.' He reached out for her again. 'Ann could cry off—'

'You would make yourself so unpleasant to her that she

no longer wants to marry you?' Kitty shook her head. 'You must not hurt her, Daniel, she is my friend. I could not bear you to do anything so dishonourable.'

'No! Listen to me—!'

She put out her hands, stepping back to put a distance between them. She said slowly, 'I will make you this promise, Daniel. If you or Ann do anything to break this engagement, I will *never* marry you.'

'And that is your final word?'

'It is.'

She kept her eyes on his face. He must not be in any doubt that she spoke with deadly sincerity. The silence stretched until she thought she might scream with the pain of it. At last Daniel spoke.

'Then there can be no hope for us.'

'None.' She added quietly, 'You told me once that we all have choices. When those choices are made we must live with them.'

He stared at her, such passion in his eyes that for a moment she feared he might drag her into his arms again and if he did that Kitty did not know if she had the strength left to resist him. Instead he reached out and caught her fingers, carrying them to his lips. Kitty blinked rapidly. She must not cry now. There would be plenty of time for tears later. Gently she disengaged her hands.

'Goodbye, my love,' she whispered as she turned and walked out of the room.

Chapter Thirteen

Three days later Kitty was back at Fallridge, where her mother's silence was harder to bear than the tears and recriminations she had anticipated. The announcement that she was not going to marry Lord Harworth had been met with bewilderment and outrage at Kirkleigh. Lady Leaconham had pleaded and Ann had begged her to reconsider: Bertram adopted the role of martyr but in Lady Harworth Kitty found an ally. The lady had never reconciled herself to the idea of her son taking a penniless bride and she showed more kindness than Kitty thought she deserved.

Lady Harworth arranged for her own carriage to take Kitty back to Fallridge, together with the trunks full of clothes that she had accumulated in London and a purse full of coins. To Kitty it felt as if Lady Harworth was buying her off, but she did not refuse the money, knowing that it would bring some relief to her family, from whom she had so cruelly ripped the possibility of comfort and riches.

A letter from Lady Leaconham followed her, detailing

how badly she had been deceived and stating that she would do no more for her goddaughter, to which Mama insisted that Kitty should reply with a very civil apology and an assurance that she would not call upon her for any further assistance.

'Your godmother has been very good but we must now think of what we are going to do with you,' said Mama, sealing up the letter and with it all her hopes. 'Mrs Midgley has put some work my way, so there is a little sewing you can help me with until you have stopped crying all the time.'

'Mama, I do not cry all the time!'

'Do not tell me that you do not water your pillow every night, my love, because the walls are very thin and even Aunt Jane can hear you, and as you know she is very deaf!'

'Very well, I confess that my spirits are a little low.'

'It is my belief that you are nursing a broken heart,' said Mama. 'But I will not ask you to tell me anything about that if you do not wish to do so.'

Kitty bowed her head.

'Oh, Mama, I am such a disappointment to you.'

'Nonsense, you are a credit to me! Why, look at you, so pretty as you are, and with an excellent education, too. I was always afraid Letitia Leaconham was aiming a little too high, hoping to catch a baron for you. I could wish that the squire had not seen the announcement of your betrothal, because it is very hard to hold one's head up knowing that everyone is wondering just what occurred to make you break off the engagement. And of course there are some ill-natured enough to gloat at your misfortune. But we shall take no notice of them.' She looked closely at Kitty. 'Are you sure there were no other gentleman dangling after you,

not even one who might be keen enough to seek you out
and come courting you?'

An image of Daniel rose before Kitty and the tears that
were never far away clogged her throat. She shook her head,
unable to trust her voice.

'Well, then, we must think of an occupation for you,'
Mama said briskly. 'I had it from Mrs Hobbs that the
squire's governess has given notice. Now I suggest you
put on your bonnet and take yourself off to the squire's
house this minute and put your name forward. You have
always been a favourite with the older girls, so I think you
have a good chance of securing the position.'

'Really, Mama?'

'Of course! I don't say I wouldn't prefer to see you married, but if it isn't to be then we must find you some other
way to support yourself.'

The weeks dragged by and Kitty fell into a regular routine at Fallridge. The squire and his lady agreed to take
Kitty on as governess, but she was not required until the
end of November, when the present governess was leaving
to live with her sister. In the meantime Kitty worked at
home and took over many of the household tasks, leaving Aunt Jane and her mother free to concentrate on their
sewing. Aunt Jane might tut and bemoan the fact that
Kitty's hands were growing rough from the hard work but
Kitty preferred the activity, because she found sewing left
her mind far too free to think about Daniel.

Even when her hands were red and sore from washing
clothes, or her eyes smarting from dust as she swept out the
cottage, she could not regret calling off her engagement. It
was not just the idea of marriage to a man she didn't love:
that might have been bearable. Given time they might even
have grown quite fond of one another, but her heart recoiled

from the thought of watching Daniel with another woman. Also, knowing that Daniel loved her, it would not have been fair to Ann for Kitty to remain. This way she could at least give them a chance of happiness. This thought was her only consolation as she dragged herself to bed every night, afraid her dreams would be filled with painful visions of Daniel, but disappointed if they were not.

She refused to discuss what had happened at Kirkleigh with her mother, and when Mrs Wythenshawe read for herself in the London newspaper the brief announcement that the betrothal was terminated, she immediately went off to visit the squire and to beg him not to pass on any further newspapers since her interest in London society was now completely at an end. Thus Kitty was spared any news of Daniel and Ann's betrothal. That part of her life was over. She must now look to the future.

August was almost over when the quiet of the village was disturbed by the arrival of a large travelling carriage. Kitty had been gathering fruit from the hedgerows and was making her way home as the elegant vehicle swept past her. She saw it stop at the green and the driver leaned down to address one of the lads tending the pigs there before setting off again, only to pull up a few yards on, outside of her mother's cottage.

Kitty stopped, her skin prickling with a presentiment of danger. As she watched she saw two ladies descend from the carriage and after a moment they disappeared into the cottage. Kitty breathed again. For a dreadful moment she thought it was Daniel come to find her. Settling her basket more comfortably on her arm, she began to walk towards her home. It must be someone with a commission for Mama. She quickened her step. It might even be a very lucrative order, since the lady could afford to travel in a coach and four.

The cottage was very dark after the bright sunshine and Kitty paused in the doorway, waiting for her eyes to adjust.

'Ah, here is my niece now!' Aunt Jane's greeting was preceded by her hacking cough. 'Come in, Kitty, come in and meet our visitors!'

Kitty stepped in, dropping a slight curtsy towards the two ladies. They were mother and daughter, she guessed, because despite the difference in their ages they were both black-haired and dark-eyed, and both had the same direct gaze that they now turned upon her. Kitty gave them her shy smile, wondering if she had met them before.

'Goodness, you have been busy, my love,' said Aunt Jane, taking the basket from Kitty. 'Wimberries, lovely— and elderberries, too!'

'Yes,' said Kitty. 'I thought it might be a little early for the elderberries, but I found some, not enough for cordial, of course, but we can put them into a pie, I thought...'

'Excellent! I shall take them through to the back. Your mama is gone to fetch down her pattern books but she will be back directly. Oh, but where are my manners? Mrs Blackwood, may I present to you my niece, Katherine. Mrs Midgley recommended us to Mrs Blackwood, Kitty, and she is come to have a gown made up for her daughter—'

Blackwood! Kitty's heart lurched. No wonder they looked so familiar. She shifted uneasily from one foot to the other, painfully aware of her old gown and fruit-stained hands. She welcomed the sound of Mama's footsteps on the stairs.

'Now, I have a number of patterns here that might be suitable, as well as a number of magazines that you might like to look at. My daughter was in London recently and brought them back for me... Oh, Kitty, there you are! I hope Jane has introduced you...'

'Yes, she has,' put in Mrs Blackwood, smiling and looking so like Daniel that Kitty wanted to cry. 'I wonder, Miss Wythenshawe, if you are not too tired from your berry-picking, if you might take a turn around the green with me? There are such a number of books and pictures for Bella to go through that it will take her quite some time, I think. I am sure I can rely upon your mother's judgement to guide her towards a suitable selection from which to make our final choice.'

'Yes, do pray leave me, Mama,' said Miss Blackwood, bending her own mischievous smile upon Kitty. 'I am sure I shall decide much quicker without you sighing over me and growing impatient!'

'You see, Miss Wythenshawe, we are quite *de trop*,' chuckled Mrs Blackwood. 'Let us walk.'

Silently Kitty stepped back out into the sunshine. This matron could only be Daniel's mother—and he had mentioned to her that he had a sister—*a minx* had been his words, and recalling the mischievous twinkle in the girl's dark eyes Kitty could well believe this was she. How unfortunate that Mrs Midgley should recommend Mama as a seamstress for them. However, it was highly unlikely that she would come into contact with Daniel. It was rare for gentlemen to accompany their womenfolk on such errands so there really was no reason to think it would ever be discovered that they had been acquainted.

Mrs Blackwood set out for the green at a brisk pace and Kitty fell into step beside her.

'Well, Miss Wythenshawe, it has been quite a task to track you down.'

Kitty started.

'Our cottage is a little out of the way...'

'That is not what I meant, my dear. I was referring to the way you disappeared after jilting Lord Harworth.'

'Oh.' Kitty swallowed. 'It…it was not deliberate. I merely came home.'

'As any loving daughter would.' Mrs Blackwood nodded approvingly. 'I am sure I cannot blame you, for you could hardly remain at Kirkleigh, could you? And I understand Lady Leaconham has washed her hands of you.' She gave a little tut of disapproval. 'I find it hard to understand why people should object to a broken engagement, when one or other party realises they have made a mistake. It is surely better they discover the sad truth before the knot is irrevocably tied.'

'It would have been a very advantageous match for me,' put in Kitty, determined to be honest. 'I have disappointed so many people by my action. I only hope that Lord Harworth can forgive me, in time.' She added, 'I do not believe his affections were engaged.'

'No, I think you are right. My son tells me he is even now turning his attentions to Miss Leyton-Smythe, a wealthy heiress who has recently arrived in the area.'

Kitty hesitated a little before asking the question that was uppermost in her mind. 'Is—does Mr Blackwood spend a great deal of time at Kirkleigh?'

'Whenever his work can spare him, yes. But that is only to be expected. He is still advising Lord Harworth on his building project, and of course he must visit Miss Harworth.'

Kitty nodded, wondering miserably why it had been so important to ask the question, since the answer only brought her more pain.

Mrs Blackwood continued thoughtfully, 'But I do not believe he is happy.'

Kitty's eyes flew to her face and found herself subjected to a piercing scrutiny.

'I think something occurred at Kirkleigh, something that my son will not divulge, but I hope that you can help me.'

'Oh, no, no,' stammered Kitty. 'I am sure I do not know…'

Mrs Blackwood continued as if she had not spoken.

'You see, when Daniel returned from London he made several references to you, Miss Wythenshawe.'

'He—he did?'

'Yes. He wanted to know if I had heard of the family. I am afraid I could not help him, but I thought perhaps he had formed an attachment, for he was quite preoccupied, you see. Oh, he did not neglect his duties, but I found him not quite so…attentive as he had been. My daughter Bella noticed it as well, and she also noted that Daniel's behaviour changed markedly when Lord Harworth brought a party to Kirkleigh.' A little smile tugged at the corners of her mouth. 'It did not take long to discover that the mysterious Miss Wythenshawe was one of Lord Harworth's guests.'

'But there was nothing—' cried Kitty. 'We hardly saw each other—I mean—'

Mrs Blackwood patted her arm.

'Oh, do not distress yourself, child. Daniel said nothing, I assure you. It was all conjecture on my part, but I think I know my son pretty well: it was very plain to me that Daniel had fallen head over heels in love.'

Kitty wrung her hands. 'No!' she whispered.

'You may imagine my surprise when Daniel came home to tell me he was engaged to Miss Harworth. Of course, he also informed me that you were to marry her brother and I began to see that something had gone terribly wrong.' She stopped, turning to look at Kitty, a mixture of sympathy and enquiry in her dark eyes. 'Am I right to think you did not know of my son's feelings for you?' Miserably Kitty shook her head and heard her companion give an exasperated sigh. 'Oh, the foolish boy.'

'Pray do not blame him, ma'am! He...he believed I wanted to marry Lord Harworth. And...and I thought so, too, for a while.' She fixed her eyes upon Mrs Blackwood, willing her to understand. 'I did not know he l-loved me, until it was too late, until he was engaged to Ann. If I had married her brother then we would have been constantly thrown together. The idea of seeing him every day and not being able to...' She pulled out her handkerchief and resolutely blew her nose. 'Once I knew he...he loved me I was sure I must not stay. If it had been only my feelings that had to be suppressed, every look, every gesture designed to conceal what was in my heart, that would have been painful enough, but to know Daniel was suffering, too—I thought it best to leave. Without me there to remind him, I thought he would soon become accustomed to his new life. Miss Harworth is a splendid young woman: she will make him a good wife.'

'But he loves you.'

Kitty closed her eyes. She said quietly, 'It is an excellent match, ma'am. I believe in the highest circles many married couples begin with mere liking but soon develop a sincere affection. I can only pray that that will happen.'

'I hope so, Miss Wythenshawe, since I can see no way out of the betrothal.'

'I am so sorry.'

'So, too, am I. You have been very foolish, the pair of you, but what's done is done and we must look to the future. Tell me your plans, Miss Wythenshawe.'

'Me? Well, I must earn my living,' said Kitty. 'I am to become a governess in November.'

'And is that what you want?'

Kitty spread her hands.

'It is a good situation; the present governess is only leaving because she is obliged to return to the family home. She has told me the squire and his lady are very considerate employers.'

'And you turned down marriage to Lord Harworth for this?' There was a note of wonder in Mrs Blackwood's voice. Silently Kitty spread her hands again, too miserable to speak. 'Well, you must let me do something for your family.'

'Oh, no, please! That is not necessary—'

'It is in some part my son's fault that you are reduced to this.'

'It was my decision,' replied Kitty, raising her head. 'I could not accept charity, especially from you, madam.'

'You must accept it for your mother and your aunt,' came the firm reply. 'They will not be able to continue with their sewing for many more years, and if they remain in that damp little house their health will soon fail. I shall set up a fund of some sort to provide them with a small income. My lawyer will arrange everything. It shall be anonymous—your mother will believe it is some benevolent acquaintance of your father's. Will that do?'

After a moment Kitty nodded.

'I want nothing for myself, but I will accept your offer for my mother's sake, Mrs Blackwood, and thank you for it.'

'Good. Then it is settled. Now let us return to the house and see what unsuitable designs Bella has chosen for her new gown!'

* * *

'...what say you, my dear?'

'Hmm? Yes, if you wish, Mama.'

Daniel had no idea what his mother had asked him. His thoughts had been far away, as they were so often these days. He knew his mother's eyes were upon him and gave her an apologetic smile across the breakfast table.

'I am sorry, Mama, what did you say to me?'

'It hardly matters, my dear. I was only saying that Cook has procured a couple of rabbits and I wondered if we should add them to the dinner tonight. Your father is bringing your uncle back to dine with us and he is very partial to rabbit.'

'Then by all means have them,' he replied. 'I regret I shall not be here; I am promised to dine at Kirkleigh.'

'Oh. I had thought that now your work on Lord Harworth's mill was complete you would have a little more time for yourself. You are looking tired, my son: I am well aware that you have spent two hours at the mill already this morning. I wish you would stay home and rest today. I am sure you are eager to hear from your uncle how Barrowford Mill is faring.'

He said quietly, 'Miss Harworth expects me.'

There was a heartbeat's hesitation.

'Of course,' nodded Mrs Blackwood. 'You must not disappoint her.'

After breakfast Daniel excused himself and went off to the study. There were letters to be answered before he could set off for Kirkleigh. He yawned. Perhaps it was not strictly necessary for him to visit the mill every morning, but when his father was away he liked to assure himself that everything was in order for the day.

He sat down at the desk and pulled the pile of letters

towards him. There was nothing urgent but he wanted to deal with them all before setting off for Kirkleigh. A tiny voice in his head whispered that he was putting off the journey. It was true. He was reluctant to spend more time at Kirkleigh than was necessary. There were too many memories. With something like a growl he forced himself to concentrate on his correspondence, working his way doggedly through the pile of letters until each one had been answered. The official documents that had arrived from London received no more than a cursory glance before being put aside to discuss with his father.

The chiming of the church clock reminded him that it was getting late. Reluctantly he sent a message to the stables to have Marnie saddled up.

The ride across the moors toward Kirkleigh usually provided him with some relief from the deadly depression that dogged him, but today he could not seem to shake it off. It was a beautiful day, the sun blazing down from a cloudless sky on the purple heather, which was fading now that summer was ending. He told himself he should be enjoying the freedom of the journey, the refreshing breeze on his face and the skylark trilling above him, but it was no good. After a brief gallop he allowed Marnie to slow down and pick her own way along the well-worn path while he gave himself up to thinking about Kitty. He rarely allowed himself the agonising luxury of wondering what she was doing, if she was happy, but that did not mean she was not constantly in his thoughts. Every waking moment conjured a picture of her: when he poured himself a cup of coffee in the morning the dark liquid was the colour of her hair; when he was surrounded by the roar and clatter of the spinning shop he could hear her asking questions about the mill and its workers. At Kirkleigh it was even worse, for everywhere he looked there were reminders of Kitty—taking her riding lesson in the park, drinking tea in the drawing room. When he sat down to dinner he expected at any moment to see her peeping at him between the epergne and the candlesticks. There was no escape from her—even at night the sky reminded him of the time he had brought her back from Chapeltown. Sometimes she was so real to him he thought that if only he looked around quickly enough he would see her at his shoulder.

Angrily he shook his head. It did no good to dwell on the past. Ann was waiting for him at Kirkleigh and not for the world would he have her know how bitterly he regretted asking her to marry him. As Kitty had said to him, the very last time he had seen her, they had to live by their choices.

He straightened his shoulders. This maudlin behaviour would help no one. Neither would being late for dinner. With a flick of his whip and a word of encouragement to his horse he settled himself in the saddle and cantered on towards Kirkleigh.

He rode Marnie to the stables and entered the house by a side door, where he was surprised to find himself accosted by one of the footmen, who informed him that Lord Harworth and his sister were awaiting him in the study.

'I thought you might be sitting in the garden on such a lovely day,' he said, tossing his hat and gloves on to a chair. 'Is there some business to discuss, my lord? I thought we had covered everything on the mill.'

'We have, Blackwood, and the building work is progressing smoothly.' Lord Harworth replied. 'This has nothing to do with the mill.'

Daniel looked from Ann to her brother, his brow contracting a little.

'Is something amiss?'

Lord Harworth picked up a newspaper from the desk.

'I need you to explain this.' He held out the paper. 'I have just read a report of the petition presented to Parliament by the West Riding Anti-Slavery Society—you did not tell me you were a member of the committee.'

Daniel's brows rose fractionally.

'The subject never arose.'

'I thought I made my views on this matter perfectly clear.'

'You did,' agreed Daniel. 'They are not *my* views, however, and I have never made any secret of that. The sooner we stop trading in slaves the better.'

'You do not know what you are saying, Blackwood. That way lies anarchy! You have seen what is happening in France. If we show weakness now...'

'It is not weakness to object to these poor souls being bought and sold and then worked to death for profit.'

'This is dangerous nonsense,' retorted his lordship. 'Who knows where it would end? Such radical views must not be encouraged. I would be obliged if you would send a note to the newspaper immediately, declaring that you have withdrawn your support.'

'I cannot do that, my lord.'

Ann rose from her seat, her manner unusually serious.

'You see, Brother, I told you he was a man of principle.' She turned to Daniel. 'Perhaps you do not understand: Bertram has explained it all to me. We have plantations in the West Indies and depend upon the slaves there to work the land. I admit I was shocked when I learned of the horrific conditions endured by some of these poor wretches, but we could work towards improving their lot.'

'I am very sorry but that is not good enough. The trade

must be ended. England will not become bankrupt, as some predict. We will find a way around the problems...'

'And what of your mills?' Lord Harworth challenged him. 'There are many who say your workers are little better than slaves.'

Daniel drew himself up.

'You have seen for yourself the conditions in my mill: I pay an honest wage and look to the welfare of my workers and their families. One does not have to be a Quaker to run a mill well.'

'Very well, very well,' said Lord Harworth testily. 'I admit that your mills are exemplary, but what of this slavery petition? My name cannot be connected to that.'

Daniel said with great deliberation, 'I will not withdraw, my lord.'

A long silence ensued, broken only by the ticking of the clock on the mantelpiece.

'Very well, Blackwood,' Lord Harworth said at last. 'I may have to accept your views and deal with you on matters of business, but this is not something I can allow in my own family. I have already discussed this with Ann and explained to her that if you will not change your mind, then the engagement between you must end. I will forbid the banns!'

He waited expectantly but Daniel made no reply. He glanced at Ann. Her eyes were fixed upon him but he could not read her thoughts.

He said quietly, 'If that is the case then I am very sorry for it, but I cannot in conscience withdraw my support for this cause.'

'Very well, if that is your final word.' Lord Harworth turned to his sister. 'Ann?'

She rose, drawing the diamond ring from her finger and holding it out to him.

'Do not feel too sorry for me, Daniel,' she said. 'Being engaged to you was not half as much fun as I expected it to be.'

He nodded, relieved. 'Perhaps that is because I am not the right man for you.'

'Perhaps not. I have thought for some time now that Garston might suit me better. He is family, you see. He understands our position.'

'Then I wish you every happiness, Miss Harworth.' Daniel picked up his hat and gloves. 'In the circumstances I think it would be best if I did not stay for dinner. Please convey my apologies to Lady Harworth.'

'I will.' Lord Harworth gave a dismissive nod. 'I bid you good day, Blackwood.'

As Daniel reached the door Ann called to him. He turned.

'When you find Kitty will you give her my love?' she said, smiling a little. 'And tell her there is no ill will in this house towards her. Is there, Bertram?'

Lord Harworth shifted uncomfortably and gazed down at the carpet, tracing the pattern with the toe of one beautifully polished boot.

'No, none,' he muttered. 'Pray tell Miss Wythenshawe I realise now that our marriage would have been a grave mistake.' He looked up. 'Tell her she is welcome at Kirkleigh at any time. As are you, sir, as long as you leave your opinions at the gate!'

Chapter Fourteen

'Oh, dear, I cannot make head nor tail of this letter.'

Mrs Wythenshawe passed the paper to her sister. 'Jane, dear, you must read it and tell me what you think of it.'

Aunt Jane coughed and put the letter in her lap.

'Well, it is from a London lawyer.' She cleaned her spectacles and settled them back more firmly on her nose. 'I do not claim to understand every word of it, but it says there is an annuity due to the widow of Mr Walter Charles Wythenshawe.' She looked up, her mouth open in astonishment. 'Three hundred pounds a year!'

Kitty gave a little gasp. Mrs Blackwood had kept her word, but Kitty had not expected her to be so generous.

'And you have no idea who is our mysterious benefactor?' Aunt Jane handed the letter back. 'My dear sister, can you recall no acquaintance of Walter's who would do this, and after all this time, too?'

'No, I can think of no one.' She looked up, her eyes shining. 'We shall be very comfortable now! We shall be able to rent a better house. Kitty will not need to become a governess! And we will not need to take in any more sewing!' Mama gave a little skip as she crossed to the little table beneath the window. 'I shall reply to this immediately, for the lawyer asks me to advise him of the bank I wish to use to receive the money. Oh, dear, how exciting! I am sure I shall not be able to set a stitch today!'

'Then do not, Mama,' Kitty urged her, smiling. 'You should take a holiday.'

'And so I shall, my love, but first we have Miss Blackwood's two gowns to finish. They are promised for tomorrow morning, and no matter how rich we may become, I will not go back on my word!'

It was Kitty's intention to be at home the following day. She wanted to meet Mrs Blackwood and thank her for her generosity, but a sleepless night sapped her courage. To see Daniel's mother again, or his sister, would only reinforce the feelings of desolation and loss that constantly dragged at her spirits. She rose from her bed, determined not to meet them. She would pen a letter to Mrs Blackwood. A much better idea, she decided, since she would be able to choose her words carefully and ensure that her gratitude was properly expressed.

Having made her decision, Kitty dressed quickly and announced that she was going out.

'I am going to see…going to see…' Kitty searched around in her mind for a name. If only her mother had not kept her quite so confined she might have comfortably spent the day with someone in the village, but her mother had never mixed with their neighbours and there was no one Kitty knew well enough to call upon unannounced. She thought with regret of Ann Harworth: by giving up the chance to marry Ann's brother, she had lost her only real friend. The pain of that disappointment gave her an even greater desire to escape. 'I am going to walk over the moors to Coldclough Valley. To collect elderberries.'

'But that is such a long way,' declared her mother. 'It will take you the best part of the day!'

'I know, but all the ripe berries around the village have been picked and the valley is particularly well stocked with elders.'

'But Mrs Blackwood is coming this morning,' protested Aunt Jane. 'Will you not stay to see her? Upon her last visit she showed you such a flattering amount of attention...'

'Then please, make my apologies, Aunt,' said Kitty hastily. 'I am sure you do not need me—indeed, it will be very cramped in here if we all stay. Besides, I fear the weather is going to break and if I don't collect the berries today they may all be ruined.' She picked up her basket. 'Do not be anxious for me, I shall be back before dark!' And with that she whisked herself out of the house.

Kitty hurried out of the village and was soon following the path across the moors. It was such a warm day that she tucked her shawl into her basket. The sun burned through the thin muslin of her gown, warming her shoulders. She loved the empty moors on days such as this when the late August sunshine seemed to acquire an added brilliance, a sudden, flaring reminder that autumn would soon arrive.

By the time Coldclough Valley was in sight she was hot and flushed with her exertion, but her spirits had risen considerably. Perhaps the future was not quite so bleak after all, and although her spirit balked at taking charity from Mrs Blackwood, she could not deny that the annuity settled upon her mother would make life considerably easier.

'And Mrs Blackwood was very right,' she told herself, coming to a halt on the path. 'We would not have been in this situation if I had never met her son. Horrid, horrid man!'

As she tilted her face up to catch the sun a sudden movement attracted her eye and she looked back the way she had come. There in the distance was the small black shape of a horse and rider. Kitty gasped.

'It could be anyone,' she muttered, trying to calm her racing heart.

She blinked and rubbed her hand across her eyes. The figure was too far away to pick out any detail, but instinct told her it was Daniel. The big black horse, the upright figure—it *had* to be Daniel. As she stared, the rider changed course and began to move more quickly. He was heading in her direction.

'Oh, heavens!'

She picked up her skirts and ran towards the clough. He was such a long way behind her, she only had to reach the wooded valley and she might be able to evade him. She reached the ridge and hurried down the path into the valley, allowing her pace to slow a little once she was sure Daniel could no longer see her. She was dismayed to see how far she would have to walk before she reached the woods, but there was no choice: the river cutting through the valley bottom might be small but it was very deep and it effectively blocked her path. She must go either up or downstream. She chose to head towards the woods. She half-ran, half-scrambled down the bank, thankful that the ground beside the tumbling waters was covered with a short, springy turf that allowed her to make good progress.

But not good enough. All too soon she saw Daniel on the ridge above her. She began to run, but he urged his horse to descend the shallow bank diagonally to cut her off. She heard the jingle of harness and the thud of hooves. Speed was useless. Kitty slowed again to a walk, turning to glare at Daniel.

'How did you find me?' she called out.

'Your mother described to me the path you had taken. You have her eyes, you know: a beautiful moss green. She is a most delightful woman: I left her taking tea with Bella and my own mother. I think they will get on very well.'

Kitty refused to be pleased.

'I do not want to talk to you. Pray go away.'

'But I want to talk to *you*.'

'There is nothing to say!'

'But there is. Kitty, listen to me—'

'Go away!' she cried. 'How dare you come here and—and torture me like this! I told you I would have nothing more to do with you.'

'But I am a free man—Ann and I are no longer engaged.'

'So you have broken her heart, too!'

'No, it was—! Kitty, hell and damnation, *will* you stand still for a moment!' He jumped down from his horse and came towards her.

'No!' Kitty stopped, putting up her hand as if to hold him off. 'Do not come any nearer. If you do I will…I will jump in the beck!'

His lips twitched. It pierced her heart to remember how much she loved his smile.

'That would be a little extreme, don't you think?'

'No!' she retorted angrily. 'You have b-brought me nothing but pain: I would walk through *fire* rather than talk to you again!'

That wiped the smile from his face, but his consternation cut even deeper into her heart.

'I did not cry off, Kitty, you have my word on it. You see—'

She said quickly, 'I made a solemn vow that I was done with you for ever, so whatever tricks you used to force Ann to jilt you they are wasted! I will not have anything more to do with you!'

She began to move again, hurrying along the riverbank. For a short while she thought Daniel had stopped following her, but a quick glance behind showed that he had merely paused to remove his coat and throw it over the saddle.

'Do you know, it is far too hot for so much exertion. I wish you would slow down.'

He spoke in a conversational tone, as if they were enjoying a gentle stroll together. Anger was warring with frustration in Kitty. How dare he torment her in this way? Ahead she could see a bridge across the stream, a series of flat stone slabs supported on boulders in the stream bed. If she could cross that, the path wound up past a small cottage where a wisp of smoke trailed from the chimney. Perhaps the owner would allow her to rest inside and shut the door upon Daniel.

'Kitty, will you please stop and allow me to explain!' He reached for her and she sprinted away from him.

'Go away, Daniel. Go away and leave me in peace!'

She had reached the bridge. Gingerly she stepped on to the first slab. It wobbled slightly beneath her. A few more steps took her to the centre, but Daniel had caught up with her. His hand shot out and gripped her arm, stopping her in her tracks. She tried to shake him off.

'How dare you touch me? Let me go this instant, you... you fiend!'

'I will let you go, if you promise to listen to me and to stop acting like some angry fishwife!' Kitty froze, furious at his insult. He was scowling down at her, his chest heaving. 'Well,' he said at last. 'If I let you go will you promise not to run away?'

'Yes.' The word forced itself out between her clenched teeth.

He nodded and released her arm. Kitty glared at him as he stood beside her on the narrow bridge. Every slight, every insult she had suffered at his hands returning to her mind, magnified tenfold. Deliberately, she put her hands against his chest and pushed.

If Daniel had not been about to step away from her it would never have happened, but he was momentarily distracted and Kitty's push caught him off balance. He twisted, his arms thrown wide as he toppled into the river. Kitty watched in a mixture of horror and fascination as he disappeared beneath the water, only to surface a few moments' later, coughing and spluttering. He rose to his feet, standing thigh-deep in the fast-flowing water.

Kitty's hands flew to her mouth. A fleeting, sickening dread that he might have been seriously hurt on the stony river bed was replaced with fear for her own safety as he stood braced against the current, glaring up at her through the heavy curtain of wet black hair that clung to his forehead. She swallowed, transported back to their very first meeting, when she had addressed him as a servant and he had scowled at her so blackly that she had been afraid he would drag her from the gig and strangle her. That fear of reprisals returned to her now. Then, to her astonishment, she saw the gleam of amusement in his eyes. He threw back his head and laughed. A deep, rich sound that drew a reluctant smile from her in response.

'*Touché,* madam! No doubt you think that a sweet justice.' He grinned up at her. 'Do you consider yourself revenged now for my dropping you in that muddy ford?'

'Well, yes,' she replied frankly. 'I do!'

She reached down her hand to him, but as soon as his

fingers curled around hers he gave a tug and she toppled off the bridge, landing with a splash in the water beside him.

'Oh! Oh, you...you...!' She spluttered and coughed as he pulled her to her feet beside him.

'You did not think I would let you get away with that, did you?'

Kitty put up her hands to wipe the wet hair from her eyes, a furious retort rising to her lips, but it died when she saw him laughing down at her. A gurgle of laughter bubbled up inside her and instead of pushing Daniel away she found herself clinging to his arm, giggling helplessly.

Still laughing, they struggled to the bank and dragged themselves out, lying side by side on the short grass. Daniel reached for her hand.

'I did not cry off from my engagement,' he said, suddenly serious. 'Neither did Ann. It was her brother who withdrew his consent.'

She sat up.

'Lord Harworth? Why should he do that—oh, poor Ann!'

'He objected to my liberal views. And you must not think Ann was heartbroken, I suspect she was as relieved as I was to be released from the engagement. She is thinking of marrying Leaconham.'

'Garston!' Kitty stared at him, astounded. 'How could she prefer Garston to...?'

'I am only too thankful that she does prefer him,' retorted Daniel, pulling her down to him. 'But that is not important now. What is important is that I am free.' He reached up a hand and cupped her face, her wet hair clinging around his fingers. 'Since neither Ann nor I cried off, you are not bound to refuse me.' He gently pulled her face down and kissed her. 'I love you, Kitty,' he whispered. 'Say yes. Say you will marry me.'

'Oh, Daniel!' Kitty stopped, unable to say more because of the constriction in her throat. Silently she nodded and with an exultant gasp Daniel pulled her back into his arms, rolling her beneath him as he covered her face with hot kisses.

'Kitty, you are crying.' He broke away. 'Dearest, what is it?

She sat up, shaking her head.

'N-nothing,' she managed, smiling mistily through her tears. 'It is j-just that I am s-so happy!' The salty tears on her cheeks were hot and made her aware of her wet gown, which was rapidly cooling. 'We must move, and quickly,' she said, struggling to get up. 'It will not do to grow chilled.'

'We will call at the cottage,' said Daniel, scrambling to his feet and nodding towards the little house at the top of the bank.

'Your horse is still on the other side,' she remarked.

Daniel gave a long whistle.

'Marnie, come on, girl! Come!' With a toss of her fine head the black mare stepped up to the bridge and daintily trotted across. 'Horses are like women,' he said, mischief glinting in his eyes. 'Better when they are well trained.'

With a laugh he dodged the blow she aimed at him. Then, as she began to pummel him he caught her wrists and whipped her hands behind her back, pulling her against him and kissing her soundly.

'How on earth am I to quarrel with you,' she said severely, when at last she could speak again, 'when you take such advantage of me?'

'I do not want us to quarrel,' he said, lightly kissing the end of her nose. 'I want only to make you happy for ever more.' He put his arm about her waist. 'Shall you walk up the bank or would you like me to put you up on Marnie?'

'Walk, I think. The exertion will warm us.'

With Daniel's arm around her they started up the bank. An old woman in a grey dress hurried down towards them, trailing a large shawl from one hand.

'Oh, my goodness, whatever has happened to you?' She demanded as she drew closer. 'Oh, my poor dears, took a tumble in the beck, did you? You must come in and dry yourselves. Quickly now.' She wrapped the shawl around Kitty's shoulders and took her arm to hurry her towards the cottage.

'Thank you, mother,' said Daniel, falling into step beside them. 'We saw the smoke from your chimney and were going to ask if we could warm ourselves by your fire.'

'Aye, of course. And you're very lucky that I have kept it in, only I fancied a drop o' soup before settin' off for t'village. It won't take a minute to get it blazing again.' When they reached the small gate in the wall that bounded her garden the old woman turned to Daniel. 'You can tie that great brute of a horse to the gate. No one will take him while you and your lady are indoors, and I don't want 'im eatin' my herbs!'

Meekly Daniel did as he was bid while the old woman led Kitty into the house. After the bright sunshine the room seemed very dark at first, but Kitty's eyes soon grew accustomed and she saw that they were standing in a small but very tidy chamber, most of the space being taken up by a large spinning wheel. The room was bare of comforts save for a small cushioned settle and a colourful rag rug before the fire. The old woman immediately set to work stirring up the coals before taking a few small logs from the basket to place on the top.

'Please, mother, do not use all your fuel for us,' said Daniel quickly.

The old woman waved aside his protest.

'Lord love ye, sir, if ye don't get warm you'll be catching your death, right enough. Besides, my son Jack brought me over a sack o' coal only last week, so we're not short o' fuel.' She pointed to a door behind them. 'Beyond there is my bedroom, sir. If you and your lady will remove thy wet things I'll hang 'em out to dry. An hour or so in the sun and with this breeze they'll be good as new. And don't you be afraid to give me your shirt and britches, young man: I have sons of my own, so you've nowt I haven't seen before!'

Kitty was aware of Daniel's eyes upon her, but she said nothing. She walked into the bedchamber and began to struggle out of her sodden gown.

'She thinks we are man and wife,' muttered Daniel, following her into the room.

'I know.'

He pulled a ring from his little finger and held it out to her.

'Here, wear this. I would not embarrass the woman by having her guess the truth.' He picked up Kitty's hand and slipped the ring on to her wedding finger. 'I hope you will allow me to replace it with the real thing soon enough.'

Kitty's cheeks burned and she turned away, giving her attention to removing her wet clothes. She stripped down to her shift and looked round for the woman's shawl to put over her shoulders but Daniel had already appropriated it to wrap around his waist, his clothes lying in a wet puddle on the stone floor. She held her breath, unable to tear her eyes from his naked torso. He seemed to fill the little room; his broad shoulders and muscled arms still glistened with damp and she was shocked by her desire to put out her hand and touch the black curling hair on his chest.

'We, um...' She swallowed, not meeting his eyes. 'We should ask our hostess if she has a towel we may use to finish drying ourselves.'

'Just a moment.' He picked up a thin coverlet from the bed, folded it diagonally and threw it over her shoulders. 'There. Do you feel more comfortable now?'

Daniel was smiling at her, and Kitty wondered if he knew that it was not standing before him in her shift that was unsettling her but her desire to feast her eyes upon his body. Quickly she scooped up their clothes and carried them into the other room. The old woman took them from her.

'You leave these to me, my dear, and sit yerself down in front o'fire until you are dry again.' She gave a little chuckle when Daniel walked in and she saw the use he had made of her shawl but she said nothing and hurried away to hang out their clothes.

'You have not yet given me an answer,' said Daniel, sitting down beside Kitty on the narrow settle beside the fire.

'An...an answer?'

'You have not said that you will marry me.'

'After this I do not think we have a choice, sir,' she said, trying to speak lightly.

'No!' Angrily he gripped her arms, turning her to face him. 'I do not want you forced by circumstances to become my wife. I want you to choose me—*me,* Kitty, do you understand? For better or worse, richer or poorer. It must be your decision, freely made. If you are not sure then I will remove myself from your presence until we are fit to return to Fallridge—'

'That will not be necessary,' she said quickly. 'I w-want nothing better than to be your wife, Daniel.' She added quietly, 'For no other reason than that I love you, with all my heart.'

She smiled, her spirits soaring when she saw the glow of delight in his eyes.

His hands tightened and he was about to drag her into his arms when the old lady came bustling in again.

'An hour, two at the most, and your clothes will be dry.' She hesitated, took a couple of steps towards the fire, then stopped again.

'Thank you, mother, but do not let us keep you from your work, if you have spinning to do...'

'Ah, well, you see I hadn't finished my spinning when Mr Jobbins called first thing this morning.' She pointed to a large cloth bag beside the door. 'I said I would take 'em on t'village as soon as they was done. I get paid by the hank, you see—in a good week I can make five shillings or more, but what with Jack comin' round yesterday, and bringin' the bairns to see me—well, they're bonny children, to be sure, but I got behind...'

'Oh, please, if you have to go out then we will leave,' said Kitty rising.

The old woman waved her back into her seat.

'That you won't. You are quite welcome to stay here while I go out. I was planning to spend the night with our Jack, so you can stay here as long as you wish.'

'Thank you, mother,' said Daniel. 'You may be sure we will lock up behind us.'

The old woman gave a cackle of laughter.

'Bless you, sir, there's no need for that.' She held out her hands and looked around. 'There's nothing here worth the trouble o' stealing. And besides it's rare that anyone passes this way. No, my dears, you sit there as long as you want, there'll be no one to bother ye. You'll find a bit o' broth in the kettle by the fire: you're welcome to that and if you want water the pump is just outside the door,' She gave another toothless cackle. 'Although I'd say you'd both had enough water today! Well, I'll bid you good day then.'

She picked up her bundle.

'Goodbye, mistress, and thank you!' called Kitty.

The woman gave them a final wave and went out, closing the door behind her.

Silence settled around them. Daniel looked down at his bare feet, suddenly feeling awkward. What was he doing here, sitting near-naked in a spinster's cottage? A glance at Kitty showed him that she, too, was uneasy.

'What a good soul,' she said with forced brightness. 'And trusting, to leave us here alone.'

'She saw the quality of our clothes. She knows we are not vagabonds.' Eager for a distraction, Daniel moved over to the fire and poked at the logs until they were blazing merrily. He glanced back at Kitty. 'Your hair is still wet. Will you sit a little closer to the fire?'

'Yes, please.' Kitty rose and rubbed her arms as Daniel tried to move the settle, which creaked alarmingly. She laughed. 'I think we should leave it where it is. I am afraid if we move it from the wall it will fall apart. But I have an idea!'

Daniel watched her pull the cushions from the settle and put them on the rug in front of the fire. Then she knelt down with her back to the fire, shaking her hair loose. His breath caught in his throat as he watched it ripple down her back like a dark waterfall. Daniel quickly turned away, knowing the shawl wrapped around his hips would not conceal his desire from her.

'Daniel, will you not sit beside me?'

She spoke softly but he heard the wistfulness in her voice. He dropped down on to the rug behind her and put his hand to her hair, allowing the dark tresses to flow through his fingers like silk. With a sigh she tilted back her head and rested against him, her eyes closed. It was irresistible: Daniel leaned forward to place a gentle kiss on the slim column of her neck. Her hand came up to his cheek. She twisted round to face him, her mouth seeking his. Daniel had intended nothing more than a tender kiss but as soon as their lips met she trembled against him and a ripple of excitement flowed between them as her lips parted and their tongues engaged in a sensuous, silent conversation. He wrapped her in his arms and eased her down on to the rug. She clung to him. The firm swell of her breasts pressed against his chest, only the thin fabric of her shift between them. He raised his head, trying to contain his excitement, then he began to kiss her again, his lips caressing her eyes, her cheeks. He trailed his tongue along her jaw and lightly over her neck. His fingers clenched on the folds of the shift. He wanted to remove it, since it was the last barrier between his body and Kitty's soft white skin. She struggled beneath him and immediately he pushed himself away from her, determined that he would in no way force his will upon her.

Kitty sat up. The cottage was silent save for the fire crackling behind her and Daniel's ragged breathing. Keeping her eyes fixed on his face, she crossed her arms in front of her and took hold of the shift, lifting it cleanly away and upwards in one smooth movement. As she raised her arms above her head Daniel reached out for her. She gasped. Her arms and head were temporarily imprisoned in the fine linen, leaving Daniel free to plunder her breasts, cupping them in his hands, burying his face between them before fastening his mouth on one tender bud and causing a shaft of white-hot desire to drive through her. She threw off the offending material and reached for him, driving her fingers through his hair, clasping him to her as she fell back against the cushions. She had no control over her body. It arched and moved against him, inviting his hands to caress her. She moaned with pleasure as his fingers traced a line from the inside of her knee and along her thigh, gasping as those same fingers moved into her and roused her to even higher realms of delight. His fingers caressed effortlessly, she was slick with desire, opening for him, raising her hips in blatant invitation. In one swift move he rolled over her and she felt his aroused body pressed against her. His hands slid under her hips, lifting her up to receive him. Kitty clung to him, her fingers digging into his back as he entered her. A tiny gasp, a tiny pain, then the joy and exhilaration of their union overwhelmed her. She tried to follow his lead, moving with him, a fierce excitement coursing through every part of her body. She was flying, soaring, her senses on fire as they moved together. She was vaguely aware that Daniel was holding himself in check, moving for her pleasure rather than his own, but she could do nothing about it, for he was lifting her to such a height of pleasure that she was helpless beneath him, crying out as her body exploded. Deep within her, muscles were clenching in spasm and with an almost painful pleasure. She clung to Daniel, whispering his name, knowing they were still joined. He held her safe in his arms as her body relaxed against his, a perfect fit. She was filled with a pleasant torpor with Daniel's hands gently caressing her body. Then he was kissing her, feather-light touches along her neck, fanning the flames of desire until her body began to pulse again. This time she pushed against him, revelling in her power to make him gasp and moan with delight. She quivered as he took her once more to the peak of excitement and this time he was with her, pushing, tensing and crying out as they soared together before falling back to earth, clinging to one another.

* * *

They lay before the fire, wrapped in each other's arms, while the sun moved across the sky.

'We must get back,' murmured Kitty.

'Soon.' Daniel nibbled at her ear.

Kitty gave a little gasp and struggled to sit up.

'We will be missed,' she said urgently. 'Your mother will be waiting...'

'No, we agreed she would take Bella home. I told her it might take me some time to...persuade you.'

Kitty turned to look at him. He was lying naked beside her, reminding her of the statues displayed in many of the grand houses she had visited with her godmother, although there was nothing cold or lifeless about Daniel. She reached out to touch him, her fingers splaying through the crisp black hair of his chest.

'And...was I difficult to persuade?'

'Very.' With a growl Daniel pulled her back into his arms. 'I am not convinced I have yet succeeded.'

They made love again and this time it was even more delightful as they explored new ways to please each other as their naked bodies tangled together. Later they took great pleasure in dressing each other, with much laughter and fevered kisses until at last they were ready to leave the little cottage. Daniel dropped a handful of coins in a cup on the hearth.

'I would give her ten times as much if I had it on me,' he declared, grinning. 'The old mother has secured a wife for me.' He caught Kitty up in his arms and kissed her. 'You must marry me now, you shameless wench!'

She wound her arms about his neck and kissed him back fiercely until with a groan he put his hands on her waist and put her away from him.

'If you do not behave I will have to take you again,' he muttered. 'Come along, we'll walk to the top of the clough, then Marnie will carry us both home.'

'I fear we will be very late,' remarked Kitty. 'And I was supposed to be collecting elderberries. What shall I tell Mama?'

'We will tell her the truth, that you lost your basket in the beck.'

'And my shawl, too! Oh dear, she will be so vexed with me!'

With a low laugh Daniel turned her to face him, catching her face between her hands.

'I doubt she will give your shawl a thought when we tell her that you are going to be married!'

It was growing dark as they rode over the moor, Kitty sitting across the saddle in front of Daniel, enveloped in his arms. The sun had disappeared below the horizon and the first stars twinkled in the sky. Daniel lowered his head to rest his cheek briefly on her curls.

'Happy?' he murmured.

'Mmmm.'

He reached for her left hand and raised it to his lips, kissing the finger that bore the little ring he had given her.

'Tomorrow I shall buy you a diamond ring. The best I can find.'

'Not too big,' she protested. 'I should be afraid of losing it, and I want to wear it, always.'

'If you lose it I shall buy you another,' he said grandly. 'And you must have emeralds to replace the ones you left behind at Kirkleigh.'

Kitty shook her head. 'Those jewels were never mine. They were intended for the next Lady Harworth.' She wrapped her arms around him and snuggled closer. 'I am so relieved it will not be me.'

'You are not sorry, then, to be marrying a mere tradesman?'

She chuckled.

'I am not, but I fear Mama might be disappointed.'

'I have news that may be of some consolation to her.'

She sat up.

'News?'

He grinned at her.

'My father is to become a baronet. He will be Sir Samuel Blackwood.'

'Oh, Daniel, how wonderful! How long have you known of this?'

'Since I left London. I had several meetings in Whitehall while I was there, you see. My father has been helping Pitt with, ah, shall we say, financial support. The baronetcy is by way of a reward. And as it is hereditary, you will become a lady after all!'

She hugged him.

'You are right. Mama will be delighted.'

'And you are not?'

'It does not matter to me at all. I only want to be your wife, Daniel.'

He brought Marnie to a halt.

'Are you sure, Kitty?'

'Perfectly sure.'

He cupped her face and kissed her.

'I love you, Kitty Wythenshawe.'

'To think we almost lost each other.' She put her arms around him, resting her head on his shoulder, gazing up at the darkening sky.

'I am afraid if it had not been for me you could have

married your baron,' he said ruefully. 'I will do my best to make sure you never regret it.'

She looked up at him, her eyes shining softly.

'You told me once I was trying to catch the moon, do you remember? What I have now is so much better, Daniel. I have your love: I have the stars.'

* * * * *

The Wicked Baron

SARAH MALLORY

Prologue

'Hell and confound it, Darvell, will you stop flirting with that lightskirt and give your mind to the cards!'

Luke Ainslowe, fifth Baron Darvell, gently disentangled himself from the lady's scented embrace and begged pardon. There were few amusements for the Army of Occupation in Paris, following the stunning victory at Waterloo: women and cards were two of the most popular and Luke was currently enjoying both. He looked at the eager, wine-flushed faces of the gentlemen around him and smiled. They all envied him, he knew, for he was sitting beside the most fashionable courtesan in Paris, the improbably named Angelique Pompadour. She leaned against him, her powdered head on his shoulder while he studied the cards in his hand.

Across the table, the officer of the Light Dragoons who had berated Luke made his discard and glanced up, his silver epaulettes glinting in the candlelight.

'I hear von Laage's wife is increasing again—she holds that you are the father, Darvell.'

Luke shrugged. 'Lady Sophia is air-dreaming, Denby.

There are at least half a dozen men more eligible than I for that role.'

'Why, then, is the lady naming you?' demanded another of the players.

A red-faced gentlemen in grey satin laughed.

'Because Darvell is the only one von Laage would not dare to call out! Well known to be lethal with swords or pistols. Never beaten in a duel, eh, Luke?'

'Not yet, Clayman, not yet.'

'So you are telling me you were never one of Lady Sophia's lovers?' cried Major Denby.

Luke shook his head. 'We had a few preliminary skirmishes, but I never breached that particular citadel. I discovered the lady was far too free with her favours.'

Sir Neville Clayman chuckled. 'A man needs to be very rich to keep an exclusive mistress, and that is not you, eh, Darvell?'

Luke grinned. 'Devil a bit!'

There was a pause while Sir Neville considered his hand. 'But you have a title, and that is certainly an advantage. I believe le Brun's widow is hoping to become the next Lady Darvell.'

Angelique raised her head. *'Mon cher...'* she pouted and placed one white hand upon Luke's velvet sleeve *'...c'est vrai?'*

Sir Neville nodded. 'Had it from the lady herself two nights' since.'

'But you have not had it from *me*,' said Luke gently. He picked up Angelique's hand and planted a kiss in the palm before releasing it. 'The woman is an upstart. Her beauty dazzled le Brun, but there is no breeding behind that pretty face.'

'If it's breeding you want, the Tregennick chit has it through several generations,' remarked the major, 'yet you cut her dead last night. She was mad as fire.'

Luke flicked a speck of dust from his sleeve. 'Her mama insisted upon throwing her in my way at Lady Gressingham's rout. I obliged her with an evening's flirtation, that is all.'

'And you could not even recall her name the very next night.' Major Denby shook his head at him. 'By Gad, you are devil, man! No woman is safe from you.'

'Nonsense. Virtuous maidens bore me, so they have nothing to fear. And you will never find me chasing innocent little *ingénues*. But a man must have a diversion now the war is over. Mine is beautiful women.'

'Yet you'll offer none of them your heart and your hand.'

'There is no room for sentiment in marriage, Denby. When I take a wife, it will be a business contract. My father gambled away the Darvell fortune; it is up to me to restore it by marrying a well-bred heiress. But not yet.' He stared at the cards Sir Neville laid on the table and muttered a laughing curse under his breath. 'Two kings! Damnation, Clayman, your luck is running high tonight. I am out.'

Angelique smiled at him. 'Well, my lord, it was agreed if you lost at cards you would worship at my feet.' She spoke in English, a charming, provocative lilt to her words. With the light of mischief in his eyes Luke reached down, curled his fingers around one slim ankle and lifted her foot on to his knee. A murmur of anticipation ran around the room, while the lady herself leaned back on her chair and smiled.

'Well, milor'? What do you propose? What will the wicked Baron Darvell do?'

He grinned. 'I will keep my word.'

His hand moved over the pink silk stocking and she

shivered delightfully when he reached the ribbon-and-lace garter at her knee. He hesitated, then his long fingers moved back to her ankle. He began to untie the strings of her pink satin slipper, calling to the waiter to bring another bottle of champagne.

'Now what are you about, Darvell?' cried Major Denby gaily. 'Do you propose to undress the lady in public?'

'Not at all, my friend. Patience and you shall see.' He pulled the little shoe free and held it aloft, the ribbons dangling over his wrist. When the waiter returned with the champagne he took the bottle from the tray. 'I wish to drink a toast to you, Angel.' He poured a little of the wine into the shoe and quickly raised it to his lips.

'You fool, Darvell, the satin won't hold it!' laughed Sir Neville.

But Luke was not listening; he had swallowed some of the champagne, the rest was seeping through the slipper and running over his hand, soaking the white ruffle around his wrist.

'It held enough,' he said. 'And witness, Angel, that none of the bubbles escaped—I drank them all.'

Angelique sat up and clapped her hands. 'Bravo, milor', I am enchanted. But we should use glasses for the rest.' She looked at him, an invitation in her dark eyes. 'Per'aps you would like to drink with me privately?'

'I regret not, Angel. I am obliged to leave you very soon.' He filled two glasses with champagne and handed one to the lady. 'I am off to England tomorrow.'

'England!' cried Major Denby, signalling for a fresh pack of cards. 'Never tell me you are going home.'

'I am indeed. Peacetime soldiering is not in my line. I have spent one winter in Paris and that is enough.'

'He's going back to Darvell Manor to become a gentleman farmer,' declared Sir Neville, smoothing the wrinkles from the sleeve of his grey silk coat.

Luke grimaced. 'Devil a bit! I plan to enjoy myself for a few more years yet. But I have a fancy to see England again. Besides, I have a commission from my brother. You may recall he was in Paris last month. He is touring Europe with his bride until the summer and wants me to make sure his new house at Malberry is ready for his return.'

'Ah, the fortunate James,' nodded Sir Nicholas. 'He married his heiress.'

'Fortunate indeed,' agreed Luke. 'Not only is she rich, but pretty and agreeable, too.'

'Perhaps you should try marriage, Darvell,' suggested the major.

'I think not, my friend. It would take a paragon indeed to make me give up my freedom.'

Angelique drew a finger gently along his cheek. 'Milor', it is not necessary that you should give up *everything*.'

For a moment he looked serious. 'Oh, yes, it is. Only a deep, long-lasting devotion could tempt me into matrimony.'

'And what would tempt the lady, his prowess in the bedroom, perhaps?' quipped an officer in scarlet regimentals.

'That and his title,' responded another.

Luke joined in the general laughter. 'Aye, that would have to do it, gentlemen, since there's no fortune to speak of.'

Angelique held up her glass. 'Then you will come back to Paris, *mon cher*?'

'Perhaps.' He handed her the wet satin slipper. 'It is past midnight: I must take my leave.'

Chapter One

The atmosphere in the morning room of Broxted House was decidedly tense. Carlotta stared at her uncle, her chin raised and a hint of defiance in her dark eyes. Lord Broxted met her look with a frown of exasperation.

'Carlotta, you are no ordinary débutante. It is no matter that your mother is the daughter of an earl; twenty years ago she eloped with a penniless Italian artist.' He paused and a faint look of distaste flickered across his aristocratic features. 'They both of them…*paint*…to earn their living.'

Carlotta clasped her hands even more tightly in her lap. 'I am not ashamed of my parents, Uncle.'

Lady Broxted, sitting beside Carlotta on the elegant little sofa, reached over to pat her hands. 'No, of course you are not, my dear, and no one is suggesting that you should disown them, only…'

'Only what, Aunt?'

Lady Broxted avoided Carlotta's eyes and fluttered her fan nervously. 'Tonight we attend Lady Prestbury's rout— your very first *ton* party. It is what we have been working for, is it not, ever since we carried you off from Malberry last June and installed you in Miss Currier's extremely select seminary? Not that I think it was necessary to send you there; no one would know you were brought up in Rome, for the English governess your mama employed gave you an excellent education, and all that was needed was a little polish—but there, your uncle was adamant.'

'I was, madam, but I fear we are straying from the point,' put in the earl, frowning at his wife.

'Yes, of course, my dear. Carlotta, now we are in London and…that is, I think it might be best if…'

Lady Broxted twisted her hands together, looking very uncomfortable.

Carlotta prompted her gently. 'If what, Aunt?'

'Well, as you know, we decided at the outset that you should take the family name of Rivington—so much simpler for us all, my love, and *quite* usual when one is taken up by relatives—but perhaps also it would be as well if we did not mention your parents. Broxted thinks it best if we merely say they live retired in the country, should anyone ask.'

'And is it the fact that my mother eloped or my father's occupation that would be most unacceptable?' retorted Carlotta, bridling.

'Well, you will admit that either of those things would set tongues wagging,' came the frank reply. 'Any hint of gossip could be quite *ruinous* to your chances of making a good match. Not that I want you to lie,' added Lady Broxted hastily. 'That would never do. Merely that you do not *offer* the information.'

'Should a gentleman show a marked interest in you, then of course it would be necessary for him to know the truth,' put in Lord Broxted. 'And if he is fond of you, then I am sure it will make no difference.'

Carlotta bit her tongue to prevent herself from saying she did not care what anyone said of her. After the kindness she had been shown by her aunt and uncle over the past year, it would be churlish in the extreme to admit how little she cared for anyone's good opinion. Part of her wished she could return to her parents, but they had been so happy to think of her going into society and making a good marriage. It was what she must do to repay all their goodness to her.

She had been in London with Lord and Lady Broxted since the beginning of May; a flurry of shopping trips and visits to my lady's dressmaker had filled her days and at last she was ready to attend her first ball. She only wished she could summon up more enthusiasm for it, but her depression was always there, just below the surface. A sadness she had tried to hard to overcome, but even now, after almost twelve months, her dreams were still haunted by a tall, handsome man with laughing, wicked eyes. Determination kept her smiling, made her hide her bleakness from her aunt and uncle. Lady Broxted was patting her hands.

'I cannot tell you how much I am looking forward to launching you into society, my love. It has been a constant sadness to Broxted and me that we did not have children and so it is doubly delightful that I have you with me now.'

Lady Broxted began hunting for her handkerchief. Lord Broxted drew out his own and handed it to her, saying as he did so, 'We are indeed delighted to take you up, Carlotta. It is the least I can do for your poor mother. When my father disinherited her upon her marriage I was shocked, but powerless to help. Then, of course, we lost touch for so many years, but now, I believe it is in my power to reinstate you into your proper place in the world.'

In the face of such kindness Carlotta's anger died away as quickly as it had come. Impulsively she hugged her aunt.

'There, there, Aunt, pray do not cry—if it is your wish, then of course I shall tell no one about my parents. Let us go upstairs and you can advise me which one of my new gowns I should wear this evening.'

In an effort to give her aunt's thoughts a more cheerful turn, Carlotta accompanied her aunt up to her bedchamber where the maid quickly brought out several of Carlotta's new gowns for inspection. Lady Broxted discarded the pink muslin with apple-green acanthus leaves embroidered around the hem, declaring that almost every other young lady would be wearing pink. Her hand hovered over the lemon satin before settling on the white sprigged muslin.

'This is perfect for your first appearance,' she said. 'You have too much of the Italian in you to appear as a typical English rose, but we must turn that to our advantage—the white muslin will accentuate your olive skin. Thank goodness you have such a flawless complexion, my love, for that means we can leave your lovely shoulders bare. My own woman shall have the dressing of your hair; when it is brushed it glows like polished mahogany and you shall have tiny white rosebuds amongst your curls. It is early for roses, I know, but the cost will be worth it and I shall have a small posy made up for your corsage, too. What do you say?'

Carlotta could not deny a small *frisson* of excitement at the picture her aunt had drawn. When she had been a child growing up in Rome she had never dreamed that one day she would be staying in one of the largest houses in Berkeley Square, preparing to attend a fashionable ball. The gown her aunt was holding up to her was of the finest muslin, embroidered all over with tiny exquisite white rosebuds. The tiny puff sleeves were gathered and fastened with satin ribbons and a wider satin band ran around the high waist. Little Carlotta running barefoot in her father's studio had never imagined owning white satin slippers with leather soles so fine that they would be worn through after one outing, but such a pair was now lying in a drawer, wrapped in several layers of tissue paper. Carlotta smiled at her aunt.

'I will look like a fairy princess,' she murmured.

Lady Broxted handed the gown to her maid and caught Carlotta to her in a warm, scented embrace.

'You will indeed, my love,' she murmured, her voice breaking. 'You will make us all so very proud of you.'

Luke glanced up at the imposing entrance of Prestbury House. Flambeaux burned on each side of the double doors and liveried servants were on hand to assist the ladies from their carriages and escort them up the shallow steps to the grand entrance hall with its soaring marbled pillars. Letitia Prestbury was a formidable hostess and invitations to her fashionable parties were jealously guarded. Luke had no gilt-edged card nestling in his pocket, but he was confident he would not be turned away. Giving his coat sleeves an infinitesimal tug, he joined the long line of guests processing up the grand staircase. From the reception rooms above came the sound of many voices intermingled with the scraping notes of several violins. No lone fiddler or squeaky quartet for Lady Prestbury—her guests would dance to the best musicians money could buy.

As he reached the top of the stairs he found his hostess waiting for him, smiling.

'Well, Cousin, we are honoured to have you attend our little party.'

He bowed over her hand. 'I promised you I would come.'

'But you are so often enticed away by more exciting pleasures, are you not?' She laughed at him. 'I did not send you an invitation because I thought my society gatherings far too staid for the Wicked Baron!'

He grinned at her. 'Perhaps I have reformed. It is not impossible, Letty.'

She twinkled up at him. 'True, Luke, but it is highly unlikely! I know just what it is that has brought you here.'

'You do?'

'Aye, 'tis curiosity, to see the latest heiress.'

He looked down so that she would not read the truth in his eyes. 'Oh?' he said lightly, brushing an invisible speck from his coat. 'And who might that be, my lady?'

'You know very well,' she said, tapping his arm with her closed fan. 'Broxted's niece, Miss Rivington. We were all agog when we heard he was bringing her to town, and he has settled ten thousand pounds on the chit! If that wasn't enough to make her a target for every young man in town, the girl is a positive beauty. But be warned, Luke, she is not for you: I have it from the countess herself that Broxted has great plans for his niece. He will be looking higher than a mere baron.'

'And so he should, but that is no reason why I should not make her acquaintance.'

'Very well, go on in with you.' Lady Prestbury waved him away. 'But you are wasting your time, Cousin.'

With another graceful bow Luke moved on. So it was already decided that the beautiful Miss Rivington was not for him; well, perhaps society's latest débutante might think differently. He walked into the ballroom and paused near the doorway, looking around him. Lounging against one wall were several callow youths standing with their mouths open as they watched the couples go down the dance and Luke saw that their eyes were following one dainty figure in particular.

Miss Rivington, he presumed.

His heart missed a beat: he had to admit she was entrancing. Her hair was curled artlessly about her head, adorned with white rosebuds that looked like stars against the night sky of her dark hair. Her white muslin dress flowed around her as she danced, showing her slender figure to great advantage. She was laughing, her huge dark eyes positively twinkling with merriment. No matter the pain it had cost him to ride away from Malberry last September, he knew now he had been right to do so. This was where she belonged, taking her rightful place in society where everyone could admire her beauty. And she looked so happy, smiling and chattering with the other young people as the music ended. He stifled a sigh. He had told himself that she would soon forget him and so it seemed. She looked so natural here, as though she had never known any other life. He was glad for her, truly. He must give her no cause to think he wished it otherwise.

Carlotta's confidence was growing with every dance. Her new sprigged muslin gown was light as air and the admiration of her dance partners was exhilarating. The ballroom was ablaze with light from the gleaming chandeliers. It bounced off the cream-and-blue walls and caused the gold-leaf decoration on the ceiling to glow like the setting sun. With the exception of the occasional blue or scarlet jacket of an officer, the men were dressed in dark coats, but the ladies presented a dazzling picture in an array of colourful gowns, from the bronze and emerald satins of the matrons to the paler shades deemed suitable for débutantes. Carlotta smoothed her hands down over the white muslin and realised what a good choice it had been. Not that she had any opportunity to tell her aunt so, for she had been on the dance floor almost constantly since her arrival.

After a few initial nerves she found that the dance steps came quite naturally and she was even able to take time to glance at the huge gilt-framed mirrors that adorned the walls of the ballroom. She saw herself reflected there, dancing with a series of attentive partners. Carlotta could hardly believe that she was the slender, dark-haired girl reflected in the mirrors, but so it was, and she was content to give herself up to the enjoyment of the moment.

She was so much at her ease that when Lady Broxted brought forward a lanky young man whom she introduced as Viscount Fairbridge, Carlotta gave him a friendly smile. She thought his expression rather vacuous, but she encouraged him to talk to her and soon they were on the best of terms. Truly, she thought, as he led her from the dance floor, it was impossible to be gloomy on such a happy occasion.

During a break in the music she was conversing with a group of lively young people when she heard her aunt's voice behind her.

'Ah, there you are, my love. Do allow me to present Lord Darvell to you.'

And the world stopped for Carlotta. The laughing, chattering crowds were forgotten. She had known this moment would come, had rehearsed it a thousand times, but still she was not prepared for the stomach-wrenching spasm that

threatened to render her senseless when she heard that
name. Of course, she had only known him as Major
Ainslowe, but she had not been living in her aunt's household for many weeks before she learned his full title. Gathering all her strength, she turned and dragged her eyes up
from the white satin waistcoat and dazzling neckcloth to
the face above. The faint hope that it might all be a mistake
withered. The gentleman standing before her was achingly
familiar. She did not need to cast more than a fleeting
glance at his lean, handsome face—it was etched on her
soul. As he bowed over her hand, she looked at the waving
brown hair that curled over his collar. She recalled the
silky feel of it beneath her fingers, tried desperately not to
remember the touch of his lips, not on her glove, but on
her own mouth, caressing, demanding—she thrust such
thoughts away. They had no place in her life now. *He* had
no place in her life now.

  She forced herself to look at him. Could he have forgotten her? No, his glance told her he knew her, but there
was no sign of uncertainty in his hazel eyes as he smiled.
He was so sure of his welcome. How could he be so complacent—did he not know what he had done to her? But
of course he did; she was aware of his reputation now. It
was rumoured that France was littered with women whose
hearts he had broken. A bitter wave of anger and unhappiness swept over her, but her training had been very
good; she buried those feelings and presented him with a
bland, polite mask. Lady Broxted was not aware of their
previous meetings, and Carlotta would not have it known
now. She withdrew her hand from his grasp, saying
coolly, 'My lord.'

  'Miss Rivington.' His self-assurance made her seethe.

He was laughing at her! 'Your aunt tells me you are not engaged for the next dance. I would be honoured if you would allow me to partner you.'

Luke observed the upright little figure before him. By heaven, she was even more beautiful than he remembered: those large dark eyes—just one flashing look sent his heart soaring again—and the soft red lips that had tasted so sweet against his own. Even as his blood stirred Carlotta lowered her gaze and the dark lashes veiled her thoughts from him. She inclined her head, accepting his invitation with every appearance of maidenly modesty and with a polite bow he turned away. This was the game they must play, of course. No one must know that they had met before.

As he walked away from Carlotta, Luke allowed himself to indulge in the pleasant memory of his very first visit to Malberry twelve months earlier. He had not expected to delay his journey to Darvell Manor by more than a few nights, and he had certainly not expected to find such an angel looking down at him from top of the scaffolding that filled the entrance portico.

He had been running up the steps to the main entrance when a soft, musical voice had stopped him in his tracks.

'Excuse me, but you cannot come in here.' The voice had come from above.

'Oh? And why may I not come in?' Luke spoke to the air.

'It is private. This house belongs to a gentleman.'

Luke spread his hands. 'And am I not a gentleman?' A slight movement on the platform close to the ceiling caught his eye and he observed a slight, boyish figure staring down at him.

'Are you the owner?'

'No,' said Luke, 'but I am come on his behalf.'

'Oh. Mr Kemble is not here.'

'So I can see. Where is he?'

'They have all gone to the inn. It is mid-day and they are always hungry by mid-day.'

'But not you?'

'No, I must finish the fresco while the plaster is still wet.'

Luke shielded his eyes, trying to get a better view of the shadowy figure so high above him. 'Are you not a little young?'

'I am eighteen.' The voice grew a shade deeper.

'Come down and let me look at you,' said Luke, intrigued.

'No, sir. I cannot leave my painting.'

'Then I shall come up to you.' Luke put his foot on the ladder and heard a squeak from above. 'Well? Will you come down now?'

'I will, but only for a moment.'

Luke stood back and watched as the figure scrambled onto the top ladder and began to climb down. He grinned. The upper body was shrouded in a loose shirt, but the tight-fitting breeches left nothing to his admittedly rather wild imagination—the figure descending from the scaffolding was most definitely *not* a boy!

Moments later she stood before him, her eyes, large and dark, regarding him with a mixture of defiance and apprehension. She was very petite with a mass of gleaming near-black hair, constrained at the back of her long, slender neck by a poppy-red ribbon. A paint-spattered shirt billowed from her shoulders, but could not disguise the gentle swell of her breasts, and the tight-fitting breeches were worn with a nonchalance that would have done credit to any actress at Drury Lane. He bit back an appreciative smile.

'Well, does my brother know he has hired a lady to decorate his house?'

'You are Mr Ainslowe's brother?'

'I am. And who are you, what is your name?'

'I am Carlotta Durini.' She clasped her hands together. 'Perhaps I should explain.'

'Please do.'

'My—my father is the artist commissioned to paint Malberry Court, but he has broken his leg and—and I am finishing the last frescoes for him, so that the house will be ready on time. Please, sir, you must not think that there is any plot to deceive, but there was no one else to do it, and, if it is not finished in time, Papa will not be paid the full amount, and then Mama cannot have her maid—and it is only this one ceiling—'

Laughing, he reached out and caught her hands.

'Peace, peace, Miss Durini! Do not upset yourself.'

Her hands were very small and soft within his grasp. Smiling, he let his thumbs gently stroke her wrists, just above the palm, and he felt her agitated fingers grow still. Her lustrous dark eyes were still wary, but he detected the beginnings of a shy smile curving her mouth. Luke found himself wondering what it would be like to kiss those soft red lips. His smile deepened; he opened his mouth to charm her with a few well-chosen words, but they were never uttered. The sound of voices drifted in on the still air. He looked out across the park and saw a group of figures emerging from the trees. Something very like disappointment passed over him.

'I think this must be the others returning now. I will talk to Kemble.'

Those dark eyes regarded him anxiously. 'You will not turn me off?'

'I have no power to do so. But if your work is not up to the standard…'

To his surprise, the worried look left the girl's face.

'It will be, sir. I have been well taught.' She stepped back, gently pulling her hands free. 'If you will excuse me, I must go back to my painting; if the plaster becomes too dry, the fresco will be ruined.'

Without another word she scrambled up the ladder and was soon lost to sight. With a sigh, Luke turned to meet the man who was hurrying towards him.

It was natural that Kemble, Mr James Ainslowe's clerk of works, should want to show his employer's brother all the renovations that had been carried out, and to assure him that the work was proceeding as scheduled. However, at length Luke could contain himself no longer.

'Is it now the fashion, Mr Kemble, to employ female painters?'

There was an uncomfortable silence.

'You refer, my lord, to Signor Durini's daughter.' Luke maintained a polite silence, and soon Kemble continued. 'I believe she has been running wild in the *signor*'s workshop since she was a babe, and learned all his techniques. Howsoever that may be, when the *signor*'s apprentice loped off back to Italy, there was no one to take over, and with the master due back in less than three weeks, the *signor* was desperate for his frescoes to be finished. I admit I was not very happy at first, having the chit here, but the *signor* assures me she can paint, sir.'

'But is she not…distracting?'

Mr Kemble grinned.

'I confess I had to give a couple o' the lads a clout 'round the ear for staring...'

Now, in the overheated confines of Lady Prestbury's ballroom, Luke thought that Kemble himself might stare if he could see Signor Durini's daughter outshining every other young woman in the room.

Carlotta watched Luke walk away from her, then stumbled to one of the cushioned benches that lined the walls of the ballroom and sank down. She was shaking. She put her hands to her temples, trying to stop the memories, but it was no good. She was back at Malberry, climbing down from the scaffolding after completing that first fresco. Even now she could remember her satisfaction at a job well done, feel the warm sun on her back...

'So you have come down at last.'
Carlotta jumped. With one hand still clutching the scaffolding, she looked around to see Luke sitting on the stone steps, leaning against the base of one of the pillars. His lazy smile made her tingle, right down to her toes.
'Mr...Ainslowe.'
He grinned. 'Yes, I suppose I am.' He jumped to his feet. 'I was taking a stroll through the park and realised you were still here. Do you always work this late?'
'Sometimes later.' Carlotta eyed him warily. The workmen had all gone back to the village, and even Mr Kemble would be in his lodge behind the stable block. Luke was smiling at her now, the twinkle in his hazel eyes making it hard for her not to smile back at him.
'I think I should escort you home.'

'Oh. I mean, um, I—I have first to clean out my brushes,' she said, backing away.

'Of course.' He nodded gravely. 'Go along, then. I shall wait here for you.'

She expected him to be gone by the time she had finished putting away her paints and tidying the little paint store, but he was still sitting on the steps as she came around the side of the house, and, with a little spurt of surprise, Carlotta realised that she would have been disappointed to find him gone. He rose to his feet.

'I was beginning to think you had run away from me.'

Carlotta's cheeks grew hot; she *had* considered avoiding him and going around the far side of the house. He held out his arm, but she gave a tiny shake of her head and began to walk down the drive, keeping a good distance between them. Safe. Sensible. Yet the truth was she did not *feel* sensible. She felt exhilarated in his company, aware of him walking beside her, matching his step to hers. She was sorely tempted to reach out her hand and take his arm, to draw closer to him. She did not understand why she should feel like this. It was all very confusing.

'Kemble tells me your father's apprentice ran away, and that is why you must finish the ceiling for him.'

'It is only two of the minor scenes. Papa has completed all the major work.'

'Yes, I was looking at the murals in the house. They are spectacular.'

'Papa is a much respected artist in Rome.'

'You must be very proud of him.'

'I am.'

'And is that what you want to do, paint life-size murals?'

She laughed. 'No, it would be thought improper.' She flushed, and glanced across at him. 'Not that my work is not perfectly good. My father would never have consented to my finishing the ceiling if he thought there would be cause for complaint.'

'You need not worry; I have seen nothing that would make me say any such thing.'

They walked together across the grass towards the edge of the park. Through the trees a short distance away the roofs of the houses at the edge of the village could be seen. Carlotta was aware of a faint disappointment that their walk would soon be over.

The sun had set and the early summer twilight was muting the colours of the park. Once they were amongst the trees the shadows deepened. When they reached the stile he vaulted over, then turned and held out his hand. After a brief hesitation, Carlotta took it. His touch disconcerted her; as she stepped down, she stumbled and would have fallen if he had not caught her in his arms. Laughing at her own clumsiness, Carlotta looked up and found his face very close. The laughter caught in her throat as she looked into his eyes. They were no longer twinkling with humour but dark and mysterious. Her heart began to pound against her ribs. No man had ever held her, let alone like this before. Her hands were resting against him; she could feel his chest, smooth and hard beneath the silk waistcoat. Even as she was wondering what to say, his arms tightened and he was kissing her.

Carlotta was at first too shocked to react. His lips fastened on hers, and there was fluttering excitement deep within her, as if her insides were dissolving. A confusion of fear and exhilaration filled her mind, making sober thought impossible. She responded to his kiss; with none of society's restraints holding her back, it seemed the most natural thing in the world to relax against him, her senses revelling in the feel of his arms about her. He encompassed her, mentally and physically. She was aware of his very male strength, crushing her against him. It was frightening, exciting, but there was something else awakening within her—a dark, dangerous attraction such as she had never known before. Carlotta had just decided that they should not be doing this when Luke raised his head and released her. She felt unaccountably bereft.

'I beg your pardon,' he said contritely. 'I did not mean to frighten you, but you looked so dashed irresistible.'

She swallowed hard, trying to regain her composure. She wondered if the world would ever be the same again.

'You did not frighten me, sir.' Her heart was thumping so loud she thought he must surely hear it. 'I…um…I must get home now.'

'Will you not take my arm?'

She shook her head, her cheeks hot with embarrassment. Until that moment she had not considered how she must look, dressed in boy's clothes, smelling of paint and resin. Mama had told her she should wrap herself in a cloak when going out, but Carlotta had always laughed at her, asking what could possibly happen to her on the short journey between Malberry Court and her home? Now she knew.

'No. No. I think I will go on alone from here, if you please.'

He seemed to tower over her, a black shadow in the gloom. Her heart flipped as she thought he might try to kiss her again—she doubted she was strong enough to resist him and was shocked to realise that she did not *want* to resist him. She did not know whether she was most disappointed or relieved when he stepped away from her.

'Of course, if that is what you wish.'

He climbed up on to the stile and sat there, smiling at her, his teeth very white in the dim light. 'Well,' he said as she hesitated, 'go along with you.'

Carlotta began to walk away, her spine tingling as she imagined his eyes raking her back. As soon as a bend in the lane hid the stile from sight, she took to her heels and ran the final few yards to her home.

'Carlotta, are you quite well?'

Carlotta blinked and looked around the crowded ballroom. Her aunt was at her side, regarding her with some concern.

'Pray do not tell me you have the headache, when everything is going so very well. Come, child, your next dance partner will be looking for you. I am so pleased for you—all but two dances taken this evening! It can be a little difficult when one is new to town, but I knew that as soon as the gentlemen saw how well you dance they would come begging to be presented to you.'

'And did Lord—Lord Darvell ask to be presented, Aunt?' Carlotta tried to keep her voice casual.

'Oh, yes. He came straight up to me and begged for an introduction.' She dropped her voice to say confidentially, 'Carlotta, Darvell is a very wild young man.'

'I know that, Aunt. The Wicked Baron. I have heard all about him.'

'Oh, well, I should not call him *wicked*, exactly,' temporised Lady Broxted, determined to be fair. 'Indeed, no one has heard *anything* of him for the past twelve months, but his conduct before that, when he was still in the army—well, it is not fitting that I should tell you everything, but you are best to beware of him, my love.'

'If he is so very dangerous, I am surprised that you should introduce him to me!'

Lady Broxted sighed. 'I know, but Broxted is well acquainted with the family and it would be very difficult not to acknowledge the connection. I think it a great pity that Darvell sold out. Mayhap he thinks to settle down.' She tapped Carlotta's arm with her fan. 'He may be looking out for a rich wife, for I believe he has not a penny to his name. If so, then he may set out to charm you, Carlotta, but your uncle would not wish for a liaison *there*, my love.'

Carlotta gave a brittle laugh. 'You need have no fears in that direction, Aunt!'

'Good. However, one cannot deny that he is very engaging and will make you a handsome dance partner. By the bye, his brother James owns Malberry Court. I tell you this so that you are forewarned; we must not let slip your family's connection with the house, must we?'

By the time Lord Darvell returned to claim his dance, Carlotta had decided she would be cool and aloof. She would treat his lordship as if they had never met. However, when he took her hand in his own firm grasp, she was not prepared for the surge of emotion that seared through her. She had closed her mind to those first long months after she had left Malberry, the lonely nights when she had cried herself to sleep. Now with one touch he had brought it all rushing back, the longing, the desire and the sheer, blinding agony of finding he had gone.

Carlotta bit on her lip; even now she could not bring herself to think too much of those dark, empty days, afraid that if she did not keep it locked away, her grief would grow and consume her. It was better to concentrate on her anger. He had betrayed her and she wanted to hurt him as he had hurt her. She set her mind to consider how best to do it. Eyes glittering, she answered his attempts to converse with monosyllables, earning a frowning look from her partner. When he suggested they should sit out the second dance she silently acquiesced and accompanied him to a quiet alcove. He smiled at her as they sat down together.

'You are looking very well, Carlotta. I hardly recognise you.'

She unfurled her fan. 'La, I am glad of that, my lord! I vow I was such a gauche little thing when we first met.'

'You were charming.'

Carlotta had not wasted her time at Miss Currier's seminary. She summoned up memories of a certain rich, spoiled, young lady she had met there, and with the sole aim of distancing herself from him as soon as politely possible, she gave a very creditable titter.

'Oh, dear me, I was utterly innocent then, and ready to make any number of mistakes. Thank heaven my uncle the earl found me when he did.'

'Do you think so?'

'O lord, yes! I had no polish at all, and no possibility of making a great match, but my uncle the earl says that now, with his backing, I can look *very high indeed* for a husband.' *Heavens,* she thought, *how vulgar that sounds!*

'And is that why you are in town?'

He was looking at her now with a shadow of doubt in

his eyes. She summoned a dazzling smile, feeling as brittle as glass inside.

'But of course. I am looking about me, but am in no hurry; I can take my time until the right man, and the right fortune, comes along.' She reached out and placed one gloved hand on his sleeve. 'Forgive me for speaking to you in this way, my lord, but I feel we are old friends.'

With bitter satisfaction she observed how he almost recoiled from her. He said stiffly, 'You will be wondering perhaps why I did not come to see you, as I had promised, at Malberry.'

Panic flared. She dare not let him near that raw nerve. She waved her fan slowly. *It is too late for explanations*, she told herself. *The damage is done, Carlotta. Do not let him see how much he hurt you.*

'I had quite forgotten about that,' she said brightly. 'When my uncle came to carry me away, it drove all other thoughts completely from my head!'

'Thus you come to town to find a husband.'

Smile, Carlotta. A smug, self-satisfied, superior smile. Put him in his place.

'Yes, indeed. My uncle has several eligible men in mind for me. All of them *extremely* rich,' she added.

He looked at her, a tiny crease in his brows. 'You have changed, Carlotta.'

She lifted her shoulders to give a slight shrug. 'I am merely being practical, my lord.'

'I thought you were above such mercenary concerns.'

'La, only a fool would claim such a thing. I know the value of a fortune, my lord. Nothing else will do for me.'

She held her breath, forcing herself to meet his gaze

with a look of arrogant unconcern. After a moment he looked away.

'Then I wish you luck in your quest, Miss Rivington,' he said quietly.

He rose and, with a little bow, turned and walked away. Carlotta's expression did not change as she watched his retreating form, but inside she felt sick to her core.

Luke stormed out of the ballroom, his jaw clenched to curb his anger. He had expected to find Carlotta altered, but he had not thought she would turn into such a heartless fortune-hunter. A year living with the Broxteds had destroyed the innocent charm that had attracted him to her. Now she was no different from all the other females with their arch smiles and false laughter. He made his way down the stairs and out into the street, where he jammed his hat on his head and began to stride back towards Piccadilly. What had changed her, or had he been mistaken all along? Perhaps he had missed something when he had seen her at Malberry Court, some clue that she was not as sweet and innocent as he had thought. He remembered trying to draw her out during one of their many picnics that summer on the lawn at Malberry.

'You are an enigma, Miss Carlotta Durini. You say you were born in Italy, and have only been here for a few years, yet your English is faultless.'

'Mama is English.' Her glance was pure mischief. 'She is the daughter of a great nobleman.'

'Oh? You intrigue me. Who?'

She laughed and shook her head. 'I shall not tell you. Mama met my father when she was touring Italy with her family. They ran away together. Mama says it was love at first sight.' She wrinkled her brow. 'Do you think that possible, Major Ainslowe? Can one fall in love so quickly?'

Luke had certainly thought so. Carlotta had stolen his heart within a week of their first meeting. Now as he strode away from Prestbury House he wondered if he had been mistaken in her. Perhaps there had never been anything more than a cold, calculating mind behind her sweet face.

Chapter Two

Carlotta gave herself a mental shake. This was her first ball; it would not do to cry. She put up her chin. She would not give Luke the satisfaction of seeing how close she was to dissolving into tears. Instead she summoned up her brightest smile to greet her next partner. She had already danced with Mr Woollatt earlier in the evening, and on first acquaintance she had found him rather pompous. However, his blatant admiration was balm to her wounded spirits and she treated him to an excess of charm as they danced together. After that she spent the rest of the evening dancing and laughing as though she had not a care in the world. It was only as she was waiting for her cloak that she discovered Luke had left early and had not witnessed her vivacious behaviour.

'Well, it really does not matter,' she told herself as she climbed into the carriage. 'We have met, the sky did not fall and I know now that we have nothing to say to one another. I can forget all about the odious Lord Darvell.'

'I beg your pardon, my love, did you speak?'

Lady Broxted's gentle enquiry made her jump and she

hastily disclaimed. Pulling her cloak about her, she subsided into one corner and stared disconsolately out of the window. She was determined not to think of Luke Ainslowe, but his image was as persistent as the man himself; she recalled how he had come to Malberry Court, armed with a picnic basket, and insisted that she take luncheon with him. She had refused at first, but she could still hear his voice, deep and seductive, persuading her to leave her painting and eat with him.

She was very conscious of her boy's attire as she seated herself on the very edge of the rug, but Luke never mentioned it as he fed her tidbits of cheese and bread and fruit. She explained how his brother James had sought out her father and commissioned him to paint Malberry Court. Luke responded by telling her something of his life in the army and of the great battle that had taken place at Waterloo. Sitting out in the sunshine with the soaring white pillars of the house at their backs and the calm waters of the lake spread out before them, she soon lost her shyness. He was very easy to talk to. She liked to make him laugh and see the merry glint in his hazel eyes. It seemed quite natural to accept Luke's invitation to join him again the next day, and the next. She was so comfortable in his company, talking of everything and nothing. They understood each other so well. Or so she had thought, until the day he had ridden out of her life forever.

With everything so new and exciting, Carlotta found much in London to divert her. Lady Broxted was determined that she should enjoy her first Season and spared no pains to keep her entertained. There were rides in the park, shopping with her aunt, promenades and balls, assemblies, masquerades and parties. Carlotta threw herself into such a round of enjoyment that she declared to her aunt she did not have a moment to think. It was not true—there was too much time to think. Even two weeks after the Prestbury ball, when she was out riding with her friends, it was so easy to allow the chatter to flow over her and to lose herself in her own thoughts, remembering how attentive Luke had been at Malberry, bringing food to share, escorting her home in the evenings—it had been an idyllic, happy interlude. She had felt safe with Luke. He had not attempted to kiss her again, even though she knew she wanted him to do so. She remembered that she had been very close to kissing *him*, the day he had climbed the scaffolding. She had peered over the edge of the platform to find him grinning up at her…

'Good morning, Major—or is it past noon now?'

He made a great show of getting out his watch, saying severely, 'It is gone three, madam. Are you so caught up in your work that you do not know the time?'

A laugh trembled on her lips but she tried to frown. 'I am very busy, sir. Pray do not disturb me.'

'Can you not come down?'

'No, sir, I cannot. What are you doing?' She laughed. 'You cannot come up *here*.'

'I can, and I will,' he said, setting his foot on the first ladder. 'I want to see you in your eyrie.'

She felt the platform shake as he began to climb and she quickly collected up her palette and brushes out of the way.

'So this is where you work.' He crawled onto the platform. 'Good God, how do you manage?'

'It is a little cramped, to be sure. There is no room to

stand and one has to work crouching or lying down. But it is easier for me, because I am so much shorter than you.'

He pointed to the large roundel in the centre of the ceiling. 'Is that your father's work?'

'Yes.' She giggled as she watched him twisting his long frame around, trying to look at the fresco. 'It is easier if you lie on your back, only you must not, of course. You will make your coat dirty.'

Ignoring her warning, he stretched himself out on the platform. 'Ah, yes, I can see it much better now. A god and his attendants.' He shifted his position. 'And the other roundel, the smaller one at the far end?'

She slid down beside him and gazed up at the ceiling. 'I painted that one. You are still too close to see it all properly; it will look so much better from the ground.'

'It looks wonderful to me now,' he said. 'I am impressed.' He rolled over and propped his head on his hand, smiling at her. 'Now, when will you come down?'

The frescoes were forgotten. His face was only inches from her own. What if she was to reach out to him, to take his face in her hands and pull him down to her, to kiss *him*? The urge to do just that had been so strong she shivered. Such wicked thoughts!

'Carlotta.'

She jumped. No longer was she lying beside Luke Ainslowe on the high scaffold at Malberry; she was ambling through Hyde Park on her docile little pony. The rest of her riding party had moved ahead and, to her dismay, she found Lord Darvell was beside her on a sleek, long-legged bay. Her cheeks grew hot—had she conjured him with her musings?

She had not expected him to seek her out after her performance at Prestbury House. She thought she had made her feelings perfectly clear, but here he was, smiling at her and causing her heart to flutter in the most foolish way imaginable.

'We had no opportunity to talk, the other night,'

'There is nothing I want to say to you, my lord.'

She urged her mount to a trot, wanting to catch up with her party, but Luke's hand shot out and caught her bridle.

'Not yet, Carlotta. Allow me to enjoy your company for a little while.'

She stiffened. 'I did not give you leave to use my name.'

'No? I told you I would do so. At Malberry, do you remember?'

She hunched a shoulder. 'I have no wish to remember Malberry.'

'No?' he said again, his slow smile slicing through her defences. 'Why should you not—did you not enjoy our time together there? Have you forgotten that I commissioned you to paint me?'

She stared ahead of her. Of course she remembered. She remembered every word he had spoken to her. She realised she would very much like to paint him, not posing statesman-like in a studio, but as he had been at Malberry Court, relaxed and reclining on the grass. For his brown hair she would use a base of raw umber and add fine brush-strokes to represent the blond sun-streaks—mixing in a little Indian yellow, perhaps. And his eyes—it would not be difficult to recreate their colour, like polished hazelnuts, but could she capture the smile that lurked in their depths, or the way his mouth quirked into a smile?

Carlotta looked away suddenly. This was too dangerous

a game—she was only a memory away from crying. She assumed a haughty look and raised her brows at him.

'You would commission me, my lord? But it is well known you have no money.'

'That will not always be the case.'

She curled her lip at him. 'But it is irrelevant, since I shall not be painting you. Indeed, I have no need to do anything, now.'

'Perhaps not, but I thought painting was your passion.'

She managed a tinkling laugh. 'Oh dear me, no. How unladylike that would be.'

She noted with satisfaction that his hand on her rein tightened, and the little mare side-stepped nervously.

'What has happened to you, Carlotta? At Malberry you were…different.'

He was watching her intently. Carlotta knew she would have to look at him, but she would die rather than show him her true feelings. He was a rake, everyone told her so. He had been her first love—her only love—and he had broken her fragile young heart. But that was what rakes did; he could not change his nature. It had taken her months to rebuild her life—only the knowledge of how dear she was to her parents and to her aunt and uncle had given her the will to carry on. She could not let him hurt her again. She raised her chin and fixed him with cold, indifferent eyes.

'At Malberry, my lord, I was a child, ignorant of the world. I thought fortune was not important. Now I know better.'

She forced herself not to look away, praying that he would not see past her icy, supercilious stare to the raw pain in her heart. For a long, treacherous moment he held her eyes; not by the flicker of an eyelid did she betray the anguish that was ripping her apart. She watched as his puzzlement turned to contempt. She had not thought she could feel any more miserable, but the disdain she now read in his eyes was almost unbearable. Almost.

He released her bridle and gathered up his own reins, saying curtly, 'Then I shall leave you to your fortune-hunting, Miss Rivington. Good day to you.'

Luke dug his heels into the bay's sides and cantered away, ignoring the stares and frowns of those who considered it unseemly to move at more than a snail's pace. Damn the chit. When he had first seen her at Malberry he had intended nothing more than a little flirtation to pass the time. By heaven, the girl had given him his own again! He scowled; it was his own fault, for he had told her of his financial problems. They had been sitting on the lawns at Malberry on one of those hot, sunny afternoons when he had persuaded her to come down from her high perch for a little while. He had been curious to know why her father was so anxious to have the frescoes finished.

'It is most important that my father fulfils his obligations, you see,' said Carlotta, stretching out on the grass and putting her hands behind her head. He tried not to stare at the way her paint-stained shirt settled over the gentle curves of her breast. 'He must be paid on time.'

'And why is that?'

'Because there are bills outstanding, expenses to be met... As a gentleman, perhaps you would not understand.'

He grinned at that. 'I understand only too well about debts; I have an abundance of them.'

Carlotta wrinkled her brow. 'It must be very unpleasant to be under such an obligation, I think.'

'But it is unavoidable,' he said lightly. 'Any gentleman living in town will tell you that his expenses are very high. There's one's house and stable to be maintained, not to mention one's tailor.'

'But surely you could cut back, economise…' She bit her lip. 'I can see that I have made you angry, I beg your pardon. The way you live is none of my business.'

'No.' He had not meant to sound so cold and he saw the sudden, anxious look Carlotta threw at him. When she did not speak, he said gently, 'What, Mistress Durini? Have you no riposte for me?' She shook her head, and looked surprised when he laughed. 'At last I have found a woman who does not want the last word!'

Carlotta sat up. She said angrily, 'I think you are making May-game of me, sir.'

'No, no, pray, Miss Durini, forgive my incivility. I was jesting when I talked of the expense of town life; I have only recently returned from Paris and I *have* no town house to maintain—and to the best of my knowledge neither do I owe my tailor a penny. The debts I do have relate to my estate, and I plan to address that problem very soon. There, will you cry peace with me now?'

His hand tightened on the reins and the bay skittered, throwing up his head. Damnation, he had never owned as much to any woman before and what good had it done him? He had given her a stick to beat him with. A short, bitter laugh escaped him. He had been within an ace of offering for her—thank Providence it had come to nothing! What a lucky escape—he had no wish to be married to such a shallow, mercenary female.

He brought his horse to a sudden stop.

The only trouble was, he could not bear the thought of anyone else marrying her.

During the following weeks it was inevitable that Carlotta and Lord Darvell would meet frequently, but a polite, distant nod was their only acknowledgement.

'I am surprised that Darvell does not pay you more attention,' remarked Lady Broxted, when they saw him in Mrs Price's drawing room one evening. 'He is generally very appreciative of a pretty young lady…a little *too* appreciative in some cases,' she added reflectively. 'He is an incorrigible flirt.'

Carlotta glanced across the room. Luke was enjoying a lively dialogue with a very pretty blonde matron and she quickly looked away again.

'I do not think I am quite to his taste, Aunt. I doubt I am pretty enough to tempt his lordship.'

'Nonsense, I have received any number of compliments for you, my love,' replied Lady Broxted. 'But I suppose we should be thankful for Darvell's lack of interest; your uncle has settled a generous dowry upon you, and he hopes you will contract an alliance with a gentleman of means.'

Carlotta raised her chin. 'You need have no fear, Aunt; I shall not throw myself away upon an impoverished fortune-hunter like the Wicked Baron.'

Lady Broxted looked at her closely. 'Oh dear, what has Lord Darvell done to deserve such vehemence? Perhaps it is his lack of attention that has piqued you. After all, you cannot deny he is very attractive. However, if you showed a partiality for him, I have no doubt Broxted—'

'Dear ma'am, I have *no* partiality for him!' cried Carlotta, an angry flush warming her cheeks. 'I am quite *thankful* that he does not notice me.'

'Well, then, there is no more to be said on the matter.' reasoned Lady Broxted. 'You are a very sensible little thing, Carlotta. I have no doubt we can achieve a very creditable match for you. Fairbridge seems to have taken a shine to you.'

Carlotta followed her aunt's gaze to observe the tall, fair-haired young man standing on the far side of the room.

'I think the viscount is more interested in our host's daughter, ma'am. Do you see how he hovers about Miss Price, and how she blushes when he speaks to her?'

'Perhaps you are right.' Lady Broxted sighed. 'Pity, for he would make you an ideal partner. His mama is well disposed towards you, too. Her late husband was a great friend of Broxted's and I think she would like to strengthen the connection.'

'Dear ma'am, is it not a little early to be contemplating marriage?'

'It is never too early,' said my lady firmly. 'I am determined to see you well established. However, we must not repine. There is time yet.'

'I hope so, ma'am,' replied Carlotta, her eyes twinkling. 'We have been in town for little more than a month!'

At that moment a young gentleman approached to claim her hand for the next set and she went off, still smiling.

The ballroom grew hotter and more crowded as the evening progressed, and in between dances Carlotta was glad to stand by one of the open windows to cool her heated cheeks. She thought with longing of her parents' cottage in Malberry village: her mother's last letter had been full of trifles such as her success in the herb garden and the diligence of the new maid, as well as news of her latest commission and her father's progress at Malberry Court. He was now decorating the little temples that littered the gardens. Carlotta wished she could be with them, but it was not possible. She was fanning herself gently when Julia Price came to join her. Carlotta said in her open, friendly way, 'Your mama must be very pleased with the success of her party, Miss Price.'

'Yes, I think she is. It is always a concern that no one will come, for there are so many concerts and entertainments.'

'Well, I think you need have no worries, your rooms are full to overflowing. Is this what they call a sad crush?' Carlotta asked. 'I believe that means it is a great success.'

She must remember to put it all into her next letter to her parents; Mama enjoyed reading about the parties and entertainments.

'Yes.' Miss Price was smiling at her. 'We are very fortunate tonight, I think. Is this your first Season, Miss Rivington?'

'It is. My aunt and uncle have been kind enough to sponsor me.' Carlotta sighed. 'They are very good, but it is all so new and there is so much to remember: I am in constant dread that I shall embarrass them!'

Miss Price was quick to disclaim, 'No, no, that could not be—you always look so calm and at ease.'

'Thank you, but I am in a perpetual quake, I assure you, Miss Price.'

'Do, please, call me Julia.'

'Very well, if you will call me Carlotta.'

'That is a very pretty name.'

'Thank you. It is—' Carlotta became aware of someone approaching and broke off, turning to see Viscount Fairbridge at her side, his pale blue eyes fixed upon Julia. He bowed.

'Miss Price, you p-promised me the next dance, I think…that is, if I am not interrupting…'

Carlotta smiled at him. 'Pray, my lord, do take your partner.'

'You shall not object if I leave you?' asked Julia, looking anxious.

'Not at all. Off you go and enjoy yourself.'

Carlotta stepped back, smiling, as Julia put her fingers on Lord Fairbridge's sleeve for him to lead her away. Too late did she see Lord Darvell standing behind the viscount's lanky form. They were only feet apart. He checked as he saw her, a slight frown in his eyes. He was already turning away when their host's jovial voice boomed out.

'Now, now, how fortunate is this, my lord!' Mr Price put his hand on Darvell's arm. 'The next set is forming and here is Miss Rivington without a partner.'

Mortification swept over Carlotta. A glance at Lord Darvell showed her that he felt very much as she did, and for a brief moment she wondered if he would walk off, but Mr Price was clapping him on the shoulder, crying, 'Well, go to it, man!'

Carlotta opened her mouth to protest, but she could not speak. Lord Darvell stepped forward, stony-faced. He held out his hand.

'Will you do me the honour, Miss Rivington?'

There was no escape. To refuse would be to embarrass them all. Tentatively she put her fingers on his sleeve.

'You are too good, my lord.'

Damnation. Luke swore under his breath. However much he tried to avoid Carlotta, it seemed she forced herself upon his notice. No, he must be honest with himself, it was not her fault. He remembered his efforts at Malberry Court, when he had realised that he was in danger of falling in love with the bewitching little sprite in her shirt and breeches. He had done his best then to keep away from her, finishing his business with the clerk of works late one afternoon and planning to set off for Darvell Manor the following morning without returning to the Court. But when he left Kemble's lodge he found the heavy storm clouds had brought an early dusk and lightning was already splitting the sky. He saw the faint glow flickering from the windows of the house and rushed in, expecting to find flames licking at the newly painted walls. Instead he had found Carlotta.

'What the devil are you doing in here?'

His voice, edged with irritation, vibrated against the empty walls of the drawing room.

'I might ask you the same, sir, when you have not been near the house for days.'

Heaven and earth, the chit was challenging him!

'I have been at the lodge with Kemble, discussing plans for moving in the furniture. I saw the light in the windows as I was about to leave and came up to see what was amiss.'

'I am sorry, then, if you thought it was intruders.'

'I was more concerned that the lightning had started a fire. Why are you not at home?' he barked the question at her, frowning.

'I wanted to have one last look at my father's work. I beg your pardon; I never meant to disturb anyone. I will go now.'

'Oh, no, you will not.'

She blinked.

He took off his hat and shook it, sending off tiny

droplets of water that sparkled in the candlelight. 'I mean the storm is too violent. It is not safe.'

'Oh.'

That one little word, spoken so softly, was his undoing. His heart went out to her; she looked so vulnerable, holding aloft the candlestick with one shaking hand. He said gently, 'You need not worry, you are perfectly safe here.' He stepped forward and took the candlestick from her. 'Let us look at your father's work together.'

They wandered through the empty rooms until they found themselves in the salon, which occupied one end of the house. There was only one painted panel, set between the two marble fireplaces. The other three walls were taken up with long windows, designed to allow in maximum light, although now they only gleamed blackly as the rain spattered against the glass. Luke crossed the room, raising the candles higher as he studied the mural.

'Your father is a great artist, Carlotta. This is really very good.'

'Thank you. May I show you something?' She took his arm and led him to the far corner of the panel. 'There,' she pointed. 'Look closely at the decoration on the lady's sandal.'

He peered closer. 'A tiny snail.'

'Yes, a *lumaca*.' She laughed. 'It sounds so much prettier in Italian. It is Papa's signature. He does not tell many people, but it is very important to him. When he was in Rome he would often paint copies of the great masters for the foreign visitors to take home and put in their grand houses. He insisted that as long as he signed them then there was no harm in it; he was not trying to trick anyone.'

'I am honoured you should share it with me.'

He looked down at her and Carlotta smiled back at him

briefly before she looked away, suddenly shy and awkward. As if to distract him, she pointed up at the chandeliers.

'When all those candles are alight this room will glow. Can you imagine how elegant it will look, with all the ladies in their finest gowns?' She sighed. 'I wish I could see it.'

'Perhaps you will.'

She laughed. 'Perhaps! I will creep up to the windows and press my nose against the glass one night.'

The thought made him angry. 'That is not what I meant,' he growled. 'You should be in here, dancing with all the other young ladies.'

'Do not frown, sir. I do not want you to pity me.'

'No, of course not, but I am determined you shall dance here.' He put down the candlestick and opened his arms to her. 'Come.'

'You are nonsensical!' She laughed, but did not resist as he took her hand and began to lead her around the room, humming a tune.

'Do you waltz, Miss Durini?'

'No, sir. I have never learned.'

'Well, the gentleman holds the lady like this.' He drew her towards him, pushed her cloak off her shoulders until it hung like a train behind her and slid one hand beneath it to rest on her back. Immediately her body tensed. A tremor ran through him as her breasts pressed again him, separated from his skin by only a few thin layers of silk and linen.

'I have been told the waltz is considered by some to be improper,' she remarked. 'It certainly feels very daring, to be standing so close.'

She looked up at him, smiling shyly, and suddenly he could not breathe.

'Well, sir, what next?'

'This.'

He placed his fingers beneath her chin, tilted up her face and kissed her, very gently. She gave a faint sigh when he lifted his head, but did not move away. Tension crackled between them. Carlotta leaned against him, a tiny movement, but it was enough. With something very like a groan he swooped down on her again and his kiss this time was much more urgent. She responded, her lips parting in surrender to his demands and her body melting against him. His arms tightened. He nibbled gently at her lip and in response she put her arms around his neck.

Together they sank to their knees and he lowered Carlotta to the floor. She clung to him as he stretched out beside her, his mouth moving slowly, sensuously, over her lips while one hand slid to her breast. Luke felt her tremble, her back arched. A pulsing wave of desire swamped him. His fingers tore at her shirt, pulling it free from those soft, clinging breeches, then his hand was on skin, caressing the gentle curve of her waist. He ran his fingers over her stomach and she drew it in, gasping. He covered her face with kisses, drinking in the sweet taste of her, a taste of summer flowers and new-mown hay. His senses reeled. He had known many women, but never had the urge to possess and protect been so strong. She moaned softly and his touch faltered. He was overwhelmed with tenderness. She was such an innocent, it was important not to hurt her, not to frighten her. He knew the heady heights that love-making could achieve, but for her it would be new, strange and bewildering. Suddenly he was aware of their surroundings, lying on the cold, hard floor. By God it was not even his house!

He raised his head and stared down at her. Carlotta gazed up at him so trustingly and with a sudden, startling clarity he knew it would not do. This was not how he would show his love to Carlotta.

'This has gone far enough,' he muttered, almost to himself.

He got to his feet and held out his hand. Her brows contracted and she looked at him with bewildered, frightened eyes.

'What is it?' she whispered. 'Have I done something wrong?'

His smile was strained as he pulled her to her feet.

'Not you, sweetheart.' He brushed his lips against her mouth in a fleeting, butterfly kiss. 'You are everything I could wish for, but this is not right, not here, on the bare floor of an empty house. You deserve so much more than that.' He looked towards the window. 'I think the rain has stopped. We must get you home.'

There was an uncomfortable silence. Carlotta did not move.

'I thought you were going to teach me to waltz.'

She sounded so lost that he had to stifle the temptation to take her in his arms again. He reached out to pull her cloak back over her shoulders.

'I am no saint, Carlotta.' He bent to pick up the candlestick.

'You are not angry with me?'

He lifted her hand, pressing a kiss into the palm. 'No, love. I am not angry with you.'

No, he had not been angry with her then, but now, as he led Carlotta on to the crowded dance floor, it occurred to him that he had been wrong about her; even then she had been trying to catch herself a rich husband.

* * *

With all the pleasure of someone walking to the scaffold, Carlotta accompanied Lord Darvell onto the dance floor. His hand beneath her arm was stiff; indeed, she thought his whole body was rigid with disapproval. She summoned up all her courage to help her through this ordeal. Anger came to her aid. What right had he to disapprove of her? When they took their places in the set she put up her chin and gazed steadily at some point over his shoulder. The music began; they held hands, moved forward until they were almost touching, the delicate flowers of her corsage trembling within an inch of his waistcoat. She must concentrate on her steps and forget her partner. There was no need for them to talk, after all. However, she soon discovered that Luke had other ideas.

'Why did you change your name to Rivington?' he asked her suddenly.

'It is in deference to my aunt and uncle. They have been very good to me.'

'And perhaps you are ashamed of your origins.'

'I am not! It is not unusual to take the name of one's benefactor.' She almost snatched her hand away as the dance parted them. Insufferable man! He was determined to think badly of her. Carlotta's head came up: she would not court his good opinion.

Luke fought down his anger. Damnation, one could not have an argument in the middle of a ballroom. The movement of the dance took him past his partner and he almost laughed aloud at the fury of her look. One had to admit those dark eyes flashed magnificently when she was angry. It seemed she planned to ignore him for the duration of the dance, but he would have none of it. The chit should learn that she must at least show him society manners.

'How are you enjoying London, Miss Rivington?'

'Very well, I thank you.'

He waited, and when she did not continue he raised his brows. 'Is that all? Have you no praises to heap upon the entertainments and the shopping to be had in town?'

'If I did so, you would write me down as a thoughtless, frippery creature.'

'You would prefer me to think you sullen, and above being pleased.'

'I do not care what you think of me,' she told him in a low voice.

Luke growled with frustration. Blast it, why should the chit anger him so? He gave a harsh laugh. 'Be careful with your scowls, Carlotta,' he hissed as they parted again. 'The wind may change and you will never smile again.'

Carlotta reined in her irritation. All around her the dancers were laughing and enjoying themselves. It would not do to let the world see she was arguing with her partner. As they came back together she said sweetly, 'Thank you for the timely reminder, my lord. Because *you* cannot help your temper, it is no reason for me to lose mine.'

His smile was as false as her own, but his eyes glittered dangerously. She sought for something commonplace to say.

'We are very fortunate with the weather, are we not? It is warm enough to make fires unnecessary, yet still cool enough to make dancing a pleasure.' He did not reply. She thought he looked very much as if he was grinding his teeth. Carlotta raised her brows. 'Come, my lord. When I go to such trouble to converse, surely you can make the effort to respond.'

'Since we are now at the end of the dance I am spared the necessity.'

She put her fingers on his arm and allowed him to lead her off the floor. 'We are both spared,' she muttered. 'We need no longer be polite to one another.'

'I noticed no politeness, Miss Rivington.'

Carlotta's eyes narrowed, but there was no opportunity to reply, since they had reached Lady Broxted, who was deep in conversation with her hostess. Lord Darvell left them without a word, but to Carlotta's relief her aunt did not appear to notice. Instead she caught Carlotta's hand and pulled her closer.

'My dear, we are discussing the most delightful scheme. Mrs Price informs me that Madame Saqui is performing at Vauxhall next week and we are minded to get up a party—what do you think of that?'

'Madame Saqui?'

'She is a rope walker,' explained Mrs Price. 'Quite a sensation. She first performed at Vauxhall last year and was so successful that she had been retained.'

'Well, Carlotta, would you like to see her?'

'Very much, Aunt, thank you.'

Mrs Price clapped her hands.

'Then it is settled. We shall all go together. And I shall find two young gentlemen to accompany us, for I am sure you and Julia will enjoy yourselves much more if you each have a handsome escort.' A commotion at the door caused her to look up. 'Now, who is this come in at this late hour? I had not expected anyone else to turn up—good heavens, it is Ainslowe and his new wife!'

As Mrs Price hurried away, Carlotta stood on tiptoe to see the couple at the door. Even from a distance she recognised James Ainslowe. He was not quite as tall as his brother, but he had the same nut-brown hair and an ease of manner that expressed itself in the charming smile he now bent upon his hostess. Carlotta could imagine him apologising for his late arrival, treating Mrs Price to the same glinting smile that Luke had shown her when they had been together at Malberry. The memory gave her an empty, hollow feeling inside. She instantly quashed it and turned her attention to Mrs James Ainslowe. She was a lively brunette with a generous figure that was shown to advantage in a low-cut gown of bronze *broché* silk and a matching jockey cap over her glossy curls. A gold tassel on the cap swung to and fro as she carried on an animated conversation with her hostess. Carlotta heard Lady Broxted's smothered exclamation.

'Is anything wrong, Aunt?'

'I could wish they had stayed in Berkshire a little longer,' muttered Lady Broxted. 'What if they should recognise you?'

Carlotta laughed at that. 'That is not possible! They were on the Continent when I was at Malberry.'

'You must be very careful, Carlotta, not to disclose your real name.'

'I thought we had already agreed that, ma'am.' She hesitated. 'Would it be so very dreadful, Aunt, if it were known that my father was an artist?'

'It would be embarrassing for your uncle, my dear, and for me. So much better that no one asks about your parents.'

Carlotta felt a little tremor of unease. 'Perhaps then it would be best if we lived a little more retired. Surely there is no need for you to puff me off quite so much.'

Lady Broxted stared at her. 'Do you not *wish* to go about, my love?'

Carlotta hesitated. Looking into her aunt's anxious face,

she realised that her aunt's pleasure in the balls and parties they attended was more than equal to her own and she could not disappoint her.

'Yes, of course I do, Aunt, but I would not embarrass you for the world. Perhaps we could avoid Mr and Mrs Ainslowe…'

'No, I am afraid that is impossible; they will be seen everywhere and you must be seen everywhere, too.' My lady drew herself up to her full, if diminutive, height. 'We must hope that your identity is not discovered, at least until we have you safely married. There is no reason why we should not carry it off. After all, there is no one here who knows you, is there?'

Carlotta knew that this was the moment to confess the truth, but she remained silent. She watched Lord Darvell cross the room to greet the new arrivals and her heart sank. It was clear that Luke was on very good terms with his brother and sister-in-law; doubtless he would tell them all about his dalliance with the painter's daughter. It seemed very likely that by the end of the evening all Lady Broxted's hopes for her would be at an end.

Luke gripped his brother's hand. 'James! When did you arrive in town?'

'This morning. Adele was desperate to buy new gowns.'

'Nonsense!' cried his wife, turning from Mrs Price. 'You were just as anxious to get to town. Luke, my dear, how are you? As handsome as ever, I see.'

'And you are even more enchanting,' replied Luke, kissing her hand. 'How did you find the Court?'

'It is beautiful; thank you for your efforts. Kemble told us you were at Malberry for weeks.'

'Yes, thank you,' said James. 'I really did not expect you to do more than look in on the place once or twice.'

'Poor Luke,' said Adele. 'Was it very tedious for you?'

Luke wanted to say that, surprisingly, it had been some of the happiest weeks of his life, but that would invite questions, and Adele was damnably perceptive. He dared not risk it.

'I endured it as long as I could,' he replied coolly. 'However, I thought you would stay there longer.'

Adele shook her head, sighing. 'We have had nothing but each other's company for the best part of a month.'

'An ideal arrangement,' murmured Luke, grinning, and earned for himself a sharp tap on the arm from Adele's fan.

'You may stop those knowing looks at once! James and I are very much in need of company before we murder one another.'

'Aye.' Her loving husband smiled. 'So we thought we would come to town for a few weeks, then take a party back to the Court with us for the summer.'

'You will come, won't you, Luke?'

'Of course, Adele. That is, unless anything better comes along.'

She gave a gurgle of laughter. 'How I have missed your teasing! We have been abroad for so long, and everyone there was so serious.' She tucked her hand in his arm. 'Come, we have not seen you since Paris. One can never say everything properly in a letter, so you must tell me all you have been doing and then we will arrange for you to accompany me to Bond Street.'

'Surely that is your husband's duty.'

She waved one gloved hand. 'Alas, James has no eye for colour.'

Luke began to back away. 'I regret, Adele, that I have a great many engagements—'

'Nonsense, you cannot be too busy to take me shopping.'

He cast a despairing look at James, who merely laughed.

'No use appealing to me, Luke. I've come to town for my own amusement. You are always at your ease with the ladies, you will enjoy yourself!'

Chapter Three

Lady Broxted emerged from the milliner's shop and stopped, blinking in the sunlight. 'Well, Carlotta, where shall we go now?'

Following her aunt out on to the flag way, Carlotta gave a little sigh. 'Must we go anywhere else, Aunt? We have bought so many gloves and shoes and hats that I dare not think what my uncle will say.'

'Tush, child, what should he say? Broxted knows how it is in town. One's gloves soon become soiled and the dirty streets quite ruin one's shoes.'

'And the bonnets, ma'am?' asked Carlotta, regarding the hatboxes carried by a wooden-faced footman.

'One can never have too many hats,' opined Lady Broxted firmly. 'Now, let us go in here, for, having seen how well you look in green, I am determined that you shall have a new silk dress for the evenings.'

'Pray, ma'am, do not go in,' begged Carlotta. 'I have been sized up, measured and pulled this way and that until I am quite exhausted with it—' She broke off, realising that Lady Broxted was not listening.

Following her aunt's intent gaze, she saw Mrs Adele
Ainslowe approaching. However, when she observed
Adele's escort she was aware of a sudden feeling of
breathlessness—her heart seemed to be fighting to escape
her body.

'Dear me,' muttered Lady Broxted, 'how did she persuade
Darvell to come shopping with her? Mrs Ainslowe, Lord
Darvell, how do you do?'

Adele stopped and gave them her wide smile. 'Good day
to you, Lady Broxted, and this must be your pretty niece
that everyone is talking of. Pray won't you introduce us?
I heard that you were at the Prices' assembly, Miss Rivington,' she continued once this office had been performed.
'I am ashamed to admit that James and I came in very late,
and there was not time to meet everyone.'

Carlotta answered as best she could. She was very much
aware of Luke standing behind his sister-in-law. She was
also a little overawed by Mrs Ainslowe's vivacity. She had
thought her very good-natured when she had first seen her
and now, at such close proximity, her impression was con-
firmed; she could see the humour twinkling in her green
eyes. Adele was looking past her, taking in the parcels
piled up in the arms of Lady Broxted's hapless footmen.

'So,' she continued, 'we are on the same errand, I
collect. We have been shopping all morning. Poor Darvell
is quite out of patience with me. Tell me, is that little
Frenchwoman still trading at the end of the street? Madame
Beaufaire, the milliner. I was always able to find something
I liked there, but last Season she was talking of returning
to Paris, now the war is over.'

'Yes, yes, Madame Beaufaire is still there,' replied
Lady Broxted, adding with a triumphant little smile, 'we

have just purchased a new bonnet of leghorn straw from her for Carlotta…'

Mrs Ainslowe laughed gaily. 'Then you will be all the rage, my dear, and we shall all be looking daggers at you when you wear it! But this is your first time in London, is it not, Miss Rivington? Tell me how you find Bond Street.'

'Exhausting,' Lady Broxted answered before Carlotta could speak. 'My poor niece is crying quits before we have completed even one side of the street, which is a great shame, because I did so want to visit the silk mercers of Covent Garden.'

Carlotta gave a rueful smile. 'I am sure one soon grows accustomed, but it is all so new to me. You must forgive me; my senses are quite overcome by so many shops, so many wonderful things displayed. I am very much afraid that if I have to make one more purchase, I shall be completely undone.'

'Well, then, I have the very thing,' cried Mrs Ainslowe. 'We shall change partners. Lady Broxted and I will finish our shopping together while Darvell escorts Miss Rivington back to Berkeley Square.'

'Oh, no, ma'am!' cried Carlotta, appalled. 'Truly I am not tired, I was merely funning.'

Luke bent a frowning look upon his sister-in-law. 'Pray, Adele, do not be so overbearing.'

She gave him a mischievous smile, but turned to address Carlotta. 'My dear Miss Rivington, I can see that you are quite done up. You must accept this opportunity to rest. Let Darvell take you home; he dislikes shopping as much as you and has been wishing himself elsewhere for the past hour. Your aunt and I can enjoy ourselves for a while longer, then we shall follow you. What do you say, Lady Broxted?'

'You *are* looking a little tired, Carlotta.'

'No, really, I couldn't leave you, Aunt—'

Mrs Ainslowe raised her hand. 'Do not think we are putting ourselves out for you, Miss Rivington. This arrangement will suit us all. And you need not fear any impropriety; one of Lady Broxted's footmen shall walk behind you.'

'Well, if Lord Darvell does not object to taking my niece home...'

Carlotta could see that her aunt was weakening. 'No, really, I could not impose upon Lord Darvell!'

She was ignored. Lord Darvell was bowing.

'Nothing would give me greater pleasure, ma'am.' He spoke with studied indifference and Carlotta cringed. 'Well, Miss Rivington, shall we leave these ladies to their hedonistic pursuits?'

She was trapped. There was nothing she could say that would not sound churlish and ungrateful.

'There, now!' cried Mrs Ainslowe, beaming. 'Take good care of her, Luke. Tell James I shall send for the carriage later to collect me from Broxted House.'

The two parties went their separate ways. Carlotta stared ahead of her. At Malberry she had wanted nothing more than to be alone with Luke but here, even with Lady Broxted's footman walking a few paces behind, she felt very tense. It was as though she was walking beside a wild beast. A tiger, perhaps, that might pounce on her at any moment. However, when he spoke, Luke's tone was perfectly polite.

'My new sister is a minx,' he remarked. 'She likes to organise everyone her own way. I must apologise for her.'

'Not at all,' murmured Carlotta cautiously. 'I like her; she is very…very refreshing.'

He laughed. 'When you have known her a little longer, you will call her exhausting. She has so much energy to expend on her friends, especially when it comes to match-making. Tell Adele your requirements, Miss Rivington, and she will have you fixed up with a rich husband before you can blink an eye.'

Hellfire! Luke swore under his breath. What had made him say that? He had been surprised at the lightness of spirit he felt at the prospect of having Carlotta to himself for the short walk to Berkeley Square. She looked so pretty with that straw bonnet framing her face, the dark brown ribbons matching her eyes. He wanted to put their quarrel behind them, but his joking remark had come too soon. He sensed her drawing away from him.

'I beg your pardon, I—'

She waved her hand, saying airily, 'Pray do not apologise, my lord, it is an excellent notion. I am sure Mrs Ainslowe must know all the most eligible gentlemen in town. And she will not be shocked by my ambition—after all, your brother married her for her fortune, did he not?'

Luke ground his teeth. 'I'll have you know that James is very much in love with his wife!'

'I am sure he is,' came the honey-sweet reply. 'But I'd wager the fortune does not detract from their happiness. Perhaps we could ask him, for he is even now approaching us.'

'We shall do no such thing,' he retorted as James hailed them from across the street.

'Luke, well met!'

James tossed a coin to the crossing sweeper and came

up to them, a look of enquiry upon his features. Luke performed the introduction almost reluctantly and Carlotta held out her hand.

'Mr Ainslowe, how do you do, sir? I was speaking to your wife but ten minutes since.'

Luke glanced down at the little figure beside him. She was smiling shyly up at James, showing no sign of the scheming minx he knew her to be. James, damn him, was beaming back at her, obviously enchanted.

'Were you, by Gad? I thought she had prevailed upon Luke here to take her shopping.'

'She did, but she has met a kindred spirit in Lady Broxted,' explained Luke. 'Miss Rivington, however, has made her purchases and I am escorting her back to Broxted House. Where are you going, brother? I did not know you would be coming out today or I would have let you escort your own wife.'

'It wasn't my plan to come this way, but I was at Brooks's last evening with a party of friends, and I am now off to collect my winnings from Sir Gilbert Mattingwood. Quite rolled up, he is. Poor Gil, almost lost his boots last night and did not have the means to pay me, so he told me to call on him today at his lodgings in Dean Street, which is where I am going now.' He took out his watch and studied it. 'By Jove, is that the time? I had best get on; there is a house sale in Curzon Street later today and I thought I might give it a look. I fancy there are one or two nice pieces of Sèvres that would look very well at Malberry Court. So—your servant, Miss Rivington; good day to you, Luke.'

James strode away and Luke set off again. He was aware that Carlotta was watching him and said irritably, 'Very well, I will admit that James could not be fitting out his house in such grand style if Adele had not brought a fortune with her. But there is a very strong affection between them.'

'I am sure there is,' was all she would say, but her soothing tones made his fingers itch to strangle her.

He took his leave of her at the door of Lord Broxted's residence, but as he bowed over her hand, a thought struck him. 'Tell me, Miss Rivington, once you have married your fortune, how do you propose to enjoy it, if you are so ill disposed to shop?'

There was a flash of anger in her eyes but it was gone in a moment. She said haughtily, 'It is the proximity of all those other shoppers that disgusts me, my lord. When I have my fortune, then the merchants will come to *me*.'

As the door closed behind her, Carlotta felt an immediate surge of remorse that her antipathy for Lord Darvell had prompted her to utter such an ill-bred comment. She ran up to her room, trying to shut out the look of surprised contempt that she had seen in his face at her words. It was the second time she had seen that look in his eyes and it hurt, even though she knew she deserved it. She sat before her mirror and tried to tidy her curls, which had been sadly flattened by her bonnet.

'What if he does think me mercenary?' she asked her reflection. 'I do not care a fig for his opinion!'

Nevertheless, the feeling of guilt persisted, even though she tempered it with anger at Darvell for being so easily persuaded to think ill of her. Had he learned nothing of her character in those weeks at Malberry Court? It was bad enough that he should consider her capable of chasing a rich husband, unforgivable that he should think that she, with so little herself, should be disdainful of others.

Such reflections made Carlotta more conscious of her behaviour, so that when Mrs Price sent a note to inform them of her plans for their visit to Vauxhall Gardens she was careful not to utter one word of dissent.

'There are to be eight of us,' remarked Lady Broxted, scanning the letter. 'That will be a squeeze at supper, but we shall manage.'

'Who is going, Aunt?'

'Let me see… Mr and Mrs Price, naturally, and Mrs Price depends upon my bringing Broxted. I shall have to work on him, for in general he is not fond of such enter-tainments, which is why it is such a joy for me to have you here, my love, to share in my pleasure. Then there is Julia, and you…oh, and she has engaged Lord Fairbridge and Mr Woollatt to join us. Splendid. How merry we shall be.'

'Yes, splendid.'

Carlotta smiled and tried to sound enthusiastic. Mr and Mrs Price's boisterous spirits would more than compensate for her uncle's retiring nature. She suspected that Julia and Lord Fairbridge would wish for nothing better than to spend an evening together, and Mr Woollatt might be a little dull, but he was perfectly respectable. Besides, there would be Madame Saqui and the fireworks to entertain them all. She told herself it would indeed be a splendid party.

An unseasonably cold spell of weather on the appointed day persuaded Lady Broxted to advise Carlotta to wear her new round gown of blue bombazine with a matching pelisse.

'I had thought it would not be needed until much later in the year, but it will not do for you to catch a chill, my love.' Lady Broxted watched her niece putting the final touches to her dress. 'And you should wear your new kid boots, too, for the rain has left the ground very wet underfoot.' She went to the door. 'Mrs Price says we are to take the water to Vauxhall rather than the new bridge—will that not be a treat?'

Carlotta agreed and hurried downstairs to join her aunt and uncle in the carriage that would take them to the river. They found the rest of the party waiting from them on the quay and they all set off in high good humour for Vauxhall.

'This is your first visit to the gardens, Miss Rivington?' asked Mr Woollatt as they alighted on the far side of the river.

'Yes, sir.'

'Then I think you will enjoy the spectacle. The Grove, you see, is before us—that large rectangle, enclosed by trees and colonnades. Mr Price has hired a supper box for us on the far side, I believe, from where you will be able to watch and listen to the orchestra while we eat. Before that, of course, there is the cascade to be seen, and later, we have the funambulist.' He smiled at her look of surprise. 'Madame Saqui, the tight-rope walker—more properly called a funambulist.'

'Oh,' said Carlotta.

His smile widened. 'You see, Miss Rivington,' he continued, 'I will endeavour to fill your evening with education as well as entertainment.'

'Oh,' she said again.

'For example, did you know that there are over one hundred supper boxes in these gardens?'

'Yes, so shall we find ours?' put in Mrs Price, coming up. 'It is far too bright yet to see the walks at their best. Instead, we shall all enjoy a cup of arrack punch.'

Carlotta made haste to agree, thinking she would need something if she was to endure Mr Woollatt's rather pompous lectures for the whole evening.

Once they had discovered their supper box, the little party passed the time watching the crowds while they sipped at their punch. Carlotta was not sure that she liked the taste of the thick, pungent drink or the way it burned in her chest when she swallowed it, but she struggled on, and had finished the whole cupful when Lady Broxted remarked that it was almost time for the cascade to be revealed.

'Pho, plenty of time yet, it is barely eight o'clock,' said her husband, consulting his watch. 'There is nearly an hour to wait.'

Lady Broxted fidgeted with her fan.

'But the cascade is only on display for fifteen minutes, my dear, and there is always such a crush. If one is late, it is difficult to see anything.'

The earl looked a little contemptuous. 'I have already experienced the spectacle, several times,' he announced. 'I shall stay here.'

'Very true, my lord,' agreed Mrs Price. 'Having seen the cascade on several occasions, I too should much prefer to remain here. No doubt you are the same, Lady Broxted, but the girls must not miss it.' She smiled at Lord Fairbridge and Mr Woollatt. 'Perhaps, sirs, you would like to escort them?'

'Indeed we would!' exclaimed the viscount, jumping up. 'That is, I can't speak for Woollatt, of course, but I should very much like to—I mean...' He trailed off in confusion, a flush darkening his fair cheek.

Mr Woollatt rose to his feet and said smoothly, 'We would be delighted to escort Miss Rivington and Miss Price to the cascade, my lady. That is, if you think you can trust us to take such precious treasures through the gardens.'

Mrs Price laughed gaily and spread her fan.

'Mr Woollatt, how charmingly you compliment our young ladies. Of course we trust you, do we not, Lady Broxted?'

'Indeed we do, my dear sir. Off you go now. You will be able to secure a good view of the cascade, and when you return we shall go together to see Madame Saqui performing.'

Carlotta regarded her aunt with a little surprise, but a moment's reflection made her realise that Lady Broxted considered both gentlemen worthy suitors and she was eager to promote them. She wondered what her aunt would say if she expressed a desire to remain in the supper box, but Julia was already standing up and the viscount was tenderly placing her paisley shawl about her shoulders. Carlotta could only acquiesce with a good grace.

With plenty of time to spare, Mr Woollatt led them all on a circuitous route through the gardens, pointing out the various statues and grottoes on their way. His tone was very much that of a man instructing a child. Julia and Lord Fairbridge were so engrossed in each other that they did not notice, but Carlotta found herself trying to think of something outrageous to say to shock him out of his complacency. Just when she thought she could no longer endure making polite conversation a bell rang out, summoning the crowds to the cascade and the wide path quickly filled up.

'Now you see how wise we were to get here early, Miss Rivington?' murmured Mr Woollatt, drawing her forward. 'We are not quite at the front of the crowd, but I think we shall have a capital view from here.'

With a fanfare, the curtain was drawn back to reveal the display; Julia laughed and clapped enthusiastically, but Carlotta was aware of a little disappointment. The metal representation of a stream and miller's wheel was ingenious, but it clanked noisily, and her artist's eye found the garish setting and lurid colours a little childish. However, as they strolled back to their box, Julia was so enthusiastic about what they had seen that Carlotta suppressed her criticism. Remembering her resolution to be charitable, she even found a few words of praise for the spectacle when they returned to the supper box and her aunt asked her for her opinion. Satisfied that she had acquitted herself well, Carlotta settled down beside Lady Broxted to enjoy a light supper of paper-thin ham, followed by fruit tarts and syllabub laced with wine, while they watched the crowds parading through the Grove.

'Goodness, I vow there are an extraordinary number of gentlemen here tonight,' remarked Mrs Price, her bright eyes surveying the throng.

Lady Broxted nodded. 'More than one usually sees here, certainly.'

'Well, that is to be expected,' said Mr Price. 'A lady performing on a rope high in the air—they have come to watch her, hoping to glimpse more than a pretty ankle, what?' He laughed loudly at his own wit. Lord Broxted, Carlotta noted, gave only a tight little smile.

Mrs Price nodded towards the latest group of gentlemen to appear in the Grove. 'We are certainly acquainted with some of them. Look.' She began to wave to attract their attention.

Like a flock of starlings the noisy crowd changed direction and headed towards their box. To a man they were dressed in the height of fashion with their cut-away coats and light-coloured trousers.

'Heavens,' murmured Julia, moving a little closer to the viscount. 'So many of them.'

'But we know them, my love,' cried her mama, still waving. 'Look, there is Mr Eastleigh, and Sir Gilbert Mattingwood...Sir Peter Ottwood...oh, and Lord Darvell, too! Good evening, my lord, gentlemen. My goodness, the gaming houses will be quite empty tonight.'

'We can always go back to 'em later, ma'am,' cried a fair-haired gentleman with florid cheeks and a twinkle in his blue eyes. He bowed over Mrs Price's hand. 'Thought we should take a peek at the incomparable Saqui.'

Luke followed his friends towards the supper box where Mrs Price was waving and smiling at them all. He had not really wanted to accompany his friends to Vauxhall, but when he saw Carlotta in the box his spirits lifted. He felt the usual tug of attraction as he watched at her. She had discarded her enshrouding domino and looked enticing in her gown of blue satin. The deep colour enhanced the creamy tones of her flawless skin. Her dark hair was curled artlessly around her head, providing a charming frame for her pale face and those huge dark eyes. The anger he had felt at their last meeting was forgotten. He moved forward, ready to smile, to speak to her warmly, but Sir Gilbert was there before him, turning from Mrs Price to fix his eyes upon Carlotta. By God, thought Luke irritably, the man's almost drooling.

'Talking of incomparable,' murmured Sir Gilbert, 'won't you introduce me, Mrs P.?'

Luke noted that Lady Broxted was tutting with disapproval at this forward approach, but Mrs Price merely laughed.

'Of course! Miss Carlotta Rivington, may I present to you Sir Gilbert Mattingwood?'

It was as much as Luke could do not to scowl with frustration as Carlotta gazed up at Mattingwood, a shy smile curving her lips.

'Your servant, Miss Rivington.' Sir Gilbert fixed his laughing blue gaze upon her face. 'Now, why have I not seen you before?'

'I have not long been in town, sir.' Still smiling, she looked past him to meet Luke's eyes for a fleeting moment. Luke knew he was frowning and he saw her smile falter, until Sir Gilbert's next words recaptured her wandering attention.

'Your first visit here, is it, Miss Rivington?'

'Yes, sir, and for Miss Price, too,' answered Carlotta. 'We are mightily impressed.'

'We have been to see the cascade,' offered Julia in her soft voice.

'And did it please you, Miss Price?' asked Luke, determined to say something, however inane.

Julia clasped her hands, a beatific smile upon her face. 'Oh, very much, my lord. It was magical—such a colourful spectacle!'

He smiled and nodded, but from the corner of his eye he could see Carlotta laughing at something Mattingwood was whispering to her. Hell and damnation, could she not see Sir Gilbert for the flirt he really was? He turned to her.

'And what of you, Miss Rivington?' he said. 'What thought you of the spectacle—did the colours suit you?'

'It is very ingenious,' she answered him carefully but her wariness only fuelled his anger.

'But not to your taste, which is for a more…classical form of art.'

Her eyes flew to his face, he could see she thought he was about to denounce her. He would never do that—did she not know him yet? He wanted to say something reassuring, but Sir Gilbert was speaking again.

'Everyone should see the tin cascade,' he remarked with a laugh. 'But only the once!' He leaned a little closer to Carlotta. 'I would be honoured to show you some of the *other* attractions of Vauxhall, Miss Rivington.'

Mr Woollatt stepped forward. 'If Miss Rivington wishes to see anything, then it will be my pleasure to escort her,' he said, his rather heavy chin jutting out belligerently.

Sir Gilbert straightened, still smiling. 'Alas, then, I feel my loss most acutely.'

Carlotta smiled. She was aware of the compliment the gentlemen were paying her and would have been more than human if she had not felt a little tremor of excitement at their gallantry. She nodded at Mr Woollatt, then turned to give Sir Gilbert an apologetic smile. 'I am sorry to disappoint you, sir.'

He inclined his head. 'Madam, you could never disappoint me.'

Her smile grew. She was very happy to indulge in this mild flirtation, conducted from the safety of the supper box where she had the protection of her aunt and uncle. It was also a refreshing change from Mr Woollat's dull lecturing. When she looked at Lord Darvell, however, his disapproving stare somewhat dimmed her enjoyment of the moment. As the group moved away, Mr Price shook his head.

'Scapegraces, the lot of 'em,' he said. 'I hear Mattingwood is done up—could not pay his gambling debts at Brooks's the other night. 'Tis a poor show when a man cannot pay his way.'

'Actually, he did pay up,' put in Lord Broxted, scrupulously fair. 'I was there myself, heard him tell Ainslowe he would settle with him the next morning.'

'Ah,' said Mr Price, winking at Mr Woollatt, 'we've all heard that one before, I dare say.'

'No doubt,' continued the earl, 'but in this case he honoured his commitment. Gave Ainslowe a painting to cover his debt.'

'A painting!'

'Aye,' said the earl. 'A Tiepolo. His father brought it back from the Grand Tour.'

'And is it genuine?' asked Mr Price. 'Has he had it valued?'

Lord Broxted looked affronted. 'Ainslowe doesn't need to do that; he has Mattingwood's word, as a gentleman.'

'Never mind that now.' Lady Broxted rose. 'Madame Saqui will be performing soon; I would like us to have a good view of it.'

They joined the crowd congregating around the fifty-foot mast erected for Madame Saqui's celebrated rope walk. Mr and Mrs Price led their party to a good viewing spot. Carlotta was not sure whether it was by accident or design that they found themselves again in the proximity of the group of young bloods that included Sir Gilbert Mattingwood. With a little skilful manoeuvring, Mrs Price managed to place herself next to Sir Gilbert and engaged him in a rather flirtatious conversation while they waited for Madame Saqui to ascend the rope. Carlotta had taken Mr Woollatt's arm and now stood patiently while he explained to her in excessive detail the number of appearances the lady had made in England. Her mind was beginning to wander when she heard a familiar voice in her ear.

'Your escort is a veritable *encyclopaedia*, Miss Rivington.'

She froze. Luke was standing behind her, pressed so close by the crowd around them that they were almost touching. Her nerves tingled along the length of her spine and she shrank closer to Mr Woollatt. Her escort patted her arm.

'These crowds are a little frightening, are they not?' he said. 'No need to be alarmed, Miss Rivington. I shall not let you go.'

'Fortune favours Woollatt in all ways.'

These next words were merely a whisper; she could almost have imagined them except that she could feel Luke's breath, warm on her cheek. Carlotta found herself trembling. She closed her lips tightly; she would not respond to his teasing. The crowd's applause alerted her to the fact that Madame Saqui had appeared. Carlotta tried to concentrate on the stocky little woman ascending the rope, but she was too aware of Darvell standing so close behind her; if she leaned back just a little, she would be resting against him. The temptation to do just that was so strong it frightened her. Her senses reeled, the blood was singing in her veins. She dare not turn to look at him, but half-expected to feel his hand on her back, or her neck. Anticipation sizzled through her—the thought of his fingers stealing around her waist, pulling her back against him, the touch of his lips on her cheek where a moment ago she had felt his warm breath… It shook her to realise how much she wanted it to happen. She wanted to scream with frustration.

Mr Woollatt was directing her attention upwards, explaining how taut the rope must be, telling her of the special slippers Madame wore to grip the rope.

'It is rumoured she is being paid one hundred guineas a week to perform here,' he said, gazing up in rapt attention at the little figure above him.

'That is nothing to a man of Woollatt's fortune,' Luke murmured in her ear. 'You will be able to command your own private performance when you are his wife—ouch!'

Carlotta smiled. Her heel encased in its soft kid boot had connected very neatly with Luke's shin. It was a small victory, but it eased some of her tension.

Mr Woollatt looked round. 'Oh, is that you, Darvell? Demmed crush, ain't it?'

Carlotta kept her eyes resolutely upon Madame Saqui. She heard Woollatt saying, 'Pray do not crowd the lady, there's a good fellow. Ah, look, Saqui's turning. Bravo, ma'am!'

Carlotta joined in the general applause as Madame Saqui turned gracefully on her high perch. She jumped as a loud cannonade commenced, and a noisy display of fireworks lit up the sky. Madame Saqui moved easily to and fro on the rope, and began a graceful descent. The crowd cheered and roared for more and Carlotta risked a look behind her. Luke had gone.

Chapter Four

'Well, well, how exciting!' exclaimed Lady Broxted. 'Did you not think so, Carlotta?'

'Yes indeed, Aunt. Even my uncle looked to be enjoying it. Is that not so, sir?'

Lord Broxted allowed himself a small smile. 'It was very unusual. I have not seen her before, but I believe she has performed at Drury Lane. A most enterprising female.'

'But she was not very pretty,' uttered Julia. 'I thought she would be dainty, fairy-like.'

'No, she was quite mannish,' agreed Carlotta. 'But very accomplished for all that. Shall we return to our supper box now, Aunt?'

Lady Broxted tucked her hand into her husband's arm. 'Oh, I think we should take a stroll around the gardens first. The lamps look so pretty now it is dark. But there is no need for us all to stay together. Mrs Price, would you object if we allowed the younger ones to go off by themselves?'

'Not in the least, ma'am!'

Carlotta's heart sank a little. 'But surely there is no need for us to go separately. I am sure you will know the most attractive walks, Aunt.'

'But we will want to take a much more leisurely pace. No, my dear, let the viscount and Mr Woollatt take you about. There can be no harm in it, when there are so many people here.'

'Yes, you can chaperon each other,' cried Mrs Price, almost bustling them away.

Carlotta turned to Julia for support, but her friend was looking positively starry-eyed at the prospect of walking through the gardens with Viscount Fairbridge, and Carlotta did not have the heart to spoil her evening. She resigned herself to accompanying Mr Woollatt and began to search for some topic of conversation. There was no lack, but since Mr Woollatt liked to turn everything into an educational lecture she soon found her mind wandering.

'…of course, the dark walks were once notorious for salacious behaviour,' Mr Woollatt remarked as he led her through one tree-lined avenue. 'You can imagine that the little recesses you see at intervals along here were black as pitch before they put up the lamps on the main walk. The gardens have been forced to shut on more than one occasion, due to complaints of licentiousness…'

Carlotta sighed and thought to herself that there was no possibility of her partner behaving licentiously. She had no idea what had happened to Julia and the viscount. They had disappeared, but she guessed they would be having a much more enjoyable time of it. 'The gardens were actually closed for a while and the proprietors were ordered to put lamps here. I think you will agree that the colourful illuminations now make it much more pleasant, although the recesses are still far too dark.'

'I think it would be very exciting to walk through here in the dark with a lover,' Carlotta said, a mood of rebellion growing within her, but her words were uttered so quietly that Mr Woollatt was not discomposed by them. She was disgusted at her cowardice. Why could she not shout at him and make him recoil at her vulgar behaviour? With an inward sigh she realised her strict upbringing did not allow her to behave in such an unladylike way. As they turned into another narrow alley, she saw a familiar figure coming towards her. Thanks to the compulsory lighting in what Mr Woollatt informed her had been a notorious trysting place, she was able to recognise Lord Darvell while he was still some distance away. He was arm in arm with a female who was displaying her ample charms very freely. In one glance Carlotta took in the improbably black curls, painted cheeks and vividly carmined mouth. Her own lips curled in distaste as she watched the woman leaning against her partner, laughing immoderately at something he said. As they drew nearer Carlotta realised she did not want Darvell to know she had seen him. She clung a little closer to Mr Woollatt and turned her face up to him.

'Do you not think it romantic here, under the trees?' she remarked. She knew Luke and his—she sought for a word to describe the wanton creature, but nothing ladylike seemed appropriate—his *woman* would be very close by now, and kept her eyes resolutely upon her companion.

Mr Woollatt regarded her with a rather startled expression. 'I—I beg your pardon, ma'am, what was that?'

Out of the corner of her eye she realised that they were about to pass Luke and his partner. There could be no doubting that he had seen her. She snuggled even closer to Mr Woollatt.

'I think this is *such* a romantic setting. The coloured lamps, the wind whispering through the leaves.' She gave an artistic sigh. 'It makes one long to be able to burst into song, or—or to write verse.'

Even as she said it, the thought of Mr Woollatt turning poet almost made her laugh, but she maintained her soulful pose, turning towards him even more, so that she could peep over his shoulder. She was rewarded for her efforts by the sight of Luke looking back at them, a heavy frown creasing his brow.

'I—um—I have never thought of it in those terms,' said Mr Woollatt, 'but now you have suggested it, I can see how some might find these coloured lights inspiring.' He smiled down at her. 'I had no idea you were such a sensitive little thing, Miss Rivington.'

With Luke now safely out of sight, Carlotta felt it was safe to draw away from Mr Woollatt, but he was holding tightly to her arm.

'Damme if I don't think you are right, m'dear—there *is* something enticing about these lamplit walks.' He nodded slowly. 'Yes, 'fore Gad I think you have made my heart beat a little quicker, Miss Rivington, I—oh—'

He stopped suddenly and released her, clamping one hand to his chest.

'Mr Woollatt, is something wrong? What is the matter?' Carlotta stared at him in concern. He was bent forward a little, his face contorted with pain. A vein on his right temple bulged alarmingly.

'Can't—quite—seem to get m'breath,' he gasped.

Carlotta looked about her, wishing that her aunt or someone she knew was at hand. There were but one couple in view and they had eyes only for each other. She took his arm.

'You must sit down, Mr Woollatt.' She guided him towards the nearest recess and was relieved to find that it was empty. 'Come along, sir. Sit down here in this little bower for a few moments.'

Mr Woollatt staggered to the rustic bench and collapsed on to it, breathing noisily. His hands were tugging at his neckcloth.

'Can't breath,' he gasped again.

Carlotta stripped off her gloves and fumbled with the knotted linen at his throat. It was too dark to see clearly, but at length she managed to untie the cravat and loosen the shirt around his neck. She glanced down at the waistcoat strained across his chest.

'If you will excuse me, sir, I will unbutton your waistcoat too, for I think you will feel more comfortable without that constriction.'

'Yes, yes, thank you, that *is* better,' he muttered. The waistcoat fell away from his chest and he took a deep breath. His frilled shirt billowed out, gleaming palely in the dim light.

Carlotta sat down beside him. His chest was rising and falling with his huge, noisy gasps for air.

'What should I do, sir?' she asked him anxiously. 'Would you like me to fetch someone?'

He reached across and patted her hand, saying wheezily, 'No, no need for that. I think if I rest here for a moment, I shall be well again.'

Carlotta sat beside him, listening to his laboured breathing and thinking miserably that if he died now it would be her fault for exciting him with her flirtatious behaviour. A little tear slipped down her cheek. Aunt Broxted would be horrified to learn how badly she had behaved. She would most likely pack her off back to her parents. At that moment Carlotta thought that she would like nothing better than to return to the little cottage in Malberry, to live in obscurity. She looked again at Mr Woollatt, slumped on the bench beside her. His breathing was much more normal now, but his eyes were closed.

'Mr Woollatt?' Her tentative call made him open one eye.

'Ah, my apologies, Miss Rivington,' he murmured. 'I seem to have been a little overcome. Pray allow me to rest for a few moments more, then I shall return you to your family. I regret this most heartily; I assure you it has never happened to me before.'

'You must not worry yourself, sir,' she replied, relieved that he was showing signs of recovery. 'Rest as long as you wish.'

He patted her hand again, closed his eyes and put back his head. A few moments later he began to snore gently. Carlotta did not know whether she was most indignant or relieved by this. She hoped Mr Woollatt would not sleep for too long, for her aunt and uncle would be growing anxious, but she did not think that she should leave him and go back through the gardens alone. It was growing late and she was aware of the sounds of raucous laughter and coarse jests coming from the adjoining walks. Occasionally she heard footsteps on the gravel path and held her breath, praying no one would look in and see her in the shadowy arbour. As the evening wore on and they remained undisturbed she began to relax, the tedium of sitting quietly in the darkness beginning to steal over her. She thought that she should put on her gloves again and was looking for them when a voice close at hand made her jump.

'Miss Rivington. What a pleasant surprise.'

Lord Darvell was leaning against the pillar at the edge of the recess, arms folded across his chest. As the lamps that lined the walk were behind him, his face was in shadow, but Carlotta thought his stance was decidedly insolent. His tone certainly indicated no pleasure at this meeting. She jumped up and went across to him, putting a finger to her lips.

'Please, Mr Woollatt is sleeping. Do not wake him.' She tried to keep her voice to a whisper.

His lip curled contemptuously. 'Exhausted your lover, have you?'

Carlotta stopped. She had been about to explain everything, but his words suddenly made her realise how the situation must look, Mr Woollatt with his clothes in disarray and her gloves lying discarded at his feet. Her cheeks flamed and she felt hot with embarrassment. 'It is not what you think.'

'No?'

He pushed himself off the pillar and stepped towards her. He towered over her, a huge, menacing black shape. Carlotta could feel the anger emanating from him and had to force herself not to retreat; something of her old spirit reasserted itself. She would not give him the satisfaction of seeing her distress.

'Woollatt looks well satisfied.' His insolent tone flayed her. 'Did you learn those skills at your fashionable academy, or does it come naturally to you?'

Carlotta gasped. Any explanation she had planned vanished from her mind. Even before he had finished speaking her hand swept up towards his face, but he was too quick for her and caught her wrist. Outraged, she tried to pull away, but with a savage laugh he captured both her hands and pinned them behind her. This brought them closer, her bosom pressed against the hard rock of his chest.

Shock rippled through her. Carlotta found herself staring at the diamond pin nestled into the snowy folds of his neckcloth. She felt an overwhelming desire to subside against him and burst into tears. She drew on her anger to support her, threw back her head and gave him a scorching look.

For a long moment they stared at one another. The poor light cast deep shadows across Luke's face and Carlotta had never seen him look so menacing. She realised that he, too, was breathing heavily, far more so than the exertion of their little tussle warranted. Pressed against him, she could feel his heart hammering in his chest as fast as her own. She was taut as Madame Saqui's high rope, heart pounding, nerve-ends tingling with excitement even while she berated herself for the way her body betrayed her. Standing so close reminded her of their dancing together at Malberry. She remembered how safe she had felt in his arms. *Then* he had been smiling and gentle. Now, as he crushed her to him, she could see only anger in his eyes. Panic threatened to engulf her. She fought it down. She would not give in.

'Release me at once,' she hissed, to be rewarded with a wolfish grin.

'Why? Do you not like being in a man's arms?'

'Not in yours!' she flashed.

His hold tightened. He lowered his head and murmured, 'You enjoyed it once, do you not remember?'

Dear heaven, why did he have to remind her! Carlotta sought to control her wayward emotions. She dared not look into his eyes and instead fixed her gaze upon his mouth, but the sight of his lips, parted slightly to reveal his strong white teeth made her recall his kisses, the way he had grazed her bottom lip, the delicious excitement he had roused within her. The urge to turn her face up to his and invite him to kiss her again was almost irresistible. Desperately she dragged her eyes away. If he did not release her soon, she feared she would give in. Or she would scream.

'I thought you such an innocent at Malberry, Carlotta.'

She managed a bitter laugh. 'You said yourself I have learned a great deal since then.'

His eyes flickered back to the sleeping Mr Woollatt. 'Enough to snare a rich husband?'

She resorted to summoning up images of the haughty girls she had known at school and said with what she hoped to be a fine air of cool arrogance, 'Oh, yes, I think so.'

She forced herself to look at him. The contempt in his eyes cut her like a knife and it took all her resolve to maintain her haughty pose, knowing it was her only defence. He stepped back suddenly, but Carlotta could not move. She was like an animal, unexpectedly released and paralysed with fear. She rubbed her bruised wrists.

'Why did you come here?' she asked him.

He looked down, smoothing his sleeves as if brushing away all signs of their contact. 'I was passing your box and saw that you had not returned. I was concerned. Foolish, is it not?'

'Extremely foolish. And the…female you had on your arm?' She could not resist the question.

'Just that. A female looking to make a few shillings from any gentleman wandering alone in these gardens. Unfortunately for her I have no interest in her charms and she has gone off in search of more lucrative company. She offers her body to the highest bidder.' He paused. 'Very much like yourself.'

This time he made no move to stop her and her open palm slammed onto his cheek with a force that made her fingers sting. She stepped back, holding up her head.

'Your opinion of me is now quite clear,' she said, her voice low and shaking with anger. 'You can have nothing more to say to me.' She turned away from him.

'What?' His jeering voice followed her. 'Do you have no response for me? Are you not going to rip my character to shreds, Miss Carlotta Rivington?'

She closed her eyes, forcing back the tears. Her shoulders slumped a little, but she managed to speak with scarcely a tremor in her voice. 'Goodbye, Lord Darvell.'

He did not reply, and after a few moments she heard the scrunch of his hasty footsteps on the gravel as he walked away.

Carlotta went back to the bench. Mr Woollatt showed no signs of waking up, so she put her head in her hands. How had it come to this? That Luke should think her capable of—she shuddered. Only one man had ever held her, had ever kissed her. There had been a violent storm at Malberry last summer, so violent that she had gone inside the house to wait until the thunder and lightning had passed before making her way home. Luke had seen the light from her candles and come to the house to make sure all was safe. She remembered how they had danced in the empty salon, how he had taken her in his arms and kissed her so long and so thoroughly that she had never wanted it to end. When eventually he had put her away from him she had been afraid that she had erred in some way and he had been at pains to assure her that he was not angry.

But he was angry now, here in one of Vauxhall's famed dark walks. She had seen it in his eyes when he looked at her, when he accused her of having a lover. He despised her. And who could blame him?

In the darkened arbour with only the sound of Mr

Woollatt's stertorous breathing to break the silence, Carlotta thought she could never be more despondent, but she was wrong.

When Mr Woollatt awoke and was well enough to escort her back to their supper box, they were greeted by Lord and Lady Broxted with a mixture of anxiety and relief. Mr Woollatt quickly explained that he had suffered a little dizziness and been obliged to rest for a while. Carlotta was relieved that her aunt and uncle accepted this explanation, but the knowing looks and smirking comments from Mr and Mrs Price made her cringe, and it was an ordeal for her to maintain her composure for the remainder of the evening.

A grey dawn was already lighting the sky as Carlotta fell into bed, and she felt little refreshed when she sat up to drink her hot chocolate later the following morning. She contemplated pleading a headache and remaining in her bed for the day, but common sense told her she could not hide for ever and she thought it better to face any criticism as soon as possible. She dressed with care and made her way to the breakfast room, where she found her aunt and uncle already at the table. It was not long before the subject of Vauxhall was broached. Madame Saqui's exploits on the high wire had to be exclaimed over, Lord Fairbridge's marked attentions to Julia Price discussed and Carlotta waited with a sinking heart for the inevitable comments on her own behaviour. She was surprised, therefore, when Lady Broxted merely remarked that she thought her niece had made a hit.

'Yes,' said Lord Broxted with ponderous humour, 'if I had not known Woollatt for so many years I would suspect him of dalliance last night, keeping you to himself for so long.'

Carlotta was not tempted to smile.

'He was suddenly taken with a shortness of breath, Uncle. I was very worried for him; he could barely walk and we were forced to sit down for a considerable time. If he had not recovered when he did, I should have been obliged to seek help.'

Lady Broxted leaned across to pat her hand.

'You did very well, my dear. Mr Woollatt was most complimentary about you. He was very impressed with your concern for him.'

Remembering that it was her outrageous attempt to flirt that had brought on his malady, Carlotta thought this could be no more than flattery and dreaded seeing Mr Woollatt again. She was relieved, therefore, when they met some days later, to find that he treated her with the same polite courtesy he had always shown her. Mr and Mrs Price only mentioned the incident once and, as Carlotta made a supreme effort to conceal her embarrassment, the matter was allowed to drop. She saw no sign of Lord Darvell during the ensuing week and Carlotta began to hope that the episode at Vauxhall Gardens would soon be forgotten.

Lord Darvell was making every effort to blot out the disgraceful scenes at Vauxhall. Never had he felt such overwhelming jealousy as he had that night, seeing Carlotta with that prosy bore Woollatt. If she was determined to marry a fortune, then let her do so—it was none of his concern. But the demon in his head told him it *was* his concern, that if he could only break through the brittle, society maiden she had become, he might find the sweet, innocent Carlotta he had known at Malberry.

'Don't be a fool, man,' he told himself impatiently. 'She

is changed. She is the same as every other woman in town, desperate to make a good match. You have seen her with your own eyes, making up to Mattingwood and flirting outrageously with Woollatt. Let her go.'

He would do just that. They must meet, of course, but he would be no more than civil to her. Carlotta had made it perfectly plain that she wanted nothing more to do with him. So be it. It was over.

Chapter Five

By an unlucky chance, Lord Broxted's party arrived at Lady Yatebury's rout at the same moment that Lord Darvell walked into the entrance hall of the magnificent Yatebury town house. Carlotta's heart sank as Lord Broxted, knowing nothing of the contretemps at Vauxhall, hailed Lord Darvell pleasantly and Luke returned the greeting with a courteous word. As he turned to Carlotta, however, Luke's eyes hardened and his bow was a calculated insult. Her cheeks flamed. How dare he treat her thus! She chose to ignore him and followed her aunt and uncle up the stairs. But despite her brave intentions she was painfully aware of him, her spine prickling with the knowledge that he was but a few steps behind her. Their hostess was standing at the top of the stairs and already calling down excitedly to Lady Broxted.

'My dear, so pleased you could come—it is a veritable crush! But I am so disappointed, the new orangery is not in use yet! I had hoped to have it ready for this evening, but they were still working on it this morning, and my plantsman has let me down and will not be bringing the flowers until next week. It cannot be helped, however, and you must come again as soon as it is ready, for I am burning to show it to you, since you are my *particular* friend.'

They had reached the landing by this time and Lady Yatebury touched her cheek to Lady Broxted's while keeping up a constant flow of chatter. She turned to greet Carlotta, exclaiming at her beauty and cupping her face in her hands while she examined her.

'Such perfect skin! I am sick with envy, my dear, for the smallpox ruined my complexion years ago, which is why I am obliged to wear these patches upon my cheek, but you are in blooming health.' She turned to smile at Lady Broxted. 'She is so pretty I vow she will have every gentleman at her feet, Celia. But you must take care of your heart, little Carlotta,' she continued, her kind eyes twinkling. 'Have a care that you do not take a liking to a rascal such as Darvell here. We would not have you losing your heart to the Wicked Baron—that would never do!'

Carlotta blushed, but said nothing; Luke was beside her, bowing over Lady Yatebury's hand.

'Miss Rivington has nothing to fear from me.'

She winced: his indifferent tone was like a blade slicing into her heart. Pride came to her aid. A half-smile, a haughty look and she murmured, 'Lord Darvell is too kind.'

They moved on to the crowded reception rooms and did not speak again. Carlotta dreaded the coming evening. Heartache, anger and nerves combined; by the time dinner was announced, she felt quite sick and unable to eat anything from the numerous dishes spread on the dining table. She drank her wine in nervous sips and accepted another glass—or was it two? She could not be sure.

* * *

However, with so many young people present it was impossible not to be in infected by their high spirits and after
dinner Carlotta began to relax a little. When the gentlemen
joined the ladies in the drawing room, the conversation
became much more animated and Carlotta even began to
enjoy herself. She tried not to think of Luke, or the fact that
he had spent most of the evening with Mrs Leonora
Daniels, a young married lady who was quite clearly
throwing out lures to him. She watched him now, bending
low over her chair, his brown hair almost touching the
matron's blonde curls as he listened to her. She hunched
one white shoulder. She was sure she did not care; there
were gentlemen enough paying her extravagant compliments and she was minded to enjoy a little flirtation. In fact,
she was feeling quite light-headed. Possibly the effect of
the wine, she thought hazily. The younger members of the
group congregated around the pianoforte where several of
them were persuaded to sing or play.

Carlotta joined Sir Gilbert Mattingwood in one duet, but
refused to perform another, despite numerous compliments
on their performance. She was sorting through the music
to find a piece for Julia Price when from the corner of her
eye she saw Luke approaching with Mrs Daniels on his
arm. She concentrated on the music sheets, but she need
not have feared, for Luke did not once look her way. Mrs
Daniels addressed Julia as they drew closer.

'Miss Price, I saw you at Almack's last night. Did you
not think it very flat?'

Carlotta had been there too and had found it incredibly
dull, although when she observed the dashing matron in her
fashionable gold robe and matching turban, hanging on to

Luke's arm in the most possessive way, nothing would have persuaded her to agree with the lady on any point. She remembered that Julia had spent most of the evening with Viscount Fairbridge, so she was not surprised when Julia declared herself very well satisfied with Almack's.

'Well, I doubt I shall go there again for some time,' Mrs Daniels purred, 'Unless, my lord, I know that *you* will be there.'

'That you will not do,' returned Luke with a smile.

'Darvell never goes to Almack's,' declared Sir Gilbert.

One of the other gentlemen laughed heartily, saying, 'Good thing, too, or he would cut us all out with the ladies.'

Luke bowed. 'Anything to oblige you, Elmwood.'

'Lord Darvell rates his charms very highly,' muttered Carlotta.

Immediately all eyes were turned on her.

'No, no,' Luke reproved her gently, 'you do me an injustice, madam. I do not rate myself above the average.'

'Aye,' cried Sir Gilbert merrily. 'It is the *ladies* who value his attentions. They are all ready to swoon at his feet.'

'Not all of them,' retorted Carlotta. Her head was bent over the music, but the words came out louder than she had intended. Mrs Daniels left her partner and moved forward a little.

'Oho,' she said softly, 'Darvell, here is a woman immune to your charms. How can this be, Miss Rivington?'

'It would be a very sad world if we all liked the same thing,' returned Carlotta, her cheeks hot. She was beginning to regret her rash words and wished someone would turn the conversation to safer channels.

'Indeed, but there are some things we must all value, and Lord Darvell has them in abundance.' Mrs Daniels was watching Carlotta, a small, contemptuous smile playing around her mouth. 'Pray, Miss Rivington, tell us what *you* find attractive in a man?'

'Yes, Miss Rivington.' Luke came forward until the candlelight was reflected in his eyes, like little dancing devils. 'Tell us what qualities you admire?'

Carlotta looked around the little group: they were all watching her, but for once she was not put out by this. She felt a little reckless and looked up fearlessly to meet the challenge in Luke's eyes.

'Honesty, integrity, a sense of honour,' she ticked them off on her fingers.

Mrs Daniels laughed; Carlotta watched her throw back her head, giving everyone the opportunity to admire her fine neck and shoulders.

'My dear, those are the attributes of every gentleman.'

'But are they the attributes of every lord?' flashed Carlotta.

A ripple of amusement ran around the group.

'Now you intrigue me, Miss Rivington,' murmured Mrs Daniels. 'Darvell, is this aimed at you? What scandalous things can she know of you? Pray, Miss Rivington, do tell us.'

Carlotta gave another of her haughty looks. Really, she was growing quite adept at this. 'No more or less than anyone has heard of the Wicked Baron.'

Luke was watching her. He said softly, 'Come, Miss Rivington, will you not give me the opportunity to defend myself?'

She put her closed fan to her lips and modestly cast down her eyes. 'A lady does not indulge in idle gossip, my lord.'

With a smile she left the group. She had not intended to be so outspoken, but it had been worth it to see the startled look upon Luke's face, to hear the whispered murmurs of those around her. She heard Julia begin her piano piece; with everyone's attention upon the music, she slipped away. The sensation of having rocked Luke from his indifference elated her and she wanted a little solitude to savour the sensation. All the reception rooms were crowded, but in one corner of the main salon, behind a silk screen, she spotted a small door. It was covered in the same Chinese paper as the walls and she would not have noticed it if it had not been ajar. Most likely it was a servants' passage, or perhaps another way to the stairs.

Desperate for a little cool air, Carlotta slipped through the door. The light from the salon illuminated the opening, but beyond that the corridor was black, the dark panelling on the walls adding to its gloom. She slipped into the darkness and took a few steps into the cool passage. In the distance she could discern a glimmer of light, but it was at the far end of the passage and Carlotta decided she should go back. As she turned to retrace her steps she saw a figure in the corridor behind her. She could see nothing but the black outline of the man, but she knew immediately it was Luke. He had followed her through the rooms! Blind, unreasoning panic overtook her. Carlotta picked up her skirts and ran.

She made for the patch of light in the distance. It was a doorway, opening into a bare, moonlit room. Carlotta ran in, glad to be out of the cloying darkness. The moonlight flooded in through long windows that filled three of the walls and showed that the room was completely empty. This must be Lady Yatebury's new orangery, she thought as she breathed in the familiar smells of fresh plaster and new paint. Her buoyant mood was fading fast; she was tired and her head was aching. After the noisy, overheated ballroom the conservatory was blessedly cool and peaceful.

She listened carefully. There was no sound from the corridor so she walked over to the window. As she gazed out on to the walled garden, she wondered what madness had possessed her to challenge Luke; surely it was better to ignore him, even to avoid him, until this pain in her heart had diminished to a manageable ache. With a sigh she rested her forehead on the cold glass.

'So, the vixen shows her teeth.'

Carlotta jumped. Lithe as a cat, Luke had come silently into the room. She swung round to face him. Words of apology sprang to her lips, but she bit them back; his face in the moonlight was as hard and cold as marble. It was too late for soft words. She lifted her chin to gaze at him defiantly. 'I said nothing untoward.'

'But you implied much,' he said, coming towards her.

She curled her lip. 'You are called the Wicked Baron; much is expected of you.'

He came closer and Carlotta stepped back until she felt the window pressing against her shoulders.

'Then I am afraid I must disappoint you,' he murmured.

He was less than arm's length from her and Carlotta forced herself not to move.

'I am not afraid of you.'

She was rigid with nerves, and her voice shook a little. Luke's teeth gleamed, but she could discern no humour in his look, no softening of those harsh features.

'Well, you should be. You should be very afraid.'

He reached out and placed his fingers on her shoulder, then drew them down along the embroidered neckline of her dress. Carlotta's nerves were stretched to breaking. At his touch her breasts tightened and rose. Against her will they were inviting his caresses. She clenched her hands, digging the nails into the palms. She wanted to run, but some instinct told her that such an action would inflame an already dangerous situation.

'If—if you try to kiss me, I shall scream.'

He came even closer. Carlotta fought down the urge of her wayward body to close the gap, to lean forward and press herself against him. His eyes held hers and she knew he would see her fear reflected in them. She could not breathe; Luke, too, was taut as a bowstring, the atmosphere between them so brittle only one wrong word could shatter their control and that, she knew, would be disastrous. They gazed at one another, Luke towering over her, dark and menacing. Carlotta's lips parted as he leaned towards her. Her head tilted; unable to prevent it, she was offering him her mouth to kiss. Then, when it seemed inevitable, when her very being was screaming to feel his mouth against hers, he stepped back and gave a little laugh.

'Oh, no, Carlotta, you shall not have the pleasure of my embraces again: that time is past.' His words, the cold tone, hit her like icy water. She leaned back against the window, the cold glass on her skin the only link with reality as he continued. 'But I shall watch your progress, my dear, and if you *should* manage to catch a rich husband, perhaps I shall disclose what delights await him. And you *were* delightful, my dear, that one time at Malberry.'

She ran her tongue across her dry lips. 'W-we did nothing wrong.'

His smile grew, but it was as cold as the moonlight. 'You were alone, at night, in an empty house with the Wicked Baron—do you think any man would believe I did nothing more than kiss you?' He took her chin between his thumb and fingers and forced her to look at him. 'You know I am right, my dear.'

Angrily she knocked his hand away. 'I know nothing of the sort!'

'Believe that if you want to, Carlotta, but I know enough about you to ruin your chances of making a good match.'

'Then you are wicked indeed, my lord.'

He merely laughed, turned on his heel and walked away. Shivering uncontrollably, Carlotta sank down against the window and wrapped her arms about her.

Luke strode back through the corridor, wondering what had come over him. He had grown used to jesting and teasing during his years in the army, so why had Carlotta's little barbs cut so deeply? He had loved and lost other women in the past and it had never been difficult to put them behind him, to see them again without a flicker of remorse. He had thought he could do the same with Carlotta, once he realised that she was intent upon finding herself a rich husband. And he had resolved to stay away from her, a resolve that had lasted only until their very next meeting! As he stepped back into the crowded reception room, he swore fluently under his breath. He would never forget the look of haughty disdain on her face the first time they had met in town, her taunts regarding his lack of fortune, but even that had not killed his feeling for her. It was seeing her at Vauxhall, behaving like any wanton in that darkened arbour with Daniel Woollatt that finally convinced him she was not the sweet innocent child he had left at Malberry.

Her behaviour this evening had been calculated to anger him, like the bitter reaction of a spurned woman, but that did not make sense—*she* had spurned *him*, telling him he was not remotely rich enough to be a contender for her hand. Yet her jibes were like a gauntlet thrown down between them. He knew he should have ignored her challenge and allowed himself to enjoy the charms of Mrs Daniels, but he could not. He had followed Carlotta through the crowded rooms and out into that bare, moon-soaked room.

His anger flared again as he remembered her standing before him, haughty and defiant. When he had moved close to her, smelled the familiar, flowery perfume, he had found her hard to resist. He saw again her face turned up to his, the dainty features so perfect, the mouth so kissable. He had been tempted. She was enticing, bewitching, almost irresistible. His muttered 'excuse me' as he pushed through the dancers was very nearly a snarl and earned for him several angry looks, but it mattered not as long as they moved out of his way. He had to get out; he needed peace and quiet to regain his self-control and work out just what it was about Carlotta that roused him to such fury.

And after that, he needed to decide just what he was going to do about it.

Chapter Six

The confrontation with Luke unnerved Carlotta and she pleaded a slight chill for the next few days until she could face the world again. Lady Broxted was very understanding.

'Poor lamb, but it is not unexpected,' she said, visiting Carlotta's bedchamber. 'We have been very busy of late, and a number of our friends remarked that you seemed pale and distracted when they were taking their leave of you at Lady Yatebury's. You shall keep to your bed for a little while.' She smiled, patting Carlotta's hand as it lay upon the bedcovers. 'I shall cancel our engagements for this week; you must be well for our little soirée.'

But as the day drew nearer it became clear to Carlotta that Lady Broxted's 'little soirée' was going to be a major event. On the eve of the party she went to find her aunt, to offer her some assistance. She found her in the morning room, surrounded by papers and making her final arrangements.

'But, Aunt, you cannot possibly wish to invite all these people,' objected Carlotta, gazing in awe at a list of guests that ran over several sheets of paper. 'You said we were to have a snug little evening—how will you find room for so many?'

'Dear child, this is only half the guests!' Lady Broxted twitched the papers from her fingers and looked at them with satisfaction. 'I think we can be sure that most of them will come; I am renowned for my parties, you know. We shall open up both the saloons and set out supper in the dining room. And if it stays dry, we shall also be able to open up the long doors to the terrace and hang lanterns around the garden. We shall have to bring in extra staff for the kitchens, of course, and we shall need more link boys in the square...'

Carlotta was not listening. One of the sheets had floated to the floor and she scooped it up, her smile dying away as she scanned the names. 'Dear ma'am, surely there is no need to invite Lord Darvell.'

'Of course he must be invited. It is unlikely that he will come, however, for he is a great favourite in town and always in great demand. And since he has shown no inclination to fix his interest with you, he may well consider my little gathering far too tame.'

Carlotta clung on to that thought. There must be far more exciting things for a wild young baron to do in London. Besides, he had made it perfectly clear that he despised her.

No, she decided it was most unlikely that he would come.

'I am beyond doubt the most contrary young woman in the world!'

Carlotta gazed at her reflection gloomily. She had no wish to set eyes on Luke Ainslowe ever again, but she had a great desire that he should see her now that she was looking her best. The thought that he might not attend her aunt's soirée was just too galling.

Jarvis, Lady Broxted's dresser, had spent a great deal of time arranging Carlotta's hair and the result was very pleasing. Tiny apricot-coloured rosebuds nestled amongst her dark curls and matched the roses embroidered around the flounced hem of her rich cream satin evening gown. An overdress of fine white net gave an ethereal, shimmering quality to her skirts and she executed a few dance steps before her mirror, watching the effect.

'Very pretty, miss, I'm sure,' said Jarvis, surveying her with a professional eye. 'We could wish that your complexion was whiter—perhaps a little powder...'

'No, no powder, thank you, Jarvis, I am quite happy with my colour. I inherited it from my Italian father.'

Jarvis tutted.

'Hush, Miss Carlotta,' she said, bending to straighten the hem of Carlotta's gown. 'You know her ladyship does not want you to be saying such things, especially tonight.'

'No.' Carlotta sighed. 'She wants everyone to think me a very English young lady.'

'Aye, she does, and English young ladies do not jig about in front of the mirror! Now, pray you keep still, miss, while I tuck away this stray curl... There, that's better. Off you go and join her ladyship, for your guests will be arriving any moment.'

Carlotta picked up her fan and ran down the stairs to join her aunt. She found her on the landing, at the top of the curling staircase that led up from the entrance hall. She glowed with pleasure when Lady Broxted exclaimed how well she looked, and took her place beside her as the first of their guests was announced. At first Carlotta found it exciting, watching the ladies come in, arrayed in satins, silks and muslins, their tassels and ostrich plumes nodding as they made their way up the stairs. The gentlemen were dressed more soberly, mostly in coats of black or dark blue with knee breeches or pantaloons, but there was an occasional splash of colour as a military man made his appearance in his regimentals. A few of the guests she had met already, such as Mr and Mrs Price and their daughter, but many were strangers, and her head was soon buzzing with names and faces that she feared she would not remember. Mr Woollatt arrived just as the orchestra was tuning up. He immediately launched into an apology.

'My dear Lady Broxted, I would have been here sooner, but my steward has arrived from the country and I was obliged to see him.' He bowed low over Lady Broxted's gloved hand. 'As a matter of fact, I wanted to be one of your first guests,' he continued, bowing gallantly to Carlotta, 'to make sure of the first two dances with Miss Rivington.'

Carlotta blushed and began to repeat the argument she had already used for several other gentlemen that evening. 'You are very kind, sir, but I shall not be dancing for some time. As you see, I must greet our guests—'

Lady Broxted interrupted her. 'Nonsense, child. All but a very few stragglers are here now. You have done your duty, no one expects you to stay here for ever.' She gave Carlotta a beaming smile. 'Take her away, Mr Woollatt. Carlotta's first two dances are free, so you shall be her reward for showing such patience.'

Reading the triumph in her aunt's smile Carlotta suspected that she had planned this. There was nothing for it but to accompany Mr Woollatt and take her place amongst the dancers.

* * *

Luke arrived at Broxted House with his brother and sister-in-law just as the first set of dances was ending. Lady Broxted had left her post at the head of the stairs, but as they entered the saloon she hurried across to greet them.

'Apologies for being late, ma'am,' said James, bowing over her hand. 'If Adele had not taken so long choosing her gown, we would have been here a good hour since.'

Adele gave him a playful tap with her fan. 'You will not blame it all upon me, James—admit that you could not tie your neckcloth!'

He grinned. 'I will admit nothing, especially in front of my brother here.'

Luke managed a faint smile. He wished he had not agreed to come, but Lady Broxted was smiling at him, holding out her hand and welcoming him. There was no escape now.

'Since you are all three acquainted with my niece, then you have missed nothing.' She smiled and added with a touch of pride, 'Except, gentlemen, that I quite fear that she is engaged for every dance.'

Luke looked across the room at Carlotta, who was at the centre of a laughing, chattering crowd of young people.

'That is definitely a severe loss, ma'am,' he said politely.

He resisted Lady Broxted's attempts to introduce him to any other young lady, and when Adele went off with her hostess the two brothers retired to a quiet corner. Luke tried to ignore James's quizzical glance, but his brother took his arm.

'Out with it, Luke—what is the meaning of this long face you are showing the world? You have been quite distracted recently, refused several invitations to dine with us—why, man you have all but given up gambling! If I did not know you so well I'd think you were in love.'

Luke felt the flush mantling his cheeks. 'Nothing so foolish!' he growled.

James gave a crack of laughter. 'Oho! So it *is* a woman,' he exclaimed. 'What happened, did she turn you down? That must be a new experience for you.'

'Go soak your head, James! Just because you are head over heels in love with Adele, pray do not think it happens to everyone.'

'Well, it should. I have never been so happy, which makes me want you to be happy, too. So tell me what is the matter.'

Not for the world could Luke tell his younger brother about Carlotta. He was not about to admit that any woman could fill his thoughts night and day.

'I have been looking at the accounts for Darvell Manor.'

'Depressing, are they?'

'Damnably so.'

'My offer of a loan still stands, brother—'

'No, it is not as bad as that. Not yet. I wish, though, that our father had told me the true state of affairs, I could have helped him.'

'He was too proud to admit that he had spent your inheritance, Luke. He always thought he could win it all back at the gaming tables.'

'Instead of which he lost even more.' Luke sighed. 'When Father died, I should have sold out, taken control of the estate, looked after you—'

James put a hand on his shoulder. 'It was too daunting a task for a young man of one-and-twenty. No one blamed you for going back to what you knew, to the army. And you found enough money to make me a generous allowance—we should not forget that.'

'But if I had begun the improvements then, five years ago, I could have been a wealthy man by now—or at least comfortable!'

'Aye, but would you have been happy, working your land while your comrades faced Bonaparte without you?'

Luke sighed. 'No, you are right, James. I would not have missed Waterloo for the world. I could not have forgiven myself. But now—'

'Now you need to take charge of your affairs, Luke. Send that rascally agent of yours to the right about.'

'I already have. In fact, I have put in motion a number of improvements at the Manor and must go back there soon.'

'Go where?' asked Adele, coming up at that moment.

'To Darvell. My estates need proper management.'

'But you are not going immediately?' She laid a hand on his arm. 'You promised to come back to Malberry with us.'

He gave her a wry smile. 'Yes, I did. And I shall come with you, you have my word.'

'Good, you will be able to see my new Tiepolo,' murmured James.

'The one Mattingwood gave you in payment of his gambling debts?'

'That's right. I sent a man down with it yesterday. I'm going to hang it in the library.'

'And we are gathering any number of people to join us at Malberry for the summer,' added Adele.

'Aye, well, make sure there are some uncommonly pretty ladies amongst the guests, my love,' said James, grinning. 'We need to provide my brother with plenty of distraction, for I think he is nursing a broken heart!'

* * *

The rooms were crowded and noisy. A sign, thought Carlotta, that the party would be deemed a success. Once it was realised that Miss Rivington was no longer busy greeting her guests, a flattering number of gentlemen began vying for her attention. Carlotta had no illusions about the attraction; her uncle had made no secret of the fact that he would make a generous settlement upon her marriage, and most of her dance partners were single gentlemen like Sir Gilbert Mattingwood, eager to improve their acquaintance with Lord Broxted's protégée. She was amused, therefore, when Lord Fairbridge claimed his dance with her. She saw his eyes following Julia, who was further down the line, partnered by a handsome soldier with bushy side-whiskers. After a half-dance of stilted attempts at conversation she was prompted to protest.

'My lord, would you not rather be dancing with Miss Price? Pray tell me truthfully,' she said, her eyes twinkling, 'I promise you I shall not be offended.'

The viscount looked at her, alarmed, but her smile re-assured him. He gave her an apologetic grin.

'She has promised me another dance after supper,' he confessed. 'To be seen dancing together more often would give rise to gossip.'

'It would indeed,' she agreed cordially. 'And so you must dance with all the other young ladies in the meantime.'

'Yes.'

His affirmation was so wistful that Carlotta almost burst out laughing. As the dance ended she gave him a specu-lative look.

'If you would prefer, we could sit out this next dance, my lord.'

'Could we?' he gazed at her hopefully.

Stifling a giggle, Carlotta took his hand and led him to the edge of the room and out through one of the long windows to the terrace.

'So many people and so much chatter, it is not conducive to conversation,' she told him as they stepped out into the lamp-lit garden. 'So, have you made an offer for Julia?'

Her direct question made him stutter.

'N-no. M-my mother thought it w-would be best if we waited until the end of the Season.'

Carlotta remembered being presented to Lady Fairbridge earlier in the evening—a colourless little woman with a small, rosebud mouth and arching eyebrows that gave her a look of permanent surprise. She had been very gracious, but in the manner of one bestowing a great honour, and Carlotta thought it unlikely that the viscountess would consider a mere Miss Price to be a suitable bride for her son.

'And what do Julia's parents say?'

'I—um—have not yet spoken to Mr Price, but Mama is sure he would agree.'

Carlotta considered it much more likely that Julia's father would want to draw up the marriage settlements immediately and make sure of such a prize, but she decided it would be unkind to say so.

'And does Julia know how you feel?' she asked him.

'Oh, yes. That is, she would do nothing without her parents' approval, of course, but I cannot think there will be any obstacle.'

'Except your mother.'

Carlotta wished the words unsaid, but the viscount was not offended.

'It is not what she would wish,' he agreed, considering

the matter. 'Julia—Miss Price—does not have a large fortune, but she is in every other way perfectly suitable.'

'She is not exactly a pauper,' retorted Carlotta.

'True, but Mama was hoping I might find someone a little nearer my own station,' he said, twisting his hands together in some anxiety.

'Hmm, someone from a noble family, do you mean? That would be more difficult, I think. I have only been in town a few weeks, but it seems to me there are very few young ladies—' She saw his anguished glance and clapped her hands to her mouth. 'Oh—you mean me? Because I am Earl Broxted's niece?' She went off into a peal of laughter. 'I beg your pardon,' she said, wiping her eyes. 'I think if your mama knew me better, she would agree that Julia is a far more suitable bride for you!'

They walked the length of the terrace and back again in an amicable silence, but as they approached the long windows Carlotta said, 'Come, the music has finished so we had best return; my next partner will be looking for me.'

They made their way back to the saloon so much at ease with each other that when Carlotta spotted a patch of dust upon the shoulder of his coat she did not hesitate to mention it.

'My lord, you have pollen on your shoulder from the bushes.'

Smiling, she was reaching up to brush it away as they walked back through one of the long windows. Then the viscount stopped suddenly and she looked up to see Lord Darvell blocking their way.

Carlotta felt the blood draining from her face. Her hand was still on the viscount's shoulder and as he stopped she was obliged to lean against him to correct her balance.

Luke stood before her, his face stony. Carlotta gathered her courage. She must be strong; he could not hurt her here, in front of all these people. She stepped away from the viscount, smiling.

'Thank you, my lord. I must find my next partner…'

He bowed and turned away. Luke's hand shot out and gripped her arm.

'My dance, I think.'

Carlotta glared at him. A young man came up, saying shyly, 'Miss Rivington, I believe you are engaged to dance this gavotte with me—'

He put out his hand, but Luke was already pushing past him, dragging Carlotta on to the dance floor. The young man looked confused.

'Miss Rivington—'

'Go to the devil!' snarled Luke.

Carlotta tried to pull her hand away, but Luke's grip was inflexible as iron. He almost flung her into position on his right, his stormy gaze daring her to run away. Carlotta ran her tongue nervously over her lips and glanced around her. Everyone was intent on taking their places for the gavotte. She must not draw attention to herself; it would not do to cause a scene. She dragged her head up. One dance, that was all. She would get through it. She knew the steps, but faltered a little when she turned to face her partner. His eyes bored into her, no longer a laughing hazel, but cold and hard as polished stone. The tense line of his jaw revealed his anger.

'What were you doing on the terrace with Fairbridge?'

Her brows rose. A tiny spark of an idea nudged at her brain. Could his anger be caused by *jealousy*? Not that she cared a jot for him, of course. She gave him as haughty a look as she could manage.

'I do not see that I need discuss such things with you, my lord.'

'Do you think he would even look at you if he knew your real name?'

His voice was low so that no one else could hear him. Knowing that the viscount had set his heart on Julia Price, Carlotta was able give him a glittering smile.

'Oh, I do not think it would make one jot of difference to him. But, naturally it is more advantageous to use Lord Broxted's family name. It confers an added dignity.' They turned away from each other, and as they came back together she added, 'Especially when one is looking for a husband.'

She noted his scowl with savage satisfaction as she completed the move.

'And has all this *added dignity* produced a suitor worthy of your consideration?' he asked.

'Several.'

His grip on her fingers tightened painfully, but she would not complain.

'No doubt they will be delighted to know the extra skills you will bring with you, just think of the savings—no expensive Chinese silks for your walls, my dear, you will have original paintings, all your own work. No doubt you will devise something…suitable for the bedroom.'

Her eyes narrowed. 'Your wit, my lord, is better suited to a tavern than a *ton* party!'

'And how would you know that, unless you were born in one?' he threw back at her. 'An Italian tavern, no doubt.'

She bit her lip, anxious that the other couples should not hear their bickering. She made her swift pirouette and the dance continued, everyone laughing and chattering as they executed the gavotte steps. Carlotta smiled until her cheeks ached. She looked up at Luke, who seemed to be smiling quite naturally, yet when they came close he snarled at her through clenched teeth, 'By God, you deserve that I should expose your deception.'

Carlotta grew cold. For herself she did not care, but her aunt and uncle—they were so anxious to conceal her history, she must do all she could to avoid embarrassing them. 'You could not be so cruel.'

He was standing behind her, their hands held high. He muttered savagely into her ear, 'Oh, I can be much worse than this, my dear. I intend to let you carry on with your little charade, but remember, I know the truth about you— I can bring it to an end whenever I wish.'

He turned her around and she glared at him, her palm itching to slap his smiling face, but he held tightly to her hands. 'Smile, Carlotta, the gentlemen like to see a happy face.'

Her eyes glittered. Mechanically she performed her steps, forcing herself to sink into the final, graceful curtsy to her partner. He bowed, then removed the white rose from his buttonhole and handed it to her.

'A token, Miss Rivington, that you may remember this dance.'

Mechanically she put out her hand, but kept her eyes fixed on his face. He looked so cold, so merciless that her fingers clenched, closing around the stem until the sharp stab of a thorn brought her to her senses. She must face the truth—it was not jealousy that made him act so. He hated her, and she had given him every inducement to do so by acting as a heartless fortune hunter. Tears burned her eyelids and she blinked them away. No one should see her misery.

Still smiling, Luke took her arm and led her off the

dance floor. Angrily Carlotta pulled away. Giving him one last, scorching look, she dropped the rose, turned on her heel and walked quickly towards Lady Broxted, who was talking with Mr Price. With his long stride, Luke had no difficulty keeping pace with her; as they approached, Mr Price beamed at them.

'There, sir, I was watching you go down the dance. Capital entertainment, eh, my lord? Miss Rivington makes an excellent partner, does she not?'

Carlotta seethed as Luke bowed and smiled at her.

'Indeed, sir, I have rarely enjoyed a dance more. She is a true artist.'

Stifling her indignation Carlotta turned away. Behind them a console table held a dish of confits and she hovered near it on the pretext of choosing a sweetmeat.

'Let me recommend the marzipan.' She heard Lord Darvell's voice in her ear. 'I believe it is an *Italian* delicacy.'

'I wish you would leave me alone,' she muttered.

'Now why should I do that, when there is such good sport to be had?'

Carlotta hunched a shoulder. She began to fan herself rapidly. So, the battle lines were drawn. At every opportunity Lord Darvell would taunt her. It seemed cruel, when he was the one who had deserted her—even now the memory of those halcyon days at Malberry still had the power to hurt her. But she would never admit that; pride would not allow it.

She suddenly felt desperately weary, longing to leave this crowded, busy life where she could not relax and be herself. In a mood of deep depression she thought of asking her aunt to take her away from London. The words hovered on her tongue.

'My dear child, you are very flushed.' Lady Broxted regarded her anxiously. 'Are you unwell, are you not enjoying yourself?'

Her resolve wavered—how could she be so ungrateful when her aunt had gone to so much trouble on her behalf?

'I am enjoying myself very much, Aunt, thank you. I am just a little warm.'

'Aye, town is grown white hot,' agreed Mr Price. 'But I have good news for you, I have just been talking with your aunt—you will not object if I tell Miss Rivington what is decided, ma'am? We are all to go away for the summer! There, you will like that, I am sure.'

'Go away?' Carlotta offered up a prayer of thankfulness. 'Aunt, that is splendid news! Where are we going, and how soon?

Lady Broxted laughed and put up her hands. 'Good heavens, my dear, how eager you are to be away from here.'

Carlotta flushed. 'Forgive me, I mean nothing against Broxted House, dear aunt, but Mr Price is right—London is growing so very warm.'

Mr Price nodded at her. 'Aye, my dear, we are all feeling it. Poor Julia suffers dreadfully. This invitation has come just in time.'

'So?' Carlotta was eager to find out more. The idea of leaving town was too tempting. 'Where are we going, Aunt— is it Brighton? Worthing? Mr Price, will you not tell me?'

Mr Price beamed at her. 'Mrs Ainslowe has invited us all to Malberry Court for the summer!'

Carlotta stared. Her dreams of escaping her tormentor crumbled away to dust. Behind her, she heard Luke laugh softly.

Chapter Seven

'Malberry Court?' Carlotta shot a swift, questioning glance at her aunt.

'Your uncle has already agreed everything,' said Lady Broxted, a hint of reproach in her voice. 'We are to travel to Malberry at the end of the month.'

'Aye,' cried Mr Price. 'And a merry party we shall make of it, eh, ma'am? If you will excuse me, now, I see my dear wife is beckoning to me, so I shall go and see what she wants.' He beamed at them again. 'I shall leave you ladies to talk about the treat in store for you!'

Carlotta knew that a crowded room was no place to discuss the forthcoming visit to Malberry Court and, by the time the last of the guests had left, Lady Broxted wanted nothing more than to retire to her room. Carlotta was obliged to wait until the morning to express her anxiety.

When she learned at breakfast that her aunt was keeping to her room after the rigours of the party, she would not be put off any longer. She found her aunt sitting up in bed, sipping at her hot chocolate.

'Aunt, do I disturb you? I need to talk to you.'

Lady Broxted waved away her maid. 'Of course you do not disturb me, child. Come, sit on the edge of the bed and tell me what is making you look so anxious.'

'Dear ma'am, surely you have guessed? The visit to Malberry Court—is it wise for us to go, do you think? I mean, with Mama and Papa in the village…'

Lady Broxted gave her an odd little look. She put down her cup carefully.

'My dear, your uncle arranged it all with the Ainslowes last night. *I* had nothing to do with it. I said it was asking for trouble to go to the Court when your parents are living so close, but he thinks there is no reason why anyone should make the connection. And, of course, it does mean that we may be able to arrange for you to visit them while we are there. Discreetly, of course. But you would like that, would you not?'

'Oh, yes, very much.' Carlotta twisted her hands together. 'But what if someone at the Court should recognise me?'

Lady Broxted shook her head, smiling. 'Now how could that be? As you have said yourself, we took you away from Malberry before the Ainslowes moved in to the Court. Silly child, I think you are worrying unnecessarily.'

'But when Papa was working, I sometimes went up to the house with him…'

Lady Broxted sat up at that. 'Mercy me! Who saw you there?'

'The—the workmen, of course, and…and Kemble, Mr Ainslowe's clerk of works.'

Carlotta waited anxiously while her aunt frowned over this, tapping her fingers together.

'But there were no household staff there?'

'No, ma'am.'

'The workmen will have been paid off by now. And the clerk of works, you say? Well, it is very unlikely that he will remember you, for you are a very different creature now. And if you visited your father once or twice while he was working, I dare say this—this Kemble scarcely noticed you.'

'It—it was more than once or twice, aunt.' Carlotta screwed up her courage. 'I—um—I painted two of the ceiling frescoes.'

'You did what?'

Lady Broxted fell back against her pillows, her colour fluctuating alarmingly. Carlotta jumped off the bed.

'Shall I call your maid, ma'am?'

'No, no, I shall be better in a moment. You may fetch my smelling salts from the table over there...ugh! Thank you. That is better.'

Carlotta watched anxiously as her aunt lay back on her pillows, eyes closed. Eventually, she sat up again, a look of long suffering etched upon her features.

'I think you should tell me the whole.'

'Papa had broken his leg—'

'Yes, yes, I know that, for he was laid up when we called upon you.'

'Well, the house was so nearly finished, there were two small ceiling frescoes to be painted and no one else to do it, so...I painted them.'

'Good heavens. And...and this was on a ceiling, you say?'

'Yes, ma'am.'

'Which entailed....climbing a ladder?'

Carlotta nodded.

'And the workmen saw you?' Lady Broxted's colour began to rise again.

'It was not so very bad. You see, I was wearing breeches, and—'

Lady Broxted shrieked and put her hands over her face. 'Breeches! Oh, heavens, we are undone!'

'No, no. Dear Aunt, you said yourself that the workmen will be gone.' Carlotta sought to reassure her. 'And Mr Kemble will not connect fashionable Miss Rivington with her curls and ringlets with little Carlotta Durini, even if our paths should cross, which is highly unlikely.' She paused. 'However, I think it might be best to cry off—could you not say that I am unwell, and we could retire to the country for the summer?'

Carlotta waited hopefully, but her aunt shook her head.

'No, your uncle would never hear of it. He was so pleased with himself for arranging the whole.'

'But why, ma'am? I know he is good friends with Mr Ainslowe, but surely it would not cause such great offence if we did not go—'

'It is not quite so simple, Carlotta.' Lady Broxted twisted the edge of the sheet between her fingers. 'Mr Ainslowe has invited a large number of guests to Malberry.'

'Then our absence will be less noticeable.'

'He has invited Lord Fairbridge and Mr Woollatt to join the party, and they have accepted.'

Carlotta smiled. 'Oh? I am sure they will all have a very pleasant time.'

'You do not understand! Broxted expects one of them to make you an offer!' The silence that greeted this statement was profound, broken only by the steady tick of the pretty little carriage clock on the mantelpiece. Lady Broxted's restless fingers smoothed over the covers. 'Your uncle is very anxious for you to make a good match,

Carlotta. He is confident that you can do so. Lady Fair-bridge has hinted that she looks favourably upon you as a bride for her son, and Mr Woollatt's standing up with you for a second time last night was most encouraging. When your uncle learned who was going to be at Malberry, he thought it could not be better; we have always said that if you should receive an offer, then your suitor must be told of your true circumstances. What better place to explain everything, with your parents so conveniently situated? And now you tell me that you were running all over the house, dressed as a...'

'I am very sorry, Aunt.' Carlotta sighed miserably.

'Well, we must make the best of it.' Lady Broxted threw back the bedcovers. 'Ring for my maid, my love. I will go and see Broxted and explain the whole.'

'Will he be very angry with me, do you think?'

'Perhaps, but we must see what is to be done. If he thinks we can still carry it off, then so be it.'

'Aunt!'

Lady Broxted regarded her, a question in her eyes. Carlotta knew it was time to tell Lady Broxted of her meetings with Lord Darvell, but even her brave spirit quailed at the thought of confessing so much. Perhaps he would not betray her. Perhaps she could persuade him not to betray her.

'Well, my dear?'

Carlotta's courage failed her, she shook her head. 'Nothing, Aunt.'

Later that day Carlotta was summoned to Lord Broxted's study. She went in cautiously, and found her aunt and uncle waiting for her. Lord Broxted's frown eased

a little when he saw how anxious she looked and he gestured to her to sit down.

'Your aunt has told me of your conversation this morning,' he said in his ponderous way. 'I admit that I had some
concerns when Ainslowe first issued the invitation, but we
have already agreed that although one cannot like the circumstances of your parents' marriage—' Carlotta opened
her mouth to protest, but he put up his hand to silence her.
'Pray let me continue. Your mother's running off to marry
an Italian artist cannot be viewed as anything other than re-
grettable, but there it is: if the truth should out then we will
deal with it. Besides, as your aunt has told you, if a suitable
gentleman should make you an offer of marriage, then he
must be told. Your announcement that you were—ah—more
actively employed at Malberry Court than we first realised
has been a shock, I confess, but the advantages of our visit
far outweigh the slight risk of your being recognised.'

'Oh. I have no wish to embarrass you, Uncle. Would it
not be better to go somewhere else this summer—
Brighton, perhaps?' asked Carlotta, hopefully.

A look of distaste flickered over his face. 'I have never
been one of the Prince's set and would prefer that you
were not brought to their attention. No, we shall go to
Malberry. Your aunt mentioned that the clerk of works had
seen you at the Court. I know from Ainslowe himself that
he has sent the man off to oversee the building of his
hunting lodge in Leicestershire. It is therefore highly
unlikely that he will return during our visit. It is my hope
that by the end of our stay at Malberry Court, it will be unnecessary for us to worry further over your origins.'

'You mean, sir, that I should accept an offer of marriage
if I receive one.'

'But of course you should!' Lady Broxted looked at her in surprise. 'After all, that is the reason we took you under our wing, is it not?'

'Yes,' said Carlotta, stifling a sigh. 'I suppose it is.'

'I do not wish to pain you, Carlotta, but you have very little choice,' her uncle pointed out. 'What does the future hold for you, if you do not marry? Perhaps you have some idea of making your living as an artist, but you must know how precarious that would be, and you must not be thinking that I should feel obliged to give you a pension,' he said, his face hardening. 'I am afraid I could not bring myself to condone your choice of a lifestyle that could only bring more disgrace upon our family.'

'So you consider Mama *disgraced* herself when she married an artist,' said Carlotta, angry colour warming her cheeks.

'No, of course he does not,' put in Lady Broxted quickly. 'I am sure—'

The earl raised his hand. 'Please, madam, I think it is time my niece realised her situation. When we offered you a home, Carlotta, it was in an effort to reinstate a branch of the family. It has never been my intention to allow you to follow in your mother's footsteps.'

Carlotta choked down the angry retort that rose to her lips. She had always known the whole point of bringing her to town was to find her a suitable husband—her aunt had never made a secret of the fact. How could she now say it was not what she wanted?

Chapter Eight

At the assembly the following evening, Mr and Mrs Price and their daughter could talk of nothing but the forthcoming visit to Malberry. They were discussing the subject when Carlotta and her aunt came up to them, and immediately drew Lady Broxted into the conversation.

'We were just saying how much we are looking forward to seeing Malberry Court,' said Mr Price in his blunt, jovial way.

'Yes, we have heard much of the refurbishment,' said Lady Broxted.

'Well, here is one gentleman who can tell us if it is worth all the fuss!' Mr Price looked past Carlotta and beckoned. 'Lord Darvell, well met, sir. We are discussing Malberry— you were there when the work was being carried out, I understand. Tell us, is it as fine as everyone says?'

Luke paused. He did not look at Carlotta, but he was very aware of her standing so close, those expressive eyes shuttered, her countenance impassive.

'Better,' he replied. 'My brother has spared no expense,

the most fashionable architect was employed, and the finest artist available…'

From the corner of his eye he saw Carlotta jump and turn away. Damnation. He had intended to ignore her, but now, standing so close, he could not help himself; he would do anything to get behind the mask of indifference.

'Aye, so I heard. An Italian.' Mr Price gave a hearty laugh. 'I hope there's nothing on the walls that will shock the ladies!'

'Oh, I would not think that likely, in the house at any rate,' murmured Luke. 'What do you say, Miss Rivington?'

Carlotta wanted to glare at him, but she was aware of her aunt's nervous looks; it would not do to raise suspicions. She shrugged. 'As I have never been a guest at Malberry, I could not say. I am sure Mr Ainslowe has commissioned everything in the very best taste.'

She turned away, but his voice followed her.

'Miss Rivington is something of an artist herself. She is very good.'

'My niece?' Lady Broxted gave a nervous little laugh. 'Wh-whatever gives you that idea, my lord?'

Unable to escape, Carlotta turned back to confront her tormentor. She raged inwardly when she saw the devilish amusement dancing in his eyes.

'She told me so herself.'

'Oh, do you draw, Miss Rivington?' Mrs Price pounced on this news.

'I prefer to *paint*, ma'am,' Carlotta replied stiffly.

'Perhaps you will take Julia's likeness. I am sure she would sit for you, my dear.'

'Miss Price will need a little patience, ma'am,' said Luke. 'Miss Rivington has promised that *I* shall be her first subject.'

An agitated murmur came from Lady Broxted. Carlotta's cheeks flamed.

'We were funning, sir. I am no portrait painter.'

'No? I thought it was in the blood.' He laughed. 'You see how she colours up, Mrs Price? Miss Rivington displays a hasty temperament. Quite *Latin*, do you not agree?'

Mrs Price chuckled and tapped his arm with her fan. 'What nonsense, my lord. You know very well it is your teasing that has overset her. Pray leave the child alone or you will make her afraid of you.'

'Thank you, ma'am, but there is no danger of that,' retorted Carlotta. 'As well be afraid of a bag of wind!'

'My dear!' exclaimed Lady Broxted, mortified at her niece's lack of manners.

Biting her lip, Carlotta excused herself and walked away. To disguise her agitation she began to tug at her gloves, which had slipped down below the elbow.

'Take care, Carlotta, you are dangerously close to flouncing, you know.'

Luke had followed her. She almost screamed with vexation.

'Pray leave me, sir. I do not care for your teasing.'

'Well, that is unfortunate for you, my dear, because I have not done with this game. When you are angry you are quite…delicious.'

He reached out and drew one finger along the bare skin of her arm between the edge of her glove and the tiny puff sleeve. Carlotta shivered as his touch awakened the memory of being in his arms, of his kiss. It had been such a sweet moment and over far too quickly. She reminded herself how little that kiss had meant to him. She jerked away.

'I will not play your game, sir!'

He bared his teeth. 'Oh, I do not think you have any choice.'

Her eyes narrowed, but even as a sharp retort rose to her lips he bowed and lounged away, laughing.

Lady Broxted came up, frowning anxiously. 'My dear, what did Lord Darvell mean? You have not really promised to paint him, have you?'

'No, Aunt, I have promised him nothing,' retorted Carlotta.

'I am so glad.' Lady Broxted gave a huge sigh of relief. 'It would not do at all, my dear, and your uncle would be most displeased. I have noticed that Lord Darvell has been paying you more attention recently; he is very engaging, to be sure, but you know that his fortune is almost non-existent. Pray do not be losing your heart to him, especially now. Your uncle has hopes for something much better for you.'

'Lose my heart?' Carlotta gave a brittle laugh. 'What an absurd idea, dear ma'am. Lord Darvell is an entertaining flirt, but when he is gone I never give him a moment's thought.'

In an effort to prove the truth of her words, Carlotta threw herself into the dancing with an excess of energy. However, when she joined Miss Price a little later, the subject of Malberry Court was raised once again.

'I am so glad you are going to be there with me,' Julia said in her shy way. 'I feel I know you so well now.' She blushed a little. 'Viscount Fairbridge has been invited, too. Did you know?'

'Yes, I had heard,' replied Carlotta. She added with a twinkle, 'Perhaps he will propose to you while we are there—would you like that?'

Julia's blush deepened to crimson. 'I should like that very much.'

'So should I.' Carlotta smiled, not at all overset at the

thought of losing one of her suitors. She only hoped her aunt and Lady Fairbridge would not be too disappointed.

'I have never received an offer of marriage,' murmured Julia. 'Have you, Carlotta? Has a young man ever proposed to you?'

'No, but—'

'But?'

Julia was watching her and Carlotta shook her head.

'Nothing. No one has ever proposed to me.'

But he was going to do so. The words ripped through her. She had been convinced Luke was going to propose…

He had escorted her home from Malberry Court after the storm. It had stopped raining and the clouds were breaking up, allowing a fitful moonlight to cast its blue-grey light over the park.

'It must be close to midnight,' he said. 'Wait here while I collect my horse, and I shall walk you to your door.'

She waited obediently, listening to his footsteps as he strode away into the gloom. She was not afraid of the dark and knew she was quite capable of making her way home alone, but she did not want to say goodbye to Luke. Luke— just thinking of his name spread a warm glow inside her, even though she knew she could not call him by that name, not yet.

When he returned, she stepped down on to the drive to join him.

'The ground is very wet,' he said. 'Shall I throw you up onto the saddle?'

'Thank you, but no. I would much rather walk with you.'

'Then give me your hand. I do not want to lose you.'

They walked in silence, the only sound their footsteps on the gravel and the drip, drip of water from the trees.

'Will you be leaving Malberry soon, sir?'

'Yes. I must go to my own house, it is in Worcestershire—Darvell Manor. I have business there. I have already delayed here too long.'

'Oh...' She hesitated. 'Your brother's affairs have taken more time than you expected?'

Glancing up, she saw his teeth gleaming in the dim light.

'No, sweet torment, I remained here for pleasure only.' She heard him sigh. 'I sought to pass the time here with a little idle dalliance, but—' Angrily she tried to pull her hand away. His hold tightened. 'Wait until I have finished, Carlotta. *But*, I found myself enchanted.'

'You cannot blame me for that,' she said stiffly. 'I never sought to entrap you.'

'No. That was my downfall.'

'Oh.'

He stopped and pulled her round into his arms. 'This is madness, my dear, our worlds are so different. I have been wild, reckless even; you are such an innocent you could not begin to understand. And yet why should we not be happy?'

He appeared to be talking to himself. Carlotta waited patiently, content to be in his arms. With a short laugh he turned and they began to walk again, but Luke kept one arm possessively around her waist.

'What are your father's plans for you, Carlotta?'

'Why, none, sir.'

'Is there no young man in Italy pining for you?'

She laughed at that. 'Of course not. We left Rome two years ago.'

'Perhaps your father wants you to marry another artist, to carry on the family business.'

'If he does, I know nothing of it.'

Puzzled by his questions, she walked on in silence. They followed the drive to the gates and turned to walk along the road towards the village. It was a much longer route than going through the woods, but she was glad of that—it gave her more time with Luke.

'Is your father well enough to receive visitors, Carlotta?'

'Why, yes, sir.'

The dark shapes of the village houses appeared through the gloom, and Carlotta could see the outline of her parents' cottage, standing square and proud in its own little garden. A candle burned in one of the windows.

'Mama has set a light for me,' she said.

'Will she be anxious for you?'

'Of course, but she knows I would not venture out until the storm had passed.'

'Then you had best go in.'

'Will you not come with me?' she asked, greatly daring. 'I am sure Mama would want to thank you for escorting me home.'

'No, no, it is very late, and I am not dressed for such an important occasion. I shall call upon you tomorrow.'

'Important, sir?'

He took her face in his hands and kissed her gently. 'Say nothing of our meetings; it would be best if I explained everything tomorrow. I would have no censure fall upon you, my dear. Any blame must be mine, all mine.' He kissed her again. 'Until tomorrow, my sweet life...'

He stepped away from her, took the horse's bridle and set off at a smart pace along the road. Carlotta watched him until the bend in the road hid him from her sight. A little bubble of happiness was growing within her. *Tomorrow*, she thought, her hand upon the latch, *tomorrow my whole life will change*.

Her life had changed, but not in the way she had hoped. She had not seen Luke again—until she had come to London. She realised Julia was still speaking, and gave herself a little mental shake. 'My apologies, Julia, what did you say?'

'I wondered why Mr Woollatt was not here tonight.'

'I believe he has gone out of town for a few days.' Carlotta smiled inwardly as she recalled her relief when she had heard the news.

'Mama says she thinks he will make *you* an offer, Carlotta,' remarked Julia. 'Would it not be splendid if we were both to find husbands at Malberry?'

'Yes,' agreed Carlotta in a hollow voice. 'Splendid.'

'Miss Rivington, do tell me that my luck is in at last, and that you are not engaged for the next dance?'

She turned to find Sir Gilbert Mattingwood at her elbow. Shaking off her sombre reflections, she bestowed a sunny smile upon him. 'I am not engaged, sir.'

He held out his arm and took her to join in a lively country dance. As they skipped and danced through the set she found herself thinking of the rumours she had heard of his impoverished state. It was a pity, she thought, for he was an engaging companion and might make a pleasant husband. He was certainly more entertaining that Mr Woollatt. Carlotta gave herself a mental shake. She was becoming positively obsessed with the subject of marriage. As the music ended Sir Gilbert took her arm.

'Let us go and find some refreshment.'

They strolled into the next room where a table was set

out with several punch bowls. Lord and Lady Broxted were standing nearby with Mr and Mrs Ainslowe, and it was only natural that when Sir Gilbert had served Carlotta with a cup of punch they should join the group.

'So hot!' exclaimed Lady Broxted, fanning herself vigorously. 'I do not know how you young people have the energy to dance. I shall be very glad to go down to Malberry next week, for it is always so much cooler in the country.'

'Aye, so it is, ma'am,' agreed James Ainslowe. He turned to Sir Gilbert. 'I was telling Lord Broxted about that picture I won from you. I have sent it on down to Malberry Court.'

Carlotta sipped at her punch, wondering that Sir Gilbert should not be embarrassed at this allusion to his gambling debts. However, he did not appear to be in the least discomposed, and merely bowed.

'The canvas is so large I have always thought it more suited to a country house.'

'A Tiepolo, is it not?' interpolated Lord Broxted.

'Aye,' Mr Ainslowe nodded. '*Maeceanas Presenting the Arts to Augustus*, or some such thing. Is that correct, Mattingwood?'

'Yes, something in that line. I was never greatly interested in art.'

'Well, it does not matter, for I shall ask Signor Durini to have a look at it while I am there.'

Carlotta stiffened. Lady Broxted looked anxiously at her husband and plied her fan energetically.

'Your pardon, Ainslowe,' said Sir Gilbert. 'I did not catch that name?'

'Giovanni Durini, the artist I have working at the house.'

'I hope you are not suggesting my painting is not genuine,' cried Sir Gilbert, feigning outrage.

'Don't be such a fool, Gil.' James grinned. 'But since Durini is at hand I shall ask him what he thinks of it.'

'Is not the work on the house complete now, Ainslowe?' Lord Broxted's tone was so studiously casual that Carlotta had to suppress a nervous giggle.

'Oh, the house itself is finished,' replied James. 'Durini has been painting the temples in the gardens this summer. His work is magnificent; I cannot wait to show it off to you all.'

Carlotta swelled with pride at this, but her aunt's anxious face sobered her. Sir Gilbert touched her hand.

'Another cup of punch, Miss Rivington?'

'Yes, yes, if you please, sir.'

'And when do you set off for Malberry, Mrs Ainslowe?' asked Lady Broxted, anxious to move the conversation away from art.

'Friday next, to make everything ready for you all to join us the following week. I would have liked to go down sooner, but we are engaged to Lady Ottwood for her entertainment on the Thursday.'

Lady Broxted nodded. 'Yes, we, too, are going. I am told we are to dine out of doors and there are fireworks planned for the evening.'

'Fireworks,' exclaimed Adele. 'How exciting. What a pity Luke will not be there. He says there is business he must attend to. But it does not matter—we will arrange something of our own at Malberry, will we not, my love?'

Mr Ainslowe patted her arm. 'I shall see what I can do.' He turned towards Sir Gilbert, who was returning with another cup of punch for Carlotta. 'You are coming to Ottwood, are you not, Gil?'

'Alas, no. I must go out of town for a few days.'

Adele looked up quickly. 'Oh, but it will not prevent you joining us at Malberry?'

Sir Gilbert bowed. 'Oh, no, ma'am.' He turned to smile at Carlotta. 'I am very much looking forward to that.'

The following day Mr Woollatt called at Broxted House. The ladies were in the morning room when he was announced; Carlotta gave him a faint smile, but her aunt flew from her chair and greeted him with uncommon warmth.

'My dear sir, you are very welcome. When did you arrive back in town?'

'Last night, madam.'

'Fie on you, sir, and it is now nearly dinner time! Why did you not call this morning? You must know how welcome you are here.'

Carlotta blinked and listened in surprise as her aunt pressed Mr Woollatt to join them for dinner.

'I would like that very much, ma'am, but my dress…'

Since Mr Woollatt was wearing a black tailcoat and knee breeches, Carlotta could not help wondering if he was half expecting the invitation. Lady Broxted was quick to reassure him.

'Pho, we stand upon no ceremony here, sir. Now if you were one of these young bucks who think it acceptable to go round sporting a spotted handkerchief instead of a necktie, an untidy coat and top boots bearing only one spur, I should not be so forbearing, but you, sir, are always dressed with neatness and propriety!'

'If I am not inconveniencing you…'

'No, indeed, Mr Woollatt. Pray sit down, sir. You will excuse me for a moment while I order another place to be laid.'

She hurried away, and Carlotta was left alone with Mr Woollatt.

'I understand the town has been very hot of late, Miss Rivington. I trust you have not suffered while I have been away?'

'No, I have been very well, sir, thank you.' She wondered if he wanted her to say how much she had missed him. She could not lie, so she kept silent. He sat back in his chair, folding his hands across his chest.

'I am very much looking forward to going to Malberry Court next week. A country-house party is the very thing to raise the spirits. Your uncle tells me you will be travelling down early next week—it is my intention to be waiting for you there.'

The smile that accompanied these words made Carlotta look away, something very like panic welling up inside her. She was thankful that her aunt returned at that moment, and she was not obliged to reply. Mr Woollatt immediately turned his attention to his hostess.

'You are not to be thinking I came here merely to beg a dinner,' he said, chuckling at his own humour. 'I have come to issue an invitation for you and Miss Rivington to join me at the theatre tomorrow night. I have secured a box at the English Opera House in Wellington Street.'

'The theatre? How splendid—is it not, Carlotta?'

'But, Aunt, I thought we were promised to Mrs Winterton.'

'A card party! What is that when there is such a treat in store for us?' Lady Broxted dismissed the hapless Mrs

Winterton with one white hand. 'You need not fret, my love. It was never fixed, after all. We will be delighted to join you, Mr Woollatt.'

'Excellent.' he rubbed his hands together. 'They are performing a farce and one of Mr Sheridan's comedies. I thought Miss Rivington might prefer that to more serious fare, and I shall be able to show you both the new gas lighting.' Carlotta thought she had misheard him, but she saw that her aunt was looking equally blank. 'Not only do they have the new lanterns at the entrance, but they are using gas to light the stage, too,' explained Mr Woollatt.

'How exciting,' murmured Lady Broxted. 'We are very much in your debt, sir. You will be able to wear your new silk gown, Carlotta.'

Mr Woollatt beamed. 'A new gown? I am sure you will look delightful, Miss Rivington, and as for being in my debt, well, ma'am, the sight of Miss Rivington in her new gown shall be my reward!'

The English Opera House gleamed in the evening sunlight, its new white stone pillars not yet blackened with the soot from the thousands of coal fires that warmed the metropolis each winter. Mr Woollatt escorted his charges to the theatre in his own carriage, informing them as he did so that the building had been designed by Mr Beazley to incorporate all the most modern comforts, as well as the celebrated gas lighting.

'You cannot appreciate this innovation while it is daylight,' he said, 'but you will see it when we leave the theatre tonight, and, of course, the stage will be illuminated. Our enjoyment should be greatly enhanced, eh, Miss Rivington?'

They took their seats in the box and Mr Woollatt hovered

about the ladies, making sure that Carlotta had a good view of the stage, offering to put her shawl about her shoulders if she should feel a chill and bringing his own chair close beside her. Carlotta turned with a look of entreaty to her aunt, who was sitting a little apart, but she merely nodded approvingly.

'Well, this is very cosy,' remarked Mr Woollatt as the play began. 'You told me you enjoy the theatre, Miss Rivington. I come to the plays regularly when I am in town. I hope this may be the first of many little outings we will make together.'

Carlotta smiled, but could think of nothing to say and after a few moments Mr Woollatt turned his attention to the stage. Carlotta wished she could go home.

When the farce ended several visitors arrived in the box, most of them friends of Mr Woollatt, but some came to pay their respects to Lady Broxted, including James Ainslowe and his wife. After Mr Woollatt's rather ponderous conversation, Carlotta was glad to see them, but her smile slipped a little when she saw Lord Darvell following them into the box. Mr Woollatt has risen from his seat when the visitors had arrived and he was now obliged to stand against the back wall to make room for them all. He directed their attention to the new gas lanterns on the stage, but no one seemed to hear him. The little box buzzed with conversation, Mr Woollatt presented his acquaintances to Carlotta and Mr and Mrs Ainslowe engaged Lady Broxted in a lively discussion. When Mr Woollatt's friends departed, he took a step back towards his chair, but Lord Darvell was there before him and slipped into the seat beside Carlotta, his knee almost touching her own. She

tensed, prepared to spring away from him should he dare
to touch her.

'Did you enjoy the farce, Miss Rivington?'

'Very much, my lord.'

She turned away, supposedly looking in the audience
for her acquaintance, but was very much aware of him,
sitting so close to her. Every nerve in her body seemed to
be on edge.

'Mr Foote's comedies are always of a superior nature,'
opined Mr Woollatt.

They ignored him.

'And what do you think of the scenery?' asked Luke.

Carlotta was immediately on her guard. She risked a
glance at his face and fancied that the devil was in his eyes.

'I did not notice. I was enjoying the play.'

'I thought it was a little crude.'

'I believe they have several renowned artists here,' stated
Mr Woollatt, on the defensive.

Luke kept his gaze fixed upon Carlotta. 'But I have seen
better artwork, have not you, Miss Rivington?'

She did not answer, merely unfurled her fan and waved
it languorously before her. He turned a little more on his chair
until his knee was in contact with her thigh. It was the lightest
touch, but it burned through the thin muslin of her skirts,
making her tremble. It was all she could do not to move away.
It was all she could do not to press against him. Carlotta swallowed hard. She dare not look at him as he continued.

'I thought the street in Rome looked a little contrived,
too—what thought you, ma'am?'

'Oh, come now,' said Mr Woollatt. 'You cannot expect
Miss Rivington to know such a thing. She has never been

to Italy.' He paused. 'That is, *have* you visited Italy, Miss Rivington?'

She began to wave her fan much more vigorously. 'I was there with my parents,' she muttered. 'A long time ago.'

'Well…' Mr Woollatt puffed out his cheeks. 'How on earth did you know that, sir?'

'I—I expect my aunt and uncle mentioned it,' put in Carlotta quickly, aware of the wicked gleam in Luke's eyes. He was going to denounce her, she knew it. She put up her chin. She would not crumble beneath his mocking glance. Whatever he did to her, she would not give him that satisfaction.

'Yes,' he said at last. 'I expect they did.'

'Luke—' Adele put her hand on his shoulder '—we must be getting back to our own box, the play will begin very soon.'

Lord Darvell rose. 'A pity,' he murmured, 'When we were all getting along so well.' He turned to Mr Woollatt. 'Your servant, sir. Perhaps we may continue our conversation at a later date.'

Mr Woollatt watched him leave, his bottom lip jutting. 'Audacious young dog! He presumes to know you very well, Miss Rivington.'

Carlotta wondered if she should confess the truth—surely nothing could be so bad as the game of cat and mouse Luke was playing with her? She glanced at her aunt; she must be told the truth before anyone else, and a box at the theatre was not the place for that. So she must put off her confession to another day. She summoned a bright smile for Mr Woollatt.

'Lord Darvell is, as you say, sir, an audacious gentleman.'

* * *

Luke accompanied James and Adele back to their seats on the opposite side of the theatre, his senses full of Carlotta, her dark beauty, the perfume of the violets in her corsage, the warmth of her thigh when his knee had touched it—only a couple of thin layers of material had separated them. It was a wicked thought.

'Well, what do you think, is it a match?' Adele walked between the two men, looking up at each of them in turn.

'Woollatt seems very much at home there,' opined James.

'She won't have him,' said Luke shortly.

'Oh, I don't know.' James rubbed his nose. 'Woollatt is as rich as Dives and Lady Broxted is giving him every encouragement. Broxted won't want to let a fortune slip away from the family.'

'Well, we shall know soon enough,' said Adele, taking her seat. 'They will all be at Malberry and we shall have plenty of time to observe them. Now, let us be quiet and enjoy Mr Sheridan's play.'

Luke sat down, but he paid very little attention to the actors. Instead his eyes kept straying to the box opposite, where Daniel Woollatt seemed to be for ever hovering over Carlotta, leaning towards her to make some comment, whispering in her ear. And she was smiling at him, damn her! Luke's reason told him that she was merely being polite, but every smile, every gesture towards Woollatt, flayed his spirits. It did not matter that he knew her to be a shallow, heartless creature; it galled him to see her giving her attention to anyone else. Now Woollatt was pointing out something on the stage to her, their heads so close together they were almost touching. Heaven and earth, how much longer did he have to endure this?

At last it was over. As the audience applauded, he watched Woollatt tenderly placing Carlotta's wrap around her. Surely his hands lingered far too long on her shoulders? What was her aunt thinking of, to let the man maul her in such a way? Smothering an oath, Luke turned away to follow his brother out of the box. As they made their way out into the street, he muttered his excuses, wanting nothing more than to be alone. Adele turned to give him her hand.

'Good night, then, Luke.' She looked up at the front of the building and said with a laugh in her voice, 'Oh, look, these must be the new lanterns Mr Woollatt described to us. What thought you of the new gas lighting for the stage, Luke? Do you agree with Mr Woollatt that it is a splendid innovation?'

He scowled. 'No, I do not. I thought the smell of the gas quite nauseating!'

Chapter Nine

As the date for leaving town drew closer, Carlotta grew ever more anxious. She knew Darvell would be going to Malberry and she could not be sure how he would behave towards her. With less than a week until their departure, she decided she could bear the uncertainty no longer. They were all engaged to spend the day at Lady Ottwood's house on the edge of the town, but Carlotta cried off, pleading a migraine and begging that she should be allowed to rest at home for the day. With some difficulty she persuaded her aunt and uncle to go without her and, as soon as the carriage had rolled away, she dashed off a note to Lord Darvell. She did not know if he would come. As she moved restlessly about the house she remembered only too well how he had promised to come to her once before.

No morning had ever dawned so bright as that last day at Malberry. Carlotta woke early, a warm glow of expectation filling her even before she remembered why. 'Until tomorrow, my sweet life.' Recalling the look in Luke's eyes as he had taken his leave of her sent Carlotta's spirits soaring. She threw herself into the morning's activities, insisting on cleaning and tidying the little parlour before she set off to the market with Jack, their manservant, to collect their provisions. She was anxious to get back, but even so the choosing of a freshly plucked chicken could not be rushed and it was past noon before her shopping was complete and she returned to the house. Jack's arms were full with baskets and parcels so Carlotta went before him to the back door to let them in. She had scarcely put down her basket when Mrs Durini put her head around the kitchen door.

'Good, you are back. Make haste and come in, Carlotta, we have visitors!'

Carlotta's heart leapt. Pausing only to take off her bonnet, she hurried to the parlour.

'Here I am, Mama…'

She trailed off, her eyes widening as she found herself being regarded by a total stranger.

With her mind in confusion, Carlotta was introduced to her uncle and aunt, Lord and Lady Broxted. She listened to explanations of renewing family connections, reinstating her in society, giving her the opportunity to make a good marriage, but all she could think of was that it was past two o'clock. Surely Luke should be here by now.

'I do not like to rush you, Carlotta, but your aunt and I must return to London tonight.' Lord Broxted turned to his sister and gave a tight little smile. 'It has taken my people a long time to track you down, Margaret. We only received word of your direction yesterday and my dear Celia was anxious that we should visit you immediately.'

'We are off to the country at the end of the week, and we would like to take our niece with us,' Lady Broxted explained with a smile at Carlotta. 'I realise that this must be something of a shock for you all, and if you would rather take your time to discuss it, then of course you must do so, but we should not then be in a position to have her join us until the end of the year…'

Carlotta gave a little curtsy. 'And I am very grateful to you, my lady—Aunt—but it is all so sudden.' *Please, Luke, hurry. I need you.*

She uttered up her silent prayer. Everyone was smiling at her, convinced she must be delighted with the prospect of being taken off to live with the Earl and Countess of Broxted.

'You will be free to return home whenever you wish,' continued Lady Broxted. 'But I intend to spoil you so much that you will want to stay with us for ever!'

Carlotta looked at the smiling faces. A net, a fine mesh of love and good intentions, was closing around her. She rose.

'I—um—if you will excuse me for a few moments, I must go and see…'

'Carla, where on earth—?'

But Carlotta did not wait to hear her mother's words. She picked up her wrap and ran out of the house.

It was only a short distance to the inn and she ran all the way. Before she reached the tap-room door the landlord came out. He stopped when he saw her, blinked, then gave her a smile.

'Well, Miss Carla, what is it now? Surely your father cannot have finished all that fine wine I found for him?'

'No, no, it is not that, Mr Hitchen. I…' Carlotta hesitated, blushing '…I was wondering if your guest is within doors; the—um—the gentleman who has been staying with you.' She twisted her hands together, hope and anxiety mixing within her as she waited for his answer.

'Ah, you'd be meaning Major Ainslowe.'

'Yes,' she said eagerly, 'yes, that's right.'

'Well, he's gone, a good half hour since.'

'Gone!'

'Aye, that he has, Miss Carla. Now what was it he said?' Hitchen jingled the coins in his pocket. 'Let me think. He said he was tired o' country ways, and country people. I think he had grown bored, miss. Said he wanted excitement. You know how these rich gentlemen can be. Miss Carla, are you quite well?'

The landlord's kindly concern brought her head up.

'What? Oh, oh, yes, thank you, Mr Hitchen.'

She forced herself to turn away and with an effort began to retrace her steps. The bubble of happiness inside her heart had burst, shattering into tiny pieces. So he had gone. He had only been amusing himself after all. But she had known that all along, had she not?

By the time she reached her father's door she had mastered the urge to cry. Instead her chin lifted a little. She went inside and found her parents sitting with Lord and Lady Broxted in uncomfortable silence. Her mother started up as she came in.

'Carla, my love, whatever possessed you to run off in that way? Such rag-manners when your aunt and uncle have come so far to see you. '

'I needed to—I had to…' Carlotta took a long, steadying breath and looked directly at the earl. 'My lord, if you still want me to come away with you tonight, then I am very willing.'

A full twelve months had gone by since then and once again she was waiting for Luke. But Berkeley Square was a long way from Malberry and perhaps, after today, she would be free of him. It was shortly after noon when he was announced.

'Please show Lord Darvell into the book room.'

Carlotta waited for a few moments, steadied herself with a few deep breaths, then went to join him. She found him standing before the empty fireplace, one arm resting along the mantelpiece. He was dressed for driving in an olive green frock coat, buckskins and top boots with a pair of York tan driving gloves clasped in one hand. She thought idly how well the country style suited him and noted how the summer sun had lightened his brown hair to a honey-gold. As she entered the room, he turned and bent a frowning gaze upon her, but although he looked serious, she was relieved that there was no sign of the savage anger she had seen in his face in their recent meetings.

'Will you sit down, my lord?'

'What is it you want, madam? I came here in my curricle, and I do not like to keep my horses standing any longer than necessary.'

His harsh tone made her heart sink; it was not a promising start. She moved to a chair and sat down. She must not allow his incivility to upset her.

'Thank you, sir, for coming here so promptly.'

He shrugged. 'You summoned me.'

'I *asked* you here,' she corrected him, holding her temper under a tight rein, 'because I want to—to call a truce.' The sardonic lift of his eyebrow brought a flush to her cheek. 'It will be difficult to avoid each other at Malberry, my lord, and—um—I have no wish to cause embarrassment to your brother or any of his guests.'

His lip curled. 'I see no embarrassment, except for you, Miss Rivington.'

'Pray do not be so foolish,' she retorted. 'Think for a moment how difficult it would be for your brother, as host, if you exposed me.'

He moved closer, towering over her. 'Very well then, tell me why you want this...truce?'

She looked down at her hands clasped in her lap. He was watching her intently and his scrutiny disturbed her.

'I have told you I want no unpleasantness—'

'You have told me nothing that would warrant you writing to me, demanding to see me.'

The brittle curb on her temper snapped. Her fingers curled tightly in her lap. 'Very well—if you want the truth, you shall have it. My uncle expects me to receive an offer of marriage while we are at Malberry.'

So there it was.

Luke caught his breath, winded, as if he had received a blow to the stomach. He kept his hands at his sides, but could not prevent them balling into fists. 'Oh? Who could be the lucky man, I wonder? Woollatt?' He gave a savage laugh. 'I take your silence for confirmation, Miss Rivington. So, you have brought your rich suitor up to scratch.'

She winced visibly at his sneering tone and paused a moment before continuing. 'Of course, if he is serious in his regard for me, then I must tell him the truth, but *I* would like to be the judge of when it is the right time, not you. I would therefore be...grateful if you would give me your word to say nothing that might j-jeopardise the situation.'

She kept her head lowered. He could not see her eyes, but her scarlet cheeks betrayed her. In the silence that followed her words, Luke could hear only the steady tick, tick of the long case clock as she waited for his answer.

'No.'

Her head shot up. 'What did you say?'

'I said no. I will make you no such promises.'

She stared at him. He turned away from those haunting brown eyes, knowing that if he met her troubled look his own defences would crumble and he might admit that he would do nothing to cause her more pain. Then he would be lost. He summoned up his anger. He was justified to feel it; by heaven, she had almost brought him to his knees! He had been on the verge of offering her more than he had offered any woman before. Thank heaven he had discovered her true nature before committing himself.

'What have I ever done to make you hate me so?' She spoke so quietly he could hardly hear her. 'I admit I was angry with you when we met again in town, but that was understandable after you had left me so cruelly last summer.'

'I *left* you, as you put it, so that you could be launched into society. And I must say you seem to have taken to it admirably.'

'I had precious little choice in the matter, since you had already quit Malberry.'

'Aye, and thank God I made good my escape.'

She jumped up, white-faced, only her eyes burning with anger as she glared at him. 'What does that mean?'

'Heaven knows what I might have done, had I stayed.'

'You had no intention of staying,' she flung at him. 'Admit it; I was a mere distraction, something to pass the time while you were buried in the country.'

'And you would know about distractions, would you not? You have enjoyed enough of them yourself!'

Her lip curled. 'You have made several hasty judgements about me, sir, but I have done *nothing* to be ashamed of.'

'No? I saw you with my own eyes, flirting with Woollatt in Vauxhall Gardens.'

'Yes, when you were parading that…that *doxy* on your arm! Can you blame me for wanting to punish you?'

He gave a harsh laugh. 'Punish me? What in hell's name have I ever done to you?'

'You abandoned me!'

Carlotta had not meant to say that. The words were wrenched from her, a despairing cry torn from her heart, where she had carried her unhappiness in secret for so many months. Angry at her own weakness, she dashed her hand across her eyes.

'How foolish of me to try to reason with you,' she said bitterly. 'I would be obliged now if you would leave me.'

'Have no fear, madam, I am going!'

He was turning towards the door when it opened and an anxious-looking footman came in.

'A letter for you, miss. Come express it has, from Malberry.'

Carlotta was still reeling from her outburst and looked at him blankly for a moment until the implications of the words penetrated her mind.

'Malberry?' She almost snatched the letter and quickly broke the seal, her fingers shaking. Luke had not left the room. He was standing by the door, tugging on his gloves, but she ignored him as she read the short note. The words seemed to jump on the page.

'It—it is my father. He is hurt, badly hurt…attacked. Mama wants me to come at once…'

Her throat dried. She looked across at Luke. Thoughts tumbled through her head but she could not make sense of them. He was watching her, his face grim.

'Fetch your wrap,' he said quietly. 'I will drive you.'

'Thank you.'

There was no surprise, no hesitation, only the knowledge that she had needed him and he had not failed her.

Pausing only to fetch her cloak and bonnet and to scribble a hasty note for her aunt, Carlotta climbed into the curricle. She did not speak as Luke threaded his way through the busy streets, her brain too shocked to think coherently, but as they left the town behind she unfolded the letter and read it again.

'I do not understand—who would want to hurt Papa? *Why* would someone do this? I cannot think—'

'Hush.' His hand closed over hers. 'Do not torture yourself with conjecture.'

'You are right. I must wait until we reach Malberry; Mama will explain.'

He squeezed her fingers. 'Try not to worry.'

A stretch of open road allowed Luke to push his team on, thundering towards a turnpike.

'Billy, sound the yard of tin,' he ordered briskly. 'We have no time to lose here.'

They were through in seconds.

'We are making good time,' remarked Luke. He glanced at the stiff little figure beside him. 'It won't be long now.'

She did not reply, merely stared straight ahead, her hands clenched together in her lap. Luke found the silence between them uncomfortable. Unbearable.

'I *did* come,' he said shortly. 'That day in Malberry. I did come to your house, but…the earl was there before me.'

Luke shifted uncomfortably in his seat. He remembered how nervous he had been, wishing he had brought his valet with him and something finer to wear than his brown country frock coat—not the ideal dress for a gentleman about to make a proposal of marriage.

'I was outside the window when Broxted said he wanted to take you to town. It was your birthright, Carlotta. I could not deny you your chance.'

Broxted's words echoed again through his head with painful clarity. *Carlotta should come back with us now and take her rightful place in society. We would treat her as our own, give her every luxury—I will even settle upon her the portion that should have been yours, dear sister. Carlotta will have the opportunity to make a good marriage—nay, an excellent match—as befits the granddaughter of an earl.*

'So you went away again.' Carlotta's quiet statement sliced into his heart.

'Yes. I'm…sorry.'

He cursed himself for the inadequacy of his words. Should he tell her how much it had cost him to ride away that day? How he had thrown himself into the improvements at Darvell Manor in his efforts to forget her? He glanced at her again. No. She was unmoved by his apology. It was too late.

Chapter Ten

They swept into Malberry High Street less than three hours after leaving Berkeley Square.

'I'd wager there ain't a cove living who could beat that,' remarked Billy as the curricle pulled up.

Carlotta barely heard him. As soon as the curricle stopped she began to climb down; by the time Lord Darvell had given his instructions to his groom, she was at the door, pushing past the maid and running up the stairs.

'Mama, Mama!'

Mrs Durini appeared on the landing and Carlotta threw herself into her arms.

'How is Papa? What happened? Where is he?'

'Carlotta! Gently, gently, my love.' Her mother hugged her fiercely. 'How glad I am that you are here, and so quickly!'

'Of course. Your note—'

'Oh dear, did I frighten you? I should have waited to write to you, but I was in such a panic, and for a few hours the doctor thought—but that was last night. Today your papa is much better and Dr Johnson is confident he will make a good recovery.'

'May I see him?'

'He is resting now, but you may come in.'

Nodding, she led Carlotta into the bedroom where her father was lying in the middle of the large bed. The sheets were pulled up to his chin, but one side of his face was misshapen and heavily bruised, the purple-and-red blotches an alarming contrast to the white bed linen.

Carlotta put her fist into her mouth to stifle a cry of anguish and sank down beside her father.

'He is sleeping,' said her mother softly. 'The doctor has given him a draught and says he must rest as much as he can.'

Carlotta reached out her hand to touch his swollen cheek. 'Who could have done this?'

She felt her mother's hand on her shoulder.

'Come downstairs, love. Bessie shall sit with him while I tell you what I know.'

Carlotta followed her down the stairs, clinging to the rail as her knees threatened to give way. They went into the little parlour, where Luke was waiting for them.

'I hope you will forgive the intrusion, Mrs Durini,' he said. 'The door was open…'

'This is Lord Darvell, Mama. He brought me here.'

Her mother moved forward, hands outstretched in welcome. 'Then you have my heartfelt gratitude, my lord,' she said. 'I dared not hope Carlotta could be here so soon.'

He bowed. 'I was with Miss Rivington when your letter arrived. It was the least I could do. May I enquire how your husband goes on?'

'He is recovering, sir. He suffered a serious beating around his head and shoulders, but we are hopeful that there will be no lasting damage.'

'Mama,' said Carlotta, 'will you tell me what happened?'

Mrs Durini hesitated, and Luke said quickly, 'Pray allow me to stay, ma'am. I may be able to help.'

With a nod Mrs Durini sank onto the sofa, drawing Carlotta down beside her.

'Giovanni was working late at the Court last night and he was set upon as he returned... Footpads. They were lying in wait for him as he crossed the stile. If it had not been for Jack he might have been—' She broke off to wipe her eyes with one corner of her apron. 'Jack—our m-manservant, my lord—was throwing rubbish on the midden when he heard Giovanni cry out. Jack went to find him and—and the attacker ran off.'

'Attacker. There was only one?' asked Luke, frowning.

'Jack saw only one.'

'And did he get a clear look at him?'

'N-no. It was too dark.'

'What is it, my lord?' said Carlotta quickly. 'What do you suspect?'

'How many people use that path and the stile?' he countered.

'The servants from the Court, when they come to the village,' said Mrs Durini.

'How often would that be, once or twice each day?'

'Possibly. It will be more when the master and his guests arrive.'

Carlotta fixed him with an anxious gaze. 'Lu—Lord Darvell?'

He hesitated. 'It seems an odd place for footpads to lie in wait.'

As his words sank in, Carlotta felt the chill running down her spine. 'You think they were waiting for Papa?'

Her mother gave a smothered gasp. 'No, it cannot be! Giovanni has no enemies.'

'You are sure of that?' he asked.

'Of course I am sure. He is very well liked here in Malberry.'

'Be that as it may, if you will permit me, I shall set my groom to make enquiries in the village—perhaps a stranger has been seen here. Can you think of anyone who might harbour a grudge?'

'My father is an honest man,' replied Carlotta, holding her head up. 'He pays his debts and has never cheated anyone.'

He regarded her steadily. 'I believe you, but until we get to the bottom of this matter, it would be as well for you to take extra care.'

'We shall do so, my lord.' Carlotta nodded at him. 'Thank you.'

'Yes, thank you, my lord, and thank you again for bringing my daughter to me so quickly. But I have offered you no refreshment, let me—'

Luke held up his hand. 'No, I will not trouble you, ma'am.' He rose. 'My groom is waiting for me at the George—I am going on to the Court, but I shall call again tomorrow, if I may.'

His words dispelled the anxiety that had been growing within Carlotta.

'You are not going back to Town?'

'No.' His look and the little smile that accompanied it warmed her. 'I shall stay at the Court now until James arrives.'

'And you will be very welcome to call here at any time, my lord,' put in Mrs Durini.

'Thank you, ma'am. Miss Rivington, it now occurs to me—we came here in such a hurry, would you like me to send Billy back to town tonight for your clothes…?'

'Thank you, sir, but I would not have you put to such trouble; I have sufficient gowns here.' Carlotta gave a little smile. 'They may not be fashionable, but they are perfectly adequate.'

Her mother nodded. 'Indeed they are, my love, for you will not be venturing out of doors while you are here.' She glanced towards the ceiling, as if anxious to get back to her husband. 'Well, my lord, we must not keep you longer. Until tomorrow, then. Carlotta, since Bessie is still upstairs, perhaps you will show his lordship out?'

Carlotta picked up his hat and handed it to him, then led the way back into the little passage. At the door she turned to him, suddenly shy. 'My lord, I—'

He put one finger against her lips. 'I will call again in the morning.' He looked at her, his hazel eyes warm with concern. 'Unless you would like me to stay…?'

The idea made Carlotta's insides tie themselves in knots. She would like nothing more than to have him stay with her for ever, but that was not what he meant. She summoned a smile. 'Thank you, sir, but we shall manage. We will check that all the doors and windows are locked, and Jack shall sleep with a thick staff beside him.'

'Make sure he does,' he said, giving her a faint smile. 'Goodnight, *cara*.'

Carlotta returned to the sitting room to find her mama looking out of the window, watching Lord Darvell's retreating form.

'Well,' she said, 'what a very kind gentleman he is, to be sure. And is he related to Mr Ainslowe, who owns the Court?'

'His brother, Mama.' She flushed at the speculative gleam in her mother's eyes.

'Ah. And is he the rich suitor your aunt has mentioned in her letters?'

Carlotta's blush deepened. 'Lord Darvell has no fortune; Uncle Broxted considers him a wastrel.'

'Well, that is a pity, for he seems a most pleasant gentleman, and uncommon kind to bring you all this way.' She sighed. 'But there, it would do no good for you to throw yourself away on a handsome face, my dear. Your prospects are so much better now.'

It was strange, after the luxuries of Broxted House, to be waking up again in the tiny bedroom of her parents' cottage. It took Carlotta several moments to collect her thoughts and separate dreams from reality. Despite knowing that her father lay injured in the next room, she felt none of the anxiety and distress that had filled her days in London. Lying very still, listening to the birdsong outside her window, Carlotta thought about the calm sense of well-being that enveloped her. The answer came to her in the form of a memory, a pair of hazel eyes smiling warmly at her. She was no longer at odds with Luke. Something had changed yesterday when she had received the letter from Malberry. Instinctively, in her need she had turned to Luke for help and he had answered her mute appeal without hesitation. And he had called her *cara*— dear one. Her heart singing, Carlotta slipped out of bed and scrambled into her clothes. Luke had promised to call again this morning!

As soon as she was dressed Carlotta went to see her father. It was clear that her mother had kept an all-night vigil at his bedside and Carlotta immediately took her place and sent her off to rest. There was little to do, for her father was sleeping quietly, but she knew her mother would not be easy unless someone was keeping watch. An hour dragged by; sitting in the quiet bedroom, Carlotta thought back to the journey to Malberry, riding beside Luke in his curricle. She had been so anxious for her father that she had given little thought to Luke's explanation that he had come to the cottage, but had turned away again when he heard her uncle's plans for her.

She closed her eyes. If only he had seen her, talked to her. She shook her head. Too late for that now. Suddenly, in the airy stillness of the little room, she thought of how Luke must have felt on that day—not the confident, strong young buck that she knew, but a nervous young man, uncertain of his welcome, knowing that, despite his title, his financial position would fall a long way short of the ideal match Lord Broxted planned for his niece.

'Oh, Luke,' she whispered, 'your fortune or lack of it did not matter to me—it has never mattered!'

She sat up with a start as her mother came into the room, carrying a large basket.

'Look, Carlotta, is this not generous?' she said, smiling broadly. 'Lord Darvell brought it himself; the fruit is from the hothouses up at the Court. He said his brother's visitors would not miss a few peaches and grapes, and when I protested he pointed out that the fruit is so ripe it needs to be eaten! What could I do, but accept it gratefully?'

'Lord Darvell has been here?'

'Yes. I was resting on the daybed in the sitting room when Bessie announced him, and you can imagine how flustered I was to be found out. I have not the slightest doubt that my cap was askew! But he was very kind, and said he only wished to leave the fruit basket and would not disturb us. He is going to call again tomorrow, to see how we go on.'

Carlotta fought down her disappointment. There was no reason why he should ask to see her—in fact, she was not at all sure that he would want to do so.

Carlotta was carrying her father's breakfast tray down the stairs when Luke arrived the following day. She heard his voice as Bessie admitted him and she hurried on to the kitchen with her dirty dishes. She hesitated only for a moment to consider running back up to her room to check her appearance in the mirror. That would waste too much precious time, so she contented herself with removing her apron and shaking out the skirts of her old dimity gown before hastening to the parlour. At the door she stopped, her hand hovering over the handle—perhaps he would not want to see her. If that was the case, she needed to know, and the sooner the better.

Taking a deep breath, she opened the door and went in.

Luke was standing by the window. His tall, broad-shouldered frame seemed to fill the little room. With his back to the light she could not see his face and Carlotta was suddenly too nervous to speak. Her mother was addressing her, and she made an effort to attend.

'So your father has finished his breakfast?'

'Yes, Mama. I left him with Jack, who has promised to shave him.'

Mrs Durini smiled and turned back to her guest. 'I think that answers your question, my lord. My husband is feeling much more the thing this morning.' She rose. 'If you will excuse me, I had best go to him; he may even now be thinking of getting out of his bed.' She added with a slightly distracted air, 'I have instructed Bessie to bring in refreshments for our visitor, Carlotta. Pray look after him.' She was gone upon the words.

Carlotta cleared her throat. 'My mother is very anxious for Papa…'

'You do not need to explain.' As he moved away from the window she was relieved to see he was not frowning. 'She has left the door open; there can be no impropriety.'

Carlotta nodded, thankful for his efforts to put her at her ease. Bessie came in, carefully carrying a tray bearing glasses and two decanters. They watched in silence as the maid put her burden down upon a side table, bobbed a curtsy and scurried out again. Carlotta looked at the tray in dismay.

'Oh dear, I expected her to bring in some small beer for you; I have no idea what is in these…'

'I am being treated as an honoured guest,' he remarked, a smile lifting the corner of his mouth. 'Allow me.' He walked over to the table. 'One is quite clearly brandy. The other…' he lifted the stopper from the decanter and sniffed it '…sherry, I think. By your leave, Miss Rivington, I shall help myself to a little brandy. May I pour you a glass of something?'

'N-no, thank you.' Already nervous, Carlotta knew it would be unwise to accept, especially when she had never tried either of those beverages. She watched him fill his glass and take a seat opposite her.

'You had no unwelcome visitors?' he asked.

'No, my lord. I explained everything to Jack and he insisted upon bringing Mack, his dog, into the house, but we have not been disturbed.'

'And have you spoken to your father about the attack?'

She nodded. 'He was well enough to talk about it yesterday. He remembers very little, except being set upon as he climbed over the stile.' She sighed. 'We can none of us think of a reason for such an attack. It must have been footpads.'

'Perhaps.'

'You sound doubtful—what do you know?'

'Nothing, but robberies usually take place upon known highways, not little-used paths.'

She shuddered. 'I hate to think that someone wishes to harm Papa.'

'Perhaps I am wrong; I do not wish to make you anxious. All I ask is that you take care.'

The concern in his voice touched her. She tried to put on a brave face.

'Well, Papa will be confined to the house for a few weeks at least, and Jack will not leave his side.' Carlotta hesitated. It was important that he realise how grateful she was for his help. She cleared her throat. 'While we are alone, sir, please let me thank you for bringing me from London—'

'It is not necessary.'

'I think it is, especially—especially when I think of what I said to you.' Her voice failed. She took a deep breath to regain control. 'I was very much at fault.'

'We were both at fault,' he responded quietly.

She clasped her hands tightly together. 'Then, is it—do you think we might be…friends?'

Luke regarded her sombrely. As the silence lengthened Carlotta's heart sank. Perhaps too many insults had been traded. Perhaps she had given him too great a disgust of her. Nervous, hurried words began to tumble from her lips.

'I am aware that there have been misunderstandings

and I regret that, very much. But—but if you could only bring yourself to forget everything that has passed between us, I…I would very m-much value your friendship.'

Her fingers were digging into her palms as she fought down the urge to weep. She could do no more. Her apology was heartfelt, but perhaps it was not enough.

'My memory is yours to command, ma'am.' He spoke lightly, and there was a strange look in his eyes, but his words gave her hope.

'Oh, yes, please, my lord! If we could begin again, from today, perhaps we could be true friends.'

'If that is what you wish, consider it so, Miss Rivington.'

Carlotta sighed and closed her eyes, feeling that a great weight had lifted from her shoulders.

'Thank you, you are very good.'

A rustle of skirts and hasty step announced Mrs Durini's return. She came bustling into the room, tutting.

'Well, what a good thing I went up. Giovanni had persuaded Jack to bring his clothes and was preparing to come downstairs! If ever I saw the like—I told him he must not even think of getting out of bed until the doctor has seen him again.'

'And when will that be, ma'am?' asked Luke.

'Tomorrow, although how we will persuade him to remain in bed until then I do not know.'

'We shall hide his clothes, Mama. Then he will be obliged to keep to his room.'

'Yes, we can do that.' Mrs Durini sank down on the sofa. 'Doctor Johnson has told me that he must rest, but he is not an easy patient. Thank goodness I shall have you to help me, Carla, at least for a few days.'

'Oh, but I shall not quit you now, Mama. Not until Papa is better.'

'But of course you must go,' exclaimed Mrs Durini, regarding her in some surprise. She put one hand to her head. 'But of course, you do not know—oh, I shall go distracted, I vow! Your aunt has written; she sent it express and it arrived while you were with Papa this morning. They are coming down to Malberry as planned and will collect you on their way.'

'No!' Carlotta shook her head vehemently. 'I cannot leave—she does not know how matters stand here!'

'Well, naturally she knows that if Giovanni was seriously ill there would be no question of you leaving us, and she says as much in her note. But that is not the case, my love. And she has explained to me about—I mean—she has explained how important it is for you to join her at Malberry.'

Carlotta flushed scarlet at the knowing look her mother gave her.

'No—I—that is—'

'Your mother is right,' said Luke quietly. 'If your father continues his recovery, there is no reason why you should not join the house party at the Court. You may rely upon my discretion.'

'That is very good of you, my lord.' Mrs Durini fidgeted uncomfortably. 'I do not know what my daughter has said to you about the arrangement with Lord and Lady Broxted…'

'Nothing to the detriment of her parents, ma'am, I assure you. However, I am aware it is not generally known that you are living at Malberry.' A noise from upstairs made him look up. 'I am keeping you from your patient. I must go.'

Mrs Durini rose and held out her hand to him. 'I am very

grateful for your kindness to us, my lord. Remember, you are welcome to call here at any time.'

'Thank you, ma'am. You are most kind.'

Luke kicked viciously at the thistles in his path as he walked back to Malberry Court. So she wanted to forget everything. Hah! If only that were possible. What he would give to banish her from his mind, to forget how sweet she had tasted, how soft and yielding she had felt in his arms, but that night at Malberry was burned into his memory. He would never forget it, even if she could. But he had agreed that they should start again as friends. Friends! His mouth twisted into a bitter smile. She wanted to keep him as a friend while she accepted an offer from Daniel Woollatt— as though he could stand by while she became another man's wife. Luke stopped. That was just what he must do: if Woollatt was her choice, then so be it. After all, what had he to offer her except an impoverished title and an estate that would take years to turn a profit? No, he could not ask that of her. She wanted him as a friend—needed him as a friend. Aye, that was some small comfort. That is what he would be, although every moment he was near her, knowing she could never be his, would twist the knife a little deeper into his soul.

When Lord Broxted's travelling coach swept through the gates of Malberry Court a few days later, Carlotta was once again dressed as befitted a member of the earl's family. Lady Broxted had insisted she put on her cream flounced gown, holly-green spencer and matching silk bonnet before setting out for the Court and now she nodded in approbation, declaring that her niece was once more fit to be seen.

'So now we shall see these famous frescoes we have heard so much about,' remarked Lady Broxted, leaning forward to gaze out of the window at the approaching house.

'My dear, I think the least said about the paintings the better,' returned the earl repressively.

Apart from an airy wave of her hand, Lady Broxted ignored him. 'You must show me the ones you worked upon, my love. What a pity it is that we cannot tell anyone about your painting, because you are a clever little puss, when all's said and done.'

Carlotta repressed a smile. 'Thank you, Aunt. I painted the two smaller roundels on the ceiling of the portico, here at the main entrance.'

The carriage pulled up at the foot of the shallow steps and a liveried footman hurried forward to open the door.

'You will do nothing to draw attention to these paintings, madam,' muttered the earl as he handed his wife out of the carriage.

'No, of course not, but I must see them.'

As they ascended the steps she glanced up at the ceiling behind the soaring pillars that supported the portico.

'Oh, my heavens!' Lady Broxted began to ply her fan furiously. 'My dear child! The nymphs—'

'They are maenads, Aunt,' said Carlotta. 'It is Dionysius surrounded by dancing maenads.'

'Never mind what they are called.' Lady Broxted lifted her fan to cover her mouth while she whispered to Carlotta, 'They are *naked*!'

'No, no, they have a diaphanous veil that covers them, a little,' Carlotta replied soothingly. 'But *my* efforts are the smaller roundels: the grapes and the lyre. I did not paint the maenads.'

'No, but you were very close to them!' Lady Broxted lowered her eyes and hurried into the house. 'Heaven and earth, Carlotta, I hope we are never found out!'

Suppressing her giggles with difficulty, Carlotta followed her aunt inside.

The hall was very crowded and Carlotta's first, alarming thought was that everyone had come to greet them, but a quick glance around showed her that they were all in riding dress. James Ainslowe separated himself from the crowd and came forward, grinning broadly.

'Welcome, my lord, Lady Broxted…Miss Rivington. We did not know what time to expect you and have this minute sent word to the stables. We could put off our ride for an hour, if you would like to join us…'

Lord Broxted put up his hand. 'No, no, Ainslowe, you must carry on.'

'Of course they do not want to come riding with us,' exclaimed Adele, stepping forward to greet the new arrivals. 'They will want to rest and refresh themselves after their long journey, is that not so?'

Her smiling question encompassed them all, and Carlotta was tempted to say that her journey had been no more than a mile, and that she would dearly love to go riding. She was obliged to press her lips together to prevent any such impulsive utterance. Carlotta glanced at the assembled group; she knew them all: Mr and Mrs Price and Julia, Lord Fairbridge, Sir Gilbert Mattingwood, Lord Darvell—Carlotta gave Luke a shy smile, hoping he would come over to her, but even as her eyes found his, Mr Woollatt was pushing past him and bustling forward, his face wreathed in smiles.

'Miss Rivington, the day is suddenly all the brighter now that you are here. I am sure our host will understand if I cry off from our ride now.'

Luke raised his brows. 'Oh, why should you want to do that, sir, if, as you say, the day is suddenly so much brighter?'

A bubble of laughter rose in Carlotta's throat and she was obliged to turn it into a cough. Mr Woollatt was in no way put out.

'I was speaking metaphorically, my lord. If you will allow me, Ainslowe, I shall not ride with you. Instead I shall go upstairs and change. Then I shall be on hand to entertain our new guests until you have all returned from your ride. There, now, what have you to say to that?'

In the face of his smiling self-satisfaction, Carlotta could find nothing to say and it was left to her aunt to speak up.

'An excellent idea, Mr Woollatt. How kind of you to think of our comfort.'

'Well, then, if that is settled, we had best get on,' declared Mr Ainslowe, shrugging.

'And I must find my man to help me change,' muttered Mr Woollatt. 'Never seems to answer my bell, whereas *your* man always seems to be on hand, Mattingwood. I'm always tripping over the fellow!'

Sir Gilbert, who had been casting an admiring glance at Carlotta, laughed at him. 'Reed is very conscientious and likes to be close by in case I need him.'

'Well, there is no need for him to be hovering in the corridors,' put in James. 'There is a bell-pull in every bedchamber so you can ring for him from your room. Perhaps you should explain that to him, Mattingwood.'

'Thank you,' replied Sir Gilbert. 'I will.'

A flurry of activity followed and for a few moments

noisy chaos reigned in the hall. The riding party made its way outside, narrowly avoiding the puffing footmen who were carrying in the corded trunks bearing the Broxted coat of arms. Mr Woollatt exchanged a final few words with Lady Broxted before disappearing up the stairs while Lord Broxted was assured by his host that the housekeeper would be down soon to show them to their rooms.

'Carlotta, my dear, are you ready?'

Lady Broxted peeped into the little bedchamber and Carlotta turned from her mirror.

'I am, ma'am. I just need my fan…'

'How quick you are,' declared her aunt, coming into the room. 'You will see that I am not yet changed. Jarvis has only now unpacked the gown I wish to wear. But if you are dressed there is no need for you to wait for me; you may go on down to the library and I shall join you shortly.' She handed Carlotta her fan and propelled her towards the door.

'Oh, but I would much prefer to sit here and read until you are ready, Aunt,' said Carlotta, resisting.

'No, you must go on. By all means take your book down with you, love. I am sure the light will be much better there and after all, the library is the proper place for book-reading.'

Smiling, Carlotta made her way downstairs. She was honest enough to admit that she was happy to have the opportunity to explore the house while most of the guests were absent. She was curious to see how the rooms looked now they were furnished. She could not linger in the hall, liveried servants were on duty there, but the new bell system, installed while her father had been working at the house, meant that it was no longer necessary to have footmen waiting in every room. She forced herself to hesitate as she reached the foot of the stairs, as if unsure of her way; after all, it was meant to be her first visit to Malberry Court.

She passed through the small ante-room where doors led to both the library and the drawing room, then went into the library, closing the door carefully behind her. The lofty ceiling was painted in shades of blue, from deepest indigo to near-white, the intricate pattern matched exactly by the huge Axminster carpet that covered the floor. She remembered her father's apprentice had carried out most of the painting in this room, for there were none of the impressive murals that were her father's trademark, any wall space not covered by bookshelves being left bare to display Mr Ainslowe's art collection. This mainly comprised family portraits and conversation pieces, but on one wall there was a single large canvas showing a more classical scene. It must be the Tiepolo, she thought. She was moving towards the picture to study it more closely when she heard the door open.

'My dear Miss Rivington.' Mr Woollatt quickly crossed the room and picked up her hand, pressing a kiss upon her fingers in an old-fashioned gesture that she found slightly unnerving. 'How fortunate that I have found you alone.'

'Is it, sir?' Carlotta withdrew her hand and moved away. 'I am waiting for Lady Broxted to join me.' She prayed her aunt would come in *very* soon.

'Of course, of course. In the meantime, we must entertain each other, eh?' He gave a series of little grunts, and Carlotta realised with a jolt that it was laughter. He began to pace up and down, his hands clasped behind him. 'Yes, Miss Rivington, I am delighted to have this opportunity to speak to you alone. You must know what is on my mind.'

Carlotta swallowed nervously. 'No, sir.'

He beamed at her. 'Ah, such innocence. Charming. Utterly charming. Then let me speak plainly, my dear. For some time now I have been contemplating a change to my situation. As you know, I am what is known in modern parlance as a *warm man*.'

'W-warm, sir?'

'Yes, full of juice—although I would more modestly call it a comfortable fortune. It is only right that at my time of life I should be looking to set up an establishment.' He cleared his throat. 'To, ah, provide myself with an heir.'

With sudden, frightening clarity Carlotta knew she did not want him to continue. Where was her aunt? 'Sir, I—'

'I have been in town for more Seasons than I care to remember and, if you will forgive my arrogance, I think I can say that I could have my pick of the eligible young ladies paraded at Almack's. But none, my dear Miss Rivington, has ever made such an impression upon me as you have done.'

'Mr Woollatt—' Carlotta put out her hand to silence him, but he merely caught it in his own.

'Your kindness, your gentle ministrations to me that night at Vauxhall Gardens, convinces me that I have made the right decision.'

Carlotta hung her head, her cheeks burning as she remembered that night, and Luke's damning accusations.

'No need to colour up, my dear, although such maidenly modesty does you credit. Lady Broxted was quite right when she told me you were totally unspoiled.'

Carlotta had a sudden, vivid recollection of the scene in the hallway when they arrived earlier that day. She remembered her aunt talking earnestly to Mr Woollatt and in that moment she realised this tête-à-tête had been arranged. Lady Broxted had told Mr Woollatt that he would find her alone. Panic welled up within her as he began to pull her towards him.

'Miss Rivington, let me say—'

'Beggin' your pardon, sir.'

Mr Woollatt dropped Carlotta's hand and jumped back at the words, uttered in a rough, country burr. Carlotta looked around to see the gardener coming into the room carrying a large vase of flowers. He placed the vase carefully upon the table, then proceeded to separate the stems in a methodical, unhurried fashion. Carlotta glanced at Mr Woollatt. His face was flushed with indignation and he glared at the gardener, who ignored him and continued to arrange the blooms to his satisfaction. Offering up a little prayer of thanks, Carlotta muttered her excuses and fled.

Once she had reached the safety of her bedchamber, Carlotta allowed herself to recall the events in the library and even to smile a little at the scene. There was no doubting that Mr Woollatt was most aggrieved to have his rehearsed proposal of marriage interrupted. However, she felt no desire to smile when she thought of her aunt and uncle. They would be very angry with her when they heard that she had run away, and rightly so—their purpose in coming to Malberry Court had been to secure for her a suitable husband, and everyone was agreed that Mr Woollatt was eminently suitable.

Carlotta stayed in her room until the dinner hour, then, steeling herself to face her aunt's displeasure, made her way downstairs. This time the doors to the ante-room and the drawing room were thrown wide and the sound of voices told Carlotta that the guests were gathering in readiness for the dinner hour. As she entered the drawing room, Lady Broxted beckoned to Carlotta.

'What in heaven's name has occurred?' she hissed, pulling Carlotta towards her. 'Mr Woollatt is quite put out—did you refuse him?'

'No, Aunt, we were disturbed,' Carlotta explained in a whisper. 'I—I panicked, and ran away.'

'Silly child, what on earth is there to frighten you? Don't tell me Mr Woollatt was anything other than a gentleman.'

Carlotta flushed. 'No, of course not, Aunt.'

'Well, let us hope all is not lost,' murmured Lady Broxted. She patted Carlotta's hand. 'There, there, child. I suppose it is only natural that you should be a little nervous. We must see what we can do to help you. Come now, do not look so downhearted—your pretty smile will help to win the day.'

Carlotta tried to oblige. She raised her head, forcing her lips into a smile, only to find herself staring straight into the eyes of Lord Darvell. Lady Broxted's fan rapped across her knuckles.

'For goodness' sake child, do you wish to drive away your suitor? Keep your smiles for Mr Woollatt, if you please! You must be careful to give him no reason to think you a flirt, my love. Behave yourself during dinner and afterwards. We must do what we can to win back Mr Woollatt's regard for you.'

Carlotta bit her lip; she was quite certain that she did not want Mr Woollatt's regard.

Chapter Eleven

To Lady Broxted's intense disappointment and Carlotta's relief, Mr Woollatt was seated at the far end of the dining table. Carlotta happily accepted Adele's invitation to sit near her, but she was disconcerted to find Luke slipping onto the chair beside her. Her aunt had warned her not to smile at other gentlemen, but it was so difficult not to respond when Luke was looking at her with that warm glint in his eyes. She sought nervously for something to say.

'Did—did you enjoy your ride today, my lord?'

'Very much,' he replied soberly. 'The countryside around Malberry provides some fine views and the park is ideal to gallop the fidgets out of horse and rider.'

Carlotta stifled a sigh. 'I wish I could have come with you. I dearly love to ride.'

'I thought Lord Broxted had provided you with a mount in town.'

'Yes, he hired a hack for me; she was the prettiest little thing, but very slow. There was no spirit in her—I doubt if she had ever galloped in her life.'

'Then we must ask Adele to find you a more lively ride while you are here.'

She thanked him warmly, and as the meal progressed she found herself chatting away quite happily. He described for her his life in the army, and was entertaining her with some of the more light-hearted moments when she caught her aunt's eye. There was no mistaking the warning.

'Ah,' murmured Luke, intercepting the exchange of glances, 'I am being too familiar.'

'No, oh, no,' exclaimed Carlotta. 'It is just that…'

She trailed off unhappily, but Luke merely nodded.

'I understand,' he said gently. 'If you are seen to be on friendly terms with me, it might frighten away other suitors.'

A spurt of anger flashed through Carlotta, burning her cheeks. 'Surely there can be no harm in our talking at dinner. I can hardly ignore you—that would be uncivil.'

He grinned. 'It would indeed. But perhaps we should restrict ourselves to the commonplace. Let me recommend the turbot, Miss Rivington.'

Carlotta lifted her napkin to hide her smile—Luke could never be commonplace!

After dinner Lady Broxted kept Carlotta by her side while she did her best to charm Mr Woollatt back into a good humour. It appeared to work, and when Carlotta retired for the night, he pressed a kiss upon her hand and squeezed it, his smile indicating that he had forgiven her.

'Well, I have done my best; it is up to you to win back your suitor now.'

Carlotta was sitting up in bed, sipping at her hot chocolate when her aunt came in the following morning.

'I have seen you in the saddle, Carlotta, I know you ride well, so I rely upon you to impress Mr Woollatt.'

'Oh,' said Carlotta, brightening. 'Are we riding today?'

'Your uncle and I do not go, but Mrs Ainslowe assures me that she will look after you, and Mrs Price says she will be riding, too, with Julia.'

'Oh, famous!' Carlotta scrambled out of bed. 'I knew nothing of this—when was it arranged?'

'It was decided last night, after you had gone off to bed. Knowing how much you like to ride, I had no hesitation in putting your name forward. Mrs Ainslowe says she can find you a suitable mount.'

'Thank you, Aunt Broxted!' Carlotta flew across the room and hugged her ruthlessly.

'Well, well, that is enough now. You may show your gratitude by charming Mr Woollatt.'

An hour later Carlotta was trotting out of the stable yard on a pretty little grey mare, trying to convey her thanks to her hostess. 'She is beautiful, and so lively. I cannot wait to try out her paces. May we gallop once we are in the park?'

'By all means,' replied Adele. 'She is called Flame and I am pleased you like her. She used to be my own favourite before I married, but James made me a present of Zephyr and I must ride her to please him.' She laughed and leaned forward to pat the glossy black neck of her mount.

'I am honoured that you have loaned Flame to me,' said Carlotta.

'Luke told me that you liked a spirited animal and Miss Price is a more nervous horsewoman. She prefers a *quieter* mount.'

Carlotta looked across at Julia. She was riding a heavy

bay hack whose dull eye and rolling gait seemed to indicate that he would not move any faster than a walk. Carlotta knew she would have disliked riding such a slug, but Julia looked happy enough, especially with Viscount Fairbridge riding beside her.

'Your horse looks very fresh, Miss Rivington,' commented Mr Woollatt, trotting up beside them.

'She is, sir. She is longing for a gallop.'

He gave her an indulgent smile. 'Do not fret, for I shall ride alongside you, and catch your bridle if she looks to be getting away from you.'

Carlotta looked at her hostess, saw her eyes were brimful of merriment and was forced to bite back her own laughter. After all, she had promised not to upset Mr Woollatt. Before she could say anything more, Mr Price's voice gave her thoughts another turn.

'My man tells me there's talk of footpads in the village, Ainslowe. Attacked your painter, I understand.'

James nodded. 'Damned scoundrels. Might have killed him, too, if his servant had not been at hand.'

'Mercy me!' declared Mrs Price, coming up at that moment.

'No need to worry, ma'am.' Her host smiled. 'I set my men to scour the area as soon as I heard of it, but there is no sign of the scoundrels. I'd say they are long gone, now.'

'Gypsies, perhaps,' said Sir Gilbert, trotting up.

'Possibly. Unusual, though. No one has reported any strangers in the area.'

'And how is your artist now?' asked Mr Price.

'A sore head, but thankfully nothing more serious. I told him to rest for a while, but I have no doubt he will be back at work in a week or two.'

'Surely there is nothing more to do at the Court,' said Sir Gilbert with a little laugh.

'Oh, not in the house itself, but there are still a few temples to be painted yet. I do not see him leaving me before the New Year.'

'My husband is determined to have every surface decorated,' called Adele from the other side of the group.

James raised his hat to her. 'In your honour, my dear, in your honour!'

Adele chuckled. 'James is determined to have everything of the finest,' she said to Carlotta. 'But I must not complain. He has bought me the prettiest little carriage to ride around the estate.'

'Dear me. Not a high-perch phaeton, I hope?' exclaimed Mr Woollatt. 'Most dangerous. There have been any number of accidents in town, you know, some of them fatal.'

'No, no, sir, mine is a gig, and perfectly safe. You must let me take you up in it, Miss Rivington.'

'I should like that very much, ma'am.'

'And you are not afraid I shall overturn you?' asked Adele, giving her a mischievous, sideways glance.

Carlotta chuckled. 'I will take my chances.'

Mr Woollatt shook his head at her. 'You are altogether too careless of your own safety, Miss Rivington.'

Carlotta quelled a little spurt of irritation and schooled her features into a smile. 'I am very honoured, sir, that *you* should be so careful of it,' she said sweetly.

Mr Woollatt blinked, then he puffed out his chest, looking very pleased with himself.

They had reached the open parkland by this time, and Carlotta's mount began to prance.

'Are you ready to gallop the fidgets out of that nag of yours?'

Luke's voice close behind her made her look round. Her eyes strayed over his horse, a raw-boned black hunter that sidled and danced, eager to be off.

'I doubt I can keep up with that rangy brute.'

He gave her a slow smile and deep within her she felt the responding tug of attraction, setting her nerves tingling.

'Try,' he murmured.

The provocation was too great, and as the hunter leapt forward Carlotta kicked her little mare on in hot pursuit, ignoring Mr Woollatt's protests.

The mare was fresh and agile, but could not match the hunter's pace. Carlotta pulled her to one side to avoid the mud kicked up by the hunter's huge hooves. She bent low over the horse's neck and gave herself up to the chase, revelling in the wind in her face, the smooth rhythm of the mare as she flew over the ground. The scent of new-mown grass and leather and horses combined into a heady mix that set her senses buzzing as she crossed the open ground, urging her mare on to keep up with Luke. All too soon they were approaching the trees that bordered the park and the hunter's pace slowed. A quick glance showed Carlotta that the rest of the party were some distance behind them, spread out across the park. Luke rode on until he was in the shadow of the trees before he pulled up to wait for her. Carlotta cantered up, laughing with sheer exhilaration. Luke was grinning.

'Well done. Where did you learn to ride like that?'

'Mama taught me, in Italy. She is an excellent horse-woman; we also used to ride bareback there, sometimes.'

'Astride?'

'Of course.'

'Miss Rivington, I am shocked!'

She put her head on one side as she looked at him. 'Are you, truly?'

'No, of course not. You have mud on your face.'

'Oh dear, have I? That is because Flame was close behind you for most of the way.' She hunted for her handkerchief.

'Bring your mare closer; I will wipe it off for you.'

'Quickly, then, before any of the others come up.' She held out her handkerchief and turned her face up towards him, smiling, but her smile faltered when he caught her fingers. The shock of his touch set her heart beating so heavily she felt sure he would hear it. 'Perhaps we should not—' She made to draw back, but his grip on her hand tightened.

'We are friends, are we not?' he said lightly.

Meeting his eyes, Carlotta saw there was nothing alarming about his smile and she relaxed a little, allowing him to take her chin with the fingers of one hand while the other gently drew the wisp of silk across her cheek. Carlotta trembled. He was so close, she could see the tiny laughter lines at the corners of his mouth, the flecks of gold in his hazel eyes. She wanted to throw her arms around his neck and beg him to kiss her, but it would not do. She had enjoyed one brief, heady flirtation with the Wicked Baron; she would not risk such pain again. She closed her eyes, afraid that he would read her thoughts.

'There, it is done.' Carlotta opened her eyes to find him smiling at her so warmly that her bones turned to water. 'Just in time. The others are coming up now.' Luke caught at Flame's bridle. 'While we are alone, I want to tell you I called upon your parents this morning.'

'You have seen my father? How is he?'

'Much better. He sends you his love.' A smile lifted the corners of his mouth. 'He hopes you are behaving yourself.'

She stifled a sigh. 'I am *trying* to do so. Thank you for bringing me news of Papa; it is very good of you to go to so much trouble for me.'

She could not read his look and was about to ask what he was thinking when she heard the thud of hooves, and a reproachful voice behind her.

'My dear Miss Rivington, was that wise, to set off at *such* a pace on an animal you do not know?'

The magical moment was gone. Luke looked up.

'You must blame me, Woollatt,' he called cheerfully. 'I could tell at a glance that Miss Rivington is at home to a peg on horseback and thought she would like to gallop the fidgets out of the mare.'

'Then I call you thoughtless, my lord, to risk the young lady in such a way.'

'No, I am the thoughtless one,' put in Carlotta quickly. 'I was very eager to try out Flame's paces, and she was raring to go. You can see that she is perfectly docile now— I could have stopped her at any time, you know.'

Having promised to behave herself, she knew it behoved her now to make her peace with Mr Woollatt. She cast a swift, apologetic glance at Luke; much as she would have liked to spend the whole morning in his company she knew her duty. She turned her horse and trotted off beside Mr Woollatt.

For Carlotta, nothing else that day could match the enjoyment of her gallop across the park and those few stolen moments alone with Luke. Even the impromptu dance that evening could not compare, for although she stood up with Luke for two country dances, Mr Woollatt hovered around her and remained in close attendance for the whole of the evening.

When Lady Broxted carried her off to bed that evening, she had nothing but praise for her niece.

'I confess I was a little anxious that Mr Woollatt might be offended, after your treatment of him yesterday, but you have made up for it today, my love, and no mistake. He was full of praise for you tonight! I have great hopes that he will declare himself tomorrow.'

'Do you think so, Aunt?'

'Without a doubt, my love. And now that you have had time to grow accustomed, you will not be tempted to run away again, now will you?'

'No, Aunt. But…should I not tell him about—about Papa before he makes me an offer?' asked Carlotta, clutching at a final straw.

They had stopped at the door of Carlotta's chamber.

'No, no, my love, your uncle will discuss everything with Mr Woollatt afterwards. There is no need for you to worry about that.' Lady Broxted patted her cheek, saying fondly, 'That's a good girl. Just think how happy your dear mama will be when we tell her of the splendid match you have made! Now, hurry off to bed, child—I want you looking your best in the morning!'

Carlotta obeyed her aunt and made haste to get into bed, but sleep eluded her. She lay between the covers, tossing restlessly while the house gradually sank into silence and at last she drifted into an uneasy sleep.

She woke again as it was growing light and lay quietly, listening. She knew it must be very early, for the house was silent, sleeping still, but Carlotta was wide awake. She slipped out of bed and went to the window. There was only the faintest line of gold on the eastern horizon, the rest of the sky ranging from flushed pink to deep blue, and the land below was still tinged with grey.

Her room was in the west wing of the house, overlooking the walled garden with its statues that gleamed in the ghostly morning light. Carlotta fumbled with the catch and quietly pushed up the sash window. The air was pleasantly cool, and she leaned her elbows on the sill, breathing deeply while she considered her situation. It could not be so very bad to be married to Mr Woollatt. He was undoubtedly kind, and so rich that she need never want for anything. Perhaps they would have a house such as Malberry Court, and a stable full of horses. She smiled to herself; she would have to ride them very quietly.

Carlotta wondered why she was so anxious; she knew that many married couples lived very comfortably together: Mr and Mrs Ainslowe certainly appeared extremely happy, and she had never known her aunt and uncle to disagree in all the time she had lived with them. There was no reason why she should not be as happy in her marriage. She thought of Julia and Lord Fairbridge; she had watched them dancing together and had seen the glowing looks they had shared. Her heart clenched. If only she could look that way upon Mr Woollatt. But she knew there was only one man who evoked such emotion from her. She gave herself a little shake. She must not think of him. It was not at all helpful.

A movement below caught her attention. She peered down into the gardens. A shadowy figure was gliding close to the wall towards the house. One of the servants, she thought, returning from meeting his lover in the village.

The thought deepened Carlotta's depression. With a sigh she went back to her bed, hoping for an hour's sleep before the maid brought her hot chocolate.

The restless night made Carlotta very tired the following morning and she sent her maid away, only to be woken some time later when the servant came back to announce that she had missed breakfast and that her aunt wished her to make her way directly to the library. She knew immediately the reason for the summons. Suddenly her sprig muslin with its tiny puff sleeves seemed far too flimsy to combat the chill that came over her. Carlotta knew this was merely nerves and resisted the temptation to wrap herself in her paisley shawl before running downstairs.

She opened the door to the little ante-room and found Lord Broxted waiting for her. He beckoned her to come forward, and as she did so her aunt came out of the library.

'Ah, there you are, my love.' She shut the door carefully. 'And in your new gown, too. Very pretty. Mr Woollatt is waiting for you.'

The knot in Carlotta's stomach twisted even tighter. 'Aunt—I—that is—'

Her uncle reached out for her hand. 'Go into the library, my dear,' he said gently. 'You know what you have to do.'

Carlotta looked from his smiling face to her aunt, who was nodding encouragement. Squaring her shoulders, she crossed the small ante-room, but at the library door she turned back. 'Aunt, I do not think I can do this.'

'Nonsense, my love. What is there to do? Mr Woollatt is not an ogre.'

'I know that, but—'

Lord Broxted put up his hand. 'Carlotta, this is no time to be difficult. Mr Woollatt's intentions have been clear for some weeks; if you are averse to his suit, then you should have made that plain to us before now.'

'No, no, it is not that...'

Carlotta twisted her hands together until Lady Broxted came up and caught them in her own gentle clasp.

'I understand, my dear; you are afraid, and that is very natural, but your fears are unfounded. Do you think your uncle has not made enquiry? Mr Woollatt is known to be a good man; he will make you an excellent husband.'

'And he has hinted that he is prepared to be very generous over the settlements,' put in Lord Broxted. 'The match will be very advantageous to your parents.'

'I am sure Mr Woollatt is everything you say, but—' She broke off as hasty footsteps approached from the hall.

'Oh, excuse me.' Luke's long stride brought him into the ante-room before he realised it was occupied. 'I left my riding gloves in here earlier.' He looked from Carlotta to Lady Broxted. 'I beg your pardon. I hope I am not inter-rupting anything?'

'Please, my lord, just go,' said Carlotta, dismayed.

'It is a delicate matter, my lord, but I think you may be able to help us.' Lady Broxted moved swiftly to close the door behind him. 'You have proved yourself a true friend to my little niece, and your advice now would be welcomed.'

'No,' whispered Carlotta, but so quietly that no one heard her.

'Aye, perhaps she will listen to you, sir,' muttered Lord Broxted testily. Luke raised his brows. 'Mr Woollatt is beyond that door,' explained the earl, pointing towards the library. 'My niece has only to go in and accept his offer of marriage and she will have every luxury showered upon her. She is a very fortunate young lady. Yet she hesitates. I pray you, Darvell, add your voice to ours, urge her to take the small step that will secure her comfort and happiness—and that of her family.'

Carlotta's cheeks flamed. She dare not look up as she waited for Luke to speak.

'Miss Rivington must do as she thinks fit,' he said at last. 'Woollatt is a good man; I believe his reputation to be unblemished.'

'There, my love, what did I tell you?' Lady Broxted beamed. 'It is a match any mother would want for her daughter. Go in now, Carlotta. You have kept the poor man waiting long enough.'

The world seemed to be tilting. Carlotta put her hand against the doorpost to steady herself. She closed her eyes. Had this been planned, that Luke should come in and add his persuasion? If that was so, then truly he could not love her. The crushing pain in her chest made it difficult to breathe. Carlotta forced her eyes open, forced herself to look across the little room to where Luke was standing. His face showed nothing but polite indifference. He gave her a little bow, saying coldly, 'I wish you every happiness, ma'am.'

She watched him turn away. He began to play with the little Dresden ornaments on the side table. She looked at his back, ramrod straight, the broad shoulders unyielding beneath the fine wool of his riding coat. The sight offered her no comfort; she read rejection in every stiff line of his body.

'My love, Mr Woollatt is waiting for you.'

Lady Broxted's words recalled Carlotta's wandering senses. She put up her chin, turned and walked into the library.

* * *

Luke moved the little porcelain shepherdess closer to her mate; he heard the door close and the soft sigh of relief uttered by Lady Broxted. Carlotta was about to make a most advantageous match and he had not stood in her way. He should feel happy for her. She would command every luxury, every comfort. But there had been no comfort in the look she had given him, only anxiety and fear and…

'Damnation, I cannot allow this—' He swung round, only to find Lord Broxted blocking his way.

'One moment, Darvell. You are not indifferent to my niece, I think. Consider, if you please, before you commit an act that you may both regret. What can you offer her, compared to Daniel Woollatt? Granted, you have a title, but no fortune, and a reputation that is not to be envied.'

Angrily Luke shook off the earl's restraining hand. 'Perhaps we should let Carlotta choose!'

'I think she has already chosen.'

The words hit him like icy water. His hands balled into fists and for a moment unreasoning anger threatened to overwhelm him. He wanted to knock Broxted to the ground, but one did not brawl with fellow guests. Besides, what would it achieve? It would merely add to his reputation as the wild, wicked baron.

Lord Broxted patted his shoulder. 'Let be, Darvell,' he said gently. 'It is best this way. She will be happy. Woollatt can give her everything.'

Unlike you. The words were unspoken, but Luke felt them in the air; they wrapped themselves around his heart, heavy as lead.

'I pray you are right, Broxted.' With a nod, he scooped his gloves from the table, turned on his heel and walked out.

* * *

Luke strode from the house, a red mist of anger, frustration and bitter disappointment clouding his thoughts. Billy was waiting for him in the stable yard.

'Mr Ainslowe has gone on ahead, my lord. Says he will wait for you in the park,' he announced formally as Luke swung himself into the saddle. 'Would you like me to accompany you, sir?'

'Of course not. I have no need of a damned nursemaid!'

Billy jumped back as Luke swung the big hunter around and trotted out of the yard. Somewhere deep inside him, reason told Luke that he would have to apologise to his groom, but that would come later. For now he just wanted to ride away and forget. So she would marry Woollatt and have everything her shallow heart desired. She had called him friend, but she had no need of him now.

A gallop across the park helped him to regain control over his temper, but did nothing to improve his mood—he found it impossible to raise a smile when he caught up with the main riding party.

'Luke! Thought you had decided not to join us.' James looked at him closely. 'Are you well, brother? You look unusually grim. Is aught amiss?'

'I am well enough—that is—urgent business calls me away.' *Why not?* he thought. *What is there to keep me here?* 'I only came here to tell you.'

'What, you are going now, *riding* to town? Luke, wait—'

But he was already cantering away, ignoring his brother's bewildered shout. He was determined to quit Malberry immediately. He would send word back to Billy and to his man—damnation, he could manage very well for one night without them and the thought of returning to the house, knowing that *she* was within its walls and unattainable, was not to be borne.

Soon he was trotting out of the gates, lost in his own black thoughts until he became aware of an unusual amount of activity on the edge of the village. Outside the Durinis' house, in fact. But he must have made a mistake; it did not *look* like the Durinis' cottage. Then he realised what was different: one half of the house was a blackened ruin.

Chapter Twelve

This cannot be real. I am dreaming. The thought echoed again and again in Carlotta's head. It was as if she was outside herself, watching Mr Woollatt as he paced up and down the Axminster carpet, outlining his circumstances and pointing out to her the advantages of becoming his wife. She felt too detached. Surely it was not her voice that was speaking, expressing her obligation, saying how happy she would be to accept his kind offer. It seemed no sooner had these words been uttered than Mr Woollatt was kissing her hand, declaring himself to be the happiest of men. Then the doors opened and her aunt and uncle came in, Lady Broxted laughing and crying all at the same time and soon Carlotta was crying, too.

'Oh, my dear, I am so happy for you.' Lady Broxted hugged her. 'And you have a ring already!'

Carlotta raised her left hand and looked at the large diamond that winked and glittered as she moved her fingers. It felt very heavy, like a manacle, shackling her to her fate.

'Yes…' Mr Woollatt came over, looking very smug. 'I know how much these little trinkets mean to you ladies, so I took the precaution of bringing it with me.'

'And it fits perfectly.' Lady Broxted beamed at him. 'How clever of you, sir.'

It was not to be expected that the engagement should be kept secret. Lady Broxted was eager to dash off to the breakfast room to tell the other houseguests and she would have dragged the happy couple with her, had not Mr Woollatt held up his hand.

'I shall come in briefly to accept their felicitations, of course, but then you must excuse me, ma'am. My mother must be informed of this felicitous event. There is no time to lose, for I would rather tell her myself immediately than risk word reaching her in a roundabout way. Naturally, I discussed my intentions with her before coming to Malberry, but she will want to know if my hopes have been realised. Lord Broxted, I shall bring my lawyer back with me to agree the settlement. After that we can send an announcement to the newspapers, make it all official.' He raised Carlotta's hands to his lips, one after the other. 'I am grieved to have to leave you so soon, my dear, but I shall not be gone above a couple of days. I shall be counting the hours until our next meeting.'

Carlotta murmured her reply and watched him walk away. All the time she felt nothing. Nothing.

Carlotta had hoped that once Mr Woollatt had departed she would be allowed some peace, but it was not to be; Lady Broxted kept her beside her for the rest of the day while the guests came in turn to congratulate her. Mrs

Price called her a sly little puss and made Julia blush by telling her that she would have to hurry up and find a husband if she was not to become an old maid. Sir Gilbert looked thoughtfully at the diamond and wished her every happiness, while Mr and Mrs Ainslowe beamed at her, declaring they felt personally responsible for her good fortune. Only Luke was missing from the happy crowd and it was not until they were all gathered in the drawing room before dinner that she learned he had left the Court.

'Urgent business in town,' explained James.

'Staving off his creditors, more like,' grinned Mr Price, winking at his host.

James's smile hardened slightly. 'No, no, it has not come to that yet,' he said gently.

Mrs Price gave a little laugh, although there was more than a hint of wistfulness about her as she said, 'I doubt we are exciting enough for the Wicked Baron.'

'I assure you, my brother-in-law is more than happy with the company here,' said Adele. 'Only a matter of grave importance would take him away.'

'It is a great pity that Mr Woollatt has left us, too,' continued Mrs Price. 'What shall we do with so few gentlemen? Methinks Lord Fairbridge and Sir Gilbert will have to work twice as hard to keep us all amused.'

The viscount flushed at this, but Sir Gilbert merely laughed.

'Oh, I am sure we shall contrive to amuse ourselves,' replied Adele smoothly. 'Now, shall we go in to dinner?'

'If I had known Darvell was going to town, I would have given him a draft on my bank,' said Sir Gilbert as everyone rose to make their way to the dining room. 'I had a little luck with the cards recently, Ainslowe, and I would buy that Tiepolo back from you. I thought this might be a good time for it, because I could have Reed take it back to town for me.'

'My, my, Sir Gilbert, how would you manage without your valet?' cried Mr Price, winking at his wife.

'Very well, sir, I assure you. I am not such a frippery fellow that I cannot dress myself for a couple of days. But I would like to get the painting back to town.'

'Oh, you would, eh?' retorted James. 'Well, I hate to disappoint you, Gil, but it ain't for sale.'

Sir Gilbert laughed. 'Surely, Ainslowe, you would not deny me my own again.'

'Unfortunately for you, Sir Gilbert, I have taken quite a fancy to it,' laughed Adele as she walked by on Lord Broxted's arm. 'I have to agree with James that it looks very well in the library—you will not get it back now, I think!'

Carlotta was thankful that her betrothal was no longer the main topic of interest and settled down to her meal, although she was so tired that every mouthful was an effort; she was relieved when Mrs Ainslowe shepherded the ladies back to the drawing room, leaving the gentlemen to their brandy. The ladies disposed themselves gracefully on chairs and sofas, Lady Broxted explaining to Mrs Price that Mr Woollatt had gone north to apprise his mother of the happy change to his circumstances.

'I think he would have been better advised to wait a little, until he could take Miss Rivington with him,' opined Mrs Price, 'When—*if* my Julia receives an offer while we are at Malberry, I should not want to separate the happy couple so soon.'

'True, but there is also a case to be made for allowing

them both to come to terms with their new situation,' replied Lady Broxted.

'Yes, poor Carlotta is looking quite worn out with all the excitement,' observed Adele.

Carlota seized her chance.

'Indeed, I am a little tired, Mrs Ainslowe. I think if you will excuse me now I would like to retire.'

'Of course we will excuse you.' Adele patted her hands, smiling at her. 'We must put the bloom back into your cheeks before your fiancé returns, must we not?'

Carlotta forced herself to smile at this, and with a little curtsy she moved towards the door.

'Poor love, would you like me to come with you?'

'No, thank you, Aunt, there is no need to disturb your-self. I shall be quite well if I can only lie down.'

Carlotta slipped out of the room and leaned against the closed door. She let out a long sigh of relief. Lack of sleep was beginning to catch up with her and her bones ached with the effort she was making to smile at everyone. The company was keeping country hours at Malberry Court and the daylight had not yet faded. However, a gloom was settling over the north-facing hall, making the glow of candles coming from a side room all the more noticeable. It was Mr Ainslowe's study. The door stood ajar, allowing the light to spill out on to the tiled floor of the hall. She heard voices and glanced in through the half-open door. With a gasp she stopped, staring. Luke was talking ear-nestly with his brother, but, as if aware of her presence, he looked up and saw her. There was no escape, so Carlotta moved forward, blurting out the words that were in her head. 'I thought you had gone!'

James opened the door wider. 'Come in, Miss Rivington.'

She walked into the study, keeping her eyes upon Luke. He looked very grim, but then he had looked no different when she had seen him in the ante-room that morning.

'I thought you had left for town,' she said again. She looked at his muddy boots and dirty coat. 'Have you been riding all day?'

'No, not exactly,' he said. 'I have this minute come back from the village. There was an attack last night, on your parents' house. A fire—but do not be alarmed,' he added quickly, 'they are unhurt.'

Carlotta glanced anxiously at James.

'You need not worry, Miss Rivington, Luke has told me your history. As yet no one knows that he has returned. The rest of the gentlemen are still at their brandy. They are not aware why I was called away from the dining room.'

She hardly heard him, but turned back to Luke.

'What of the maid, and Jack?'

'Both safe.'

'Thank heaven. What happened?'

'Someone piled wood and bracken against the back door and set fire to it, but the dog's barking woke the servants in time to put the flames out before anyone was hurt. Half the house is damaged, but it is not irreparable.' A faint smile tugged at his mouth. 'That is why I am so filthy, I have been helping your father to salvage what he could from the wreckage and move it into the undamaged part of the house. There is room for the servants to sleep there, but I have taken your parents to the George.'

Carlotta put her hand to her throat as she looked at the two men. 'But who would do this? I mean—coming so soon after the attack upon Papa...'

James hesitated.

Luke said quietly, 'I think we should tell Miss Rivington the truth, brother.'

The silence was unnerving. Carlotta forced herself to speak. 'Thank you. Yes, if you please. Do you know who—who would do this?'

'No,' said James gravely, 'but there was something. Whoever started the fire left a message painted on the wall of the house.'

'A message?'

'Two words,' said Luke, watching her. *'Leave now.'*

'I—don't understand.'

'Someone wants your parents to quit Malberry.'

'B-but why?'

'That is what I have been asking Signor Durini.' Luke regarded her sombrely. 'Perhaps you can help us?'

She shook her head, frowning. 'I have no idea why anyone—it is preposterous. Papa has no enemies.'

'It would appear that he does,' Luke corrected her gently.

'But who could it be?' she challenged him. 'Why would someone want him to leave here?'

James looked uncomfortable. He glanced at his brother, then said diffidently, 'Forgive me, Miss Rivington, but it would be less embarrassing for Lord Broxted if your parents were not living quite so close.'

She stared at him. 'You cannot think my uncle capable of this!'

'Since he brought you to town, he has been careful to keep your parentage a secret,' Luke reminded her.

'Yes, but only because he is afraid any eligible suitors will be discouraged.'

'Any man who truly cares for you will not care a button that your mother married an artist,' muttered Luke.

'Yes, that is what my uncle thinks,' she said eagerly. 'He has always said that once a man shows a true regard for me he will explain everything. He would have told Mr Woollatt if he had not been in such haste to get away this morning.' She fixed her eyes upon James, pleading silently with him to understand.

'Broxted is very conscious of his own importance,' murmured Luke, 'but I do not think him capable of this.'

Carlotta gave an emphatic shake of her head. 'No, of course not.'

'But if that is not the reason for the attacks, what is?' asked James.

'Until we find that out, we must do something to protect the Durinis.' Luke looked at his brother. 'Well, James?'

'I shall move them to my Leicestershire estate. The gatehouse there is empty. Then we will spread the word that they have fled we know not where.' He turned back to Carlotta. 'You may rest easy, Miss Rivington. I shall look after your parents.'

'Thank you, sir. You are very good. How soon will they leave?'

'As soon as they can be packed and ready. Tomorrow, I hope.'

'I must go and see them—'

'No! It is too dangerous.'

Luke's vehemence startled her. She began to protest until James said gently, 'It would be best if you did not visit them, Miss Rivington. Few people here know your background—to own it now might put you in danger, too.'

'But I could visit them after dark. They would not be asleep. Mama never retires before midnight, and sometimes Papa works through the night—'

'And do you truly believe it would relieve their worries to think of you wandering abroad at night? No, be guided by me, it is best that you do not see them.' James raised his head, listening. 'I hear voices. The gentlemen are on their way to the drawing room, and I think we should join them—that is, you and I should join them, Miss Rivington, Luke must go upstairs and change. He is not fit to be seen.' He held out his arm to her.

'I—I was about to retire,' she confessed.

'If that is what you wish. However, we could tell everyone that you overheard the news and are too disturbed to sleep, if you go now, you may be obliged to hear the story several times over in the morning.'

'Very well, sir, you have persuaded me. And it is the truth that I could not rest now.' She laid her fingers on his sleeve. 'Will you tell them everything that has occurred?'

'Only that someone tried to set fire to my artist's house. The rest shall be our secret. You may wish to confide in your aunt and uncle, of course, and with your permission I should like to tell Adele that you are Signor Durini's daughter, but you may be assured it will go no further.'

'Yes, of course.'

He patted her hand. 'Very good. Now, shall we go in?'

Carlotta lay on her bed and counted the chimes from the clock tower on the stables. Eleven o'clock. It was time. She dragged her cloak around her and went to the door. The landing was deserted, but she knew that some of the guests might still be downstairs. She strained to listen for footsteps, but all she could hear was the thudding of her own heart. It was only a few yards from her bedchamber to the backstairs, but it would not do to be discovered creeping out of the house so late at night. Nothing stirred. Carefully she closed her bedroom door and flew across the landing to the backstairs. Her soft kid boots made no noise on the wooden treads, but she was fearful that a creaking stair might betray her. By the time she reached the door leading out into the garden, her nerves were stretched to breaking point and when a dark figure detached itself from the bushes beside her she almost fainted. She turned to flee, but even as she drew breath to scream a pair of strong arms wrapped about her and a hand was clamped over her mouth.

'I have been waiting for you.'

Carlotta stopped struggling. The hand was removed from her face and she swung around.

'Luke,' she hissed. 'What are you doing here?'

He looked down at her, his face in deep shadow.

'I told you, I was waiting for you. I knew you would go to see your parents, with or without consent. I saw it in your face when James forbade you to go.'

'He did not forbid it, he merely advised.'

'And your uncle? I assume he knows the truth now about the attack.'

'Yes, I explained it all to him and to my aunt when we retired. They were deeply shocked.'

'And did they condone this night-time escapade?' He waited. 'Well?'

'I did not tell them,' she replied in a small voice.

'I thought as much.'

'How did you know I would be here?

He reached up and cupped her chin with his hand. Gently he ran his thumb across her bottom lip. Despite her anxiety, the familiar flame of desire stirred at his touch.

'I have seen that obstinate look before—it was a simple

matter to ascertain the nearest way out of the house from your chamber.'

'I suppose you will insist that I return.'

She heard him laugh softly. He pulled her hand on to his arm.

'No, but I insist you let me accompany you.'

Relief flooded through her. '*Thank* you!'

'Save your thanks until we are safely indoors once again,' he muttered. 'And pull your hood up to cover your face. That's better. We will take the longer path, through the trees to the far side of the lake. I would not expect anyone to be looking out of the window at this time of night, but we will take no risks.'

After the attacks upon her father, Carlotta had not been looking forward to walking through the dark grounds of Malberry Court, but with Luke beside her she was no longer afraid. They left the shelter of the walled garden and followed the path around the perimeter of the park. They walked in silence with only the occasional screech of a fox or hooting owl to disturb the peace.

When they reached the stile, Carlotta glanced around her anxiously, knowing that this was where her father had been attacked. The trees and lush undergrowth made the area particularly dark, and she was glad to have Luke's comforting presence as they made their way past her parents' house, one side of it blackened and damaged. The gaping black holes where the windows had been made her shudder, and she was pleased that Luke hurried her on towards the George, where lights still blazed from the taproom despite the lateness of the hour. He led her under the arch, but at the doorway he stopped, pushing her behind him.

'Wait here. I will make sure there is no one on the stairs… Good, it's clear. Come along.'

Carlotta could hear voices and laughter coming from the taproom. The smell of stale cabbage and onions permeated the dark corridor. Taking her hand, Luke led her up the narrow staircase and along a dimly lit passage, stopping at the end to knock on a solid door. A bolt scraped back, the door opened, and Carlotta fell into her father's arms.

Carlotta sat between her mother and father, looking from one to the other to assure herself that they were safe while they explained what had happened.

'It is not so very bad.' Her father shrugged. 'We lost some clothes, a few pots and pans—'

'A few pots and pans!' cried Mrs Durini, 'My whole kitchen was destroyed.'

Signor Durini threw up his hands. 'Hah, of what importance is a kitchen?'

'Of great importance, if you want to eat,' returned his wife, drily. 'Not only that, the flames reached the room above it, where most of my gowns were stored.'

'I shall buy you more gowns, *cara*. But if it had reached my *pittura*, or the *miniatura*, now *that* would have been serious. As it is, Signor Ainslowe has said he will send his carriage tomorrow morning to take us to another, safer house, and we can continue to work there. Signor Ainslowe says the final two temples can be completed some other time, he has enough for now.' He squeezed Carlotta's hand. 'So you must not worry about us, Carla. In fact, I think we should celebrate our good fortune! I shall fetch a bottle of wine, if our landlord is not abed!'

'I'll go with you,' said Luke.

'Papa is remarkably calm about all this,' said Carlotta as the two men left the room.

'Your father is an artist. He lives for his painting. Besides, Lord Darvell and his brother have promised to help us, and they are good men, I think. Although I cannot condone his lordship bringing you here tonight, and so late.'

'It was my idea, Mama.'

'Well, you should not have come, my love. It is not safe.'

Carlotta put up her chin. 'I had to come; I could not let you go away without seeing for myself that you were unharmed. Please do not be angry with me.'

'Of course not, my love.' Mrs Durini smiled fondly at her. 'And you have something to tell us, too, have you not?' She lifted Carlotta's hand, turning it so that the ring on her finger glinted in the candlelight.

Carlotta's cheeks grew warm. 'Yes, Mama. I—I am betrothed.'

'Oh, my dear, that is wonderful! To…?'

'M-Mr Woollatt.'

Mrs Durini blinked. 'Mr Woollatt? The man your aunt mentioned in her letters, the rich suitor?'

'Yes, Mama. The *very* rich suitor.'

'Then why are you with…?'

'Lord Darvell is m-my friend,' Carlotta replied, flushing.

Mrs Durini frowned. She took Carlotta by the shoulders and pulled her round to face her. 'My love, listen to me. A young lady cannot have male friends, especially when she is betrothed. People will talk.'

'Let them; I do not care what they say!'

'Of course you do not, but your fiancé might well care.'

'Please do not worry, Mama. Luke only came with me to

protect me; no one knows we are here, and we shall be careful to make sure we are not seen as we go back through the park.'

Her mother did not look very reassured. 'We will have no more than one glass of wine together, *cara*, then you must go home as quickly as possible. Do not tarry. Promise me.'

'Of course, Mama, but there is no danger, Luke is with me.'

She pulled Carlotta into her arms and hugged her tightly. 'Oh, my sweet child,' she murmured, 'there is every danger!'

'Well, are you happy now you have seen your parents?'

Carlotta and Luke were walking back through the park, their path through the trees dappled with moonlight.

'Yes, I am.'

'Then what is worrying you, Carlotta?'

She looked up quickly, but Luke's face was in shadow. 'Is it so obvious?'

'It is to me.'

She sighed. 'Mama says…I must… She says you cannot be my friend.'

'She is right. That is why I was going to leave Malberry today.'

'Then why did you return?'

'Because I could not leave knowing you might be in danger.'

A bubble of happiness began to grow inside her; she reached out for him. 'So you *do* care.'

'Yes.'

He squeezed her hand, and the fragile little bubble burst as Carlotta felt Mr Woollatt's ring pressing into her fingers.

The gibbous moon was high above them, sailing through the clouds, serene and untroubled. Luke had a sudden impulse to throw back his head and howl, letting out his despair and frustration.

'It is too late. I would to heaven I had declared myself.' He was not aware that he had spoken aloud until he heard Carlotta's heavy sigh.

'My uncle would not have countenanced it, he—he deplores your loose ways. Besides, Mr Woollatt is far richer than you, is he not?'

Luke hesitated. Should he tell her how much he loved her? What good would it do now? If she broke off the engagement to Woollatt, she would be labelled a jilt and lose her place in society—her rightful place and one that she had known for such a short time. He could not do that to her—and if he did, would she not come to hate him for it? He forced himself to speak lightly.

'Yes, Woollatt is a much better man than I am, in all ways.'

The little hand in his trembled. He stopped. Something about the stance of the slender figure beside him stabbed at his heart. Her hood had fallen back, but she stood with her face averted. He took her shoulders and pulled her into a patch of moonlight. Still she would not look at him and he cupped her chin with his hand, tilting her face up. As she raised her eyes to look at him, he saw that they were glistening with tears.

'Ah, love, don't cry.' The words were wrenched from him. He folded her in his arms, felt the stiff little body resist for a moment before collapsing against him, sobbing piteously.

He held her, crooning softly and caressing her hair, hating her pain, but at the same time revelling in the closeness, the feel of her leaning against him, dependent upon him for comfort. Desire stirred; her nearness was arousing him, but he tried to ignore it. He rested his cheek on her hair, breathing in the fresh, flowery scent. If only this could go on for ever, if they did not have to face the morning. If only…

He realised she had stopped crying and was standing passively within his arms, her head resting against his chest. He loosened his hold and reached into his pocket.

'Here,' he said, holding up a handkerchief. 'I would rather you wiped your eyes on this than my shirt front.'

A watery chuckle greeted his words. 'Thank you.' She raised her head, smiling slightly, but as she reached for the handkerchief he pulled his hand away.

'No, let me do it.' She stood quietly, her face uplifted, while he wiped her cheeks. 'There, that's better.' He kissed the tip of her nose. She stood mutely looking up at him, her eyes huge and dark in her pale face, her lips full and lush. Irresistible. Gently, he slid his lips over hers. Just one kiss, he told himself, just one moment of happiness before he gave her up for ever.

Carlotta closed her eyes as his mouth found hers. It was supremely comforting, having Luke so close to her. Her hands slid up around his neck. Just once, she told herself, just one last, treasured moment to remember in the bleak years that stretched ahead of her. It was her last conscious thought. Luke's mouth became harder, more demanding and she gave herself up to the pleasurable sensations he was arousing within her. She pressed herself against his hard, aroused body and felt her insides liquefy. An urgent and irrepressible need consumed her. Luke pushed aside her cloak, his hands sliding over her shoulders, then he was cupping her breast, his thumb circling, teasing until she was pushing hard against him, her thighs aching, her body tingling with an anticipation she did not understand. His mouth trailed lightly across her neck, his breath tickling her skin, his touch sending little darts of heat through her body. She drove her fingers through his hair and gave a little moan of pleasure.

Desire surged through Luke, fuelled by elation as Carlotta leaned against him, her body inviting his caresses. He pushed her back gently, trapping her against a tree. His tongue flickered over the silky smooth skin of her shoulder, nibbled gently at her collarbone before his mouth moved on to explore the soft swell of her breasts. He pushed aside the thin muslin and took one hard erect nipple in his mouth, his tongue circling slowly while Carlotta arched against him, her responses driving all other thoughts from his mind. Her hands tangled in his hair, then, as the fingers of her left hand slid down to caress his cheek, he felt the hard, unyielding metal of the ring upon her finger.

It was a little touch, but it was enough. It reminded him that Carlotta was to be another man's wife. Slowly Luke raised his head, listening to his own ragged breathing. He would not do this. He would not take what did not belong to him. Carlotta was looking up at him, her eyes large and luminous with desire. He could take her now; he knew she was willing, but he remembered the vow he had made to himself twelve months ago, that he would not ruin her. His own private devil whispered that no one need ever know, she would not be the first bride to go to her husband without her virginity, but it would not do. *She* would know, and she was too honest, too innocent to live with that secret—it would ruin any chance she had of happiness with her husband.

'Luke, what is it?'

He kissed her, one final, light touch of the lips. 'No more, sweetheart. I am promised to protect you, and I must get you back to the Court before I dishonour you completely.'

She was watching him, the signs of doubt on her face. 'Do you not…want me?'

He heard the uncertainty in her voice. It tore at his heart. 'Want you! Heaven and earth, love, you'll never know how much!' He cupped her face with one hand, saying gently, 'I will not take another man's bride, Carlotta. It would bring us all pain. Believe me, I know, I have seen it happen too many times.' He moved away from her, away from temptation. 'I will not lie to you—I have had my share of mistresses, but it has always been a game understood by both parties. We enjoyed each other, then moved on, with no regrets, no broken hearts—until now. I will not risk yours.'

Carlotta was confused. Her heightened senses were aware of the balmy stillness of the night and the moon sailing overhead, so calm and serene. Yet here, within the shadow of the trees, there was an atmosphere of suppressed passion. She felt as if she had been rudely awakened from a lovely dream, where she and Luke loved each other, and nothing else mattered. Now he talked of risks, and broken hearts. She gave a shaky laugh. 'It is too late for that, I think.'

'But not too late for you to be happy.'

She put a hand to her head, trying to think clearly. 'I—I do not understand.' She heard him sigh.

'No, you are too innocent, but believe me, it is for the best. You must marry Woollatt with a clear conscience. You deserve that. *He* deserves it.'

A line from a poem darted into her head and she murmured the words,

'"I could not love thee, dear, so much, loved I not honour more."'

He looked at her. 'What was that?'

She gave him a sad little smile.

'You are a good man, Luke Ainslowe.' She held out her hand. 'Will you take me back to the Court, now?'

Hand in hand they walked through the park; as Luke opened the gate into the walled garden, Carlotta looked up at him.

'You will not go?' she said. 'Even though my parents are moved to safety, you will stay?'

'I am promised to help James track down the attackers.'

'Then I won't lose you just yet.'

He followed her into the garden. 'It would be less painful if we did not see each other.'

'But we must grow accustomed,' she reasoned. 'We move in the same circles, we cannot avoid seeing each other.'

'I will not be in town so often in the future. I have spent much of the past year on my estates, trying to bring them back into shape. I have made some progress, but there is a great deal yet to do.'

She sighed. He had withdrawn from her, as he must. They were moving silently along in the shadow of the garden wall towards the side door of the house, creeping along like a couple of robbers, or lovers. With a gasp Carlotta stopped and reached out to grab Luke's sleeve.

'I have just remembered something. Last night, I did not sleep very well and was looking out of my window—it was just before dawn, the sun had not risen, but it was growing light—I saw someone here, in the garden. A cloaked figure keeping to the shadow of the wall. It could be nothing. At the time I thought it was a servant, coming back from a tryst with his maid—'

'You are sure it was a man?'

'Yes, I think so…that is—yes, it was a man; it moved like a man.'

Luke frowned. 'The figure was coming towards this door? This wing is used only for guests and their personal servants.'

'Do you think someone from here set fire to my parents' house?' She shivered, suddenly fearful.

'That is what we must discover,' murmured Luke. He pulled her into his arms for a brief moment. 'You must try not to worry, *cara*.'

'I am not at all afraid when you are with me,' she murmured into his coat. Gently he disentangled himself from her arms.

'You must go back to your room,' he said softly. 'Let us see if the side door is unlocked, as we left it.'

Chapter Thirteen

'Carlotta, my dear, are you ill? You are looking very pale.'

No wonder, thought Carlotta, entering the breakfast room, *I spent half the night wandering the park with Luke, and the other half lying awake, thinking about him. Damn the man! Oh, Luke…*

'I slept ill last night, Aunt.' She smiled at the guests gathered around the table, as if to apologise for not looking her best for them. Luke, she noted, was not present.

'Too much excitement, perhaps, Miss Rivington?' Sir Gilbert waved away the footman and held the chair for her himself. Carlotta would have preferred to sit beside her aunt rather than across the table, where she must face her close scrutiny, but she could not bring herself to refuse Sir Gilbert's courtesy.

'I know what it is,' declared Mr Price. 'She is missing her swain. Am I not right, Miss Rivington?'

'Perhaps.'

'I am afraid I cannot divert you with any outdoor pursuits,' announced Adele. 'The inclement weather has put an end to hopes of that.'

Everyone present glanced towards the windows and the steady rain pouring down.

'I only hope we will not have to cancel our shooting party,' remarked Mr Price, addressing himself again to his breakfast.

'Lord, no.' Sir Gilbert laughed. 'That is two days hence; the weather will have changed by then.'

'But it will be excessively muddy,' pointed out Mrs Ainslowe.

'Then it is a good thing we shall not be dining with you.' Her husband laughed.

'The gentlemen have decided that when they have finished shooting they will retire to the bathhouse,' explained Mrs Ainslowe, observing Lady Broxted's puzzled look. 'We shall be left to enjoy a quiet dinner here at the Court, where we may gossip and chatter to our hearts' content.'

'It means we shall not be bringing our dirt back to the house.' James grinned. 'There is nothing that annoys the ladies more than to have our muddy footprints all over the floors.'

Lord Broxted turned to his wife. 'Ainslowe mentioned it to me yesterday, and I had meant to tell you, my dear— I hope you do not object?'

'Not in the least. I am sure you will all enjoy getting excessively dirty, and we shall spend a very pleasant day without you, I have no doubt.'

'I just wish it was fine today.' Adele sighed. 'I did so wish to take Carlotta for a ride in the gig.'

'Perhaps it is for the best that you do not go,' put in Lady Broxted. 'Mr Woollatt is very anxious for Carlotta's safety.'

'Then we must hope tomorrow is dry, so that we can drive out before he returns,' retorted Carlotta. Her aunt's look of surprise made her flush and she added more gently, 'I am sure it is perfectly safe, ma'am, and I would not have him worry over me.'

'Of course he will worry!' Mrs Price put down her piece of toast and shook her head at Carlotta. 'Lord, what a strange notion! It is a very good sign that Mr Woollatt is concerned for you, my dear, it shows he means to take very good care of you when you are married!'

Carlotta pinned on a smile, but inside she was already feeling constricted by that invisible mesh of solicitude.

The rain was succeeded by a drizzling mist that kept the house party indoors. Adele invited everyone to the library to play charades, an idea eagerly taken up by most of the younger guests and improved upon by Sir Gilbert, who suggested that the ballroom would offer more scope for their theatricals. Lady Broxted and Mrs Price decided to adjourn to the morning room and Carlotta chose to remain close to her aunt, determined to avoid all male company. The older ladies settled down to while away the afternoon with their books and desultory conversation, and Carlotta carried her embroidery frame to a chair by one of the far windows where she was not overlooked. She kept her head bent over her work, and, if the memory of Luke's embraces sometimes made her set a stitch awry, at least there was no one to observe it.

However, she was heartily bored with her occupation by the afternoon and was relieved when Adele came in and announced she was going out.

'The weather is clearing and I am going to take a walk before dinner. Who will join me?'

'Dear me—walking, so late in the day?' said Lady Broxted, glancing at the pretty ormolu clock on the side table.

Adele laughed. 'There is an hour or more before we need to even think of changing for dinner, that is time and enough to take the air.'

'I stand in awe of your energy, Mrs Ainslowe,' said Mrs Price, waving her fan. 'I vow I am quite fatigued, and was about to suggest to Lady Broxted that we should retire now to rest until the dinner hour.'

'An excellent idea, ma'am,' agreed Lady Broxted. 'I fear you will have to excuse us from your little outing, Mrs Ainslowe.'

Carlotta wondered how they could possibly be tired when they had done nothing but sit down since breakfast. Something of her thoughts must have shown in her face, for Adele was looking at her with a very decided twinkle in her eyes.

'Then Julia and I will be going for a walk on our own, unless I can persuade Miss Rivington to join us?'

'Just the two of you, ma'am? No gentlemen?'

'Alas, no. They have decided they would prefer to play billiards. So you see, it will be a very small little party. Will you come?'

Reassured that there would be no danger of meeting Luke, Carlotta gladly put aside her embroidery and accepted the invitation.

'How fresh the air is!' declared Adele as they set off into the park. 'I declare I am quite *stifled*, being confined to the house all day. We are all wearing very sensible half-boots, I see. I thought we might take the path around the lake, it is newly completed and should not be too muddy, despite the rain. Are we agreed? Good. Onward, then!'

Adele's brisk walking pace suited her young companions very well. A stiff breeze had blown away the low cloud and after the recent rain the colours of the park seemed enhanced in the sparkling sunlight. Carlotta was very glad to be out of doors. The exercise soothed her ragged nerves and she walked along in silence, happy to allow her mind to wander freely. Adele was drawing Julia out, gently encouraging her to talk, but Carlotta paid little heed to them or to their direction until the meandering path brought them in sight of a large square building, its fluted columns and stone portico reminiscent of a Greek temple. When she had seen it last it had been little more than a neglected shell, but now the windows had been glazed and the solid oak doors repaired.

'Ah, the bathhouse,' said Adele. 'There are some very fine murals in here, I understand. Shall we go in and look?'

Julia stopped. 'Oh, but…is this not the gentlemen's bathhouse?'

'Well, certainly the gentlemen use it, but they will not be here today,' replied Adele. 'Come.' She squeezed Carlotta's arm. 'I am sure *you* would like to look inside.'

'Indeed I should,' agreed Carlotta. It was one of the last buildings to be decorated by her father, and she was eager to see it, eager for some link with her parents. With a jolt she realised how much she was missing them.

Adele led the way up the shallow steps to the double doors situated beyond the pillars.

'Perhaps it is locked,' said Julia, not unhopefully.

Adele reached into her reticule and pulled out a large key. 'I came prepared!'

The doors opened smoothly and they stepped inside. They found themselves in a square, vaulted room with windows set up high in the walls. There was a rectangular plunge bath in the centre of the floor with a flight of shallow stone steps leading down into it. Adele stooped to put her hand into the water, sending little waves rippling across the surface.

'I am told it is deep enough for swimming. It is very cold, of course, but the gentlemen do not seem to mind that.' She giggled. 'The high windows mean that they cannot be spied upon.'

'I—I am sure we should not be here,' stuttered Julia, staring wide-eyed at the walls.

Carlotta looked around her; a series of murals depicted classical scenes, men and women bathing in a river. She had been brought up in an artist's studio and was quite at home with the near-naked figures, but Julia was clearly shocked. Adele merely laughed.

'Of course, we should not be here, but you are not children; I do not believe you will be irrevocably harmed by what you see. Besides, we need not tell anyone.'

Julia gave a nervous giggle. 'No, I suppose not.'

'Come along, then; let us go into the warm room.'

They moved on past the plunge pool and through the doors beyond. Carlotta was surprised to find herself now in a very different space. There was a large fireplace set into one wall and a number of padded couches placed around the room. The windows here were also high and the walls beneath them were covered with scenes of what Carlotta suspected might be an orgy. She smiled to herself; Papa was very liberal, but he would never have allowed her in *here* while he was working!

'The gentlemen come in here to relax,' explained Adele. 'There is a little room at the side where water can be heated for the hip baths. Then, when the gentlemen have finished their day's shooting, they can bathe and refresh themselves in the plunge pool before taking an informal dinner here, before the fire.'

'It sounds very…decadent,' observed Carlotta, her lip quivering.

'Yes, but amusing,' replied Adele.

The three ladies looked at one another and giggled.

'P-perhaps we should hold a dinner of our own here one day,' suggested Adele.

Julia put her hand to her flaming cheeks. 'Oh, no, I could not…!'

Carlotta took her arm. 'You need not be anxious, Julia. I do not think it would be allowed.'

'Certainly not for *unmarried* ladies,' agreed Adele, twinkling.

Carlotta returned from the walk with her spirits much improved and looking forward to her dinner. At the back of her mind there were nagging doubts about her engagement to Mr Woollatt, but he was not expected to return for a few more days and in her present buoyant mood she found herself reluctant to think too much about the future.

As the ladies hurried up the stairs to change they found James waiting for them on the landing.

'Ah, there you are. Did you enjoy your walk?'

'Very much, my love,' replied Adele. 'And we are now ready for our dinner!'

James grinned. 'Then you had best go and change, but perhaps Miss Rivington would spare me a moment? I have a message for her.'

Carlotta looked at him in surprise, but Adele patted her arm.

'From Daniel Woollatt, I don't doubt. Very well, James, but do not keep her too long!'

'Is that it?' asked Carlotta, 'Do you have a message for me from Mr Woollatt?'

James beckoned to Carlotta to follow him to one of the deep window embrasures that overlooked the south lawn. He waited until the other ladies were out of sight, then he pulled a note from his pocket and handed it to Carlotta.

'Better than that—it is from your father. My coachman returned from Leicestershire this afternoon and he has brought a note for you from Signor Durini.'

Eagerly she unfolded the paper and scanned it. 'Thank you, Mr Ainslowe. I had asked Papa to let me know that they were safe.'

'Well, now you can rest easy.' He smiled down at her. 'And when Woollatt returns we shall see the smile back in your eyes, I hope. Oh don't colour up, my dear; Adele noticed that you had lost a little of your sparkle, but that's to be expected, with your fiancé gone away.'

Carlotta blushed, confused, and strove for something to say. 'May I write a letter to my parents, sir?'

'Of course—give it to me when it is finished and I will see it safely delivered.' With a final reassuring smile James stepped quickly out of the embrasure. 'What the—!'

Carlotta heard his exclamation. As she moved forward she saw he had come to a halt at the head of the stairs.

'Reed! What the devil are you doing there?'

Sir Gilbert's manservant was almost at the top of the grand staircase, but at these words he stopped and made a low bow.

'My apologies, sir. My master sent me to the library and I thought, this being the shortest route and with all the guests in their rooms, dressing for dinner—'

'Well, quite clearly they ain't all in their rooms,' retorted James coldly. 'Please use the service stairs in future.'

'Yes, sir.'

Watching from the window, Carlotta observed the smirk on the man's ferret-like features as he bowed again.

'One moment, Reed!'

'Yes, sir?'

'Where's your book?'

'Sir?'

'If Sir Gilbert sent you to the library, it must have been for a book.'

'I was *returning* a book for him, sir,' Reed said quietly. Then, with another bow, he continued on his stately way.

'Insolent dog,' muttered James.

'I understand that all valets think themselves superior,' murmured Carlotta.

'Aye, they do, but most of 'em make a better pretence at subservience than that creature. In fact, most of 'em keep out of sight. Ah, well, Mattingwood tells me the man has been with him for many years and long-serving attendants are the very devil, Miss Rivington. Now, I had best let you get on, or we shall both of us be late for our dinner!'

Luke wished the interminable day would come to an end. He had spent his time avoiding Carlotta, as much for his sake as hers. It was bad enough that he couldn't get the thought of her out of his mind; when he walked through the hall the perfume from the flowers on the console tables made his step falter and for a moment he was back beneath the trees, burying his face in her hair and breathing in her sweet, flowery fragrance. Just going out of the front door and looking up at the frescoes reminded him of Carlotta.

Now, at dinner, he had to steel himself to face her. He had deliberately come down late to the drawing room, but not late enough, for James was laughingly informing the assembly that his wife had kept the young ladies out of doors for far too long, and they were even now at their dressing tables.

Luke positioned himself in a far corner and watched the door, waiting for a first glimpse of that beloved, heart-shaped face. When Carlotta did come in, he thought how well she looked, the effects of the walk still discernible in her glowing countenance. He had hoped to avoid her, but it was as if some magic thread drew her gaze to his. She looked away immediately, as anxious as he was to avoid detection, but that one fleeting glance set his pulses racing, made the blood course faster through his body.

With an effort he turned his back to her and joined Sir Gilbert and Mr Price for a lively debate on horses, but he was aware of her presence and found himself straining his ears to hear the soft words she was exchanging with Adele. Luke soon realised that he was not the only gentleman showing an interest in Carlotta. He noticed how often Sir Gilbert's eyes wandered over to the little group, and when the ladies engaged upon an argument regarding *The Mysteries of Udolpho* and Carlotta was about to run to the library to fetch Mrs Radcliffe's novel, Sir Gilbert swiftly stepped in, offering to go in her stead. Damn the man, he had not shown such great interest in Carlotta before she became engaged to Woollatt. Was he trying to set up as her flirt even before she was married? Scowling, Luke tried to give his attention to Mr Price, but from the corner of his eye he watched as his brother joined the little group.

'So, my love,' said James, 'did you and your young friends enjoy your stroll through the park?'

'Very much. We completed a full circuit around the lake. The new path makes it a most pleasant walk with beautiful views across the park. We passed the bathhouse.' Adele threw a mischievous glance towards Julia, who blushed vividly. 'We were *most* impressed.'

The devil, thought Luke. They have been inside. He imagined Carlotta looking at the bathing scenes. Had they also visited the inner sanctum? He glanced across at Carlotta and immediately looked away again, biting his lip. Of course they had. Her sparkling eyes and the telltale flush on her cheek gave her away. He wondered if she, too, was imagining how delightful it would be to swim together in that cold pool—could she swim? If not, he would teach her. Afterwards they would lie naked in front of the roaring fire in the warm room. He turned away suddenly. It could never be, of course—she was Woollatt's fiancée. But still the thought was far too arousing.

'We are very tempted to join you in the bathhouse when you have done with your shooting,' murmured Adele.

Luke swung back in time to see the look of horror on Miss Price's face. James wagged a playful finger.

'We have entertained you with dancing and rides and I know not what every day thus far, madam wife. You will now allow us to enjoy ourselves in peace! Besides, have we not promised that we shall join you here for supper?'

'Your wife is teasing you, Mr Ainslowe,' put in Mrs Price. 'We have plans for our own entertainment that day, I assure you. More to the point, is anything arranged for tomorrow? If it remains dry, I would very much like to take the lakeside walk—Mrs Ainslowe's description has given me a desire to try it.'

'Yes, I, too, would like to see it,' added Lady Broxted.

'Let us all go,' suggested Sir Gilbert, returning from the library.

'Yes, James may escort you,' declared Adele. 'And since we have already seen it, I shall take Julia and Carlotta out in the gig.'

'Th-thank you, but Lord Fairbridge has already promised to take me out for an airing in his curricle,' stammered Julia.

James laughed. 'Miss Price has seen your driving, my dear, and is in dread of being overturned! And you, Miss Rivington—will you risk life and limb?'

'I understand it was you who taught Mrs Ainslowe to drive,' replied Carlotta in the same bantering tone. 'Have you no faith in your pupil?'

'Bravo, Carlotta! James knows I am a very good driver, else he would not have given me my own carriage.' Adele nodded at Carlotta. 'I thought we could drive up through the woods to the south of the house; there is a fine view from top of the hill. We will set out directly after breakfast, if you would like it.'

'I should,' said Carlotta. 'I should like it very much.'

A bright, sunny day greeted Carlotta when she awoke the following morning, but despite the promise of driving out with her hostess, there was a tiny shadow over her anticipation. Mr Woollatt might well return that day. With a sigh Carlotta slipped out of bed. The diamond ring was resting on her dressing table, a physical token of the promise she had made. She forced herself to slip it onto her finger. She should be happy; she was betrothed to a good man with a handsome fortune. If she had not met Luke—she cut off the thought. She *had* met him, nothing could change that, and nothing could change the fact that she was engaged to Daniel Woollatt. There was no going back. Therefore she must make the best of it. Perhaps if she and Luke were not in the same house, if they did not see each other every day, then it would be easier to bear. She could forget him—well, perhaps not quite forget him, but at least this crippling, aching longing might ease a little. Carlotta decided that she must persuade her aunt to take her away from Malberry. Away from Luke. The thought made her eyes prickle with hot tears, but she brushed them away, resolutely turning her thoughts to the more pleasant prospect of driving out with Mrs Ainslowe.

Adele drove the gig from the stables at a smart pace, sending up a shower of gravel as she swung sharply around the corner to bring the equipage to a halt at the front steps.

'There,' cried James, waiting on the steps beside Carlotta, 'do not say I did not warn you! My wife is a demon when she is handling the ribbons.'

Carlotta heard the affection and pride in his voice and said nothing as he helped her up into the gig and tucked the rug around her.

'Have I kept you waiting?' said Adele. 'I beg your pardon—Perkins was nowhere to be seen and Little Jones, the stable boy, was struggling to yoke poor Brigadier all on his own. But we are here now, you see.'

'Will you return to take luncheon, my love?' asked James.

'Oh, I am sure we shall be back by then.' Adele arranged

the reins between her fingers. 'When do you set off for your walk around the lake?'

'As soon as we are all ready,' said James. 'But I doubt we shall make such good time as you did yesterday.'

'No. We set a very smart pace, did we not, Carlotta?'

'Well, go a little more slowly today,' he said, stepping back. 'Be careful, my love.'

Adele smiled at him. 'Am I not always? Stand aside, sir!'

With a flourish of her whip she set the team in motion. Carlotta turned to wave to Mr Ainslowe, her smile slipping a little when she spotted Luke staring out of the study window.

'Tell me, Carlotta,' said Adele. 'If you and my brother-in-law are so in love, why did you accept an offer from Mr Woollatt?'

Carlotta jumped. 'H-how did you know? We have been so careful…'

'That is what made me suspicious. You both prowl around each other, being far too rigidly correct. Oh, have no fear, I doubt if anyone else has noticed, even darling James.' Adele paused while she guided the horse out of the gates and turned away from the village to drive up the hill. 'Perhaps it is being so in love oneself that makes one especially aware—or perhaps it is being with child.'

'You are—oh, Adele, that is wonderful news!'

'Yes, isn't it?' she laughed. 'That is why James is so concerned that I should be careful. He would have me lie abed all day if he could, but I am not such a poor creature.'

'But you will drive steadily, will you not?'

'Pho.' Adele laughed at her. 'I will not overturn you, I promise. But you have not told me why you are marrying Daniel Woollatt.'

Carlotta had twisted slightly in her seat with her right

hand resting along the back rail, but as the gig swayed alarmingly on the uneven road she hooked her arm around the rail and held on tightly.

'Well?'

'It is a very good match.' This sounded lame even to Carlotta, and she added, 'He is extremely rich.'

'But you love Luke.'

'Yes.'

'And what does he say about this?'

Carlotta felt the hot tears burning her eyes. She swallowed the lump in her throat and tried to speak lightly. 'H-he agrees it is a good idea.'

'The devil he does!' exclaimed Adele in a most unladylike manner.

'He told me so,' said Carlotta miserably. 'When…when he knew Mr Woollatt was going to make me an offer.'

'Then he is a fool, and I shall tell him so to his head!'

'Oh, no, pray, Adele, you must say nothing of this. We are agreed that it is too late, and we must forget each other.' She sniffed. 'L-Luke will soon find himself someone else.'

'Unfortunately, my dear, I am afraid that is more than likely,' said Adele. 'Luke has something of a reputation.'

'I know.' Carlotta gulped back a sob.

'You could cry off from your engagement.'

Carlotta shook her head. 'I have thought of that, but it would not do. I would be labelled a jilt; my aunt and uncle would be mortified and Mama and Papa would be very disappointed in me. There would be gossip; everyone would learn about m-my parents and I should not be welcome in polite society.

'But I could bear all that, I really could, if only… You see, if Luke married me, everyone would blame *him*, too. We w-would be outcasts. That would not trouble me very much, because I have not lived in society very long, but I could not ask Luke to give up everything he has known. It would make him unhappy, and he would end up hating me for it.'

Carlotta gazed ahead, considering her future and unappreciative of the bright sunshine or beautiful woodland that surrounded them.

'I must say it is a pretty coil,' confessed Adele after a moment. 'I was very fortunate, you see. I fell in love with James the first moment we met; although he was a younger son and not the most important of my suitors, Papa could see how much in love we were and eventually gave his consent.' She sighed, but after a moment she turned her head to give Carlotta a reassuring smile. 'You must not be cast down, my love. I am a firm believer that everything happens for the best. Something may yet turn up. And if it does not, and you do marry Mr Woollatt, well, just think how much pin money you will have to spend!'

Carlotta did not find much to comfort her in this thought, but she nodded and tried to enjoy the drive. They had emerged from the trees and were now travelling through open grazing land towards the summit of the hill. As the road levelled out, Adele gave an expert little flick of the whip and the horse picked up its pace.

'There are some outstanding views up here,' she said. 'They will make you forget—'

The sentence was never finished. The gig gave a sickening lurch. Carlotta's arm was still hooked around the back rail and instinctively her fingers clung on as the carriage dropped away from her. Her arm was almost wrenched from its socket; the gig tipped onto its side and Adele tumbled past her.

Chapter Fourteen

Carlotta scrabbled to find some ledge for her feet since the footwell of the gig was now tilted at a steep angle. She managed to push her toes against the side wall of the carriage and relieve some of the strain upon her arm, but her tentative foothold was shaken as the gig shuddered, then lurched again. She looked up to see that the horse was trapped in the tangle of harness and gig shafts and was frantically lunging forward, trying to pull free. She was not that far from the ground, and thought she might well be able to jump down if the gig would remain still. She was aware of voices, heavy footsteps running up. Turning her head, she saw one man drop his shepherd's crook and run to the horse's head, calming the frightened animal. Another was reaching up for her.

'It's all right, miss, I've got you!' Strong hands were around her, trying to lift her down.

'Wait, wait—my hand!'

The muscles of her right arm had seized up and would not obey her brain. With a great effort she managed to uncurl her fingers from the back rail and ease her arm free. She felt herself being lifted bodily from the carriage.

'Adele,' she panted. 'Where is Mrs Ainslowe?'

'Let's be sure you's taken no hurt first, miss,' her rescuer replied in a soft country drawl. 'Can 'ee stand on yer own? Good. Now then, let's look to yer friend.'

'Adele!'

Carlotta staggered a few steps and fell on her knees beside the still form stretched out on the grass verge. Adele had lost her bonnet and was lying on her back with one hand thrown above her head. To Carlotta's terrified gaze she looked extremely pale.

'She's stunned, miss. Took a nasty tumble, I'd say.' The man scratched his head. 'We needs to get 'er to a doctor. Are you from the Court?'

'Yes, yes, we are,' said Carlotta, taking off her spencer to make a pillow for Adele's head.

'Well, I'll run down and fetch some help. T'ain't far if I goes down through the trees. Abel will stay with 'ee.'

'Aye.' The man holding the horse's head nodded slowly. 'An' I'll try to get the poor 'oss out of this tangle.'

Carlotta turned a grateful gaze upon her rescuer. 'Yes, please, fetch help as quickly as you can!'

'Don't you worry, miss, I'll be back in two shakes of a lamb's tail.'

Carlotta watched him set off at a lumbering run down the hill and he was soon lost to sight amongst the trees. The man he had called Abel was talking soothingly to the horse, at the same time quietly grappling with the buckles and straps of the harness. Carlotta struggled to her feet and fetched the rug from the gig. It had fallen to the ground when they had crashed and was lying abandoned on the track. It was only a few steps, but Carlotta felt very unsteady and she was glad to sink down again beside Adele once she had covered her with the rug. Adele stirred.

'Carlotta?'

'Hush, now. Pray be still.' Carlotta put her hand on Adele's shoulder to prevent her from rising. 'We have sent for help.'

'What happened?'

'You lost a wheel, ma'am,' called Abel.

Only then did Carlotta notice that one of the gig's wheels was lying some distance away.

'Oh, good,' murmured Adele. 'James cannot blame me for overturning us.'

'Miss'll be relieved to hear you talkin', ma'am,' continued the shepherd. 'She was afraid you was a goner.'

Adele lifted one hand and Carlotta grasped it.

'No,' said Adele with a weak smile. 'I'm not gone yet.'

Even as Carlotta squeezed her fingers, Adele's eyes closed again as she sank into unconsciousness.

Carlotta had no idea how long she sat beside her friend at the roadside. She was aware that Abel had managed to move the horse from the shafts of the carriage. Once the animal was securely tethered, the man made no attempt to approach, but remained at a respectful distance, chewing on a straw. She was glad of the summer sunshine, but the hillside was quite exposed and without her spencer the fresh breeze felt chill on her bare arms. She was aware of how quiet it was; only the whisper of the wind in the distant trees and the exuberant trill of a skylark disturbed the stillness. Then she heard the faint but unmistakable sounds of a carriage approaching at speed and a few minutes later the silence was replaced by a bewildering amount of noise and bustle. Two carriages hurtled up the hill and came to a stand, the horses stamping and blowing. James Ainslowe ran to his wife, barking commands. Carlotta tried to rise, but her trembling limbs would not work. She staggered and fell against a comfortingly solid body. She was lifted off the ground by a pair of strong arms. Raising her eyes, she found herself looking up into Luke's anxious face. He smiled down at her.

'It's all right, you are safe, *cara*.'

She snuggled her cheek against his shoulder. 'I am now,' she sighed.

Carlotta was aware of an intense disappointment when she came to her senses and found herself lying on her own bed rather than in Luke's arms. Lady Broxted hovered about her and tried to insist that she should rest until the morning, but Carlotta would have none of it. Her right arm ached quite dreadfully from being wrenched when she had clung on to the overturning gig, but she had sustained no other injury and was determined to go down to dinner. This could be the last opportunity for her to speak to Luke before Mr Woollatt's return. Surely it could not be thought improper for her to thank him for his kindness?

As she entered the drawing room, Mrs Price immediately sprang to her feet.

'Ah, dear Miss Rivington! Is this wise—should you be out of your bed?'

'Why yes, I am very well now, I assure you. I was a little shaken, but nothing serious—nothing to compare with Mrs Ainslowe. I believe she is still laid up in her room.'

Mr Price sighed and shook his head. 'Indeed she is. When Ainslowe carried her into the house she was as white as her lace, and the poor man looked exceedingly grim. As he is not here, I can only suppose that he is still with his wife—what do you say, Darvell, am I right?'

'I believe my brother intends to join us for dinner and is even now in his room, dressing.'

Carlotta observed the anxiety in Luke's face. She wanted to go to him, but Julia was urging her to sit down beside her.

'You must have been very frightened, Miss Rivington.'

'There was no time for fear, the gig collapsed so suddenly.'

'We were on the far side of the lake when we heard the news,' said Mrs Price. 'You can imagine our surprise when Lord Darvell's groom came running up to tell us what had occurred.'

'Aye,' declared Mr Price. 'By all accounts, Sir Gilbert's man was ready to dash off immediately to the rescue, but Darvell's groom insisted on fetching his master and Mr Ainslowe.'

'And a good idea it was,' nodded Mr Price. 'The carriages were ready and waiting by the time we arrived back at the house, so there was little time lost and the four of us could set off to find you.'

Carlotta frowned, trying to hold a fleeting memory. 'Were there four of you? I remember only Mr Ainslowe, and Lord Darvell…'

'Bless you, my dear, how could you be expected to know what was going on?' said Mr Price. 'Lord Fairbridge and I came along to render what assistance we could. And I dare say Sir Gilbert would have joined us, too, if he had been there.'

'I had decided to take a ramble in the woods,' explained Sir Gilbert, coming forward. 'I was never more shocked than when I returned and Mrs Price told me of the accident—' He broke off as James came in. 'Ah, Ainslowe—we were just talking about the dreadful events this morning. How is Mrs Ainslowe?'

'Sleeping.' James looked tired and strained, but he came towards Carlotta and took her hand. 'I am glad to see you are up and about, Miss Rivington. Can I assume you were not hurt in the crash?'

'I bruised my arm a little, nothing more. I trust Mrs Ainslowe has suffered no *lasting* injury?'

She raised her eyes to his face as she spoke and he seemed to understand her, for he gave a tight little smile and returned the slight pressure of her fingers.

'The doctor is hopeful, but it is too soon to tell.'

The meal dragged on. Carlotta had found herself sitting at some distance from Lord Darvell and it was not until the gentlemen came into the drawing room after dinner that she found the opportunity of speaking to him. Mrs Price had persuaded Julia and Lord Fairbridge to sing a duet; while the little group arranged themselves around the pianoforte, Carlotta moved across the room to stand beside Luke. She dared not look up at him and could only hope her voice would tremble less than her hands, which were clasped tightly together.

'I have not been able to thank you for your assistance this morning, my lord.'

'It was my pleasure, Miss Rivington.'

The cool note in his voice brought her head up and she saw the reason for it. Mr Price was standing very close to them.

He nodded at Luke, saying cheerfully, 'I beg your pardon, my lord, if I could just reach past you and take these candles to the pianoforte—my wife needs more light to read the music…'

Luke waited until he had moved away. 'I have never been more afraid,' he murmured. 'The shepherd said one of the ladies was unconscious, but I had no idea which of you was hurt until I came upon you.'

Carlotta put one hand up to her throat. His nearness unsettled her; she found it difficult to breath and her heart was beating such a tattoo that she was sure he must hear it. They were standing in shadow now, but even so Carlotta could see the glow of desire in his eyes, feel the longing emanating from him. It was like a magnet, a force beyond her control, pulling her in. She edged closer and put out her hand. His fingers closed over hers and she trembled. Her whole body tingled, her skin felt very tender, aware of the slightest touch. They were only inches apart; she need only take one little step and she could rest against him, put her cheek on his chest and listen to his heart.

Abruptly he released her hand and stepped away. 'You must not tempt me, *cara*,' he muttered. 'If you stand too close, I cannot think properly. When I carried you to the carriage this morning, you do not know how much I wanted to keep you with me for ever. I wanted to whip up the horses and drive off with you, to take you far away from here, from everything.'

He gave a ragged sigh and walked away. Carlotta watched him through curtain of hot tears.

'How I wish you had,' she whispered sadly.

A cold, grey dawn reminded Carlotta that the summer was coming to an end. She gazed out of her window at the blanket of low cloud shutting out the morning sun. The dull scene reflected her depression. Today she must persuade her aunt to take her away from Malberry, away from everything that could remind her of Luke. With a sigh she made her way downstairs and was about to cross the hall to the breakfast room when she saw Luke coming in through a side door. She dragged up a smile. 'You are up and about early, my lord.'

'Yes. I have been in the stables, looking at the gig.'

Something in his tone caught her attention. She stared at him, frowning slightly. He hesitated, then drew her away from the breakfast room. After a quick glance at the footmen standing motionless around the hall, he escorted her to his brother's study and carefully shut the door upon them.

'When I looked at the carriage yesterday, on the hill, I was surprised that the wheel had come away so cleanly. James commissioned that gig for Adele only months ago. It is of the very latest design—you will know by now that my brother likes to have everything of the best. The gig was brought back to the stables and I have been to check: the wheel is fixed with a pin and two nuts. If Perkins was in a rush, I can imagine that he might forget to put in the pin, or to secure one of the nuts, but he would never miss all three.' He paused. 'James's coachman—Perkins—insists he went over the gig thoroughly the previous day because Adele had warned him she might want to go out at a moment's notice. Now we know Perkins left the Jones boy to fetch the gig yesterday and the lad did not remove the axle caps to check the wheel nuts and pins were in place. After all, why should he, knowing his master had already done so?'

'What—what are you saying, Luke?'

'The grass where you took your tumble is kept very

short by the sheep that graze it. The men who brought the gig back found the wheel nuts, but not the pin. I think someone removed it and loosened the nuts before replacing the axle cap. It was only a matter of time before the wheel would work itself free.'

Carlotta felt the blood draining to her feet. 'You—you think it was deliberate? Someone was trying to harm Adele?'

'No, Carlotta,' said Luke slowly. 'I think someone was trying to harm *you*.'

'Oh, heavens.' Carlotta sank down on to a chair. 'You think, then, that this is connected to the attacks upon my father?'

'I do—it is too great a coincidence.'

'But *why*? What have we done?'

He shook his head. 'That I do not know, but it would appear to be the work of someone within the Court. The doors to the stable yard are locked at night; no one from outside could gain entry. It could be the same person you saw returning to the house the other morning.'

'What should I do?' Instinctively she reached out her hands.

Luke took them in a comforting grasp. 'I am not sure. I must talk to James. I wish we were not obliged to go shooting, but if we call it off it might make your attacker suspicious; he may go to ground, and I do not want that. I want to find him.' He dropped to his knees in front of her. 'Promise me you will not leave the house today. I will tell Billy to remain here. If you need anything you may send for him, but you are to stay in the house, and with your aunt, wherever possible. Do you understand?'

Carlotta gazed at him. Her heart flipped over at the anxiety she saw in his eyes. Knowing he cared so much was a tiny crumb of comfort she would squirrel away for the future. For the time when she would not see him.

He spoke again. 'Promise me, *cara*. You must stay indoors and in company.'

'I promise.'

'Good.' He rose, pulling her to her feet and into his arms. He made no attempt to kiss her, but held her tightly for a moment. She felt his mouth on her hair.

'I will not let anything happen to you, sweetheart, but we must find out who is behind this. I cannot bear the thought of sending you away from Malberry with this riddle unsolved, with the threat still hanging over you.' He drew a deep breath and resolutely put her away from him. 'You must go now. Tell no one. I will talk to James and we will decide what to do.'

'Oh, but I need to know—'

He put a finger to her lips, a rueful smile lighting his eyes. 'Hush, little termagant. We will do nothing without consulting you, never fear.'

The low cloud persisted all day, but it did not rain, and the ladies amused themselves indoors with their books, their painting and their embroidery. Carlotta found it difficult to settle to anything and in desperation she asked if she might be allowed to sit with Mrs Ainslowe for a while. The suggestion was put to Adele's dresser, who graciously agreed to let Carlotta visit her mistress while she took a short rest in the afternoon. Carlotta duly presented herself at the door of the bedchamber and entered to find Adele awake, and smiling a welcome.

'Carlotta, my dear. So my gorgon has permitted you to come and sit with me, has she? You are honoured, for she has refused admittance to everyone else.'

A slight smile softened the dresser's severe countenance. 'Now, ma'am, you know the doctor said you was to have complete rest. And you, miss—' she turned her fierce eyes to Carlotta '—you are not to be overtaxing the mistress.'

'No, no, of course she will not,' said Adele. 'She will sit here and tell me all that is going on downstairs; I shall not move a finger.' She watched as her handmaiden left the room, and then beckoned Carlotta to come closer. 'Pull up that chair beside the bed, Carlotta, where I can see you. I have been so quiet today without James, but I told him he had to leave me, for his guests could not go shooting without their host, now could they?'

'I think he would have preferred to stay here with you, ma'am.'

'Perhaps, but there is nothing he can do for me. The doctor says I shall be well again presently, but for now I am to lie very still. Not an easy thing for me, my dear. You know how much I love to be out and about. But he says it is necessary, if I am to save the baby.' Adele paused, placing her hands on her stomach. With a sigh and a smile she looked up. 'So now, my love, tell me all that is going on downstairs. Has Viscount Fairbridge proposed to little Julia yet? Has Mr Woollatt returned?'

'No, and no, ma'am, but both events are imminent.'

They talked for some time and when the conversation began to flag, Adele waved towards the table at the side of the bed.

'I have Mrs Radcliffe's story here that I would dearly like to finish, but reading makes my head ache so. Would you read to me, Carlotta? Just for a little while.'

Carlotta readily agreed and they spent a pleasant hour

immersed in *The Mysteries of Udolpho*. They had just started on the second volume when Adele's formidable maidservant returned and suggested her mistress should now rest. Carlotta rose immediately, giving Adele no opportunity to argue. With a promise to return again tomorrow, if Adele should still be in her bed, Carlotta went off to take the first, finished, volume of Mrs Radcliffe's tale back to the library.

The house was very quiet and Carlotta saw no one except the statue-like footmen in the hall as she made her way to the library. It was Mr Ainslowe's orders that all rooms should be kept in readiness for his guests, and candles were already burning, casting a warm glow over the library. It was a stark contrast to the gloomy dusk that was settling outside the long windows. Carlotta paused at the door. She had spent very little time in the library and was unfamiliar with the book-lined shelves. She walked slowly around the room, reading the titles engraved on the spines. Most were learned tomes, but at the far end of the room she found what she was looking for, volumes of popular novels tumbled together on a shelf. She smiled, recognising Adele's disregard for order. She slotted the book back in amongst its fellows and turned to make her way back to the door.

As she crossed the room, the low sun burst forth from the clouds and for a brief moment it shone in through the long windows and illuminated the large canvas that dominated the far wall. It was the painting James had won from Sir Gilbert. Carlotta remembered Papa talking often of the artist, Tiepolo. He had died before Papa was even born, but she thought her father would like to know that she had seen it. As quickly as it had come, the sun disappeared again, plunging the room into comparative darkness. Carlotta picked up a branched candlestick and moved towards the wall to study the picture. It was a classical scene: Maecenas at the feet of the Roman Emperor. Carlotta held her candles aloft, staring at the painting. She frowned. There was something very familiar about the style, the vivid colours and flowing brushwork. Stepping closer, she peered at the richly patterned cloak that tumbled from Maecenas' shoulders and filled the centre foreground of the picture. She gasped. There, nestling amongst the patterned folds, was a tiny, delicate little snail.

Carlotta stepped back, her heart and mind racing. Her overriding thought was that she must tell Luke, and quickly. She ran back to the hall and ordered one of the footmen to fetch Lord Darvell's groom. She was in the morning room finishing off her brief note when Billy knocked on the door. She ran to him, folding the paper as she went.

'You must take this to your master at once—will you be able to find him? They may still be shooting.'

The groom glanced out of the window at the heavy clouds. 'The light is fading now, miss. I reckon they might have gone back to the bathhouse by now.'

'Very well. You must hurry, but do not attract attention to yourself.'

'Best if I run down, then,' he replied, putting the note in his pocket. 'But my lord did say I was to stay here and look out for you, miss.'

'I know, but this is very important—' She broke off, glancing out of the open door. 'What was that? Is there someone out there?'

Billy stepped out into the hall and looked around. 'There's no one there, miss, only the lackeys on the far side.'

'I should have told you to come in and close the door,' Carlotta scolded herself.

'Well, no harm done, miss,' Billy reassured her. 'All the guests have gone to their rooms to prepare for their dinner, and the servants know better than to dawdle here.'

'You are right; I am stupidly nervous tonight. Very well, you must be off now.'

'But the master said—'

She shook her head at him. 'I promise I shall go to my room directly, and remain at my aunt's side for the rest of the evening. I cannot possibly come to any harm. And it is important Lord Darvell receives my message as soon as possible.' She hesitated, biting her lip. 'He might be in danger.'

Billy nodded. 'Very well, miss, I'll go now, but you promise me that you will stay with Lady Broxted.'

'Yes, yes. Now *go*!'

The dinner hour dragged by. Carlotta had no appetite for the stuffed fish or the lamb's feet prepared so carefully by Mr Ainslowe's expensive French chef, although she did take a little veal ragout. Her nerves were at full stretch: she strained her ears for any sound of an arrival and her eyes flew to the door each time it opened, which happened frequently as the servants brought in each fresh dish. Carlotta tried to calculate how long it would take Billy to find his master. Surely once Luke had read her message he would understand and be on his guard. She was struggling to give her attention to her neighbour, who was advising her to try the blackberry sauce with the apple pie, when she felt something brush her arm. Her heart leapt to her throat as she looked down to see a small, folded paper in her lap. Trembling, she dropped her napkin over the note and looked around. Who could have put the note there? Several footmen were behind her, all intent on their duties. It must have been one of them, she reasoned. Perhaps Luke had slipped unnoticed into the house and bribed one of them to pass the note to her.

The agony of sitting with the note unopened was almost unbearable, but she dare not risk detection. At last she saw the signal to withdraw, and as the ladies filed out of the dining room she excused herself and found a quiet corner where she could scan the paper unobserved. She recognised her own writing immediately: it was the note she had given Billy, but now on the bottom was a short scrawl.

Come to the bathhouse at eleven o'clock. I will wait for you. Tell no one, and avoid the main path. You must not be seen. D.

With trembling hands Carlotta pushed the note into her reticule. Her heart pounded wildly. Luke had sent for her! He had promised nothing would be decided without consulting her—*that* must be the reason for a secret meeting. Eleven o'clock—it would be very dark, but she dare not take a lantern. She would have to trust to the moon to light her way to the bathhouse. A shiver tingled down her spine at the thought of it, then she straightened her shoulders. Luke needed her—she would not let him down.

Carlotta pulled her cloak around her shoulders. Outside the stable clock was chiming the half hour. Ten thirty. She turned to the maid appointed to wait on her.

'Remember, Mary, if anyone asks for me, you must tell them I am asleep and not to be disturbed.' She slipped a silver sixpence into the girl's hand. 'Do this for me and you shall have another upon my return.'

As she opened her bedroom door she could hear the faint murmur of voices from the drawing room, where the ladies were waiting for the gentlemen to join them for supper. No one had questioned her decision to retire early, pleading a headache, but they would want to know what she was doing now, so late and out of her room. Thankfully she met no one on the back stairs and was soon standing in the darkness outside the side door.

A chill breeze had sprung up and was dispersing the cloud, allowing a pale moon to peep through. Carlotta ran swiftly through the walled garden and out into the park where she hurried to gain the cover of the trees and began the long walk down to the bathhouse. The knowledge that Luke was waiting for her spurred her on and helped her to overcome any fear of walking through the park alone. It was difficult to see the old worn path and Carlotta was forced to go carefully to avoid tripping up. She put out her hand to guide her and the diamond in Mr Woollatt's ring flashed. Quickly she pulled back her hand and buried it in the folds of her cloak. She had not gone far when she heard voices, and the scuffing of boots on the main track. In the fitful moonlight she could see little more than black shapes, but she knew it was the shooting party, on its way to the house. She shrank back into the shadow of the trees as Mr Price's laugh boomed out across the night. She waited until they had passed, then, when there was no chance that they would see her, she pressed on, anxious to reach Luke.

The square shape of the bathhouse gleamed palely in the moonlight, the columns at the entrance were silver-grey against the black shadow of the porch. She thought she could make out a dim glow from the windows, but it could have been the reflected moonlight. As soon as she reached the clearing she ran across the short grass and up the steps. The door opened easily to her touch. She stepped inside.

The bathhouse felt warm after the chill of the autumn night air. Candles in two of the wall brackets were burning, giving a soft glow to the stonework. As she entered the sudden draught made the flames flicker wildly and Carlotta stopped as the figures on the walls seemed to move. Her nerves skittered in panic even as she told herself not to be foolish.

'Luke?' She whispered his name softly and the word echoed around the room. 'Luke?'

The door closed behind her. She swung around and found herself face to face with Sir Gilbert Mattingwood.

Chapter Fifteen

As the gentlemen walked back across the park Luke wanted to stride on ahead. He had enjoyed the day, but there had always been an underlying anxiety for Carlotta. He told himself she was perfectly safe in the house with so many people around her, and Billy would be keeping watch, too, but he was eager to get back, to see her for himself. It was irksome in the extreme to have to dawdle at this slow pace.

'Not a bad day's work,' said James. 'Of course, next month we shall be able to go after pheasant, but I hope you agree we had good sport today.'

'Aye, but I wish we had not sent the cart on ahead,' grumbled Mr Price. 'I had not realised it was such a walk, and uphill, too.'

Some of the gentlemen laughed at that.

'What, sir' Lord Fairbridge grinned 'would you want to sit in the cart with the duck, partridge and snipe?'

'Better that than walk another yard in these boots,' grumbled Mr Price. 'New, you see. Decided to try that new bootmaker in Davies Street. He's a damned charlatan, for they pinch my toes like the devil! The sooner I can take off the damned things the better.'

'Well, we are nearly there now,' said James. He touched Luke's arm. 'I like to thank the servants at the end of each day's shooting,' he murmured. 'I order a bowl of punch to be prepared for them all, but as it is—Adele—'

'I know, you are anxious to see your wife as soon as may be,' replied Luke. 'Leave it to me, brother. I will see the servants for you.'

When the party reached the house, Luke made his way directly to the servants' hall to pass on his brother's thanks. He was a little surprised that Billy was not there. He looked into the kitchen as he passed on the way out to the stable block; that too was empty save for the cook and the kitchen maid carrying a large kettle to the fire. Outside the stable yard was in darkness with only a low light showing in the carriage house. Luke crossed quickly and found James's coachman there with the stable boy affectionately known as Little Jones.

'Oh, it's you, my lord.' Perkins lifted one finger to his head in brief salute. 'We was just finishin' up here, hanging up the cleaned tack ready for another day.'

'Have you seen my groom?'

'No, my lord.'

'I seen 'im,' piped up the stable boy. 'I was fetchin' our dinner from the kitchen and 'ee was there.'

'Are you sure?'

The lad nodded. 'One of the footmen came in and said Miss Rivington was wanting 'im.' The boy cast an anxious look at the coachman, who clapped a fatherly hand on his shoulder.

'Little Jones is pretty reliable, my lord'

Luke frowned. 'Very well—I will enquire in the house.' He turned to leave but at the door he stopped. 'Oh, The master has ordered rum punch to be served to you all. It is being prepared now, in the kitchen.'

'If it's all the same to you, my lord, I won't, not after last time.' Perkins shifted uncomfortably. 'The wheel on the mistress's gig... Master has said he will turn me off if I can't do my duty. I wouldn't blame 'im, neither.' He added fiercely, 'It's never happened to me before in all my years in service. That ashamed of meself, I am...'

'Ah. I see.' Luke turned to go.

'You said it might've been a bad bottle o' rum,' said Little Jones, helpfully. ''Acos Mr Reed told you 'ee had a bad 'ead, too.'

Luke swung round. 'What was that?' His gaze swept over Perkins, whose countenance showed a mixture of anger and embarrassment. 'Well?'

'I promised 'im I'd say nothing, me lord, Reed's that afeard of his master—'

'Are you saying you were drinking with Reed the night before Mrs Ainslowe's accident? You had best tell me,' he added as Perkins hesitated.

'Reed and me, we'd been chatting, you see. He seemed a friendly sort, not high and mighty like some o' your household staff, who holds up their noses at those of us as works outside.

'Well, we found we was both partial to a game o' cards now and then, so t'other night Mr Reed brings down a pack o' cards and a bottle o' rum after dinner, and we had a few games. Only...' Perkins shrugged, his ruddy face turning a deeper shade of red. 'Well, I misremember what 'appened, me lord. Put to bed in me boots, I was, and woke up with such a fearful 'eadache there was no getting up, so when the mistress ordered the gig, Little Jones here had to get it ready.'

'An' I did me best, sir, 'onest I did,' added the boy, staring anxiously at Luke.

'Can't blame the lad for not taking off the axle hubs and checking the wheels was secure,' said Perkins. 'I told master that, when he came back from fetching the mistress. The blame is mine, though I'd swear I checked both wheels the day before.'

'And it was Reed who brought the rum?'

'Aye, me lord, but when we was both bad on it, he asked me not to tell anyone that he'd been drinkin' with me, 'cos his master would turn him off. Right scared he was.' Perkins looked anxiously at Luke. 'I wouldn't want to get 'im into trouble, me lord…'

'No…' said Luke slowly. 'No, of course not.'

Luke ran back into the house and met his brother's stately butler in the servants' passage. 'Where is Sir Gilbert's man?' he asked him tersely.

'I believe he is gone back upstairs, my lord. He has just brought his master's boots downstairs for cleaning.'

'And Miss Rivington?'

'She retired early, my lord.'

Luke went on up to the hall, where he saw his brother coming down the stairs. James smiled.

'I have just left Adele. She is much better today and is even talking of coming downstairs tomorrow… Luke? Is something wrong?'

'Come into the study and we will talk.' He followed

James into the room and closed the door carefully behind him. 'I have found our villain.'

'The devil you have! Who is it?'

'Mattingwood's man, Reed. Perkins says they were drinking together the night before the gig crashed. I believe he drugged Perkins by slipping something into the bottle of rum he brought with him, then he tampered with the wheel. Perkins was the only person who might possibly go over the gig again before sending it out, and he was too sick to get out of bed.'

'That would explain the crash,' said James, 'but there is nothing to bear out your suspicion that the target was Miss Rivington.'

Luke shrugged. 'Two attacks on Durini, then the wheel comes off the carriage bearing his daughter—that is too much of a coincidence to my mind.'

'But what in heaven's name does the man have against the family?'

'Perhaps it is not just Reed, perhaps it is his master,' said Luke slowly.

'Gil?' James gave a little snort of laughter. 'How could he possibly be involved with an artist and his family? Why, he told me he has very little interest in art—' He broke off and fixed a sudden, intense look at Luke. 'The Tiepolo?'

Luke made for the door. 'Let's go and see.'

'But, Luke, can you tell if it is real?' said James they hurried to the library. 'Have you acquired some special knowledge of art in the past few years?'

'Not exactly, but there is one thing I know to look out for.' Luke strode into the library, picked up a branch of candles and carried it across the room. Holding the candles close to the painting, he began to study it closely.

'What are we looking for?'

'Something… Ah. There it is.' He pointed 'Look there, on the cloak.'

James peered closer. 'It's some kind of snail…'

'Yes. A *lumaca*. It's Durini's mark. I remember Carlotta telling me that he used to copy paintings for visitors doing the Grand Tour. She was adamant that they were not forgeries, because he signed each one.'

James stared. 'Do you mean Mattingwood gave me a worthless painting?'

Despite his anxiety, Luke smiled. 'Not worthless, James—Durini is a fine artist.'

'But Mattingwood tricked me over a debt of honour.' James gave a low whistle. 'He would be ruined if this got out.'

'That is why he has tried to stop Durini or his daughter seeing this painting.'

James was already heading for the door. 'Very well,' he said grimly. 'Let us find him!'

As they crossed to the stairs a figure emerged from the servants' door. 'My lord!'

Luke swung round. Billy was coming towards him. His clothes were dishevelled and he was gingerly feeling the back of his head with one hand.

'What the devil has happened to you?'

'Attacked, my lord. I was on my way to the bathhouse when someone clobbered me from behind. Pushed me down a culvert, too—must have thought I would be drowned, the drain being quite full after all the recent rains, but I came round to find myself caught by my belt on a tree root.'

'I told you to stay here and look after Miss Rivington.'

'That you did, my lord, and I was doing so, but Miss Rivington insisted I bring a note to you, urgent like.' He reached into his pocket, a look of consternation growing on his bruised face. 'Funny, I know I put it in here…'

'When did she give you the note?' asked Luke, a chilling suspicion growing within him.

'Just before dinner, sir. I was to find you and give you the note as soon as I could.'

'Damnation!' Luke raced up the stairs, James and Billy following. 'Tell me which is Carlotta's room,' he demanded as James caught up with him.

'Is she not in the drawing room with the ladies?'

'No, Wicks told me she retired early. Will you show me her room?'

James looked at him for a long moment, then silently led the way towards a door at the far end of the west wing. Luke knocked softly. After a few moments Carlotta's maid peeped around the door.

'I must speak to Miss Rivington.'

Perhaps it was Luke's brusque tone that caused the maid to look so frightened, but it roused his worst fears.

'She—she is asleep, my lord. I—'

Ignoring her feeble protests, he walked into the room. A few candles glowed about the room, but in the dim light it was clear that the bed had not been slept in. He turned back to the maid. 'Where is she?'

'I—I…'

'Come, girl, you must tell us what you know,' said James, following Luke into the room.

The maid shook her head, twisting her apron nervously in her hands. 'She didn't say, sir, only that she was going out and I was to tell anyone who asked that she was asleep.'

Luke stared at his brother, who nodded.

'We must talk to Reed.'

Seconds later Luke was banging on another bedroom door. Reed's ferret-like face appeared.

'Sir Gilbert is sleeping, my lord. I must ask you to—'

He got no further. Luke pushed past him, walked up to the bed and threw back the hangings. The bed was empty. He heard a scuffle behind him and found James and Billy struggling with the valet. They forced Reed onto a chair.

'The fellow tried to make a dash for it,' grunted James, holding him down.

'Because he knows you will want to thrash him for trying to kill your wife,' retorted Luke.

'No, no, it wasn't me,' squeaked Reed, alarmed by the ugly look on James's face.

'Oh, I think we can safely say it was you,' said Luke, dragging his arms roughly around the back of the chair.

'No, no, it was not my idea—I was o-ordered to do it.'

'Then you'd better tell me everything, if you want to save some of your hide,' growled James menacingly.

The valet licked his lips, looking fearfully at the three men standing over him.

'It—it was my master. He—he heard that Mrs Ainslowe had ordered the gig for the morning and he t-told me what he wanted me to do.'

'And the attack on Signor Durini in Malberry village?' asked Luke.

The valet shook his head. 'No, I swear, sir, that was not me—Sir Gilbert came on ahead of me.'

'What about the fire at the Durinis' cottage?' barked James.

Reed hesitated, as if deciding on what to say, and James took a step towards him.

'You came back through the walled garden just before dawn,' said Luke. 'Do not deny it—you were seen.'

'All right, it *was* me. But I was acting on orders. S-Sir Gilbert said he wanted Durini scared off. He didn't want him to come to the house again.'

'Because the Tiepolo is a copy,' growled James.

The valet nodded miserably. 'The master purchased it from the *signor* in Rome several years ago.'

'And he found out that Miss Rivington is Durini's daughter,' Luke persisted. 'Well, man, how did he do that?'

James put his hand to his head. 'It was that day on the stairs,' he muttered. 'When I gave Carlotta the note from her father—Reed was there. You overheard us.'

Reed swallowed hard. 'Aye. Sir Gilbert pays me well for any information I can bring him.'

'So where is Mattingwood now?' Luke demanded.

'He—he's still at the bathhouse.' Reed's ferret-like eyes darted to Luke's face. 'Waiting for Miss Rivington. She thinks she is going there to meet you.'

The chill that had been growing in Luke seemed to sharpen into ice.

'Billy,' he said quietly, 'go to the stables and saddle a horse for me, quick as you can.'

'Make that two,' called James as Billy ran out of the room.

Luke pulled loose the cord from the bed-curtains and began to tie Reed's hands to the chair back.

'I'll call a couple of my people to watch him until we return,' said James, going to the door.

'Thank you. And, James—fetch your pistols.'

Chapter Sixteen

'I—I was not expecting to see you here, Sir Gilbert.' Carlotta tried to sound innocent and bewildered. Could she convince him she was involved in a romantic intrigue? She thought not, since he showed no surprise at her presence. She began to talk rapidly. 'I thought everyone would be gone by now. Were you delayed?' She glanced at his stockings and buckled shoes. 'L-looking for your boots, perhaps? One can hardly walk back through the park without them, can one?'

'Reed has taken my boots back to Malberry Court. By now they will be lined up with all the others, waiting to be cleaned.' His growing smile made her shiver. 'Everyone will assume I am in my bed.'

'R-really?' She began to back away. 'I—um—I told my maid I was coming here to collect something. She will be anxious if I am not back soon—'

He laughed at her.

'You are the most delightful little liar, Miss Rivington. We both know you did no such thing. The note said "tell no one." You will have followed the instructions to the letter.'

Carlotta stared at him. 'How do you know what was in the note?'

'Because Reed took the original off Darvell's groom and brought it to me. *I* wrote the reply.'

Her heart dropped. There had been a faint, unacknowledged hope that Luke might rescue her, but now that hope died. She swallowed painfully. 'What is it you want with me?'

'Not your virtue, if that thought is making you clutch your cloak around you so tightly. Unfortunately, you know my secret.'

'Secret?'

'Come, come, Miss Rivington—or should I call you Miss Durini? Let us pretend no longer. You of all people should know that the Tiepolo is a copy.'

'Yes…but it is not so very bad; I dare say if you explained everything—'

'Explain it? I have *cheated*, my dear—cheated on a debt of honour. The *ton* would have no mercy, I should be shunned, no member of society would acknowledge me, and how long do you imagine it would be before my creditors started hounding me? I would be ruined.'

'But no one else need know of it,' she said quickly, 'I will say nothing—'

'I am afraid, my dear, I cannot take that chance. You must be disposed of.'

'You—you would not dare,' she whispered, still moving away from him.

'Oh, I would.'

'But it will do you no good. Sooner or later someone else will notice, too.'

'Before that happens I hope to have the picture back in

my possession. I am sure I can persuade Ainslowe to sell it back to me.'

Carlotta shook her head. 'I doubt it; Mrs Ainslowe has already told you she has grown to like it.'

'That is, of course, a minor problem, but she is not yet recovered. I think if Mrs Ainslowe were to take a turn for the worse, her husband might be far too overset to care about a mere painting—in fact, he might be pleased to be rid of it, if it reminds him of his wife. Yes, that might work out very well. At the time I thought it a pity that she should be in the gig with you, but now I see it could be an advantage.'

'So the crash was your doing?'

'Yes. I was waiting in the woods, ready to administer the final blow, should either of you survive, but those damn fool shepherds were up on the hill and decided to come so gallantly to your rescue. But there is no one here this time to rescue you.'

Carlotta's lip curled. 'You are insane if you think you will get away with it.'

'But I *am* getting away with it. The attack on Durini has been blamed on gypsies, and as for the gig—Ainslowe's coachman was too drunk to do his job. If he were my man, I would have turned him off immediately for such gross ineptitude.'

An icy chill spread through Carlotta as she listened to Sir Gilbert. He was rambling on, and she began to think he was truly deranged. She forced herself to consider her situation. Mattingwood stood before the entrance, blocking her escape. She guessed there would be a smaller, servants' door beyond the warm room. If she could only reach the back room, then perhaps she could get out into the park. She turned on her heel and ran, heading for the inner door.

She felt the tug as Mattingwood caught at her swirling cloak, but the ties were loosened and it slipped easily from her shoulders. The door was only feet away, if she could get through and slam it shut—it would give her precious seconds to find a way out.

'Got you!' A strong hand gripped her shoulder, yanking her backwards.

'Let me go! Help! Help me!'

'Scream all you like, there is no one to hear you.' He pinioned her arms at her sides and held her against his chest. As she stared up at him, she saw the look in his eyes change. 'Hmm, shame to kill you before I have sampled your charms.' He leered down at her. His hold tightened and his head came down towards her. She turned her face away, squirming as she felt his lips on her skin. She tried to struggle, but he was too strong for her, pulling her closer until she could feel his body pressing against hers. Revulsion and fear shuddered through her. She stopped struggling, gathering her strength for one final, desperate push.

'That's right,' his voice was muffled as he nuzzled her neck. 'Relax and enjoy it, my dear.'

His arms slid around her, binding her to him. She turned her head against his; the smell of the oil on his blond hair made her feel sick, but she ignored it. She reached round and sank her teeth into his ear. He yelled with pain.

Savage satisfaction raged through her and she fought desperately to break away. She freed one hand and clawed at his cheek, her nails drawing blood before he pinioned her arms again and dragged her with him into the plunge pool.

The shock of the cold water paralysed Carlotta, but it took only a moment to realise that Sir Gilbert's vice-like grip on her had slackened. She kicked out and felt the stone steps beneath her feet. She struggled towards them, but before she could crawl out of the pool he had grabbed her again, pulling her back into the deeper water. She scrabbled wildly, her legs entangled by the clinging skirts of her gown. Sir Gilbert's weight was on her shoulders, pushing her down. She ducked away from him and came up to the surface, gasping. Then he lunged at her once more and forced her head under the water again.

Carlotta's lungs were bursting, burning with the effort to hold her breath. She knew it must end soon. The blood was pounding in her ears. She began to exhale, allowing the air to slip from her body. She could see the bubbles rising past her face. Soon she would have to breathe in and the cold, deadly water would fill her up. She would drown. She tried to hold back, but it was impossible; the last of the air escaped her and the empty, burning void of her lungs screamed for her to take a breath. *Give in*, said the tiny voice in her head. *Give in—a moment's pain and it will be all over*. She knew she was weakening as the blood and water pounded in her ears. It was too much effort to fight any longer.

Then, miraculously, the weight above her was gone. Strong hands were lifting her, dragging her out of the water. She lay face down on the cold stone, coughing and gasping. When at last she dared to open her eyes, she saw she was lying in a pool of water that was expanding outwards as more dribbled from her clothes and hair.

'Just in time, thank God.' Luke's voice was shaking, but his hands were firm and comforting on her shoulders as he helped her to sit up. Raising her eyes, she saw Sir Gilbert on his knees with James standing over him, a pistol in one hand. James met her eyes and gave her a little smile.

'Thank heavens we did not have to jump into the pool to rescue you.'

She shifted around to look at Luke. 'How—how did you know?'

'Billy came to find me—'

Sir Gilbert raised his head. 'Impossible. He's dead.'

'No, he is very much alive,' retorted Luke, nodding towards the door where Billy stood, legs slightly apart, looking belligerent. 'Reed thought he had disposed of him, but my man is not so easy to kill.'

Carlotta reached up to touch Luke's hand. 'I wrote a note. I thought you had sent for me…' Her voice trailed off and she began to shiver.

Luke helped her to her feet. 'There will be time for talking later. Take Mattingwood back to the house and secure him, James. Billy will help you.'

'You are not coming?'

Luke swung Carlotta up into his arms. 'No. I must get her warm, and quickly. I do not care if that villain catches a deadly chill, but I'll not risk Carlotta. Tell her maid to pack up some dry clothes for her mistress and send them down in the carriage.'

James nodded. 'Very well, brother.' He reached out to grab the back of Sir Gilbert's collar. 'Come along. It's Newgate for you, my man—and a fate far worse than being shunned by society, I think.'

He dragged Sir Gilbert to his feet while Luke carried Carlotta through the doors to the inner room. It was very dark, only moonlight from the high windows and a faint glow from the dying fire illuminating the furniture, but Luke did not hesitate. He walked swiftly across the room and gently laid Carlotta down on one of the couches.

'First, we need some light, then we must get you out of those wet clothes.'

Dazed, Carlotta watched as he pushed a taper into the embers and proceeded to light the candles. Soon a golden glow illuminated the disordered room. It was still littered with the remains of the gentlemen's dinner party. Dishes, bottles and glasses covered the side tables. Luke moved to one of the chests and pulled out a large bathsheet and a brightly patterned dressing gown. 'Here, take these. I will make up the fire; we shall soon have you dry again—and me.' He grinned as he dragged off his frockcoat and threw it over a chair. 'Just carrying you in here has soaked through my coat.'

Carlotta struggled with the buttons of her spencer while he crouched before the hearth, feeding the glowing embers with kindling and small logs.

'That's better.'

She glanced at the flames leaping upwards in the hearth. She had managed to remove her spencer, but was still struggling to unlace her sodden boots. She was shaking so much that her fingers would not work; they felt clumsy and terribly weak. Luke came across to sit beside her.

'Here, let me do that.' Gently he lifted her foot onto his knee, deftly loosened the laces and tossed the boot on to the floor. 'I have had years of practice at removing a lady's clothing,' he said lightly, lifting her other foot. 'One learns it from an early age, if one aspires to be a rake.' The second boot followed its partner to the floor. He glanced up, a hint of a smile in his eyes, but she could not respond to it. Silently he pushed aside the wet skirts and gently moved his hand up to remove the silk stocking. She noticed how his fingers trembled as he tugged at her garter, but they did not linger. As soon as the ribbon came loose he quickly stripped off her pink stockings. 'Can you stand?' he asked her gently. 'We need to remove your gown.'

Obedient to the pressure of his hand on her arm, she rose. 'I am afraid I have ruined the couch,' she murmured, looking down at the damp mark where she had been sitting.

'It makes no odds, there are plenty more in here. Turn around for me.'

Soon gown, stays and chemise were all removed and Carlotta was wrapped in the heavy brocade dressing gown. It was much too big for her and crumpled in thick folds around her feet.

Luke removed the remaining pins from her hair and spread it over her shoulders. He paused, a smile tugging at one corner of his mouth. 'You look a veritable urchin, Miss Rivington.'

For the first time that evening Carlotta managed a little smile.

'You are still shivering.' Luke pushed her gently down onto the rug. 'Sit there, the heat will soon warm you.'

She looked up at him. 'You will not leave me?'

He hesitated, then dropped down beside her. 'I am here as long as you need me.' He put his hands on her shoulders and, twisting her away from him, began to comb his fingers through her hair, lifting and separating the tresses so that they splayed across her back. Carlotta sighed. The combined effects of the fire and Luke's gentle caresses began to relieve the tension in her muscles. She could even think about the events of the evening.

'So Sir Gilbert was responsible for all the horrid things that have happened?'

'Yes. He attacked your father and sent his man to set fire

to their house and to loosen the wheel on the gig. Reed confessed it to us when we went looking for you.'

She sighed. 'All because of a painting. And he was willing to—to kill rather than lose face?'

'Mattingwood lost what little fortune he had at the gaming tables and now exists on the goodwill of his fellows. To be pronounced a fraudster would ruin him.'

She began to shake again. 'D-despicable man.'

His hands rested on her shoulders. 'He is gone now, *cara*. You are safe.'

'I know it.' She dropped her cheek on his hand and rubbed it gently, closing her eyes. Luke's grip tightened. He was very close behind her, so close that when she leaned back she found herself resting against him, the ruffles of his shirt pressing on her hair. She felt rather than heard his ragged sigh.

'Carlotta.' His breath was warm on her cheek. 'Carlotta, I—what the devil is that noise?'

Carlotta, too, heard a commotion in the outer room— voices and swift, heavy footsteps, growing ever closer. The door flew open and she smothered a gasp. There in the doorway stood Daniel Woollatt.

Chapter Seventeen

'In heaven's name, what are you doing here?' demanded Luke, helping Carlotta to her feet.

Mr Woollatt pointed at Carlotta, a look of horror on his face. 'More to the point, my lord—why is Miss Rivington dressed in that—that—?'

'It is a gentleman's dressing gown,' explained Carlotta. 'My own clothes are too wet, you see.'

James slipped into the room, carrying a portmanteau. 'It is as I told you, Woollatt. Mattingwood tried to drown Miss Rivington.' He gave his brother an apologetic look. 'Woollatt arrived just as I got back, Luke. He insisted upon coming with me.'

Luke nodded and looked again at Mr Woollatt. 'I am sorry, then, that you had to return to such bad news.'

'I was never more shocked in my life,' said Mr Woollatt heavily. He was still staring at Carlotta. 'You came down here *alone*?'

Carlotta found herself blushing. 'It was very foolish of me, I know, but thankfully Mr Ainslowe and Lord Darvell arrived in time—'

'Ainslowe tells me you thought you were meeting Darvell here.'

'Yes, I had written a note, you see—'

'A note?' Even in the candlelight she could see the vein in Woollatt's temple was standing out. He was clearly very annoyed. 'What in heaven's name possessed you to do such a thing? You are an unmarried lady, you should not be writing notes to a gentleman. One, moreover, of Lord Darvell's reputation.'

Carlotta blinked. 'It was very urgent; I needed to tell him—'

'You should have gone to your aunt and explained the situation. And then to compound your folly by stealing out to keep an assignation—!'

Carlotta stared at him. A sharp retort arose to her lips, but she felt the pressure of Luke's hand on her shoulder.

He said coldly, 'Surely at this stage you should be expressing your relief that Miss Rivington is safe.'

'Well, I am thankful for that, of course, but such unbecoming behaviour—I am deeply shocked.' He shook his head, a look of distaste twisting his countenance. 'Not only that—Ainslowe was obliged to tell me of…your parentage.'

Carlotta's head went up at that. 'Indeed?' And just what is wrong with my *parentage*?'

'I do not think you need me to tell you,' retorted Mr Woollatt. 'A runaway match, and to an artist, no less! I must say, madam, I think you have been less than honest with me.'

Luke took a step forward. 'Miss Riv—Miss Durini's lineage may be a little unusual, but it is perfectly respectable. Lord Broxted would not be sponsoring her if he was in any doubt of it.'

'I am well aware of that!' replied Mr Woollatt testily. 'But there is something repellent about the way this matter has been handled. What my mother will say when I tell her—and it will have to be explained to her—I dread to think.'

Carlotta heard Luke's angry hiss, saw his hands form themselves into fists and she quickly touched his arm, giving him the tiniest shake of her head.

'You are quite right, Mr Woollatt,' she said quietly, stepping forward. 'It would have been much better if I had been honest with you from the outset. I have no doubt that your mother would be most distressed to learn the truth about my—my family. Indeed, I am sure she would find such a connection most abhorrent. It is not to be thought of. Perhaps it would be best if you told her that it had all been a misunderstanding, that there is no engagement.' She drew the diamond ring from her finger and held it out to him.

There was a long silence. Carlotta knew that Luke, James and Mr Woollatt were staring at her and it took all her willpower to remain still, her arm outstretched. At last, with a little nod, Mr Woollatt reached out and took the ring. It was only then that Carlotta realised she had been holding her breath. Now she exhaled as quietly as she could, hoping it would not sound too much like a sigh of relief.

'Perhaps we were a little hasty,' muttered Mr Woollatt. 'But all is not lost, nothing has been announced yet. We will take a little time to consider.' He pursed his lips and looked thoughtful. 'Perhaps next Season I shall bring my mother to town and introduce you to her. Naturally, she will find it hard to forgive you for crying off, but once you are acquainted, and if you behave with becoming modesty, I have no doubt she will warm to you in time.'

She forced a smile and was grateful to be spared a reply when James stepped forward, saying in a hearty voice,

'Well, then, if that's settled I think we should all drive back to the house. I have dry clothes for you here in this bag, Miss Riv—I mean, Miss Durini.'

Luke took the portmanteau. 'You go on, James, and take Woollatt with you. Miss Durini is still very pale. I would not risk taking her into the night air just yet. You may send the carriage down later to collect us.'

A look passed between the two brothers; Carlotta saw it and a little voice in her head urged her to protest, to say that she was perfectly well enough for the short journey to the house. But it was a very *little* voice and easily silenced. James was already at the door.

'Yes, of course. Come along, Woollatt. Come back to the Court with me. I have a fine cognac in my study that is just the thing for these occasions.' He ushered Woollatt out of the door before him.

'James!'

'Yes, Luke?'

'Do not rush to send the carriage back.'

James looked towards Carlotta.

She reached up to touch the dark locks curling over her shoulders. 'It would be most unwise for me to venture out of doors with my hair still wet.'

His knowing grin made her cheeks burn. 'As you wish, then.'

Carlotta did not move. She listened to the voices dying away, heard the outer door slam, then there was silence. At length Luke spoke to her.

'You are very pale.'

'Yes.'

'If I pull a chair closer to the fire, will you sit down?'

She nodded, and watched him drag a velvet-covered sofa to the very edge of the rug.

'This might help.' He went across to the side table and poured her a glass of wine from one of the open bottles. 'The servants will not come in until it is light. We may as well make use of what is here.' He came back and sat beside her, handing her the glass. 'Now, drink it.'

His arm was about her shoulders. It seemed the most natural thing in the world to lean back against him.

'Your hair would dry quicker if you were to kneel before the fire again.'

'But this is so much more comfortable.' She took a sip from the glass. The wine was dark and warm and tasted of berries. 'Do you think he will?'

'What?'

'Introduce me to his mama next Season.'

'Very likely, but you will be Lady Darvell by then.'

Carlotta was in the act of taking another sip of wine and choked. She was obliged to hand the glass to Darvell, who placed it carefully down on the floor beside the sofa.

'Are—are you asking me to marry you?' she asked when she could command her voice.

'No, my sweet life, I am informing you that we will be married, even if I have to drag you screaming to the altar.'

Her lips twitched. 'What about my—um—unfortunate birth?'

'There is nothing unfortunate about your birth. Your father is a great artist. I only hope he will think me worthy of his daughter. I have very little fortune, as you have reminded me on several occasions.'

She blushed at that. 'It was very bad of me to throw that up at you. I am ashamed of myself.'

His arm tightened around her. 'I had hurt you. I did not understand how much.'

'That day last summer...' She began to play with the cord of her dressing gown. 'Did you—were you going to propose to me?'

'Yes, until I heard Broxted offer to take you away with him. I thought you deserved a taste of society.'

A great wave of unhappiness rushed through her. She bowed her head. 'I was so miserable! I d-did not wish to go and live with my uncle. I—I thought you did not l-love me.'

With something very like a growl he gripped her shoulders, pulling her round to face him. 'Not love you—do you know what it cost me to leave Malberry that day? I felt as though I was cutting out my own heart!'

Carlotta looked up. His eyes scorched her; she trembled under the intensity of his look. She wanted to reach out to him, to pull him closer and feel his lips on hers but he continued to hold her at arm's length, to subject her to that burning gaze. 'I left Malberry and buried myself on my estates, taking charge of them as I should have done years ago. I wanted to be prepared, so that when Broxted brought you to town I would have something more to offer you than a mountain of debts. And I succeeded, too. Darvell Manor is beginning to pay its way, the land is in good heart, the tenants prospering—but all the time I was there I lived in dread that you might find someone else, that I would be too late.'

Carlotta blinked rapidly, determined not to cry. 'There was never anyone else,' she said simply. She reached up and gently touched his cheek. 'I have never loved anyone but you, Luke.'

He turned his face towards her hand, pressing his lips

to the palm, then in one swift movement, he gathered her into his arms and kissed her.

All Carlotta's pent-up longing of the past twelve months was released. She flung her arms around his neck and kissed him back hungrily, responding to the demands of his mouth, her lips parting willingly to allow his tongue to explore ever deeper. Her body pressed itself against him and they slid from the sofa until they were kneeling together on the rug. Luke broke away, but only to ease her down on to her back, all the time holding her gaze, mesmerising, willing her to trust him. She answered him with a tremulous smile and he kissed her again, but this time it was slow and languorous, melting away the tensions in her body. His teeth grazed her bottom lip and she almost groaned at the intense, sweet desire that welled up inside her.

Luke tugged at the cord around her waist and the dressing gown fell free. She trembled as he touched her naked waist. Gently he moved his hand upwards, smoothing over her ribs and on until he was cupping her breast, which tightened beneath his fingers. His thumb began to circle the nipple, and a wave of pure heat began to build within her. Her bones seemed to melt as she arched her back, offering herself up to him. He kissed her chin, then her throat, his tongue leaving a burning line on her skin as it trailed downwards. His hand was still fondling one breast, and when his mouth fastened over the other she gasped at the unexpected surge of pleasure. His tongue circled the taut bud at its peak, causing the wave of heat that had been building inside her to grow stronger, threatening to overwhelm her. So intoxicating were the sensations he was awaking in her that as she felt his hand moving down over her belly she felt only growing excitement. Her eyes flew open as his fingers moved between her legs, easing her apart. She was very hot down there, and moist. Her body was pulsing, opening to receive him. She had never felt so out of control before, but there was no panic; Luke was holding her, his hand gently stroking her; and her body responded of its own accord to the rhythm of his caresses.

Sighing deeply, Carlotta opened her eyes for a moment. She looked up at the painted walls of the room. Suddenly the pictures made sense to her, the men and women touching each other, pleasuring each other. Her eyes dwelled on one particular couple: the woman was crouched between the man's legs, her head bowed over him while he lay with his head thrown back in ecstasy at her touch. Gently Carlotta pulled Luke's head from her breast. Immediately those pleasuring fingers on her body stilled and he looked at her, a question in his eyes.

'You are still dressed, sir.' Was this her voice she could hear? It was unfamiliar, deeper, richer. An exultant wave of wanton happiness bubbled up inside her. She tugged at his shirt, helping him to pull it over his head, then with eager hands she unbuttoned the fall flap of his breeches.

Luke gave a shaky laugh. 'Careful, sweetheart. There is no rush.'

Oh, but there is, she thought, her groin aching for him to touch her again with those magic fingers. As he slipped off the rest of his clothes she struggled free of the brocade dressing gown, wondering at her daring as she lay before him, naked. Luke was on his knees, staring down at her.

'Is—is anything wrong, my lord?' A little doubt shook her.

'Nothing is wrong, sweetheart. You are so very beautiful.'

She reached out for him, but he caught her hands.

'If you want me to stop, if you want to wait until our

wedding night for our first full union, you must tell me now.' He added with an attempt at humour, 'I can cool off in the plunge pool.'

His voice was unsteady and Carlotta's heart swelled with love at his concern for her. She pulled one hand free and reached up to place her palm on his smooth cheek. 'You held back once before and I almost lost you,' she said softly.

Still he did not move. 'After this there will be no going back,' he warned her. 'You will be mine, body and soul.'

'And will that be the same for you, my lord?'

'I am already yours, Carlotta.'

His slow smile reassured her and, when she saw how aroused he was, her desire returned to fever pitch. She pulled him down to her and kissed him, but even as he leaned into her she twisted around, pushing him on to his back. The surprise in his eyes gave her another rush of pleasure. She began to kiss him, her hands caressing his body, then, remembering his effect on her, she began to work her way downwards, planting gentle kisses on his throat and the hard smooth skin of his chest. His long, slow sigh made her feel all-powerful. She revelled in the taste of his flesh, the enticing mixture of spicy, aromatic fragrance and clean male skin that inflamed her senses. She explored him with her hands and her eyes, marvelling at this male body that was as beautiful, exciting and strange to her as a foreign land. The crisp hair below his navel tickled her as she kissed his flat stomach while her hands continued to caress him. She heard Luke gasp. He gave a little groan and with an exultant laugh she glanced up again at the wall-painting. She ran her tongue around her lips. It was only fair that she should give Luke as much pleasure as he had given her.

Luke moaned softly as she applied her mouth to him. She heard his endearments, little words of instruction. Suddenly he was pulling her away, rolling her over on to her back. 'No more for me,' he murmured thickly. 'We will finish this together.'

Luke's mouth captured her lips again and once again his fingers slid down to find that magic spot. Her hips tilted up to meet him, welcoming his touch. He eased himself over her and she opened for him, eager now to receive him. She gave a little gasp as he entered her and he moved with slow, steady movements, stroking her gently. He watched her closely until she began to move with him. He restrained himself, curbing his own desires until she was gasping, her body arching, beyond her control. Carlotta threw back her head, her lips parted slightly as she clung to him, her fingers digging into his shoulders. Only then did Luke allow himself to give the final push, to drive into her, uttering her name as they clung together for a final moment of intense, shuddering ecstasy. They collapsed together on the rug, breathing heavily. The fire had died back to a golden, glowing mass, enveloping them in its comforting warmth. Luke rolled onto his back beside her. He reached for her hand, threading his fingers through hers.

'I never expected anything so wonderful,' he murmured.

'Was I...did I please you?'

He raised himself on one elbow and looked into her eyes, his own glowing. 'You were...magnificent.'

He kissed her, but when he broke away she chuckled. 'I followed the paintings.' She pointed to the walls.

'The devil you did!' Luke laughed and kissed her again. 'Perhaps your father will paint these scenes in our bedroom at Darvell Manor. Would you object to that?'

'If it is what you want, my lord.'

He ran a finger over her lips and trailed it gently down between her breasts. 'No, I want only you, night after night!' He grinned at her. 'We must be married by special licence, as soon as possible. I cannot bear to sleep alone after this.'

She touched his cheek. 'Nor I, my lord.'

He kissed her gently, his naked body hardening as it rested against hers. 'You see the effect you have on me?' he murmured, nibbling her ear. 'After tonight your aunt and uncle will keep you well away from me.'

She put her hand down to caress him and felt a soaring elation as he responded to her touch. She drew him closer. 'Then let us not waste a moment, my lord,' she whispered.

Chapter Eighteen

On a bright, spring morning, Lord Darvell's elegant travelling carriage swept through the gates of Malberry Court. Unable to contain herself, Carlotta leaned out of the window.

'We should be able to see the house soon… There it is! Can you see it, Luke?'

'I see something I like much better.' He caught her around the waist and pulled her back.

She collapsed onto his lap, laughing. 'Behave yourself, my lord.'

He kissed her, causing a bolt of excitement to shoot through her. Would she ever become immune to his touch? Carlotta hoped not.

'How can I behave myself, my lady, when you look so adorable?'

Carlotta settled herself back beside him and made her voice suitably severe. 'Well, you must try, Luke. Your brother will not think us respectable enough to be godparents for little James.'

Luke gave a mock scowl, but as the carriage pulled up at the steps of Malberry Court he jumped out and turned to help her alight, every inch the respectable husband, as James came hurrying out to meet them.

'You have made good time,' he said, gripping his brother's hand. He turned to greet Carlotta, kissing her cheek and giving her an admiring glance. 'You are looking very well, my dear. Am I to take it my wicked brother is looking after you?'

'Alas, sir, he abuses me quite dreadfully.'

'Baggage!' Luke grinned. 'Tell me truthfully, James—does she look like a neglected wife?'

'No. In fact, you both look very pleased with yourselves! Have you been to town yet?'

'No. As you know we went to Rome directly after the wedding—my father-in-law wanted to show me off to all his relatives!'

'And why not?' declared Carlotta. 'He is very proud of his new son—a baron, no less!'

Luke grinned at her and kissed her hand. 'Since then we have been at Darvell Manor. I now take my responsibilities as a landowner very seriously.'

'Aye, and about time, too! Come along in—Adele is in her room with the baby, but she has instructed me to bring you both to her.'

'How is she?' asked Carlotta as James led them through the hall.

'In good health. You will remember I was a trifle anxious when she decided she would not have a wet nurse for the baby, but you will see that they are both thriving.' He led them up the stairs and into the main bedchamber. 'Here you are, my love, I have brought them straight up to you, as you see—they have not even had the chance to put off their coats.'

Adele was reclining on a daybed, wearing a blue satin wrap and gently rocking the cradle at her side. She smiled and held out her hands to them.

'Carlotta, my love—and Luke! Come and see your little godson. Is he not beautiful?'

Luke glanced at the little bundle lying in the cradle and murmured indistinctly.

Carlotta met Adele's eyes and giggled. 'He is adorable,' she said, pushing Luke out of the way. 'I hope he is a good baby?'

'He sleeps a great deal, but when he is awake he is very demanding, just like his father,' replied Adele, her eyes twinkling. 'And everyone says he has the Ainslowe look.'

'Dashed if I can see it,' muttered James. 'We have had so many visitors I am beginning to wish we had turned the morning room into Adele's bedchamber; Lord and Lady Broxted called on us yesterday and Mr and Mrs Price the day before that. They are on their way to town to order Julia's bride clothes.'

'Ah, yes, she marries Viscount Fairbridge this summer.' Carlotta nodded. 'I am glad; I think they are well suited.' She paused. 'And what news of Mr Woollatt?'

Adele's eyes brimmed with merriment. 'My spies tell me that his mama has found him a very suitable bride— excellent breeding, reasonable fortune and from a *very* respectable family.'

'Sounds exceedingly dull,' said Luke. 'But then Woollatt is a very dull dog.' He pulled Carlotta into his arms. 'You are much better off with me, you know.'

Carlotta blushed, then giggled as James grimaced at this open display of affection. A snuffling cry from the cradle brought their attention back to the baby. Adele began to rock the cradle again and James moved over to gaze at his son.

'I was very much afraid I should not see this day,' he said, reaching down to stroke the sleeping baby's fat cheek. 'When the gig overturned, I was afraid I should lose you both.'

Adele reached out her hand, smiling fondly at him. 'You knew when we married that I come from tough yeoman stock, my love. It would take more than a little tumble to hurt me.'

'Nevertheless, I was never closer to doing a man harm than when I found out it was Reed who tampered with that wheel. I am glad he was sentenced to hard labour—any lesser punishment and I should have been tempted to take the law into my own hands.' He scowled at the memory.

'And Mattingwood—is he still awaiting transportation?' asked Luke. 'He was the bigger villain; Reed was working on his orders, after all.'

'He was transported for life soon after you left for the Continent.'

They were silent for a moment, then little James set up a cry and broke the spell. With infinite care, James lifted the baby and handed him to Adele, who rocked him gently in her arms until he settled back to sleep. James watched them for a few moments, then turned back to his brother.

'And is Durini to paint Darvell Manor for you?

'Devil a bit! He is far too busy. They have taken a house in Brighton for the summer; he is working at a certain royal palace at present.' His laughing eyes flickered towards Carlotta. 'However, he has promised me that he will paint our new bathhouse. Which reminds me, James…we would like to make use of yours while we are here—I want to teach Carlotta to swim.'

It was said blandly, but Carlotta felt Adele's eyes upon her and could not prevent the blush stealing into her cheeks.

'What an excellent idea. Once the baby is weaned, I think we should do the same, James. I believe the exercise would be very beneficial.'

'Well, perhaps, perhaps,' said James, looking flustered. 'We shall have to wait and see.'

'You know, my love, I am quite as aware as Carlotta of the wall paintings in the bathhouse,' said Adele, choosing a bonbon from the little dish on the table beside her. 'We peeped into the warm room, you see, when we were walking in the grounds last summer.'

'You never told me that!'

'No, well, I thought you would be too shocked. However, Carlotta is a married lady now, and Julia almost a wife, so I doubt if there is any harm done.'

'Quite the contrary,' murmured Luke, casting another wicked glance at Carlotta, who blushed to the roots of her hair. She was relieved when James suggested they should leave Adele to rest, and they were shown to their own guest room.

'James is quite the family man now,' observed Luke when they were alone. 'Marriage undoubtedly agrees with him.'

He watched Carlotta untie the ribbons of her bonnet and toss it aside, swiftly followed by her pelisse. As she stood with the light from the window behind her, he could see the curves of her body outlined through the thin muslin of her gown.

'And what do you think of the state, my lord, now that you have had several months to sample it?'

He held out his arms and immediately she walked into them.

'I think it agrees with me, too.' He put his arms around

her. Looking down into the dark eyes that gazed so trustingly up into his own, he felt his heart tighten—she was so damned irresistible. 'No, it is not marriage,' he said slowly, 'it is *you* that agrees with me, *cara.*'

His mouth slid over hers and she responded immediately, her lips softening and her body leaning into him, arousing the desire that was never far away. He swept her up into his arms and carried her over to the bed.

'Luke! We have only just arrived.'

'No one will disturb us. I have locked the door.'

'But will not James be expecting us?' Her voice sounded husky, breathless—a sign that she wanted him, too.

'No, love. He was going back to sit with Adele. We need not appear again until the dinner hour.' He tugged gently at the ribbons securing her bodice. 'You will be wanting to change your gown…'

They undressed each other slowly, taking pleasure in arousing each other in the ways they had learned during the passionate days and nights since their marriage.

'*With my body, I thee worship,*' Luke murmured as they continued with their sensual rituals until they reached the final, fulfilling climax, clinging together as their passion spilled over, a great wave of blinding, gasping exhilaration that left them both exhausted.

The spring day was coming to a close, the light fading. Soon they would be summoned to the dinner table. Luke raised himself on one elbow and looked at Carlotta. She was curled on her side, her hand cradling her cheek. He leaned over and kissed her.

'It is time to get up, *cara*. Your maid will be banging on the door soon.'

A sleepy chuckle greeted his words. 'She knows better than that.' She sat up and reached for her wrap.

He heard her sigh. 'Carlotta? What is it?'

'I was thinking of Adele, and her fortune. I brought you so little…'

'You cannot call your uncle's ten thousand pounds a paltry sum!'

'No, but he insisted upon so much of it being tied up in settlements and jointures.'

'And quite rightly so. He is protecting you from the Wicked Baron.'

'Were you ever really wicked?'

He grinned and pulled her back on to the bed. 'No. I was more….wild. But I am tamed now.'

'Not completely, I hope.'

'No, love, not completely.'

She wound her arms about his neck, sighing again, but this time with contentment. 'I am so fortunate, so—so blessed—to have a man like you, who loves me so much. It is the best feeling in the world to be so beloved.'

Luke's heart swelled at these words. He held her even tighter. 'And I intend that you shall continue to feel beloved,' he murmured as he prepared to kiss her again. 'For ever.'

* * * * *